SHE SAID SHE'D NEVER GO BACK.
NOW, SHE DOESN'T WANT TO LEAVE.

Forever After All

SHELBY STORME

Content Warning

This book contains content that may be troubling to some readers, including, but not limited to:

Death

Grief

Toxic familial relationships

Narcissism

Gaslighting

PTSD

Substance abuse

Alcohol

Sexual choking

Contents

To my Sweet Courage.

There's no love story I love more than ours. Thank you for inspiring this one.

Chapter One

Dear Sissy

IF YOU'RE READING THIS, I'm not here anymore. I'm sorry for not reaching out more these last few years. I wish I could have made it out to visit you in California like we'd always talked about. There's a lot of things I wish happened differently, but one thing I want you to know is I don't blame you for leaving. Maybe if I were braver, I would have too. I always admired how you went to the beat of your own drum. You carved your own path, regardless of how some people (Mama) would say that you'd fail.

Your strength is exactly what Cason needs right now. I know this is a huge ask of you and that you're not going to be happy or understand. I hope one day you can forgive me, but I need you to take care of him, to support him and love him—to help him move on. He needs someone who will be there for him to watch him grow up. You know just as well as I do how bad Mama's arthritis was before you left, and it's only gotten worse in the last five years. She can't take care of a five-year-old. She says she can, but she doesn't deserve that, and neither does Cason.

So please, Sissy… *please* do this for me. Love him for me. Be there for him since I can't. He's the sweetest, kindest, funniest, most amazing little boy in the whole world and you two are going to have such an amazing bond—I just know it.

This isn't ideal, especially with you all the way in California, but I think it would be best if you came back here for a bit. At least until the end of the school year. You can stay at my place. I've already worked things out with my landlord. I just think it will be easier on Cason if things are stable during the transition. As stable as they can be, at least. Again, I am so incredibly sorry. I hope one day you can forgive me. Just know that I love you, I miss you, and I can't wait to see you again.

Sheldon

CHAPTER TWO

Temporary Home

CHARLIE

I'M NEVER GOING BACK.

How many times had I told myself that over the last five years? Every Christmas, Easter, summer vacation, birthdays... It was a mantra now, with how many times I'd said it. Yet, here I was, driving down Main Street toward the only bar in town.

Crazy how in five years literally nothing changed. Sweet D's diner still had those god-awful checker and lace valances hanging in all the windows. Mr. Cooper's old Chevy sat in the first spot from the door of the hardware store. I'd kissed Alden Hicks on the tailgate during the Fourth of July parade in eighth grade—still one of my cringier moments. And the "a" was still out on the neon sign of Jack's. It'd been that way since I was a kid.

That's the thing about small towns. Change might as well be the devil.

I sighed and looked down at the folded-up letter on top of my purse in the passenger seat. Tears pricked in my eyes—ones of downright fury or confusion, or devastation…. I wasn't sure anymore. Maybe a bit of all three? How could Sheldie do this to me? As if my sister dying wasn't already hard enough to deal with, but now there was a kid in the mix?

I need a drink…or three. Yeah, three sounded like a good place to start.

Turning into the lot, I parked quickly before grabbing my phone, purse, and keys. I checked my home screen for the hundredth time since leaving the hospital, but nothing. No call from Mama, no texts from Cal. I pushed down the trickle of sadness that niggled at me like a damn worm on a hook.

He's probably busy. He'd told me earlier he had showings and meetings all day. *A text takes less than ten seconds, though.*

No. I wasn't going down that road right now. I didn't need to think about that on top of the shitshow that had become my life in the past few days. Shoving my phone into my purse, I pulled open the door to Jack's. A wave of nostalgia and the acrid scent of cigarettes hit me, taking me down memory lane to when I spent too many nights here doing homework in the back corner while Mama worked her shift.

I didn't recognize the girl behind the bar, thank God. I wasn't in the mood to talk to anyone. I didn't want the questions. *How's Miss Sheldon doing?* Or, even better, *how's big ol' California treating you? How long was I in town? Is it for good?*

I bit back a sigh. As if any of them would understand why I left.

I didn't want to *people.* I just wanted to drink in peace. Despite it being a Friday night, it was just me, the bartender, and a few old guys sitting on the opposite end of the bar. For now, at least.

Give it time—it was a Friday Night. Jack's was always busy on the weekends. At least by the time familiar faces trickled in, I'd have a bit of alcohol in me.

Chatty Charlie would probably come out about three drinks in.

"What can I get ya, Miss?" the bartender asked as I took a seat at the bar top.

"Whiskey sour, please. Make it a double."

"Yes, ma'am," she said with a soft smile before turning to make my drink.

I bit back the urge to tell her not to call me that. I was maybe a year or two older than her—definitely not old enough to be ma'am, that's for damn sure. Couldn't really blame her though, I'd been raised the same way. Funny how quickly those manners wore off after leaving this place. Daddy would be rolling in his grave. What happened to his polite little girl?

Some old George Strait song drifted on the air from the speakers, muffling the chatter from the basketball game playing on the TV in the corner. How was it possible to feel so uncomfortable and right at home all at once? It was like two halves of myself were warring for dominance. The old me, and then the new.

"Here, you go, Miss," the girl said, placing my drink in front of me.

"Thank you, ma'am."

Okay, so I guess some habits did die hard. Maybe Daddy wouldn't be completely embarrassed of his little girl after all.

I took a long sip and sighed. What the hell was I going to do? I had no business raising a child. Like, *none*. I couldn't even keep a succulent alive. A *succulent*. Weren't they supposed to be basically kill-proof? Other than pictures and the occasional facetime call, I hadn't even seen Cason. We were essentially strangers. And Sheldie wanted me to raise him? He needed someone who knew him, and his wants and needs. He needed someone to love, support, and help him grow. He needed a mother. Not me. He needed *Sheldon*.

But that wasn't an option anymore.

It was weird…I hadn't cried since leaving the hospital. When I walked into her ICU room and saw her lying there two days ago? You bet. When they took her off life support? Like a damn baby. When she finally passed away, my hand gripping her frail, lifeless body? Abso-*fucking*-lutely. But since leaving the ICU, it's like that well had run dry. The tears would come again, it was only a matter of time. We still had the funeral to plan—and when I said we, I meant me. Mama would be useless. At least she had been with Daddy's. Sheldon and I had done everything, while she cried and cried and cried to our family and friends, acting like she'd worshiped the very ground Daddy walked on. She should've been a damn actress.

I had no doubt she'd be the same way this time around. She'd just been beside herself after losing the love of her life and now her perfect, kind, selfless first-born? What would she do now with her ungrateful youngest who gave up on her family the moment she got a scholarship to California?

I rolled my eyes and pulled out my phone from my purse. Opening up my calls, I pressed on Cal's name. *Please answer. Please answe*—nope, voicemail. My heart sank and I hung up without leaving a message before thumbing through my texts.

Me: Love you. Miss you. I'm a mess. Can you talk?

Three little dots showed up on my phone screen, fluttering there for a few long seconds.

Cal: Sorry Babe. At a work dinner now. Gonna be late. Call you in the morning.

Tears stung in my eyes as I all but threw my phone across the room. Of course, *of fucking course*, he couldn't spare three damn minutes. How many times had we argued about this? How many fights had we gotten into after I brought up how unseen and invalidated he made me feel. How my feelings were constantly belittled or brushed off as dramatic. Was I being dramatic now? Was asking him to call me then and there too much? I didn't think so. My sister just *died*.

I didn't have Daddy to go to, and Mama was absolutely *not* an option. Might as well just talk to Cal at that point. It would go just about the same.

Blowing out an exhale, I picked up my phone and opened up Instagram to scroll through pictures, memes, and posts from friends. Cal's story icon showed up as one of the first on the top of my screen and my stomach plummeted. A feeling of dread coiled in my chest like a cottonmouth gearing up to strike.

Don't click it. But like a bad car crash, I found myself unable to stop looking.

At least he'd been telling the truth that he was at dinner. I'd recognize the restaurant anywhere. Duke's—an oceanside grill off the coast that we'd dubbed our Friday night restaurant. All of our friends were there. *Work dinner, my ass.* This was why he couldn't answer my calls?

His stupid, handsome face took up most of the screen as he panned left and right, giving a roll-call of everyone. Sloan and Axel were there. Jay and Kate.

The Instagram story ended, leaving a weight as heavy as an eighteen-wheeler settling on my chest. *What the hell?*

I don't remember exiting the app and opening up my calls. I don't remember clicking on his number, or hearing his voicemail greeting. I don't even remember what exactly I'd said. I think there were a few *how could you's* in there. At least one *fuck you.* And a *don't call me.*

Why did he lie? He couldn't spare a few minutes to call me, to reassure me that everything was going to be alright, but he could post a fucking Instagram story?

My phone buzzing in my hands dragged me from my thoughts. Cal. Of course, now he wanted to talk. He sure couldn't be bothered before. I sent the call to voicemail. *Give him a taste of his own medicine.*

I was so done. So done of constantly bending over backward to be there for him. To support him. Help him. Do his job for him, even. All I wanted was a five-minute phone call. To hear his voice. To have him tell me everything would be okay. Was that too much to ask?

I turned off my phone. I didn't want to deal with his calls and texts. Tomorrow I'd figure out whatever the hell I was going to do. Right now…right now I wanted to forget all about him.

"Want another, Miss?" The bartender's voice pulled me from my thoughts. God, when did I finish the first one? I didn't even have it in me to say yes, I just gave her a nod.

A flurry of guilt welled up inside me. I should be at Sheldon's, getting ready for when her friend dropped Cason off in the morning. He'd been splitting time between there and Mama's the past few weeks. Although now, with the letter folded up in my purse, he wouldn't be staying at Mama's anymore.

The thought of going into Sheldie's house, being around her things and not seeing her there… That wasn't something I could do sober.

So, yeah. I needed another drink.

CHAPTER THREE

Looking For You

RYDER

I POCKETED MY KEYS as I made my way to the bar. Oddly quiet for being a Friday night, but that was the thing about Jack's, it never stayed quiet for long. Especially not with the Mav and Cash coming in soon. Before long, it'd be loud as hell in here, so I reveled in the quiet for the moment.

"Evenin', Miss Grace," I said, tipping my ball cap to her as I settled onto a bar stool. "How's your day goin'?"

A smile blossomed on her lips. "Oh, you know, same ole. What can I getcha, Ryder? Same as usual?"

"Yes, ma'am."

With a nod, she busied herself behind the bar. I glanced around and waited, noting the woman a few stools down. Her long hair fell over her shoulder in loose curls, hiding her face. Between the dim lighting and neon signs, I couldn't quite tell the color of her hair. Probably a brown or red of some sort, if I had to guess. Her slim left arm was wrapped in tattoos. Even from a distance, I could make out mountains and flowers and storm clouds, all drawn in intricate detail. *Probably spent a pretty penny on that.*

I'd never seen her before. She must be passing through or new to town. Didn't get too many newcomers that often, so it was likely the former.

Then I noticed the glasses in front of her. One empty, the other nearly there, and a third on the way. Grace slid her some sort of mixed drink before handing me my beer. Now what was she doing drinking all alone in a place like this? *Just leave her alone.* She hadn't come to be bothered. She'd come to drink away whatever was running through that mind of hers. And who the hell was I to interrupt her from that? Cash and Mav would be here soon enough.

But as I drank my beer, as I watched that basketball game on TV, I found myself glancing over at the girl way too often. She hardly moved. She didn't check her phone. Didn't talk to anyone. Didn't look anywhere other than straight ahead, all the while draining drinks like they were water on a hot summer day.

Who was this girl?

Leaning toward her, I finally gave in and called over the music, "Nice tattoos, miss."

The woman jolted, her head whipping to me, and for a moment it was as if the damn world stood still. She was beautiful. Honestly, truly, despite the sadness that lurked in her light eyes. A light dusting of freckles were smattered over a button nose and high cheekbones. Wait—I knew her. It had been, what, at least six years since I'd last seen her. Probably more, honestly. I'd been closer in age to her sister, Sheldon, who'd been two grades older than me. But I'd recognize that pretty face anywhere.

Charlotte Evans.

Time sure had been good to her, not that it hadn't been before she'd left for California. She still had the same heart-shaped face and curves made for holding, but the tattoos were new.

She sure as hell ain't a kid anymore.

"Wha–? Oh…thanks." She offered me a polite smile, her light gaze fixing on mine. Did she like what she saw? Did she recognize me? I wouldn't be surprised if she didn't. We'd only hung out a few times at parties and bonfires, but she'd never given me or any of the rodeo kids much attention.

And though I already knew, I asked, "You're Charlotte Evans, right? Sheldon's little sister."

Something flickered in her gaze, her smile seeming forced as she nodded. "Yes. And you're…" Her brow furrowed a moment before recognition smoothed the lines of her face. "You're Ryder, right?"

"Yes, ma'am. Ryder Wright, that's me."

Her lips tugged up in the corners and a soft chuckle escaped her. "Your daddy sure had too much fun coming up with that one, didn't he?"

I laughed. "Shit, he still gets a kick out of it."

Those lips bloomed into a full-fledged smile. One of those heart stoppin', make the world stand still, bright as sunshine smiles. "I'll bet he does." She took a swig of her drink, looking me up and down. "You know, a couple girls in school said you sure lived up to your name. That true?"

I damn near choked on my beer. Dear Lord, was she that forward or just buzzed? I couldn't quite tell. There was something guarded in her gaze.

I should walk away. Walk away before I did something stupid. Because, I *would* do something stupid. It was in my damn blood. She was trouble with a capital T, and I didn't need trouble. Not right now. Not with things finally going right.

But that stupid running through my veins won out in the end.

Pressing my beer to my lips, I replied, "Would you like to find out?"

A low chuckle bubbled up out of her. "Oh, someone's cocky."

I shook my head. "I ain't claimin' nothin'. I'm a firm believer that actions speak louder than words."

She laughed, the smile she flashed me damn near blinding in its intensity. "You're quick. I'll give you that. But I guess you have to be with a name like yours." She settled into her seat a bit more and took another sip of her drink.

I pulled out the stool beside her and moved closer. She noted the movement, but didn't seem to mind. This wasn't the same doe-eyed seventeen-year-old I'd talked to at parties on occasion. Something sharp, almost predatory lingered in her gaze. Age, wisdom, and time away from this small little town would do that to you. I welcomed that look. Found it intriguing. Captivating.

"It's been a while since you've been back here," I said.

Charlie looked into her near empty glass a moment before polishing off the rest of her drink. "Five years."

Damn. Longest I'd been away was, what, half a year? I drained the rest of my beer and waved to Grace for another round for the both of us.

"How's your sister?" I asked. I knew she was sick. Our moms went to the same church, and my mom had mentioned a few weeks ago that Miss Sheldon was in the hospital with cancer. That could be the only reason Charlie was back here. Most people who left this town didn't come back.

Her face fell, the light in her eyes dying out like a shooting star. "She's dead," Charlie said matter-of-factly. "She died this afternoon."

Shit. "Ah, damn, Miss Charlotte—" I pulled off my ball cap and ran a hand through my hair. Shit, I hadn't expected that. "I'm–I'm really sorry."

Charlie's eyelids fluttered shut and she let out a loud sigh. "You don't have to apologize, and please don't call me Charlotte. Charlie's fine. Preferred, actually."

"Yes, ma'am."

Charlie grimaced and shook her head. "And please don't call me ma'am."

"Yes, ma'—shit, sorry."

A sad, little laugh escaped her as she met my gaze. "No, I'm sorry. I should go. I'm awkward as hell and buzzed and just a complete fucking mess." She slid out of her chair and leaned against the bar, motioning Grace with a wave. "Can I get the check, please?" she asked.

I glanced over at Grace who still held our newest round of drinks in her hand. "Put it on my tab."

Charlie's head snapped toward me, a scowl marring her face. "You don't have to pay for my drinks."

"Don't worry about it. It's the least I can do after ruinin' your night."

She looked skyward, exhaling loudly. When she met my gaze once more, tears hung in eyes. "You didn't ruin my night. It's just…today was shit, and I'm…so. Fucking. Done. I came here…I don't know, to drown my sorrows? To get so fucked up I forgot who I was? To forget why I'm even in this tiny town? I don't know at this point. It's all pointless anyway, and isn't going to help. Besides, my mother will just try to use it against me if she finds out I came here. So, I should go."

I didn't know what to do. What to say. She was a mess. Understandably. Who the hell wouldn't be in her situation? I couldn't imagine being in her shoes. And even though I had no business, even if she likely didn't want it, I wanted to help.

From the minute I'd recognized her, something drew me to her. Nostalgia? Fate? Who the hell knew? But the thought of leaving her right now didn't sit well with me.

"Want me to take you home? I'm good to drive." I already had my wallet out of my back pocket and my card on the bar top. I glanced over at Grace. "I'm ready to close out, Miss Grace."

Charlie shook her head beside me. "Honestly, it's not a big deal. I'll just get an uber or something."

I laughed. "There ain't an uber this side of San Anton that'll be here in any less than three hours. If you want to leave, you're either walking or I'm driving you."

She groaned. "I forgot how much I hate small towns."

I huffed a laugh. I wondered if she really meant it? Five years was a long time, but long enough to hate this place? Sure, it had its problems, but you'd never convince me that some big city in California had shit on this itty-bitty town. "What's it going to be, Miss Charlo—Charlie," I corrected.

Charlie sucked her bottom lip and bit it. With a sigh and a shrug, she replied, "A ride would be nice. Thanks."

CHAPTER FOUR

What He Didn't Do

CHARLIE

RYDER WRIGHT.

How could I have forgotten about him with a name like that? To be fair, he'd definitely gotten better looking with age. Not that he wasn't cute in high school, but now… Let's just say, he wore the hell out of a plain black t-shirt and blue jeans. The boots and ball cap were just icing on the damn cake. And when I mean cake, I mean a gorgeous specimen with a *fit* build—not the kind of washboard abs you got from spending hours in the gym, but from working and riding and lifting bales of hay all day.

He looked damn good. His dark hair was longer, the ends of it curling slightly where it brushed his shoulders. He somehow still had a tan despite the fact Spring wasn't even here yet, and I spied a quarter sleeve tattoo on his right arm peeking out from beneath his t-shirt.

Stop staring.

I tore my gaze from him for what had to be the dozenth time since we'd gotten into his truck. It was immaculate, by the way. Because of course it was. Hot, respectful, had a sense of humor, clean. He may as well have been Prince Charming… If Prince Charming's noble steed was a white RAM 3500.

God, why did I care? I had a boyfriend…*for the moment.* I still wasn't positive what to do on that front. Breaking up with Cal over text or a phone call just seemed so high school. But it's not like he was going to come out here. *That's a future me problem.* One current me had no desire to think about. Besides, I'd sworn off cowboys the minute I left Texas five years ago. I wouldn't be going back on that after less than a few days back in town. No matter how good-looking Ryder was. And kind. Really kind.

"You didn't have to do this, honestly," I said, filling the silence.

He glanced over at me, those dark eyes flicking up and down my body. "Don't worry about it. I wasn't busy, anyway."

"So, you weren't there on a date?" I cringed inwardly. Did I seriously just ask that?

He glanced over at me, a smile curling on his lips. "Why, you interested?"

My cheeks burned. Thank God it was dark out and he couldn't see me blushing. "No. I was just curious."

He chuckled, eyes settling on the road once more. "Don't worry, Miss Charlotte, there was no date. Just meeting up with the guys."

I don't know why, but something loosened in my chest. Relief settled around me like a blanket. *Wow. Desperate, much?* And why did I even care? I wasn't planning on staying here long, anyway. Long enough to sort things out with Cason, and sure as hell not long enough to fall in love.

Who said anything about love? I shouldn't even be thinking about this when Sheldon had literally just died today. What was wrong with me? God, I was a horrible person. A shit sister. Just an all-around piece of shit.

Tears pricked in my eyes. This was too much. All of it. I just wanted to go home. Wrap up in my blankets and sleep until the pain and heartache went away. But did I really want to go back to Cal? Where was home if I left him? *Future me problem, remember.*

"You stayin' at one of the hotels in town or your mom's?" he asked.

Shit, I hadn't told him where I was going. I fished out my phone to look up the address in my maps and remembered I'd turned it off. Powering it up, I replied, "Actually, neither. I'm staying at Sheldon's house. I can give you the address."

He frowned. "Really? That ain't gonna be hard on you?"

I shrugged. "I've never been there, so hopefully not, but I've gotta be there by tomorrow. Sheldon's son, Cason, is coming back from his friend's house."

"Ah, I've seen him around. He's a cute kid. Does he know what happened?"

The tears hanging in my eyes finally slid free, leaking down my face. I sniffled and wiped them away quickly. "My mother didn't want him there to say goodbye. She said it would be too traumatic for him. I disagreed. I still regret not getting to tell Daddy goodbye. Cason's five—old enough to understand what happened—he should have gotten the option. He knew she was sick." I blew out a shaky breath. "I'll just have to tell him tomorrow that she's actually gone now."

How the hell I was going to do that was beyond me. I'd heard the panic in his little voice even all the way across the room when my mother had been talking to him on the phone earlier in the day. She and I had a huge fight right after that. I thought Cason had the right to say goodbye. She didn't. She won in the end. Just as she always did.

And now it was up to me to tell him what happened to his mom. "That's…" Ryder began.

"Shitty?" I offered. "Because yes, it *is* shitty. Shitty and selfish of her." Rage bubbled up in me like boiling water. And maybe it was the whiskey or that I was just so incredibly done with everything that had happened today, but I found myself saying, "A part of me is convinced the only reason she said no to Cason being there, is basically because I suggested he should get the chance to have some closure. When I mentioned Daddy, I swear, she had downright wrath in her eyes." I wiped furiously at my tears and shook my head as I went on. "That woman is petty as petty can be. Time's only made her worse."

Ryder met my gaze. I expected some sort of reaction from him. Shock, surprise, but he just nodded and asked calmly, "You two don't get along?"

"She's the reason I left Texas." I sighed, a wave of exhaustion washing over me. "She's manipulative and selfish and completely uncaring of anyone else's feelings other than her own. So no, we most definitely don't get along."

Ryder looked like he wanted to say something, but refrained. His gaze returned to the road. We slipped into silence for a few moments. Not long enough for me to get completely lost in my dark thoughts—he dragged me back to the present before I drowned in them. "How long are you going to be in town for?"

"That's a good question, and one I don't really have an answer to. Sheldon, uh, named me Cason's guardian." I ran a hand through my hair and blew out a deep breath. "She also wants me to stay here long enough to let him finish out the school year. She thought it would make the transition a little easier if as many things were as normal as possible for him."

"Did you know about that when you came out?"

"Nope. Sure didn't. She had a will made up, which means she'd been planning this for a while. My mother gave me a sealed envelope today from Sheldon with a handwritten letter from her asking me to take care of Cason, and then the actual will."

Guilt welled in my chest. Here I was complaining about having to take care of my nephew and help out my dead sister. Even with the distance, even with the strain on our relationship, I know Sheldie would have done the same for me had the roles been reversed.

Ryder offered me a reassuring smile. "That's good that he has you. So, you think you're gonna stay til summer then?"

I shrugged. "Honestly, I don't know. Technically, I'm still living with my boyfriend...though I'm pretty sure that relationship is over after tonight. But I don't want to stay here. My mother is already furious about Sheldon naming me Cason's guardian. She's going to make life a living hell for me here if I stay."

I couldn't ignore the way his hand gripped a little tighter around the steering wheel, but his face remained relaxed, devoid of any emotion other than mere curiosity. Hm, interesting. I wondered if that had to do with finding out I had a boyfriend, or at the mention of not wanting to stay here.

"You have a boyfriend?" he asked, still staring out the front windshield.

"Yeah. Well, kinda. For the moment."

Ryder huffed an incredulous laugh. "What the hell does that mean?"

I groaned and wiped a hand across my face. "When I got the call from my mother that Sheldon wasn't doing well, he told me he couldn't come because he was super swamped with work. Fine, I get it. But I've talked to him once in the past three days. He hasn't checked in on me, reassured me that everything would be okay. He didn't even respond to the voicemail I sent him about the guardian situation. When I tried calling him earlier tonight, he told me he was at a work meeting. Turns out he wasn't. He was at dinner with our friends. The fucking idiot posted a story to his Instagram. I called him out on it and he's been trying to call me since."

"Guy sounds like an asshole."

I huffed a bitter laugh. "Tell me about it."

"You gonna leave him?"

I shrugged, unable to meet his gaze. "I don't know. I need to talk to him when I'm not so buzzed and after I get Cason settled in."

"What's there to talk about? He let you come here to deal with your sister's death. All alone. You should leave his ass."

I frowned, my brows knitting together in annoyance. "I don't need you telling me what to do with my love life, thank you very much. I'm a big girl, I can handle myself."

Ryder's brow rose, a shit-eating smirk tugging on his mouth. "*Yes, ma'am.* But I'll tell you right now, Miss Charlotte, you deserve someone who'd drop everything for you. Especially in your current situation."

My blood boiled even as something stirred within me at his words. "Oh, and I suppose you would be that someone?"

"Well, I'm here and he ain't. What does that say?"

"Oh, fuck off," I snapped. "You saw me in that bar—a shiny new belt buckle to add to your collection. That's the only reason you came over and talked to me. Had you known all this at the start, I highly doubt you'd be saying the same thing." The moment the words spewed from my lips, regret flooded through me.

Ryder met my hard stare, his face a mask of calm, his gaze guarded. I pressed a hand to my mouth. What had gotten into me? God, I was all over the place. "I'm…I'm so sorry. That was really out of line for me to say. I—"

He surprised me then, reaching his hand over the center console to rest it on top of mine in my lap. The calluses on his palm scraped against my skin and a shiver danced down my spine. "Sometimes, when an animal gets scared and feels like it's backed into a corner, it'll attack anyone that goes after it, even if they're only trying to help."

"Are you really comparing me to an animal?" I asked with a huff.

That was something my dad would have said. He *had* said something like that to me before. He was always using stupid analogies about animals to explain people's behavior or why certain things happened. I guess when you worked with horses and cattle all day, it seemed second nature. Some of the anger withered away at the thought of both him and Daddy doing that.

An earnest smile lit up Ryder's shadowed face. "Sorry, force of habit. What I'm tryin' to say is that you've been through a lot today. Your emotions are…shot to shit, essentially. I didn't mean to poke the bear."

"I'm sorry. Thank you, again," I said softly, unable to rip my gaze from his. It was like a magnet pulled me to him. But why? Because he was attractive and nice to me? Had my relationship with Cal gotten so bad that the first hot guy who gave me any attention seemed like a catch?

Silence swallowed us for a few moments before I said, "He's not a bad guy, Ryder. An idiot, yes, but he's not all bad."

"I didn't say that. But he sure as hell ain't the guy for you," Ryder said, glancing over at me.

God, the confidence in this man. It was refreshing. Intriguing. Exhilarating. And even though my mind shouted at me to shut the hell up, I found myself asking, "And I suppose you are?"

His dark eyes burned me to my very core, awakening a part of me I hadn't known existed. "I could be, Miss Charlotte." His thumb brushed over the back of my hand. I'd completely forgotten he was still holding it.

My breath left me in a whoosh.

I'd always hated being called Charlotte. Mama had loved the name, which was the main reason I never used it. But the way Ryder said it...*Dear Lord.*

What about Cal? Was I really going to leave him?

Yes, he was an idiot. Yes, he was selfish and we fought. A lot. Yes, he hadn't been there for me and made me feel small and unseen. *I need to break up with him.*

But I didn't want to deal with that tonight. I had enough on my plate. *Get through tomorrow. Get Cason settled in.*

"So, what are you going to do about Cason?" Ryder asked, his voice dragging me from where I'd been lost in thought. "You going to keep him here or leave?"

Leaning my head back against the headrest, I sighed. "I honestly don't know. I really don't have any business raising a kid. A part of me wonders if maybe he would be better off with my mother. She knows him better than me, and then he wouldn't have to leave this town."

"That's bullshit."

I glanced at him, surprised at the anger in his voice. "Excuse me?"

Ryder leveled me with a hard stare. "That kid's world got turned upside, and his mother, *your sister*, entrusted him to you. She obviously believed you'd be the better fit. Do you believe he'd be better off with your mom?"

Fury and confusion and guilt ate at me. As if I didn't already feel like shit about this whole situation. Now Ryder was making me feel even worse? Cool.

Tears spilled down my cheeks once more. "I–I don't know. I have no experience with kids, but I'm willing to try."

Something softened in Ryder's hard gaze; his grip on the steering wheel loosened. "That's all Cason needs. Someone willing to fight for him."

It wasn't until Ryder put his car in park that I realized we'd stopped. Beyond the windshield, his headlights lit up my sister's little rental.

"Wait. How did you know—" I'd never actually shown him the address.

"Small town, remember? I know the people Sheldon rents from."

"Makes sense," I said with a shrug.

I hadn't even unclipped my seatbelt before he'd gotten out of the car and walked around the front to open my door. Had Cal ever done that for me? I couldn't even remember. So, that was probably a no.

"You didn't have to do that for me," I said, sliding out of the passenger seat. "But thank you."

"Yes, ma'am," he replied with a half grin.

I rolled my eyes, but a smile tugged on my lips. "Well, thank you for putting up with me. I'm sorry for being a hot mess and I appreciate you taking time out of your night to drive me here."

"You aren't that much of a hot mess."

"But I'm still a hot mess," I replied with a smirk.

He held up his forefinger and thumb. "Just a bit. In a good way."

I couldn't help the laugh that fell from my lips. Why was I flirting with him? I mean, was that so wrong? The more I thought of Cal, the more I knew I was done. It wasn't just because of the past couple days. Looking back now, our relationship had been dying for a while. It was far past time to wave that white flag and call it off.

I looked at my sister's house, and whatever lighter emotions fluttering around in my chest because of Ryder withered to ash. At least that drained some of the traitorous desire pumping through my veins, even if tears welled in my eyes at the thought of being in my sister's home. With all her things. I was so not looking forward to this.

"Well, goodnight, Ryder." I took a deep breath and made my way towards the front door. Each step felt both way too fast and too damn slow.

I don't know how long I stood there, the key halfway in the lock. Would it be a disaster? Would Mama have come and cleaned up at some point? Sheldon had been in the hospital for about a month.

That thought alone pissed me off. She'd been sick all that time and Mama hadn't even told me. Sheldie not telling me made sense. She'd always hid a lot. But Mama had no right to keep that from me. What was worse, is I knew *why* she kept it from me. She wanted to use it as ammunition against me at the most opportune moment. Yet another example of how I was a horrible person. First an ungrateful daughter who'd up and left her family to move out of state, now a terrible sibling who couldn't even be bothered to come back and see her sister before she died.

A warm hand on mine pulled me from my thoughts. "You okay?" he asked.

I turned to Ryder, tears blurring my vision. I didn't have words. How could I possibly explain how I was feeling? Guilt and anger and devastation and hatred and helplessness and…I could go on. So, I just shook my head.

I choked out a sob as he pulled me into his arms. He smelled of sandalwood and a hint of leather. His strong arms held me there, anchoring me in place. I was lost at sea, and he was the life raft keeping me afloat. That should have worried me. How easy it was with him. But I didn't want to think about that right now. Not when the night wasn't over, and I hadn't even gotten to the hard part yet.

"I can't do this," I muttered into his chest. I couldn't go in there and sort through her things. I couldn't begin to think of how I was going to take care of Cason. I couldn't deal with my mother. I couldn't stay here in this town. It was too much. All of it. Too damn much.

Ryder's fingers brushed beneath my chin, tilting it up so that our gazes clashed. "Hey…hey. Look at me. Just breathe."

I tried to breathe, but it was like a ton of bricks sat on my chest. Panic writhed to life inside me, threatening to swallow me whole. I hadn't had a panic attack since leaving Texas, but not even three days in and they were back. All the while, four words kept playing over and over in my mind. *I can't do this.*

"Breathe," Ryder repeated, his voice soft yet stern. He gripped my shoulders and ran his hands down all the way to my wrists then back up again, over and over, all the while repeating that single demand.

With each stroke of his hands against my bare arms, with each rumbled word from his lips, my heart rate slowed, my shallow breathing evened out. When I finally managed to look up into his eyes, I inhaled sharply

The way he looked at me. Like I was the only person in the world. I'd never felt so exposed and yet so seen in my life. It was like he'd seen the ugly in me that I tried to keep hidden and hadn't been scared. Hadn't shied away.

"You don't gotta do it alone," he said, resting his hands on my shoulders once more. "I can help."

A shiver shot through me. His voice was little more than a deep grumble, reminding me of gravel as it scraped underfoot. His breath fanned my cheeks. My gaze dropped to his mouth before flicking back up to those dark eyes. God, he was hot and kind and I wanted to kiss him.

Do it, the little devil on my shoulder whispered.

What about Cal? Guilt reared its ugly head, and I bit back a groan. Even if I fully planned on breaking up with him tomorrow, he still technically was my boyfriend. Besides, the alcohol likely had something to do with these traitorous thoughts. Yeah, Ryder was a whole other breed of man, but would I feel as enamored tomorrow?

Let's be honest, probably.

But still, now was not the time nor place. With far more self-control than I thought I possessed, I took a step back. His hands fell away from my shoulders, and the answering cold that brushed my skin sent shivers through me. "Thank you." I sighed, placing a slightly trembling hand on the front door. "Last chance to leave and go have some fun with your friends."

His lips pulled up into a grin as he pulled his ball cap off and ran a hand through his hair before slipping it back on backward. "I ain't going anywhere."

As I turned the door knob, I couldn't help but think that what those girls in high school said might have actually been true. Maybe he did know how to ride em' Wright. He sure knew how to charm a girl.

CHAPTER FIVE

More Single Than She Was

RYDER

WHAT THE HELL WAS I doing here?

She's got a boyfriend. Though, I doubted that'd be the case much longer. She didn't act like a woman in love. She didn't even bother defending him when I called him an asshole. She'd even agreed.

Between that, the fact her sister just died, and she was the new guardian of a kid, she had enough to worry about without me messing shit up for her. And yet, when she'd given me an out, I'd jumped at the chance to stay.

Idiot.

But Charlie Evans was the most interesting woman who'd come into this town for years, and like a desert needing rain, I thirsted to know more about her.

I followed her into her sister's house, bracing myself for, well…for anything really. The house was a mess, though not as bad as I expected. A pile of laundry took up the entirety of the smaller sofa, toys littered the floor, and dishes were piled up in the sink. I glanced at Charlie. Her lips were drawn into a frown, gray eyes brewing with anger like a summer storm. Her jaw twitched as she exhaled through her nose.

"You okay?" I asked, reaching for her hand, before dropping mine at the last second. Shit, I hadn't even meant to do that. But touching her, being close to her, it just felt right. Damn, I was in trouble.

"It just pisses me off that my mother couldn't come over here once to clean up. I guaran-fucking-tee you she has a key here and has been getting clothes for Cason. But God forbid she actually put in the hard work. No, why do that when you can have your daughter do it for you?"

What happened between her and her mom? She mentioned they didn't get along earlier. I wondered if it had always been like that or if a certain event catapulted that sort of animosity from her. I didn't say anything though, not with that angry look in her eyes. I spied a couple bottles of whiskey on top of the fridge and brushed past her, ignoring her sweet scent. Something with a touch of lavender? Yeah, she reminded me of the lavender fields at my parents.

"What are you doing?" she asked as I opened and closed the cupboards until I found some small tumbler glasses. Flicking the top off the bottle, I poured us both a drink and offered one to her.

"Here. It'll help take the edge off."

Her lip quirked up in one corner as she took the glass from me. "I'm sorry again for being a hot mess and for bitching about my mother. She just—she pisses me off."

"You ain't gotta apologize."

Who was I to judge her? She was going through hell. Her sister had just died earlier today. I'd never lost anyone before, but I don't think I'd be able to do what she was doing now the very same day.

Charlie blew out an exhale, sending her bangs fluttering around her face. In the warm light of the living room, I could finally tell the actual color of her hair. A pretty copper with golden blonde pieces and streaks of crimson woven throughout. It reminded me of a sunrise.

"Alright. Well, I guess the best way to go about this is to divide and conquer," she huffed, meeting my gaze.

I nodded. "I'll go through and get all the trash and wash the dishes."

Charlie nodded and slammed her tumbler back, draining all of its contents. "And I'll start some laundry and get the rooms situated."

Following her example, I downed my drink. We set to work, Charlie mostly lost in her thoughts as she started a load of laundry and began picking up toys. Every now and then, she'd stop to pour herself another glass. She always found mine and silently poured me another.

My phone buzzed in my pocket for at least the dozenth time as I took the last of the trash out to the garbage cans. Cash's name shone on my home screen as I pressed answer. "What's up, Cash?"

"A little birdie told me you left the bar with a girl 'bout two hours ago."

I huffed, rolling my eyes. I had no doubt Grace had said something to one of the boys. "It ain't like that."

I could practically hear Cash's shit-eating grin through the phone. "Sure it ain't. Well, bud. You have yourself a good night. Tell me all about it tomorrow."

I didn't bother to say that there wouldn't be much to tell. Not in the hookup department. Drama, well, that was a different story. Charlie's life was damn near brimming with drama, whether she wanted it or not.

I made my way back into the house, noting that she'd made a good dent in the living room. She'd found some laundry baskets and taken all of the clothes to be washed again.

"Your friends checking in on you to make sure you haven't been kidnapped?" she asked, lighting a candle on the dining room table.

"Somethin' like that." I chuckled.

Her lips curved upward a moment before dropping into a frown. "It's not too late. You could still go hang out with them. You've already done more than enough. Another hour or two and I'll be done."

I went to the half-empty bottle of whiskey and poured both of us another glass. Shit, I hadn't realized we'd drank so much. "I ain't goin' nowhere for a bit. Don't wanna drink and drive."

She bit her lip a moment before a sly smile lit up her face. Dear Lord, she was gorgeous. I wondered if she realized how devastating that smile was. Did her boyfriend tell her that? I highly doubted it from the way she talked about him. But, damn, that smile. It'd make a man do just about anything.

She shook her head and huffed a laugh. "You're crazy, you know that?"

My brow quirked up as I drank from my tumbler, savoring the burn of the whiskey. "Now, why's that?"

"What guy would rather spend his Friday night cleaning some random house with a stranger than hang out with his friends?" she asked, grabbing her own glass and taking a sip. She didn't even grimace at the taste. My kinda girl.

Nope. That was a dangerous road to go down. She wasn't my girl. Probably never would be. But a cowboy could dream, right?

Maybe it was all the whiskey giving me liquid courage, or the fact she did something to me that gave me more confidence than I should have, but I replied, "When the company is this pretty, cleanin' ain't half bad."

She dipped her head down, her long hair falling in a curtain around her face, but I noticed how flushed her cheeks were. She took an audible breath and looked up at me. "You're just saying that."

I moved closer to her, eating up the distance between us. I'd fought the pull long enough. Like a damn magnet, I was drawn to her. "I ain't a liar," I said, pushing her hair off her face as I slid a hand through the soft strands and rested it against the back of her neck. Her gray eyes snapped to mine, some emotion flashing through them so quickly I couldn't make out exactly what. But she didn't pull away. "Do you know just how gorgeous you are, Miss Charlotte?"

Her lips parted and a shaky breath fanned across my skin. She smelled of whiskey, no doubt tasted like it too. I was so close. So damn close I could kiss her if I moved but an inch.

She's got a boyfriend. She clearly wasn't happy with him, but the thought served as an ice bucket to the lust pumping through my veins.

Shit. I wouldn't put her in that position. Maybe they'd break up, maybe they'd work things out. But I wouldn't cause any more problems in her life. Biting back a groan, I let my hand fall from her hair and took a step back.

I needed some air.

I T WAS CLOSE TO midnight by the time we finished. The bottle of whiskey was nearly gone, and I'd be lying if I said I wasn't feeling its effects. Damn, I should have stopped a while ago, but she kept pouring and I kept drinking. Now, I'd have to sleep it off in the backseat of my truck after I left. I'd slept in worse conditions, but it didn't mean I had to be happy about it.

"I should probably get goin'," I told her as she collapsed onto the sofa.

A scowl formed on her face. "What? No, you can't drive."

"I'll sleep it off in my truck, then leave."

"Absolutely not." She shot up, her hands going to rest on her hips. My gaze drifted up and down her body. Over the black crop top and a pair of black leggings that hugged her curves in all the right places. *Stop it.*

"I'm not having you sleep in your car," she said. "You can sleep on the couch."

"I—"

"I'm not taking no for an answer."

I knew a losing battle when I saw one. She had that same stubborn look in her eye that my buddy Maverick's mare usually had. Blowing out a breath, I sighed. "Yes, ma'am."

Charlie narrowed her gaze at me. "Don't call me that."

"Why not?"

"It makes me feel old."

I scoffed. "You're what twenty-one? Twenty-two?"

She crossed her arms over her chest, failing to bite back a grin. "Almost twenty-three, actually."

"You're just a kid."

She scowled. "You're, like, four years older than me. You're not old enough to call me a kid."

"Yes, *ma'am*—Miss Charlotte," I said, tipping my hat to her.

She rolled her eyes, but that grin bloomed wider. "You cowboys and your manners."

"You say it like it's a bad thing."

"Because it is." She let out a half laugh. "You guys go parading around town, wooing us women with your chivalry, making us think that all men are like you. And then we get to the city and realize that chivalry is dead, and now we're ruined for life."

I bit my lip, trying my damnedest to hide the smile on my face. I liked seeing her riled. There was a wildness in her eyes that I wanted to see more of. I drifted closer to her, unable to keep my distance. Meeting her gaze, I said with more confidence than I deserved to have, "Well, there's an easy fix to that problem."

"Oh yeah?" she asked. I wondered if she even knew how her body seemed to lean into mine. Like a flower looking for sunshine. "What is it?"

My hands drifted to her hips, even as my mind screamed to stop. But I couldn't. What was worse was I didn't want to. I wanted her. To taste her. To touch her. I wanted her like a kid in a damn candy shop…and I'd bet she'd taste just as sweet as any candy.

This was dangerous. Dangerous and downright stupid. But I found myself saying in a low, smooth voice, "You need to get yourself a cowboy."

She wrapped her arms around my neck, surprising the hell out of me. Her gray eyes were bright and glassy. *Definitely buzzin'.* Which should have been reason enough to walk away, but the laugh that rolled off her tongue sent a shiver through me. Dear lord, I was in trouble, and I didn't mind one bit. Stupid really did run through my veins.

"And I suppose you could be that cowboy?" she replied, her voice breathy.

Shit. Desire pumped through me. I needed to get out of here. She had a boyfriend. I had no business provoking her like this. But it'd been hard enough to resist her sober. Now? I was screwed. "I could be. If you wanted, Miss Charlotte."

She sucked her bottom lip into her mouth, and I bit back a groan. She couldn't be doing things like that. I'd always thought myself a strong man, but damn. This woman, this little spitfire who guzzled whiskey like sweet tea and had eyes the color of storm clouds, could bring me to my knees if she wanted.

"I know I shouldn't—" she said softly, her words little more than a sultry whisper. "But I want to kiss you. I've wanted to all night."

"You're goin' to regret it in the mornin', darlin'," I replied, fighting the urge to pull her against me.

She leaned in, so close that her lips brushed mine in the ghost of a kiss. "Maybe. But I think I might regret not kissing you more."

Charlie pressed her mouth to mine, and damn if every ounce of self-control I possessed didn't turn to ash in that moment. One of my hands slipped up the column of her spine, settling around the nape of her neck. She deepened the kiss, opening to me before flicking her tongue against mine. I groaned; she tasted like whiskey.

Damn.

I needed more. All of her. Whatever she was willing to give… Which was exactly why I couldn't have her. At least not tonight. Not until she didn't have a boyfriend and I was sober. With far more resolve than I thought possible, I broke the kiss and pulled away from her. I placed my hands on her shoulder, needing that little bit of distance between us. "I'll stay here tonight, Charlie. But we're not doing that again. Not until you don't have a boyfriend."

It was like a switch went off in her right then and there. Her name on my lips had the glazed-over look in her eyes disappearing, and when she spoke the words weren't husky and breathy, they shook. "I…oh my god. I can't believe I did that. I…I'm so sorry."

"It's o—" But before I could even finish my sentence, she raced down the hall. I didn't miss the tears in her eyes.

Well, shit.

CHAPTER SIX

Last Night Lonely

CHARLIE

I'D KISSED HIM. DEAR god, what the hell was wrong with me? What about Cal?

Oh, stop with that bullshit. There was no more Cal. At least, there wouldn't be by tomorrow. I shouldn't have kissed Ryder, but if it showed me anything, it was that Cal was definitely not the guy for me.

I wanted the butterflies fluttering in my ribcage that I felt when I looked at Ryder. I wanted the banter. I wanted the sincerity. I wanted someone who put my needs above their own in a situation like this. How was it that Ryder—a complete stranger, essentially—had been there for me far more than my own boyfriend? If this was how my relationship with Cal was going to continue, I didn't want it.

A part of me wanted to just call—no, text him right then and there and end things.

But I couldn't do that. I needed to at least give him the courtesy of a phone call. Right?

I stood beneath the scalding spray of water in the primary bathroom's shower, my hot tears mingling with the droplets sliding down my face. Tears of embarrassment, tears of guilt, tears of anger.

I wasn't honestly sure anymore. But the floodgates had opened, and now there was no stopping them.

Here I was, kissing a guy in my sister's house not even twelve hours after she died. God, I was terrible. Pathetic. Bile rose in my throat, and I couldn't stop myself as I vomited all over the floor of the shower. *Ew*. At least it would be easy to clean. *Again, ew*.

Still sobbing, I cleaned up myself and the shower, before toweling off and walking into my sister's room. Oh god, my clothes were still in my rental car at the bar. There was no way I was getting back into the grungy clothes I'd worn all day. The smell of the hospital clung to them over the scent of cleaning supplies and smoke from Jack's. No, those were definitely not an option.

I glanced at Sheldie's dresser and new tears burned twin paths down my cheeks. I opened up the top drawer to find rows of neatly folded shirts—so opposite of the chaos that lived in my drawers. Hers were even color-coordinated. I huffed a laugh, even as I cried. She'd always been so funny about her drawers being organized. She said it was easier to pick out something to wear. Not that that should be hard for her. It was mostly varying styles of black t-shirts. A few gray or navy here and there. A random white one.

I grabbed one and brought it to my chest with trembling hands. It smelled like her, and that just about broke me. I hadn't seen her in five years, but I knew her scent anywhere. I'd never forget it. I couldn't even properly describe it—something flowery, though. But that scent brought me back to Mama and Daddy's. To summers in the backyard and at the river. To Friday night football games. To riding horses in the green pastures behind Grandma and Grandpa's.

It hit me then like a ton of bricks, knocking the air from my lungs so thoroughly that I thought I might pass out.

She was gone. *Gone.*

Why? Why her? She'd only just turned thirty. Too young to get cancer and die. Why hadn't she told me? She'd mentioned the headaches often in the last few months, but I hadn't thought anything of it. I should have noticed. I shouldn't have been so dismissive whenever she'd told me they were nothing. I could have come back sooner and helped her. Dealing with Mama would have been a pain, but I'd have done it for Sheldon.

What I'd give to see her smile again. To see that light that shone in her blue eyes. To hear her laugh. God, it sounded like a seal dying, but I'd give anything to hear it once more. At the very least, she wasn't suffering anymore. I had to believe that. God couldn't be that cruel. To take her so young, then make her suffer even after.

Sheldon had always been more religious than me. We'd gone to church and done bible study, and while I believed in a heaven and hell and a man upstairs, I wasn't the kind of believer Sheldon was—had been.

She's okay. She's happy. She's not hurting.

At least she would be with James now. He'd died overseas during one of his tours in the Army. He hadn't even gotten to meet Cason. They'd only been married a year.

Even though all of that was supposed to make me feel better, I couldn't help the crushing weight on my chest. Through shaking sobs, I slipped the shirt over my head before checking the other drawers for a pair of sleep shorts or leggings. Finding the latter, I pulled those on as well.

I turned and looked at my sister's bed. Everything about it—the pale blue comforter with daffodil stitching, the lacy accent pillows, even the Be Kind sherpa lined throw—were all so positively Sheldon I almost smiled through my tears. A part of me wanted to climb into the bed, curl up in her blankets, and just sob. But the scent of her on me was already too much. Sleeping in her bed...I couldn't do it.

I don't remember collapsing to the floor. I don't remember anything other than the crushing grief that pressed down on me with each breath, each passing moment. I withdrew into myself. To some dark place where time and space and color didn't exist. But through the darkness, I remember warm hands and a deep voice calling to me. Beckoning me back.

"Charlie? Hey. Charlie. I need you to breathe. Breathe."

My eyes fluttered open, his dark gaze greeting mine.

"Breathe," Ryder repeated.

I obeyed, forcing cold air down my lungs over and over. My head pounded. God, it had been a stupid idea to drink so much. I don't know what possessed me to think that would be a good idea.

"You okay?" he asked as he pushed my wet hair back off my face. I'd somehow ended up in his lap, my body cradled in his. The smell of sandalwood and leather muted some of my sister's scent, and some of that crushing grief eased if only just a bit.

I bit back a snarky reply. Did it look like I was okay? My sister had just died. I'd basically cheated on my boyfriend, and I was completely drunk. I settled on just shaking my head. "No, I'm not."

"That's okay, too. I can't imagine goin' through what you're goin' through." He ran his hand through my hair again, the gesture soothing. "Do you want to talk about it?"

I shook my head. Talking was the last thing I wanted to do. But one thing was for sure. I needed to get out of this room. Seeing pictures of her, being surrounded by her lingering presence in this room…I needed out.

"Can we go to the living room?" I asked, my words little more than a ragged whisper. Even that was too loud for the headache brewing at the back of my skull.

Him picking me up and carrying me to the couch was answer enough. He still cradled me to his chest as he sat down and grabbed the blanket off the back of the couch. How he managed to drape it over my shoulders was beyond me—I was useless at that point. Hollow. There but…not. I felt numb. So damn numb and it should have scared the hell out of me.

"What can I getcha?" he asked. That deep voice rumbling in his chest. "Water? Food? I doubt there's much, but I can go through the cupboards and find somethin'. Or I can go get you somethin'."

The light of the living room was too bright, and honestly, it was just too much effort to keep my eyes open, so I closed them and nestled further into Ryder's warmth. And I don't know why, but I asked, "Will you sing to me?"

A surprised chuckle escaped him, then. "I ain't much of a singer, but I can try. Any requests?"

I shook my head.

"Alright," he replied, loosing a deep breath. "If I give you nightmares, just know you asked for it."

My lips twitched at that, but even that was too much.

He started singing some old Dean Martin song. I recognized it as one Daddy used to listen to. Ryder's voice wouldn't give me nightmares, but he wasn't the next King of Country either. It worked for him, though, especially with that deep voice of his.

His singing did the trick, and soon thoughts of Cal and my sister and this whole mess I was in faded away into nothingness until I descended into a deep, deep sleep.

I awoke to a knock on the door. My head pounded; my body ached from the position I slept in. Rubbing sleep from my eyes, I sat up, momentarily confused at the random living room I was in. *Where the hell—oh.* I was at Sheldon's.

Memories flooded my mind of the previous night, bringing guilt and shame and heartache along with it. I glanced around the room. Ryder was gone. Disappointment rippled through me, but I brushed it aside as a feminine voice accompanied another firm knock on the door.

"Is anyone home?"

Realization dawned on me like the sunrise on a new day. Shit, shit, shit. How could I have forgotten about Cason? Oh my god. I wasn't ready for this. I wasn't even dressed. Panic settled in my gut like a brick, and I fought the urge to throw up. Dear God, no. I couldn't do that again.

My heart pattered wildly in my chest, and I swore the temperature in the house rose about fifteen degrees in that instant. *Breathe.* Damn it, where the hell was Ryder when I needed him?

The thought shocked me. How was it I'd come to depend on him that much in just a single night? I shook my head. *Deal with that later.*

I took three deep, calming breaths. *I've got this. I can do this.* He was Sheldie's son. My nephew. I could take care of him. I could do this.

"Coming!" I managed to croak out, my voice hoarse and raspy.

God, my head hurt. I'd need to take something ASAP.

I ran trembling hands through my hair, hoping to God I didn't look like a train wreck as I strode to the front door. Taking one last breath, I opened it.

A blonde woman, a few years older than me, stood on the porch, along with two kids. A wave of recognition hit me. Layla Wilkins. She'd been in the grade below my sister. My gaze drifted to the boys, and my heart just about stopped as it settled on the one closest to me.

He looked just like *her*. Sheldon. Same chocolate brown hair. Same bright blue eyes. I didn't know what to expect from him. Maybe an awkward hi. A smile, even. But to my downright surprise, he launched into my arms, squeezing me with every ounce of strength in his little body.

I squeezed him right back, clinging to him with all that I was. I'd never met him in person, but right then and there I knew he was mine. That I would do anything for him.

"Hi, Auntie Charlotte." He pulled back far enough to look up at me.

I smoothed his hair back off his forehead and smiled down at him through tears I fought like hell to hold back. "Hi, bud," I choked out.

He hugged me once more, and I lost track of time for a few moments as I clung to him. How was I going to tell him what happened to his mom? How did I even approach that? Did I ease into it or just dive right in? My chest tightened, my heart squeezing at the idea of having to ruin his day in just a few minutes. I hated that our first meeting had to be like this. What horrible trauma would today cause him? What if I screwed him over royally for life?

Fuck, I hated this.

Sinking into a crouch, I held him at arm's length. "Do you want to go inside with your friend for a few minutes so I can talk to Miss Layla? We'll be right in, I promise."

He smiled and nodded, but his eyes held a hint of worry in them. I forced my lips up into a smile as well, praying like hell it seemed reassuring, even if it felt more like a grimace.

"Come on Jace!" Cason waved to the other boy. "Wanna play legos?"

The two barreled past me into the house and down the hall.

"I'm surprised you remembered me," Layla admitted once the boys left. Her tone held more surprise in it than accusation.

I turned to look at her and gave a soft smile. "We might not have hung out much, but you and Sheldon were close. I wouldn't forget you that easily, Layla."

She smiled. "How is she today?"

My throat tightened, words failing me. My stomach twisted in painful knots; it hurt to breathe. I couldn't speak, so I just shook my head, tears spilling down my cheeks.

Layla's pretty face morphed into a mask of grief as tears of her own slipped from the corners of her eyes. She clasped a hand to her mouth, a muffled sob escaping her. "W-when?" she asked, voice quaking.

"Yesterday afternoon," I managed through my tears.

Layla croaked out another sob. "Was it…Did she…" Her words trailed off into quiet cries.

I inhaled deeply and shook my head on the exhale. "She wasn't in pain. She just...slipped away."

Layla pursed her lips together, trying to bite back more sobs as tears continued streaming down her face. They'd been close. Obviously, since Sheldon had trusted her enough to watch Cason. But seeing the pure devastation reflecting in her hazel eyes was proof enough.

"I'm sorry," I whispered, feeling the need to console her as I gripped her hands and squeezed softly.

She huffed and shook her head. "Oh my god, I'm the one who should be sayin' sorry to you. Here I am cryin' like a damn baby. You're her sister."

I shrugged. "Yes, but that doesn't mean that you can't grieve for her as well."

Layla sniffled and squeezed my hands back before letting go. "Have you read the letter from Sheldon yet?"

I rocked back at that. I hadn't expected that little revelation. "She told you about it?"

Layla nodded. "She told me right before she got really bad about a month ago. I'd asked her what was going to happen with Cason, since, well, you know James isn't here anymore, and his parents passed away years ago. And then your mother isn't in the best of health…"

I exhaled through my nose, fighting back the ember of anger that flickered to life in my chest. Why hadn't Sheldon told me? Did she seriously think I would have said no? That I would have fought her? *Would I have?* That gave me pause. I might have questioned it for, like, an hour or two, but I'd have come around pretty quickly to the idea of taking care of him. I would have done anything for Sheldon, no matter how far apart we lived. A streak of jealousy clawed through me at the thought of Sheldon confiding in Layla instead of me.

Stop it. It wasn't Layla's fault. Being angry with her wouldn't do any good. She'd been nothing but kind to me.

"I'm not sure exactly how to tell him she's gone," I said, running a hand through my hair. "How much does he know about what's going on?"

"He knows quite a bit. She's been preppin' him since she found out a couple of months ago."

"I'm sorry, months?"

Sheldon had known for *months.* Why hadn't she told me? Why would she keep that from me? I could have come back here and spent time with her. I could have helped her out.

Layla's eyes swam with sympathy. "She went to the doctor's four months ago because she was gettin' horrible headaches. She had a few tests and scans done, and within a few weeks, she found out it was glioblastoma. The tumor that they found was inoperable, and the chance of chemo even helpin' was so low, that Sheldon decided not to go through with it. With how bad everythin' had already progressed, they gave her a few months to half a year."

More tears sprouted from my eyes. "Do you know why she never told me? Did she happen to say?"

Layla offered me a sad smile. "She wanted to give you as much time away from here as possible. She said it was gonna be hard enough on you to come back here and deal with your mom."

"I don't care about that!" I snapped, then sighed. "I'm sorry. I know it's not your fault. I just…I would have dropped everything. Literally, *everything* to spend just one more minute with her."

"I'm sorry," Layla whispered, reaching out and squeezing my hands this time.

Sobs wracked my body like waves on a shore. So many emotions writhed within me that I couldn't even keep them straight anymore. Guilt, anger, regret, bitterness, helplessness. So much fucking helplessness.

Breathe. I forced air in and out of my lungs. Forced my clenched muscles to relax. Forced my heart to slow. *Breathe.*

I met Layla's stare. "So, Cason knew what was happening?"

She appreciated the subject change as much as I did. I didn't want to think about the fact my own sister hadn't wanted to tell me she was dying. Sure, she'd done it because she wanted me to have more time, but that didn't make me feel better. That just made me feel selfish.

"Cason knew she was sick. That she was dyin'. She already explained to him that you'd be takin' care of him and that hopefully you two would still be livin' here for a bit. She made him a video he watches on his tablet every night. She honestly thought of everythin'."

I nodded through my tears, wiping uselessly at them with the back of my hand. "She always liked to be prepared. She had a checklist for her checklists. I used to make fun of her for it."

Layla let out a weak laugh. "I remember her drivin' us all crazy in school when we'd study for tests. Her study guides were so ridiculously extensive. She always passed with flying colors."

"Yep, sounds like Sheldon." A smile cracked my lips. She was ever the perfectionist and overachiever. She never left anything up to chance. I wiped my eyes again and took a deep breath. "Thank you for watching Cason, and for everything you've done for my sister."

"Of course." Layla offered me a genuine smile. "There's a list of phone numbers on the fridge, mine's one of them. Cason also has mine saved into his tablet. If you need me at all, please feel free to call or text. I put together a meal train through church for your mother, but now that you're here, I'll make sure that we get you set up as well. If you need any help, anything at all, please…please don't hesitate to reach out. I meant it."

"Thank you." I offered her what I hoped was some semblance of a smile.

"Jace!" she called, before meeting my gaze. "I mean it, Charlotte. Please feel free."

The boys came storming out the front door a moment later. Cason stopped at my side, while Jace made his way over to his mom. They had the same hazel eyes and light hair, though his held more of a reddish tint to it.

"I will, definitely. Thank you again, Layla."

"Of course. Jace say goodbye to Cason and Miss Charlotte."

I didn't correct either of them as they left. I just smiled and waved, wrapping an arm around Cason. He leaned into the touch, and something warmed inside of me. How could that feel so natural already? And would that change when I told him his mom was gone? I know she'd been prepping him, but being told she was going to die, and then her actually being gone were two very different things. Would he cry? Get angry? Would he withdraw into himself like I had last night? I took a deep breath and held it for three long seconds then exhaled.

Only one way to find out.

"Hey, bud," I said softly, looking at Cason. "Did you have fun at Miss Layla's?"

He nodded, his blue eyes meeting mine. "Yep. Did you know Jace has *ten* many goats?"

I laughed. "Ten many? Do you mean ten?"

He nodded, his brow furrowing slightly, even though a smile lit up his face. "Yeah. That's what I said."

"You did. I'm sorry," I agreed with a laugh. "That's a lot of goats. Did you feed them?"

"Yep. And chased them," he replied, matter-of-factly.

"Sounds fun." I moved to one of the chairs on the front porch and sat. "Want to sit with me?"

He plopped down into my lap without any warning. I grunted, adjusting to his added weight. Dang, the kid was solid. Cason curled up in my lap, even though he wasn't that little. But I didn't mind.

We sat there quietly for a moment before his little voice drifted on the breeze. "You're even prettier than in your pictures, Auntie. Mama showed me them."

Tears slid down my cheeks and I squeezed him just a little tighter. "And you are the most handsome little dude I've ever met."

He giggled and turned to meet my gaze. His smile dropped into a frown. "Why are you sad, Auntie?"

Oh god, how the hell was I going to do this? I couldn't. *You have to.*

I blew out a deep breath. "C-Cason, I n-n-need to t-tell you something. Your mommy…she um…she went to Heaven. Do you…do you know what that is?"

He nodded, his brows knitting together once more. Sadness melted over his features and turned his eyes glassy, but he didn't cry. "Mama told me she'd be leaving soon to go to Heaven, and when she did, you would come. She said you're my guardian angel."

That just about broke me. Shattered my heart into a million pieces. I pressed a kiss to his forehead and pulled him tightly against me. "That's right, bud," I choked out. "I'm here to take care of you now."

"Will Mama come back from Heaven?"

A sob escaped me. I couldn't bite it back in time. The earnestness in his voice, in the question. My heart couldn't take this. "N-no, bud. She has to stay in Heaven."

Cason pulled back to look at me. His bottom lip trembled and tears welled in his ocean-blue eyes. *Sheldon's eyes.* "But I miss her."

"Oh, sweet boy." I cupped his little face in my hands, noting the light dusting of freckles on his tan cheeks. I wiped a solitary tear from his face. "I miss her too. But, guess what?"

Lip still quivering, he sniffled and asked, "What?"

I pressed a hand to his heart, feeling the steady thump against my palm. "She's right here, in you. Every time you look in the mirror, she's staring right back at you. You have her eyes, her nose, and her dark hair. She's always with you and she'll never ever leave as long as you live."

The sadness in his face lightened just a fraction as he offered me the smallest ghost of a smile. *I get it, kid.* So much of how I felt reflected in his face. I wished like hell I could take all the pain away. That I could make everything better for him. I'd been older than him when Daddy died, but I still remembered that pain and sadness, and I'd do anything to ease that for him. There wasn't even a question now. I *had* to stay. I needed to make this as easy and comfortable as possible for him. I could deal with my mother, at least for the next few months. After that...*I'll think about that later.*

I hugged him once more, and his little body just molded to mine. How was it that someone who wasn't even mine fit so perfectly? How could I love him already more than life itself?

"Hey," I said after a while. "Want to go grab some food?"

He didn't speak but nodded against my shoulder.

Sweet D's had the best cinnamon rolls, and if he was anything like his mama he'd love them. She'd always eat so many she'd make herself sick when we were younger. But even as the idea came to me,

I bit back a groan. How the hell would we get there? I'd left my ca—*wait*...I spied my little black rental in the front yard. But...but how? I hadn't driven it here last night.

Urging Cason to get up, I strode into the house, finding the keys and my bag neatly piled on the table.

Ryder.

It had to be. He'd managed to do all of that—slip out without waking me up, grab my keys, go get my car, and bring it back and unload my stuff—all without me knowing? Had I been that drunk I'd slept through it all? Dear god, he was perfect. Absolutely perfect and kind and hot…and I didn't even have his number to thank him.

My heart squeezed. I was sure I'd see him in town at some point. It wasn't very big, and that was the thing about small towns, everyone ran into everyone. But damn if I didn't want to wait.

"What's wrong, Auntie Charlotte?" Cason asked.

"Nothing," I said, turning to look at him with a reassuring smile. "Let me just change real quick and we can go."

Cason meandered down to his room, while I went and changed in Sheldon's. I bit back tears as I walked in once more. Everything about it was just so…her. If I was going to stay here, I had to change it. I needed to make it *me*.

Right now, it felt like I was replacing her. Filling her shoes, and if Mama had taught me anything in life, it was that I would *never* be Sheldon. So, I needed to make this space mine, at least the room. The rest of the house could stay the same so that Cason didn't feel too overwhelmed.

Get breakfast. Then go to Walmart.

I pulled on a pair of leggings and a new shirt before tying a white and black flannel around my waist. I slipped on my Vans and gave myself a final once-over in the mirror. My hair was a wild, tangled mess, so I pulled it back into a ponytail and grabbed one of Sheldon's hats.

I shrugged at my reflection. *Eh, that'll do.* We were just getting food and running some errands, after all. Nothing worth doing my hair and makeup over.

"Alright, bud," I called, walking down the hall. "You ready?"

Cason hurried out of his room—already a mess by the looks of it—and grinned. "Yep!"

Grabbing my keys, I opened the front door.

And ran smack dab into a hard, warm body.

Ow.

"Good morning, Miss Charlotte."

I recognized that deep timbre. That gravelly tone. My heart fluttered as my gaze slid up his body to meet his. His dark eyes met mine—I still couldn't quite make out what color they were. They couldn't be all black. No one had black eyes, but I'd never seen a shade of brown so dark before.

"Dear God, you scared the hell out of me!" I gasped.

"Ooh! You said the Lord's name in vain. Mama said that's a penny in the swear jar." Cason exclaimed!

Right, no swearing in front of the kid. "Shit," I muttered on instinct.

"Ooh! That's two pennies!"

I groaned. This was going to take some getting used to. I'd never censored myself before. Never had a need to. But if Sheldon went so far as to have a swear jar, I guess I *had* to at least try, even if I felt there were far worse things in life than a kid swearing.

Ryder chuckled, a sly smile tugging on the corner of his mouth. "Didn't mean to startle you. I uh, I brought you some things in case y'all were hungry."

My heart danced in my chest. He'd brought food? First the car and my clothes, and now this? "You didn't have to do that," I said for what had to literally be the dozenth time since seeing him last night. "Thank you."

He flashed me a lopsided grin and dipped his head. "Not a problem."

I moved out of the doorway. "Well, come on in. Cason," I said, glancing over my shoulder. "This is Ryder. Ryder, meet my nephew, Cason."

"Howdy, mister Cason," Ryder said, holding out a hand.

"Howdy, sir." I grinned as Cason held his own hand out and gripped Ryder's firmly. "How do you know Auntie Charlotte?"

"Well, she and your mama and I grew up together here. I went to the same school as them."

"Oh," Cason said with a shrug. "I thought you were her boyfriend."

I choked back a gasp, my cheeks heating. "Cason!" I laughed, sinking my head into my hands.

"What?" he asked, glancing up at me innocently.

I gripped his shoulder, gave it a reassuring squeeze, and smiled. "Ryder isn't my boyfriend. I mean he is a boy and he's my friend, but he's not my *boyfriend.*"

"Do you want him to be?"

My stomach clenched. Were all kids so damn blunt? God. I bit back a groan, catching Ryder's lips curving up into a smug grin. He was having entirely way too much fun with this.

"Yeah, Miss Charlotte. Do tell," he asked, his deep, gravelly voice sending butterflies dancing around my ribcage. How could he affect me so much by just saying my name? But dear God, if he said it like that every time, he could say my name forever.

Pushing down the desire brewing within me, I threw a playful glare his way and walked toward the dining room. "We should probably eat before it gets cold."

Ryder gave an answering chuckle as he and Cason followed.

chapter seven

Me to Me

RYDER

I WAS IN TROUBLE.

I'd sung her to sleep and held her in my arms for most of the night before sneaking out to get her car back. Then I had to practically beg Mav and Cash to come pick me up so I could grab my car after. But now I was back, bringing her breakfast. And we weren't even dating.

Shit.

I had it bad. For a girl who still had a boyfriend. Who might still decide to stay with him now that she wasn't pissed and buzzin'. Asshole didn't deserve her. I'd never met the guy, but I knew that for a damn fact.

I was in so deep, I didn't know which way was up and which was down. But one thing was for sure, I hadn't stopped thinking about her since she'd kissed me last night.

I followed Charlie and the kid to the dining table. She'd changed out of the oversized t-shirt and sleep shorts, and I couldn't help but admire her figure as she moved through the house. She was on the shorter side but no amount of fabric could hide those lovely curves. She wasn't just skin and bones. She had meat on her. I liked that.

"So?" Charlie asked, going to the kitchen cabinets to grab a couple plates really quick. She placed them on the table and pulled out a chair before sitting in it. "What'd you bring?"

I set the plastic bag on the table, rifling through it to grab out the box of cinnamon rolls first, followed by a to-go bag with breakfast sandwiches in it. "I wasn't sure if you had a sweet tooth or liked somethin' more hearty for breakfast, so I got both."

Charlie shook her head and bit back a grin. Dear lord, why'd she have to do that? "You really thought of everything, didn't you?"

I shrugged. "Better safe than sorry."

She huffed a laugh and tore her gaze from mine, looking at Cason. "So, what's it gonna be, bud? Cinnamon rolls or a breakfast sandwich?"

Cason's eyes flicked back and forth between the bag of sandwiches and cinnamon rolls. With a sigh, he pointed at the to-go bag. "I'll take a sandwich."

Charlie frowned and reached a hand out to touch his shoulder. "What's wrong?"

"Grandma's always telling me I eat too much sugar. And Mama would say that the breakfast sandwich has more protein…whatever that means."

I watched all the light leave Charlie's gaze, her face hardening, storm clouds forming in her gray eyes. Her jaw feathered a moment before she exhaled deeply. "Cason, I'm only going to tell you this once… You eat whatever you want to eat. You don't need to worry about eating too much sugar or not having enough protein. That's my job. I don't see anything wrong with having a cinnamon roll every now and then. It's no different than having cake. And I know for a fact that your grandma still makes one every weekend. Doesn't she?"

Cason nodded.

I didn't miss the embers of rage burning in her gaze. I didn't know what to do. What to say. Obviously, this was some point of contention between her mother and her. Was that why she left?

"That's what I thought," Charlie replied, grabbing the tin of cinnamon rolls and opening it up. She scooped one out, placed it on a plate, and handed it to Cason. "If you want a cinnamon roll, you eat the cinnamon roll."

Cason glanced at me, his dark brow rising in question. "You gonna eat one too, Mister Ryder?"

I met Charlie's gaze. And though cinnamon rolls weren't my usual pick, I knew that this was important to her, even if it didn't seem that big of a deal. There was something deeper going on here, so I nodded. "May I have one, Miss Charlotte?"

A soft smile graced her lips and the storm in her eyes broke. "You may."

She dished us all up one and for a few moments the room descended into silence as we ate. Cason's voice broke the quiet. "This is the best cinnamon roll I've ever had," he said, licking every last bit of frosting off his fingers.

Charlie grinned and looked at me. "These from Sweet D's?"

I nodded.

Her grin spread wider. "You know, Cason, your Mama used to love these cinnamon rolls. One time she ate so many, she was sick for three days."

"Really?"

"Yep. Your grandpa used to take us there every Sunday after church. It was tradition. Her and I would always race each other to see who could finish theirs first."

"Who won?" he asked.

"Mostly me." She laughed. "I was a lot more competitive than your mom."

Cason frowned. "What does that mean?"

"It means she don't like to lose," I replied before she could.

Charlie shrugged. "It's true. I don't like losing."

That made two of us.

"I don't either," Cason admitted. "Mama says it's okay to lose, though. That winning isn't everything."

"It isn't everything," Charlie admitted. "You can learn a lot from losing. But you should always try your hardest. You should always strive to win."

I liked that. I'd learned far more from my failures than I had from my successes, but if rodeoing taught me anything, it was that I'd always look for that win.

Cason nodded and glanced at the bag of sandwiches. "What are you gonna do with those now?"

"Eh, I'll give 'em to Dutch," I said with a shrug.

"Who's Dutch?" Cason asked.

"My dog. She's in the truck." I glanced toward the front of the house and out the window. Not that I could see her. Girl was probably sprawled out on the backseat.

"What?" Charlie gasped, a scowl forming on her lips.

"Don't worry. I left the window down, and it ain't warm out. She'll be fine."

But Charlie was already standing. "You have a dog and you didn't bring her in here?"

My brows knit together. "I didn't want to just assume. Some people don't like dogs."

"Anyone who doesn't like dogs is a damn idiot. Bring the poor girl in."

"Oooh that's another penny."

I laughed. Pretty, competitive, loved dogs. She couldn't be any more damn perfect. Cash would say wife her up before someone snatched her up. Too bad she already had been, at least for the moment. Maybe that would change, though. I hoped like hell it did. "Yes, ma'am."

"Don't ma'am me. Get your as–butt on out there and get her."

I laughed, rising from my chair and making my way outside. Dutch's brindle head popped out of the window as I walked toward my car. "Hey, girl. Wanna meet some new friends?"

Her excited leap out of the car was answer enough. Though, Dutch did everything excitedly. After getting her calmed down, we made our way back toward the house. Cason and Charlie both stood on the porch, bubbling with anticipation. I couldn't tell who was more excited.

"This here is Dutch," I said as I came to a stop before them and motioned for her to sit. She did, her tail brushing against the dirt in a frantic sweep back and forth.

"Oh my God, she's gorgeous!" Charlie gasped. "Can I pet her?"

"Yeah, me too!" Cason chimed in.

I nodded as Charlie sunk down into a squat and ran a hand over Dutch's back. "Who's a pretty girl?" she cooed, completely unbothered by Dutch's aggressive kisses. "You're a pretty girl."

I swear, if that girl didn't have my heart already, she sure damn did now.

"She's so soft, Auntie Charlotte."

Charlie grinned, continuing to pet Dutch even aftershe leaned into Charlie and knocked her over before plopping into her lap. Charlie just laughed and looked at Cason. "I know. And doesn't she have the prettiest coat?"

"She looks like a tiger!" he giggled as Dutch pawed at him, demanding more pets. Not like she needed any more attention. She got it everywhere we went.

"Do you know what her markings are called?" Charlie asked Cason.

He shook his head.

"It's called brindle. She's got a brindle coat."

"Brindle," Cason replied, trying the word out. "She's pretty."

"She sure is," Charlie grinned, managing to stand up. I bit back a smile. She was covered in dog hair, her black leggings revealing it all, but she didn't seem to mind. Charlie met my gaze. "She's a Dutch Shepherd, isn't she?"

I nodded, a little shocked she'd guessed it so quickly. Most didn't. A laugh escaped her before she replied, "I used to work with dogs. I've met a few Dutchies. Also, very original name, by the way." A smirk pulled on her lips. "Really, I couldn't have thought of something more unique myself."

I laughed, pulling my cowboy hat off and running a hand through my hair before placing it back atop my head. "Hey, it's a step up from Dog. That was my first choice."

She rolled her eyes, but a smile broke on her lips like a sunrise peeking out across the horizon. God, she was beautiful, and the fact she still had a boyfriend wasn't enough enough to stop me anymore. I just…didn't care. I wouldn't do anything with her, wouldn't let it go any further than this back-and-forth flirting, but I'd be damned if I didn't make my intentions clear.

Cason's voice dragged me from my thoughts. "Does she like to play fetch?"

I grinned. "There's a ball in the back seat. Go grab it and see for yourself."

The kid tore off for my truck. The moment he pulled that green tennis ball out of the backseat, Dutch was at his side, tongue lolling out of her mouth. With a laugh, Cason threw the ball along the long driveway and Dutch shot after it, kicking up dirt and gravel as she went.

I watched them for a few moments, thinking back to when I was a kid doing the same thing. Oh, to be that young again. What I'd give to go back to my biggest worries being staying up past bedtime and having to stop playing with the dog because the sun went down.

"Thank you. He needed this." Charlie's voice drew my attention. She'd shifted to stand beside me. I hadn't even heard her.

I turned to face her. "Did you tell him?"

She nodded, sucked in a shuddering breath, and exhaled slowly. "Yeah. He took it well, I think. Sheldon's been preparing him for this, though. She made a video for him to watch every night explaining it all. She even went so far as to tell him I'm his guardian angel and that I've come to take care of him since she had to go to Heaven."

Her words remained even, but pain laced her features, lining the planes of her pretty face and lingered in her stormy eyes that brewed with unshed tears.

I grabbed her hand and gave it a squeeze. "I'm glad he took it well. How're you doin'?"

She shrugged and wiped at her eyes. "I'm okay. Tired and hungover as fuck, but I'll be okay."

I chuckled. "Careful, or you may have to put another penny in the swear jar."

"Dear God." She huffed a laugh, her gaze finding Cason across the yard. "Give me a few months and that damn jar will be overflowing."

I grinned. "So that mean you're stayin' then?"

She met my stare and raised her shoulders in a shrug. "Looks like it. Everything's changed so much for him, I don't want to make this any harder than it already is."

I nodded. "Makes sense. You gonna need a job?"

She blew out a sigh. "Yeah. I'll probably start focusing on that after the memorial. I need to meet up with my mother and get that sorted out first."

"I can ask around in town, see who's hiring. What all can you do?" I asked.

"Well, I have a business degree. I was the social media manager of an animal rescue…also waited tables through college and have personal assistance experience. I'm great with computers, and I even did a bit of event planning here and there."

"A jack of all trades." It wasn't surprising, though. She'd always been smart and driven in school and sports. I'd only been around during her freshman year when I was a senior, but she and her sister had both been similar.

Her cheeks flushed a pink color, and I fought the urge to run my fingers across her freckled skin. "I wouldn't go so far as to say that. But I pick things up quick and work my ass off."

"That's another penny," I replied with a wink.

"Oh, fuck off," she muttered, though a smile quirked her lips. "And if you tell Cason, I'll murder you."

"Whoa there, pump the brakes darlin'." I chuckled. "Maybe I won't put in a good word for you with my friend at the shelter, after all."

Her brow furrowed and she cocked her head to the side. "What? You'd do that?"

I shrugged. "Yeah, why not? You need a job, and there ain't no harm in me askin' if they're hirin'."

She shook her head, an incredulous laugh falling from her lips. "Why are you doing this? Why are you being so nice?"

"Have you been gone from here so long you forgot what some southern hospitality looks like?"

She pegged me with a hard stare and scoffed. "There is southern hospitality, and then there is—" She waved a hand at me. "Whatever you are doing, Ryder Wright. The two are absolutely not the same thing."

I bit my lip, trying to calm the beating of my heart. When was the last time a woman made me feel like this? It reminded me of that thrill I got right before a run. That second before the cow chute slammed open and that steer went tearing off for the other side of the arena. Or that rush I got when I settled onto a bull's back, waiting for that gate to open. Terror and excitement warring for dominance. Charlie Evans both terrified and excited me, and I needed more of her.

"I'd be lyin' if I said I didn't do any of this for selfish reasons. From the minute I saw you in Jack's last night, I've been drawn to you."

"So I *am* a new, shiny buckle you want to put on your shelf?" she asked. There was no anger or animosity in her tone though. In fact, it almost sounded teasing.

She'd moved closer, her lavender scent drifted to my nose, and I could feel her body heat. Dear Lord, I wanted to reach out and pull her against me. But I resisted. How the hell I did, I can't even begin to explain. I settled on brushing my thumb over the back of her hand, though. "You ain't just some prize to be had, Miss Charlotte. If I wanted you for that, I wouldn't have stopped you last night."

Her answering gasp damn near did me in.

"I want to make my intentions clear right now. I'll do anything I can to be around you, even if I have to go get your car, butcher Dean Martin songs, and bring you cinnamon rolls."

Her teeth dragged against her bottom lip as she bit it a moment before saying, "I still have a boyfriend." But there was no conviction in her voice.

I'd been worried this morning that once the alcohol had worn off, she'd go back on her feelings about him. But she was just as unconvincing now as she had been last night. She wasn't in love with him. At least, not anymore.

Leaning in close to her ear, I murmured, "I'd bet good money that by this time next weekend, you and him won't be together."

"Bold words, cowboy," Charlie replied, taking a step back to peg me with a narrowed gaze. She placed a hand on her waist, jutting one of her hips out in a defiant stance.

I offered her a confident smirk. "Tell me I'm wrong. Tell me that you're in love with him. That he makes you happy. That that kiss last night was a mistake. Tell me that, Miss Charlotte, and I'll walk away right now and leave you alone for good."

She huffed a bitter laugh, unable to meet my gaze as she slid her tongue over her teeth. A shiver went through me. Oh, I'd riled her. Good. It was about time she saw how much better she could do. And while I knew I had my own plethora of problems, I could make damn sure she never felt the loneliness she'd experienced last night if she were mine.

I reached for her hand on her hip and brushed my thumb over the back of it once more, whispering, "That's what I thought."

And though her gaze remained hard and narrowed, her fingers brushed against mine in the barest of touches. "You're an arrogant bastard," she breathed.

I tipped my hat with my free hand and winked. "Confident, darlin'. There's a difference."

Charlie snickered and shook her head, the sound like music to my ears. Her cheeks flushed once more, and she pressed a hand to her lips. "I don't know how I can be so incredibly annoyed and attracted to you all at once, but it's infuriating."

"Well, I apologize for that," I replied with a grin, brushing my fingers over hers once more. I reveled in the rush of the forbidden touch.

Something in her eyes flared, her breath hitching in her throat. I bit back a groan. Funny how such a small gesture could cause such a strong reaction.

"Hey! Hey guys!"

I turned just as Dutch and Cason came skidding to a stop at our sides. Shit, I'd completely forgotten about the two of them. I cleared my throat as Charlie fiddled with her long braid.

"Hey, bud. What's up?" she asked as he barreled into her. Her arms wrapped around him on instinct as he clung to her side. I smiled. A motherly role suited her, even if she probably would argue about that.

"Look what Dutch can do!" he exclaimed, letting go of her long enough to turn to Dutch and say, "Sit!"

Dutch obeyed. Cason looked up at us expectantly. Charlie recovered quicker than me, a smile lighting up her face. "Wow! That's awesome. I wonder if she can lay down."

I whistled, drawing Dutch's attention. "Down." She obeyed once more, gaze flicking between me and Cason.

Cason excitedly hooted. "What else can she do?"

Dutch and I went through our list of commands and tricks, each one impressing both of them just a bit more. Good. I'd worked my ass off with Dutch, glad to see all that hard work paying off. Even if it was only to impress a six-year-old and his gorgeous aunt.

"Impressive." Charlie grinned when I'd finished.

I shrugged. "She's impressive, I just give her commands."

"Auntie Charlotte, can Dutch and Mister Ryder hang out with us today?" Cason asked, already back on the ground rough housing with Dutch.

As much as the thought of spending the day with Charlie enticed the hell out of me, I had the rodeo tonight. *Oh shit.* I grabbed my phone out of my back pocket. *Shit.* I had to go. I'd told Cash I'd be at the ranch to get him and Maverick in less than an hour. I still had to go get Boone and my trailer. Damn it. What I'd give to spend the day with Charlie and Cason. "Aw, bud. I wish I could hang out with y'all for the day, but I gotta get goin'."

Cason groaned, the same disappointment reflecting in Charlie's face.

Invite them to the rodeo. But something in my head said to stay quiet. On second thought, having her there might be a distraction I couldn't afford. I had to see her again, though. I wanted it—no, needed it, about as much as I needed this win tonight.

I looked at Cason. "How 'bout sometime this week you and your aunt come over to the ranch and you can play with Dutch? Maybe even ride a horse?"

"Really?" he asked, bouncing up into a stand. "You'll teach me to ride? Oh, please! That would be so cool."

I huffed a laugh and met Charlie's stare. "If it's alright with your aunt."

A coy smile toyed on her lips as she played with the end of her braid. "I think we could maybe find some time."

"Well, good then. I really best be goin'. Y'all have a good day now." I whistled low, and Dutch moved to my right side. Tipping my hat at Charlie and Cason, I said goodbye and made my way to the truck.

I was almost all the way backed out of the driveway when I noticed her running toward my truck. What the hell? Putting it in park, I rolled down the window just as she approached.

"How am I going to get a hold of you?" she asked, her voice breathless.

She'd run all the way down the driveway for that? I bit back a grin. That gave me too damn much satisfaction. "I went ahead and wrote my number on that paper on your fridge."

She huffed a laugh. "You really thought of everything, didn't you?"

I shrugged. "I told you, I'm a man of clear intentions. I ain't leaving anything up to chance or fate. I want to get to know you, Charlotte."

The smile that bloomed on her lips sent my heart skittering. I'd never get tired of that smile, especially when it was aimed my way.

"You're something else, Ryder Wright."

"I'll take that as a compliment."

She took a step back from the truck. "It was meant as one. Maybe I'll see you tomorrow."

It wasn't a question, but a statement. One I planned to wholeheartedly make damn sure happened. I tipped my hat to her. "Yes, ma'am. You have a good day now, Miss Charlotte."

Cash and Mav were going to give me a ration of shit, but some things were worth it. And that woman standing there on the dirt and gravel driveway definitely was.

Shit, I was in trouble.

CHAPTER EIGHT

Highway Boys

Ryder

I PULLED UP TO the Mooney ranch at ten on the dot. Technically still on time, but punctuality was kinda my thing. Not even a day with Charlie and she was already flipping my world upside down. Why was I so...enamored by her? Yeah, enamored was a good word for how I felt. I'd dated plenty of girls. Not that that was something to brag about, but I hadn't met a single one that made me *feel* the way she did. She stirred something in me. Something exhilarating. Terrifying. Addicting.

I made quick work of backing up the trailer and opening up the doors. Boone stood there, tied up in the front slot, unfazed as he ate from his hay bag.

"Ohhh shit! Look who finally showed up!" Cash, my best friend and biggest pain in my ass, brayed his most infuriating laugh as he led Playboy, his roan gelding, out of the barn.

"Shut up." I huffed a laugh as he made his way toward me. "I said ten, it's ten."

"If you're on time, you're late, if you're early, you're on time," Cash's million-dollar grin somehow spread even wider as he threw my own words against me. *Damn bastard.*

I shook my head and pinched the bridge of my nose. "One time. I show up—*on time,* I might add—one time, and somehow that's worse than literally every other damn time you've been late because you're hugging a toilet in some random buckle bunny's dad's house."

A low, deep voice, like rolling thunder, sounded from the barn. "It is," Maverick said as he walked out, leading his massive black mare.

See!" Cash chuckled, walking Playboy into the trailer.

"How do you figure, Mav?" I asked, flicking the brim of my hat up so I could see the tall cowboy and his stupid mare better.

"The standards are lower." Maverick shrugged. "We expect more from you. All we can expect from Cash is that he shows up every once in a while."

"Hey!" Cash boomed as he hopped out of the trailer, his spurs jangling as his boots hit the dirt. "Big Daddy *always* shows up!" He threw his arm around Maverick's shoulder, but shied away as Black Betty squealed and tried to bite a chunk out of him.

"When are you goin' to send that nag to get made into dog food and get a *real* horse?" I asked. I didn't hate many things, but I hated that mare. Damn near everyone did—except Mav. He loved her and doted on her, and she loved him right back. Probably the only damn thing she loved. I'd never met a rider and horse quite so different, him being so quiet, gentle, and patient, whereas that mare was all fire and brimstone. Piss and vinegar. But they worked well together. Mav liked to say they balanced each other out. I couldn't help but agree.

"After she kills Cash," Maverick replied with a grunt as he led her up into the trailer.

"It'll never happen!" Cash swaggered his way around my trailer to the ice chest to grab a Monster. "I'm too fast. That old nag would never see me, let alone be able to kill me."

"*Okay,* John Cena. Get your ass in the truck," I groaned. I should've just trailered up there on my own. Car ride Cash was even more obnoxious than every day Cash. Not to mention, pre-rodeo pump up Cash...he was another beast entirely.

Cash plucked his massive pink polarized sunglasses out of his shirt pocket and slipped them on before cracking open his drink and taking a long swig. "Where is she?" he asked.

I frowned. "Who?"

"The girl! I want to see what the girl who can make Ryder Wright late looks like."

"She ain't comin'." I immediately kicked myself. *Way to set him up for that one.*

Cash's mouth spread into a shit-eating grin. "Ah, don't beat yourself up about it, you can't please 'em all. Well, I can. But that's besides the point." Cash let out another braying laugh.

"You're an idiot," I pointed out, motioning for him to toss me a Monster as well. I'd need one for the two-hour drive with him. "She's got a boyfriend, dipshit. We're just friends."

"*Oh-kay!*" Cash sent a can flying my way before pulling down his sunglasses to wink. "We definitely believe him, don't we, Mav?"

Maverick closed up the trailer doors, ignoring Betty screaming and kicking angrily. Damn mare. "*We* don't believe it's a good idea to make fun of the only one of us that's got a trailer at the moment." Maverick pegged Cash with a pointed stare. "And *we* believe we're goin' to be late if you don't shut up and get in the truck."

"Don't get your panties all twisted up." Cash grinned and winked at Mav. "No cowboys will want to take you home if you cry too much."

"Fuck off." Maverick scowled. "I'll have to take home a cowboy because you use up all the buckle bunnies."

"What can I say?" Cash stood with his hands on his hips and his feet spread wide apart. "Everyone wants a piece of Big Daddy!"

I had to give it to any man who could refer to himself as Big Daddy with a straight face. Cash Mooney didn't hold a shred of shame. He was handsome and confident as hell, buck wild, charming, and just self-deprecating enough to not be an asshole—well, not a total asshole. He was my oldest friend, and, truly, one of the best men I knew. A pain in the ass, yes…but I'd rather have that pain in the ass in my corner when push came to shove.

"Just get in the fuckin' truck or I'm leaving your ass here." I turned and headed back for the driver's seat, cracking open my Monster and downing half of it. My heart could hate me later.

"We need to stop and get some chew," Cash said.

I turned to look back at him, catching him spitting off to the side before he touched my passenger side door. "I've told you not to chew that shit in my truck. You get drunk and spit that shit on my floor again, I'll tie you onto Mav's mare and hit her with a hot stick."

"Well, damn—" Cash whistled, sliding into the back seat where he sprawled out. "This new mystery woman's got you *all* riled up."

I got into the front seat, pleased to find Maverick already in the passenger seat. Him and I shared a long look before he looked back at Cash and said curtly, "Shut up. Now."

Cash let out an obnoxious laugh as I put the truck in drive.

This was going to be a long day.

CHAPTER NINE

You Ain't No Cowboy At All

CHARLIE

G OD, I HAD IT bad.

I couldn't stop thinking about him. It didn't help that Cason couldn't stop *talking* about him. But even if every other word that came out of his mouth wasn't Ryder's name, I'd be just as doomed. He'd consumed me. Mind and soul. I thought of that kiss last night. Of how he'd sang me to sleep. How he'd gotten my car and breakfast...and god, how he'd interacted with Cason.

I'd never been more attracted to someone in my life.

I really needed to call Cal and break up with him, but just the thought was so damn exhausting. I knew he'd start a fight, then try to keep me on the phone and continuously gaslight me until I was so overwhelmed and anxious that I just said whatever I could to appease him enough to get off the line. It's how all of our fights went.

God, that realization was horrible. How long had I let myself be treated like that?

I glanced down at my phone as Cason and I walked through Walmart. Twenty missed calls. Five voicemails. Who the hell knew how many text messages. *Oops, make that twenty-one calls.* Ugh, you'd think he'd take a hint. *Apparently not.*

I sighed and hit the end button, sending it straight to voicemail before sliding my phone into my purse. "So, bud," I said, looking at Cason. "What do you like to eat?"

We made our way up and down the aisles, Cason pointing out his favorite foods and snacks. I'm sure Sheldon would have thrown an absolute fit at the amount of crap food that ended up in our cart, but hey, she'd put me in charge knowing cooking wasn't my area of expertise. Besides, Hot Pockets weren't too bad, and according to the box, they had like ten grams of protein. That counted for something, right?

We ventured over to the home goods section, when a familiar voice called out my name. I turned to find Layla Wilkins and her son Jace in the aisle just behind us.

"Oh, hi, Layla...Jace," I said with a smile.

Layla smiled back. "How are y'all doin'?"

"Good," I replied. "Just getting some things for the house."

"Y'all have plans for the evenin'?" she asked as the boys played tag around the carts.

I was about to say something, but if she didn't feel the need to stop them, then maybe I was just overthinking it. Mama had always been ridiculously strict on us. She'd probably have a whole earful to say about it if she were here, but if they weren't hurting anything then I'd allow it.

I shrugged. "Honestly? Nothing." I hadn't even thought about what we'd do for lunch. Planning out my days wasn't something I was used to at the moment.

"Y'all should come out to the rodeo. There's good food and it's somethin' to do on a Saturday night."

The mere mention of the word rodeo sent my stomach into knots. Flickers of images passed through my mind. *Daddy running down that steer. Him jumping off. Him and the steer colliding, rolling on the ground...and then nothing.* The steer got up, trotted off. But Daddy didn't so much as move. He'd gotten injured before. Blown kneecaps. Torn shoulders. Broken collar bones. But I never thought he'd die. Didn't even realize it was possible. He'd done it for so long with no serious accident, and then...boom. He was gone. Ten years now.

I hadn't been to a rodeo since. Not because I hated it or thought it was inhumane or anything like that. It just gave me too much anxiety now. The thought alone had my heart thumping.

"Uh, I don't think—" I began.

"Oh, please, please, please, please, *please*!" Cason cut in, practically begging. Those puppy dog eyes of his reminded me of an ASPCA commercial.

I took a deep breath. I didn't want to let him down. Didn't want to say no when he was so clearly excited about it. Besides, the rodeo would be a good distraction for him.

It's been over a decade. I could deal with one night.

I sighed. "Okay."

His whoop of excitement was infectious. I couldn't fight back a small grin at the sheer happiness on his face. *It's going to be okay. What's the worst that'll happen?*

"**A**LRIGHT. YOU EXCITED, BUD?" I asked, opening the back seat passenger door. Cason had already unbuckled his seat belt and slid out of his booster seat the moment I'd put the car in park. I swear, the only reason he hadn't gotten out yet was because of the safety lock I'd made sure to put on in the car.

Why did kids have to touch buttons and knobs and car doors that they *knew* they shouldn't touch? Also, why did car companies insist on putting buttons and levers where kids could easily get to them?

"Yes! Yes! Hurry!" Cason squealed, almost knocking me over to get out of the car.

"Excuse you." I laughed, shaking my head. "Is that any way to behave?"

Cason offered me a sheepish smile and wrapped his arms around me. "Sorry, Auntie Charlotte."

I'd debated correcting him on what to call me all day today. Part of me wanted to groan or cringe, but Auntie Charlotte sounded better than Auntie Charlie or Aunt Charlie. Besides, Ryder called me Charlotte and I didn't correct him.

"It's okay. Wanna go in?" I squeezed him back and ruffled his dark hair. He went for the whole cowboy get-up this evening, minus the hat, and that was only because he didn't have one. I told him if they were selling them tonight I'd get him one. I didn't know how big this rodeo was. Some of the ones I'd gone to as a kid had vendors. If not, I promised I'd get him one soon. His blue and white checkered shirt brought out the color of his eyes, and he looked absolutely precious in his little Wranglers and cowboy boots.

He nodded and grabbed my hand in his small one and dragged me through the parking lot, toward the crowd walking through the front gates.

It's just one night, I reminded myself, even as anxiety wound its way around my heart, constricting it like a snake. *Stop.* I was being ridiculous. It wasn't the rodeo itself that killed my dad. It was a fluke accident.

"Auntie Charlotte? Are you okay?"

I shook off my intrusive thoughts and looked down at Cason. Only he wasn't by my side. My worried gaze scanned around for a couple seconds before landing on him. He stood a few feet in front me. Had I stopped walking? I didn't even remember.

Breathe. And though it was my own voice in my head, I remembered Ryder telling me that numerous times last night. That seemed to do the trick, and after a few deep inhales and exhales the tingling in my nerves dulled, while the vice-like grip on my heart eased up just a bit.

I nodded and moved to his side. "Yeah, bud. Sorry."

I paid for us and we made our way into the fairgrounds. A few booths had been set up—mostly food and beer, one from a local radio station, and another for raffle tickets to win the souped-up Ford F-150 they had on display.

"Sorry, bud. There's no hats. Want an ice cream, though? Or maybe some nachos?" I said, nodding at the concession stand.

Cason shrugged, a smile still lighting up his face despite his disappointment. "It's okay, I don't like nachos."

"You don't like nachos? They're so good!" He just made a face, and I laughed. "Okay, well what do you want to do? Wanna walk around or go grab a seat? It's going to start in about twenty minutes."

He tilted his head to the side and thought for a moment. "Can we find Jace and Miss Layla?"

I nodded, impressed with how well he'd taken that. Weren't kids, like, notorious for meltdowns when they didn't get what they wanted? Was he just *that* good, or was he over that phase? Regardless, I was happy I didn't have to deal with a crying kid. I didn't know if I'd ever be ready for that.

"Sure, bud."

"You think we'll see Mister Ryder here tonight?" he asked as we made our way to the main covered arena.

I frowned. "I don't know. Maybe."

It seemed like everyone from every single surrounding town and their family was here tonight. I wouldn't be surprised if he was, but I'd think he'd mention it if he were going to be here. At least I would have thought he would with how we'd interacted earlier. Or maybe he was competing and hadn't told me about it because he didn't want a distraction. Oh god, I hoped it wasn't that. That would stop any potential for us right then and there. I couldn't watch someone I loved get hurt again.

And he *would* get hurt. They all did. Some worse than others.

Maybe, I'm just overthinking all of this entirely. Maybe, last night and this morning meant nothing. Maybe, he actually was just being nice and I was romanticizing everything that happened between us.

What about the kiss? The finger brushes? That wasn't just being nice. True, but maybe it wasn't as big of a deal as I'd made it in my mind either. One thing was for sure, though, I wanted it to be a big deal. I wanted to get to know him. Wanted to find out what he did for work, for fun. Find out his likes and interests. What that faint scar on his cheek was from that I'd noticed today. Anything about him, honestly.

As we made our way into the main arena, everything got louder. Country music blasted from speakers, people talked and shouted as they ambled about and found their seats, cattle mooed and shuffled around in their pens. We'd entered on the side nearest the contestants. Cowboys and cowgirls were busy prepping for their rides.

That weight on my chest tightened up again, but I forced deep breaths through my nose. *You can do this. You can do this. Breathe.*

"Miss Charlotte?"

My heart fluttered wildly at that deep, familiar voice behind me. A grin formed on my lips before I'd even turned to look at him. "Well, hello there," I said, spinning to face him.

He looked good. Too damn good. He rocked the hell out of a black long sleeved button up, Wranglers, cowboy boots, and a black felt cowboy hat.

"Mister Ryder!" Cason yelled excitedly.

Ryder mussed up Cason's hair and tipped his hat to me, his gaze traveling up and down my body, sending shivers down my spine. How did he do that? Make me feel so exposed despite the fact I was completely clothed. "How're y'all doing tonight?"

"Good." I smiled, tucking a strand of hair behind my ear. "I don't know why, but I wasn't expecting to see you here. Which I realize is dumb, because, like, basically all of town is here."

"Ah, yeah, this is one of the qualifiers for the big rodeo in Austin comin' up in a couple weeks. I need a win tonight in either of my events to go."

The butterflies dancing in my rib cage died then, disappointment setting in like a storm cloud around me as I registered his words.

All men had a flaw. Everyone did, really. I'd been hoping, praying, that Ryder was as perfect as he seemed to be. But I'd found his flaw. And damn it, if that didn't absolutely kill me.

Ryder Wright had never been more off limits than he was now.

I would never fall in love with a rodeo cowboy.

Chapter Ten

Should've Been A Cowboy

Ryder

Damn, she looked gorgeous. I swear, the minute she'd walked in, my gaze was drawn to her. She wore a sleeveless, mustard-yellow crop top. I'd never liked the color, but on her...well, I think she could probably wear a potato sack and look good. Her ripped, black flare jeans hugged her curves in all the right places. Long, copper curls fell down to her waist, nearly brushing her hips as she walked.

Maverick had been talking to me when I'd seen her, but I don't remember anything he'd said. One minute, I leaned against the pipe-stall, talking with him and Cash, then the next, my boots ate up the distance between her and I.

"Miss Charlotte?"

"Well, hello there." That sunshine smile she pegged me with sent a shiver through me. I hadn't told her about tonight, but I'd hoped like hell she'd come. Fate worked in mysterious ways, I guess.

I fought the urge to pull her against me. I hadn't stopped thinking about her since leaving this morning. But she still had a boyfriend, at least that was the case when I'd left. Last thing I needed was to go and do something stupid and scare her off.

"Mister Ryder!" Cason called excitedly.

I grinned and ruffled up his hair even as my gaze came to rest on Charlie. "How're y'all doing tonight?"

"Good," she replied, offering a shy smile as she tucked a piece of hair behind her ear. "I don't know why, but I wasn't expecting to see you here. Which I realize is dumb, because, like, basically all of town is here."

"Ah, yeah, this is one of the qualifiers for the big rodeo in Austin comin' up in a couple weeks. I need a win tonight in either of my events to go."

The light in her grey gaze turned dark and stormy, and that smile on her lips dropped into a frown.

She blew out a breath. "Oh, um...what, uh, what events are you competing in?" Her words were friendly enough, but there was a coldness in her tone that hadn't been present a moment ago.

Shit. What did I say? What did I do?

"Steer wrestlin' and bull ridin'."

"Oh." She dropped her gaze from mine and glanced at Cason. "Well, good luck. Cason, tell Mister Ryder good luck as well. We need to go find Miss Layla and Jace."

"Charlotte," I said, grabbing her hand. "Did I say somethin' to upset you?"

She closed her eyes and took a deep inhale before letting it out slowly and pulling her hand out of my grip. When she opened her eyes, sadness glimmered in them like a star-flecked sky. "It's Charlie. Please, just call me Charlie."

I frowned. Okay, something was seriously wrong. She'd not once corrected me about earlier today. In fact, a few minutes ago she hadn't either. Maybe she changed her mind about breaking up with her boyfriend, after all. Maybe they talked it out, worked things over. I don't know… Something. But then why had she seemed so interested up until I'd mentioned needing a win tonight?

I wanted to ask, to press, but Cash's loud, obnoxious voice rose over the speakers. "Woo! Get some, Ryder!"

I glanced back toward him. The damn idiot sat balanced on top of the pipe-stall, his neon shirt matching his pink sunglasses. Maverick stood beside him, arms draped over the top rail. He gave me one of those *'I tried'* looks that he used when Cash did something stupid. I scowled at Cash, shaking my head once. I was going to kill him. Absolutely fucking kill him.

I turned back to Charlie, noticing her flushed cheeks. She dipped her head, refusing to meet my gaze, but I swore unshed tears lined her eyes. "I need to go," she choked out.

"Charlo—Charlie," I corrected myself, grabbing her hand once more. "What'd I do?"

She opened her mouth, closed it, and shrugged, a heavy sigh escaping her. "You didn't do anything. See you around, Ryder." And with that, she turned away. Cason waved goodbye, confusion shining in his light eyes.

That makes two of us.

I watched her and him walk towards the stands, up the stairs. Not once did she look back.

Bewilderment rocked through me. *Shit.* I scared her off and I still didn't know what the hell I'd done.

The walk back to Mav and Cash was worse than any walk of shame or failed run I'd ever had. Mav's scowl deepened, worry slithering across his features as he met my gaze, but Cash—fucking Cash—was as oblivious as ever.

"Well, damn, Ryder. She don't look too happy with you. No good luck kiss?" he crowed, from his perch.

"Shut the hell up and get down. Now," I growled through gritted teeth. *That's it.* I was going to murder him. I shared another look with Maverick.

He gave me a single nod, before smacking Cash on the back of the head, the force of it knocking Cash's grey felt cowboy hat off. "Get down, idiot. Learn to read the fuckin' room."

Cash raised his hands in an innocent shrug. "What? I was just—Ow!"

I didn't even look over as Maverick smacked Cash again. I just made my way through the labyrinth of pipe-stall and rodeo contestants until the evening sun greeted me. I walked to the stall I was keeping Boone in and grabbed his halter. We'd already warmed up, but I needed a moment to cool down. To get my mind and emotions sorted. There never was a better way to do it than while in a saddle. Leading him out of the stall, I headed for the practice arena.

I'D ALREADY RIDDEN A couple laps by the time Maverick came out to check on me. "Well, Cash may be a fuckin' idiot, but he was right about one thing. This girl's got you riled."

I grunted a response.

"Hey." The intensity of that single word from him gave me pause. Boone and I slid to a stop, my gaze snapping to Maverick. "Whatever the hell happened doesn't matter no more. You do whatever you gotta do to get her outta your mind. You needa focus. You're one win away from Austin. One damn win, Ryder. And I'm not babysittin' your sorry ass tonight if you lose cuz your head wasn't in cuz of her." He pegged me with a hard stare.

I blew out a slow exhale. He was right. Like he always was. Charlie had been on my mind for a day. But this...I'd been working toward this since I was a kid. I wasn't going to drop the ball just because of whatever the hell happened between her and I. *Focus on tonight. Worry about Charlie later.*

Nudging Boone into a walk towards Maverick, I said, "Alright. I'm good."

"You sure?" His brows disappeared beneath the brim of his black cowboy hat.

I nodded, exiting the arena. "Come on. Let's go find Cash. Lord fuckin' knows what sort of trouble he's gotten himself into without a chaperone."

And even though he didn't press, I noted the concern still lingering in Mav's gaze. He'd ask me about it later, when I had the chance to cool down and the stakes weren't so high, but for now he'd leave me be. "Your best friend's a pain in my ass," he said as we walked toward the fairgrounds arena. No use putting Boone away now, we had our first event after bronc riding.

"At least he ain't my family. You ain't gotta choice but to put up with him."

Mav huffed, though the cacophony of the rodeo starting drowned it out. I tied up Boone in one of the waiting stalls for steer wrestling, and we went to find Cash, who, shocker, was busy flirting it up with a barrel racer.

"Don't you have an event to be gettin' ready for?" Maverick snapped, pegging Cash with that familiar, withering stare. The one he always gave him.

"Yes, mama." Cash's lips pulled up into an answering smirk before he turned it on the girl he was talking to. "Whatcha think, darlin'? How 'bout givin' me a good luck kiss?"

I didn't hide the groan that escaped me. I almost preferred him flirting with the buckle bunnies. Barrel racers were a whole damn new level of crazy. Add it to Cash's chaos, and that was like putting a match to kerosene.

"Come on, Mooney," I said, smacking him in the stomach as I passed by. "Leave the poor girl alone." He grinned, blocking my hand, but the interruption distracted him from the pretty brunette.

"Miss Jaycee, good luck tonight," I said.

She flashed me a smile that rivaled Cash's million-dollar one. "Thanks, Ryder. Good luck to you, too."

I tipped my hat to her and grabbed Cash, leading him away by the shoulders. "You dumbass, do you wanna scratch for your event? You're about to start."

"Shit, man. I was just on my way. I got distracted."

"No, shit." I'd never understand how easily Cash could turn his focus on and off. One second he could be chasing tail, and the next he'd be hopping on the back of a bronc or throwing a rope with ridiculous accuracy. It was like a switch went off in him. I envied that.

We made our way to the staging pens, and with each step further from Miss Jaycee, something centered within Cash. By the time he stopped in front of his bag and pulled on his vest, his face was drawn into a mask of steely resolve.

"You ready?" Maverick asked, coming to stand directly in front of Cash. He placed his hands on his cousin's shoulders and peered at him from below the brim of his hat.

Cash took a deep breath and placed his hands on Mav's shoulders in return. Maverick's voice dropped even lower, somehow, as he murmured something I couldn't hear. It was a part of their little ritual they had going on. I wasn't a superstitious person, but for the most part, it worked.

One of the event organizers called Cash's name, breaking up their moment. "Cash Mooney. You ready?"

Cash pulled away first, clapped his hands together, and grinned at me and Mav. "Big Daddy's in the house!"

I shook my head even as a smile spread across my face.

Maverick and I situated ourselves where we could easily see Cash and get to him once his run was done or he got hurt. He was the third to go out of seven. The first rider, a young local guy we'd run into a few times, went first and made his eight seconds. The second didn't.

"Come on, Cash," Mav muttered under his breath, eyes glued to the gate Cash would come out of.

"He's got this," I said, my voice filled with certainty. Funny how I could be so confident in my friends, but I was always getting into my own head and second guessing myself.

Cash didn't disappoint.

That gate flew open. That bronc went bucking, and Cash fucking nailed it. Maverick and I shouted over the buzzer as he threw himself onto the pickup man's horse, before hopping to the ground. Grabbing his hat in one hand, Cash launched himself into a backflip, landing perfectly on his feet, shouting, "Big Daddy's in the house!"

"Ever the fuckin' performer," Maverick said with a shake of his head.

It was true, though. The whole crowd loved him. It was just how he was. You *knew* he was a cocky sonofabitch just looking at him, but you loved him anyway. Charisma, magic, or charm, whatever the hell you wanted to call it, he had it. In fucking droves.

He sauntered over to us, that wide grin slicing across his face. "Tonight's gonna be a good night, boys."

I sure as hell hoped.

CHAPTER ELEVEN

Hope That's True

CHARLIE

SADNESS AND ANXIETY WARRED within me as the rodeo commenced. They thrashed and writhed through my veins and heart, making my chest tight and it difficult for me to breathe.

Of course, he had to be a cowboy. Looking back now, I should have seen the signs. Maybe I had, and I'd just ignored them. I was pretty good at missing red flags, apparently.

Stop thinking about him. It only made things worse.

But that was pretty damn hard when my gaze was drawn to him like a fucking magnet. Everywhere I looked, I noticed him. I couldn't do this.

We'd found Layla and Jace. Him and Cason ate popcorn as they watched and cheered for the bronc riding event. Layla and her husband sat beside me, their two-year-old daughter switching back and forth between their laps. I glanced at Cason, just about ready to tell him I needed to leave, but the smile on his little face stopped me dead in my tracks. That smile dropped into a frown a moment later. "What's wrong, Auntie Charlotte?"

I couldn't leave. Couldn't take him away from this. He was having fun. Just earlier today he'd found out his mom died. He needed this.

This little bit of joy and fun. Who was I to take that away from him?

I was being selfish and dramatic. I'd spent one night with Ryder. And nothing had even happened. Not really. Besides, I hadn't come back to Texas to meet a guy. I still had to deal with Cal, after all. He was still calling and texting.

I'd come back here for Sheldon, and now I was staying for Cason. Even if it was only until the end of the school year. I still wasn't sure I could stay here long-term. We'd see how the next couple months went. But one thing was for sure, I didn't need to add guy drama into the mix.

I offered Cason what I hoped was a sincere smile and nudged him affectionately. "Nothing, bud. You having fun?"

He nodded, shoveling a handful of popcorn into his mouth.

I'd finally managed to calm myself down when they announced steer wrestling. Whatever progress I'd made went straight out the window then. Each run set me further on edge, until I felt like I was nothing more than a bundle of nerves wound so tightly together that I might just snap.

And then they announced *his* name.

My stare went straight to him. Ryder sat atop a buckskin, poised to start his run behind the starting line. A cow mooed in the chute to his left. *Please, don't let him get hurt.*

The chute opened, the timer started, and they were off. My stomach clenched in tight, painful knots that made me glad I didn't eat any nachos, and, I swear, my heart almost beat out of my damn chest.

It took all of two seconds. Two point nine, actually. He was fast. Faster than Daddy. There was so much power and precision and purpose in how he moved. A large part of me couldn't help but admire him. My heart nearly bursting with how proud I was of that run. But that was the thing about rodeos. It only took one bad run to end a career or a life.

"Charlie, are you okay?" Layla asked, her hazel eyes shining with concern.

Something dropped into my lap, and I noticed a small, dark spot on my jeans. I pressed a hand to my cheek, finding it wet. When did I start crying? My heart raced, my nerves completely shot, even as my gaze sought out Ryder once more. And even though there had to have been at least five hundred people in that stupid building, his eyes met mine.

I dragged my gaze from him and wiped at my tears, sniffling. "I'm fine," I lied.

Her face softened. "Sheldon had a hard time during this event as well."

I don't know why, but that was somehow oddly comforting. She'd been able to get over it, even if this event had still been difficult for her. Maybe one day I could get over it too.

Ryder went on to win that event. He had the best time of the night, and apparently solidified his spot for the Austin rodeo in a couple weeks. As the rest of the events went on, I found my nerves unwinding bit by bit. A small win, but I'd take it. I wasn't a crying mess anymore, so there was that.

I recognized Ryder's friend, the bronc rider decked out in neon pink—from his shirt, to his chaps, even his boots—in the team roping. Him and his partner won that event too.

By the time bull riding started, I felt more like myself again. Calm, stable—for the most part. I'd even come out of my shell enough to conversate with Layla and her husband, Will. Their daughter Braileigh wound her way onto my lap after I'd won her over with a couple games of peekaboo.

"Looks like you've made a new friend," Layla said with a grin.

I laughed. "I guess so."

"You should feel special. She hardly goes to anyone other than Will or I." She leaned into her husband for emphasis. As if on instinct, his arm wrapped around her, even though his eyes were glued to the arena.

The gesture was so sweet, so wholesome. It made a trickle of sadness well within my chest. I couldn't remember the last time Cal and I had acted like that in public. He was usually off with his friends and I was talking to mine. But even before then, even in the 'honeymoon' phase, we'd never been like that. He'd never been one for PDA. But I realized, watching Layla and Will, that I wanted that… That silent, simple touch of affection. That secret smile. That brief kiss here and there. Little reminders of the love they shared.

I smiled and looked down at Braileigh, remembering what Layla and I had been talking about. "This is honestly, like, the first time I've really been around kids, so I'm just as surprised."

"Really? I'd never have guessed. I always like to think kids are the best judges of character. They're honest. Brutally honest, most of the time." She laughed softly. "So if they like you, you've earned their trust."

"Well, I'm honored." I bounced Braileigh on my knees, causing a giggle to erupt from her.

My phone buzzed in my back pocket for what had to be the dozenth time since getting to the rodeo. Funny how Cal couldn't be there for me at all over the last few days, but the moment I became unavailable, he was blowing up my phone. Anger rippled through me, like water in a pond.

I looked at Layla. "I gotta answer this. Can I give—"

Layla didn't let me finish, instead just grabbed Braileigh and urged me to go while she watched Cason.

I walked down the stairwell and off towards the front of the building, further away from all the commotion. With a steadying breath, I clicked the green button. Hearing his voice didn't stir any confusion in me; it didn't change my feelings. I think a part of me was scared that if I heard his voice, I'd only be able to remember all of the good times and try to make excuses for him. But that anger, that...rage, didn't dissipate as I snapped, "What?"

I could barely hear him over the crowd and the music coming from the speakers, but I did pick up on the annoyance in his voice as he asked, "Where are you?"

"At a rodeo, Cal. What do you want?"

"I want to talk to you. You went all crazy last night and then stopped answering my calls or texts. I've been worried." His voice was calm, placating, but his words sent my blood boiling.

So, I'd gone crazy. Me getting upset that he'd lied to me was being crazy. *Good to know.*

A bitter laugh erupted from my throat. "That's really rich, Cal, especially considering you couldn't be bothered to talk to me for three days when I was dealing with my sister dying. You lied to me and told me you were at a work meeting when you were actually at dinner with our friends. I just wanted to hear your voice. I just wanted you to tell me you loved me and you were sorry that I was going through this. You couldn't even do that. Not until I caught you lying."

"Oh stop, babe. You're just being dramatic. It was a little white lie. I didn't want you to feel bad that I was at dinner without you."

"You told me you had to stay back in California for work. Which is bullshit, because your parents own the real estate company and would have easily given you a couple days off."

"I told you—"

I cut him off. "Did you even ask them if you could take some time off and come back here with me?"

"Babe, it's been super busy. It's peak selling time right now—"

"Your parents let you take off for an impromptu booze cruise boys' trip for a week that you planned the night before. You're telling me they told you no you couldn't come support me as I deal with the death of my sister?"

"You weren't even close with her!" he shouted through the phone. "Honestly, Charlie. You're being really fucking psychotic about this."

Tears burned in my eyes before falling in twin paths down my cheeks. I took a deep breath, hearing Ryder's voice in my mind whispering, *breathe.* "Wow, Cal," I said, my voice far less shaky than my trembling hands. "Thank you for making this even easier. I'm done."

"What?" he growled. "No! Babe. What are you talking about? You're just upset and emotional and—"

"Yes, I'm upset. Yes, I'm emotional. But I know exactly what I'm talking about when I say that I'm done. I'll arrange for my stuff to be picked up. Don't call me back, Cal." And with that I hung up.

My phone buzzed and his name showed up on the screen a second later, but I promptly pressed the end button. Asshole could go to voicemail.

Taking a few slow, centering breaths, I calmed my breathing. My tears slowed enough that wiping at them wasn't completely useless. I realized then that they weren't tears of sadness. They were tears of anger. He'd tried to turn this around on me *again.* He belittled my feelings…*again.* Tried to paint me as the villain…again. I wasted two years of my life letting him treat me like this. Hell, at the worst of times, I found myself defending his behavior.

I wouldn't shed another, single tear over him. Wiping at my eyes a final time, I sighed. He didn't even deserve my anger. Making my way back toward the stands, ignoring my phone buzzing in my pocket, I realized something. The weight on my chest, on my heart, that I'd been carrying around so long, had vanished. I felt lighter.

I was free.

I TOOK MY SEAT between Layla and Cason once more. Layla gave me a questioning look, her brows furrowed together. "Everythin' alright?"

"Yes, ma'am." Oh, dear God, I'd gone and said it without even thinking.

Cason nudged me, staring up at me with my sister's kind eyes. He didn't say anything, just leaned his head on my shoulder. The gesture was so sweet, so earnest, it almost brought tears to my eyes again, though for a very different reason than a few moments ago.

The bull riding event started shortly after, and I found my eyes glued to the arena. It was one of those things that was both exhilarating and terrifying to watch. There were eight riders in the event—Ryder being among them. Seven riders loaded into those bull chutes, seven riders got bucked off. Not a single score. By the time they announced Ryder's name over the loudspeaker, my heart thumped so hard and fast, I didn't know how it hadn't come out of my chest yet.

"Auntie Charlotte! It's Mister Ryder!"

I glanced down at Cason while rocking Braileigh in my arms—she'd maneuvered her way onto my lap again and passed out at some point. "It is."

"Do you think he'll make it eight seconds?"

"I'm not sure," I replied honestly. "The bulls tonight have been really good. What do you think?"

Cason's face scrunched up in concentration. "I think so. I believe in him," he said after a moment, conviction ringing in his voice.

I smiled. Everyone needed a Cason in their life. Sheldon did good with him. I nudged him gently and smiled. "I think you're right."

Some ACDC song came on as the gate flew open. That bull launched out into the arena, mad as hell, Ryder clinging to his back. It bucked and kicked and spun. *One. Two. Three. Four. Five. Six. Seven.*

Cason and Jace shot up out of their seats, cheering loudly. I even found myself standing, still holding a sleeping toddler in my arms—how she could sleep was beyond me.

Would he make it? My heart lodged in my throat. It hurt to breathe. *Please, let him make it. Don't let him get hurt.*

Seven point five.

I cheered as the buzzer sounded. The whole arena did. Ryder slipped from the bull's back, crashing to the floor. The excitement I felt for him turned to dread as the bull rounded on him and trampled over him before being distracted by one of the rodeo clowns.

Oh, dear God. The breath left my lungs, dread paralyzing me in place. Seeing him like that, laid out on the ground...It was just like Daddy. But a second later, he was up and moving. The pinked-out cowboy and his roping partner were already in the arena helping him out. He limped only a step or two before evening out, a wide grin on his face as he grabbed his hat off the ground and righted it atop his head, but that did little to calm my racing heart.

In fact...

"I think I'm gonna be sick," I said, turning to Layla, handing her Braileigh. She whined, but I was already shoving my way out into the stairwell, rushing for the nearest bathroom.

I barely made it into a stall before throwing up. That was twice in as many days. Was this how it was always going to be? How did Sheldon get over it? I didn't want to be this way. To feel this way. Some of my best memories as a kid were at the rodeo. But I couldn't stop seeing Daddy.

After cleaning myself up and taking a moment to stop the tears from falling, I made my way back towards the stands. Layla, Will, and the kids waited for me at the foot of the stairs.

"You okay?" Layla asked, holding a cranky Braileigh in her arms.

I took a deep breath and nodded. "I'm better now. Did I miss anything else?"

"No, they're just wrapping things up. Interviews, mostly. You uh, want us to take Cason, tonight?" Will said, offering me a sympathetic look.

I looked at Cason. "It's up to you, bud. Do you want to go or stay with me?"

He glanced between Jace and I before coming to my side, leaning into me. "I want to make sure you're okay, tonight."

Tears pricked in my eyes as I ran my hand through his dark hair. I was the adult. The one who should be making sure he was okay, and yet, this sweet little boy was trying to take care of me. "Thanks, bud."

He smiled up at me in answer.

I looked at Layla and Will. "Sorry about that. PTSD's a real bitch—"

"Ooh that's another penny!"

I grimaced, my shoulders shooting up to my ears. "Oops, sorry. Little ears...still getting used to that."

Layla and Will just laughed. "Oh, don't worry," Will replied. "You should hear Braileigh when she gets frustrated. Looks like an angel, but I swear that little miss has the mouth of a sailor. She gets it from her mama."

"Shut up! She does not!" Layla giggled, aiming a playful glare her husband's way. "Okay, maybe she does."

I grinned and glanced down at Cason. "Should we get going?"

He nodded.

We said our goodbyes and made our way through the fairgrounds back towards my car. We'd almost reached the front gates when a hand on my shoulder stopped me.

"Excuse me, miss?"

I whirled around at the deep voice, taking in the cowboy before me. Holy God, he was tall. Like, really tall. Even beneath his all-black ensemble, I could tell he was cut, chiseled. Yeah, chiseled worked well. He could've been carved from stone. From the severe, stoic look on his face, to the muscles rippling in his exposed forearms where he'd rolled up the sleeves of his shirt to his elbows. He was handsome, in a harsh, broody type of way. A bit too dour for my taste, but I knew plenty of girls who liked his type. He had kind eyes though, a soft, pretty jade that were a complete paradox to his harsh features.

"Yes?" I asked.

"Did you...uh, did you enjoy the rodeo?" he asked, a bit awkward. Almost like talking was a chore for him.

I nodded, my brows drawing together. "You could say that."

"Hey! Aren't you one of the team ropers?" Cason asked, bubbling with excitement.

The man's lips crooked up into the smallest ghost of a smile. "Yes, sir, I am. What's your name?"

"Cason Briggs. You won first place. didn't you? With that cowboy in the pink shirt, right?"

"I sure did. My name's Maverick. Maverick Holstrom."

"Nice, to meet you, Maverick, and congratulations on the win." I offered him a polite smile. "We should probably get going, though." I was already in the process of trying to turn Cason away when his deep voice stopped me in my tracks.

"Wait! Please, miss. Just...just one minute."

I had no energy left after throwing up my guts in the bathroom. I needed food, a shower, and a bed. I didn't want to be hit on by yet another cowboy. Especially, when it wasn't the cowboy I wanted.

No, I needed to stop thinking like that.

Tonight served as a blatant reminder that me and Ryder just wouldn't work. But my heart and mind rarely communicated when it came to him, apparently.

"Look, Maverick. You are very attractive, and you seem nice, but I'm going to be straight up with you. It's been a long night and I'm just not interested."

Somehow, I managed to wrangle a smile from him. Not a ghost of one. Not even one of those half smiles. A full-fledged smile, complete with a little chuckle escaped him. "Oh, uh, darlin', I didn't come over here for you. I came over here to stop you for someone."

"For wh—"

But a familiar voice cut me off. "Miss Charlotte, wait."

Butterflies erupted in my chest, a trill of excitement thrumming to life within me, even as my mind told me to just keep walking. I was getting really tired of my head and my heart not being on the same page.

"Mister Ryder!" Cason shouted, pulling out of my grip. "You were so awesome!"

I met Ryder's intense stare. He broke it for only a second to smile at Cason. "Thanks, bud. Did you have fun?"

Cason nodded. "So much fun! I don't think Auntie Charlotte had as much fun as me, though. She got sick."

Ryder's dark eyes fixed on me. "You alright, Miss Charlo—Charlie?"

I appreciated the attempt to call me Charlie. But, not going to lie, something about the way he said my full name just...did something for me. Which was exactly why I needed him to *not* call me that.

"I'm fine," I said with a polite smile. "Congratulations on your wins, tonight. Are you alright? That bull landed on you pretty good back there."

"Oh that? It was nothin'. A little sore, but no broken bones." He shrugged as if it were no big deal, and that made my heart break a bit.

The things these cowboys did to their bodies just to win an event. Was the thrill really worth it? Was it worth the broken bones? The torn ligaments and tendons? The threat of death? There were sports, and then there was rodeoing. Just the thought set my sensitive stomach on edge.

"Well, um, I should probably get Cason home. I'll—"

"Wait," he said, reaching out a hand as if he were going to grab mine, before letting it fall. And though I had no right to, my body yearned for his touch. Correction, *I* yearned for it.

Ugh. God, I needed to leave before I did something stupid.

I sighed and met his pleading stare. "What, Ryder?"

"What did I do? Just tell me, please. I just…I need to know what I did wrong."

I blew out a breath, my long bangs fluttering from the exhale. Cason glanced up at me, confusion written on his face as plainly as on Ryder's. "Honestly, you didn't do anything wrong," I admitted in a hushed voice. "It just…It's not going to work. I don't know what all's going to happen after Cason finishes his school year, and I should really be focusing on him, anyway."

Ryder opened his mouth to reply, but I cut him off. I knew he'd try and give me some reason to give him a chance. He'd promise that we could make it work. But it wouldn't.

I couldn't date him if he rodeoed, but I would never make him choose between that or me. So I would take that choice from him.

"Look, if you need a reason, I don't date rodeo cowboys, okay?" I offered him a guilty shrug, fighting back tears for the third time tonight. "It's better this way," I choked out before looking down at Cason. "Alright, bud. Say goodbye to Mister Ryder and Mister Maverick."

Cason muttered a half-hearted goodbye and grabbed my hand.

I nodded at Maverick and gave a weak wave to Ryder. "I'm sorry," I all but whispered.

"AUNTIE CHARLOTTE?" CASON ASKED sleepily from the back seat. He'd been dozing for a bit now, since finishing the milkshake he'd sucked down from Whataburger.

I glanced in my rear-view mirror, meeting his gaze. "Yeah, bud?"

"Are we not going to live here much longer?"

My heart sank. Shit. I shouldn't have said that in front of him. The whole point of me staying here was to make this transition easier. Now, he'd be worrying about if we were actually going to move or not. *Way to go, Charlie.*

"I shouldn't have said that earlier. To be honest, though, I don't know what's going to happen this summer. I need to figure out if we can rent your house from the landlords once the school year's over, and I need to find a job." I offered him a soft smile in the rear-view mirror. "I know that all of that grown up stuff probably doesn't make a lot of sense, but I will promise you this. I will do everything to make life as easy and happy for you as I possibly can."

He returned my smile with a soft one of his own. "You're a good guardian angel, Auntie Charlotte."

My chest squeezed as tears brimmed in my eyes. "Love you, bud," I croaked, meaning every word of it. I don't know how it was possible to love something that wasn't mine so much, but I did. And I would do anything to make him happy.

Looked like there would be plenty of opportunities now for mine and Ryder's paths to cross now that I was staying. And while a part of me—a far larger part than I wanted to admit—trembled with excitement, the logical part screamed at me to stay as far away as possible.

I was so fucked.

Chapter Twelve

Letting Someone Go

Ryder

Cash, Mav, and I had a long-standing tradition after a rodeo win. Drinks at Jack's 'til last call. Well, Cash and I would drink, usually until we were stumbling drunk, Maverick would just babysit us and beat us at pool. He'd never had so much as a sip of liquor, and never would. It worked out well, though. Especially, when we needed a designated driver.

Tonight should have been an absolute cause for celebration, and yet you'd think by the way I sat there nursing a bottle of beer that I'd lost big time.

I had, though, if I were being honest. I won my events, but I'd blown it with Charlie. Blown it and still didn't even really know how.

"You sure know how to pick 'em, Ryder." Cash laughed, clapping me on the back as he came to stand beside me, pool cue in hand.

I grunted, in no mood for his chipper attitude.

Of course, I'd meet someone who did something to me, who made me feel alive, who gave me that same thrill I got when rodeoing, only for her to hate the very thing I did for a living.

I still didn't understand why, though. Why specifically rodeo cowboys? She'd been very specific, and the way she said it, I felt like I should know the reason behind it.

"Leave him alone, Cash," Maverick warned as he set up for a shot, his jade eyes focused on the pool table.

Cash had no such plans. *The asshole.* "Charlie Evans sure is pretty, though. Aged like fine wine..."

I took a deep swig from my beer, guzzling it nearly down to the dregs. Cash grabbed another from the bucket sitting on the table beside me and cracked the top off before handing it to me. "Shame she don't date our kind, though. I wonder why that is? Afraid to be called a buckle bunny, you think?"

Maybe, but somehow, I felt it was more than that. Something lurked in the edge of my mind, but it was like looking for a fish in a murky pond. I knew it was there, but I couldn't quite see it.

Maverick made his shot, sinking the last of his solids in the furthest pocket. Without even looking at us while he lined up his shot for the eight ball, he said over the music, "Wait...Evans...I recognize that last name."

"Makes sense. She grew up in town," I replied, pressing the new bottle to my lips. "She has—had an older sister a couple grades before Cash and I. She was only a year younger than you, I think. Sheldon Evans."

Maverick's face scrunched up into a frown—a feat as his face was almost permanently set in one—and made his shot.

That was game.

He didn't even react to his victory, just stood up and leveled me with an intense stare. "I remember her, but that ain't it. I feel like there's a bigger reason I know that name."

I nodded. "Me too."

Cash opened up another bottle for himself and chugged it down as he stumbled his way over to the table to help reset it. Tapping his bottle to his lips, he said, "Hey wait...ain't her daddy the cowboy who died when we was kids?"

I snapped my finger, a flicker of a memory sparking to life in my mind. "Weatherford rodeo." I snapped again. "When was it...'09?"

I'd been there. I competed in the youth rodeo the day before. That day was definitely something ingrained in my mind. That accident had rocked me for a bit. Steer wrestling was my main event at the time.

Maverick met my gaze and shook his head, disappointment gleaming in his light eyes. "You're a damn idiot, you know that?"

It hit me right then and there. Why it didn't immediately register was still beyond me. But I finally had my answer. "Well, shit."

Cash let out one of his obnoxious laughs as he came over and smacked me on the back. "How is it that I figured that out before you, bud?" He placed his beer on the counter with a loud thud, a smug grin on his lips. "And y'all say I'm the dumb one."

Maverick's lips cracked into the weakest semblance of a smile. "I'm wondering the same damn thing."

I blew out a breath and drained my beer. Well, that explained everything. The reason she'd gotten quiet when I'd mentioned rodeoing, the way her face fell when I'd said I was a steer wrestler. Why she'd been so concerned if I was alright after the bull riding event tonight.

I was an idiot.

How could I change her mind? I knew it was preemptive and she'd just come into my life. I knew next to nothing about her, but I *wanted* to know more about her.

I drained the rest of my beer and cracked open another. I should just leave her alone. I needed to focus on Austin anyway, and didn't need a distraction—no matter how pretty she was.

This is for the best. She said, herself, she doesn't know how long she's staying here. Ain't no use startin' somethin' with a girl who's already plannin' on leavin'.

"Enough talk of women," I said over the music, snatching Cash's pool cue. "Mav, you and me... Loser cleans out the trailer tomorrow."

Maverick's usually soft eyes sharpened, hardened to stone. His lips twitched. "Go ahead and break, bud."

CHAPTER THIRTEEN

I Run To You

CHARLIE

CASON STAYED AWAKE THE whole car ride—a feat I still couldn't believe he managed. We'd played a tame version of twenty questions, asking each other lots of things, ranging from more serious—on my end—to silly—on his. Even though we'd laughed so hard we cried at times, I felt like I'd made some serious progress with getting to know his likes and dislikes.

The minute we'd pulled up to the house, he was already asleep. Of course. I'd tried to wake him, but the kid slept like a log, so I ended up carrying him to his room. By the time I'd pulled off his boots and tucked him underneath the covers it was close to midnight.

Closing the door, I trudged to Sheldon's—*my*— bedroom.

I'd switched out the light blue comforter for one with a black and white geometric design. Throwing in some earthy brown and black pillows in the mix. But the room still felt like Sheldon. Which was to be expected. It was her room, after all, but I didn't know how I'd be able to stay in here if I couldn't start making it feel like *me*.

No. Stop it. You're being a baby. It's a fucking room, Charlie.

Rifling through my suitcase, I pulled out a change of clothes, slipping into a pair of spandex sleep shorts and my favorite oversized

In This Moment shirt. I let out a content sigh as I glanced in the mirror. This. This felt so much more *me* than those boots and flares I'd worn tonight. Yes, I looked great, but I felt like a fraud. Like I'd lost the privilege to wear them once I'd moved out to California.

I grabbed my phone off the corner of the bed and slid under the new covers. Cal hadn't called in over an hour—thank fuck for that. *Maybe he finally got the hint.* Somehow, a part of me doubted that.

God, I didn't want to think about him. Forcing him to the back of my mind, I settled further under the blankets and turned off the bedside lamp and closed my eyes, willing unconsciousness to drag me under.

But sleep didn't come...because of course it didn't.

Even though I'd washed all the new blankets and sheets, everything smelled like *her*. That familiar floral scent clung to me, stirring up memory after memory. Each second, each minute, that passed by sent my heart thumping a fast, frantic beat.

I miss you, Sheldie. Tears slid down my cheeks. *Why did you have to go? I feel so lost. Everything's falling apart and I don't know what to do.*

Time slipped away as sob after sob wracked my body. I couldn't do this. I just...I couldn't. With a deep, shuddering breath I rose from the bed and raced out of the room.

I gulped down lungfuls of cool, crisp air as I paced on the front porch. Guilt gnawed at me, turning my stomach in knots. Why did I feel like this? Why was I reacting this way? I didn't have a problem with going into Daddy's office in the tack room after he'd passed away. I never got so overwhelmed that I'd started sobbing just because of his scent. Why was it so different this time?

Breathe, I reminded myself for, like, the millionth time. I swear, if I thought it anymore, I might need to get the damn thing tattooed on me.

I forced another deep inhale, savoring the cold air as it sliced down my throat and settled in my lungs. *Breathe.* Glancing up at the starry midnight sky, I repeated the mantra over and over. And I don't know how or why, but soon that word didn't sound like my voice at all, but a certain dark-haired cowboy's, whose eyes were as dark as the sky above.

My breathing hitched for a whole new reason, but at least I wasn't thinking about my sister. At least the guilt threatening to consume me was replaced by a deep, hidden desire for Ryder. God, why did he have to be so hot and perfect and kind? Like, seriously?

Why send him into my life to distract me, only for him to be completely off limits? I wished that it was something I could get over, but I just couldn't. Tonight proved that. Seeing that bull trample him sent me right back to those stands when I was twelve years old. I was so terrified and helpless. I couldn't see someone I loved get hurt like that. Plain and simple.

But what if...

There couldn't be any what ifs. No exceptions. It was a dangerous path—one I knew I would get absolutely lost on if I even attempted to navigate it. Best to just steer clear. It was a small town, but we hadn't run into each other much as kids. It would likely be that way now.

I wiped at my face and sniffled before managing to walk into the house. One glance down the hallway, and I knew I wouldn't be staying in Sheldon's room. I couldn't. Maybe a drink would help calm some of the nerves. Nothing wrong with a little night cap. I made my way to the fridge and reached for the bottle atop it. Ryder's name and number practically glowed on the paper on the fridge. A shiny beacon beckoning me.

Ignore it.

I took a long pull straight from the bottle, hoping, praying it would ease some of the tumultuous emotions raging through me, but it did nothing. Not a damn thing. I don't remember when the tears started once more. I don't remember how I got my phone. I don't even remember sliding to the floor, my phone in one hand and the bottle in the other. All I remembered was a deep, familiar voice answering the phone. "Hello?"

"Ryder," I choked out.

Chapter Fourteen

Crash My Party

Ryder

Eight beers deep and three losses to Maverick later, my phone buzzed in my back pocket. Dread trickled down my spine. Nothing like a phone call at close to two A.M. to slap the drunkenness right out of you. Was it Mom and Dad? The Mooneys? Was something wrong with the horses? I could think of only a couple potential reasons for a call this late, and none of them were good. Grabbing my phone, I checked out the caller ID. I didn't recognize the number, even with the Texas area code. My finger hovered over the end button. *Probably just a spam call.*

How or why I ended up with the phone to my ear saying hello, was beyond me. I could blame it on being buzzed or just a bit too paranoid at the late hour, but I sure as hell wasn't expecting the familiar, feminine voice on the other end of the line.

"Ryder?"

My stomach somersaulted. In excitement or dread I wasn't quite sure. Why would she call so late? "Miss Charlotte, is everything okay?"

"I...I think I'm h-having an anxiety attack." Her voice sounded so weak, so small, through her sobs.

"Hey...hey, it's okay. I'm here. Take a deep breath." Covering my other ear to hear better, I asked over the music, "Is Cason okay?"

"He-he's asleep."

"Good. Where are you?"

"Outside. I-I didn't want to wake him."

I turned to look at Maverick, sharing a silent look with him. "I'm on my way," I told her. "Do you need me to stay on the phone with you?"

"You don't have to come. I—I'm sorry for calling. I just. I had no one to call and this house reminds me of Sheldon, and I broke up with my boyfriend, and I keep thinking of the rodeo and how you got trampled, and then my daddy and—" With each word her voice rose and rose, getting more breathless and shrill as it went.

My heart clenched, hearing the panic in her voice. "Charlie—Charlotte, I need you to slow down, okay. Deep breaths."

"I can't...I can't breathe. It f-feels like a weight's on my chest."

I glanced over at Maverick, who was already making his way over to the bar to settle the tab. Cash stumbled over to me from his spot by the pool table. "Oh shit! Is that your girl, Ryder?"

A muscle ticked in my jaw as I threw a glare his way, gesturing with my hand to knock it off. Maverick was there a second later, a withering glare glued to his face as he scolded Cash like a mother hen. Ignoring them, I said to Charlie, "Okay, I need you to do me a favor, Miss Charlotte? I need you to take a deep, deep breath and hold it in for five seconds, then let it out slowly, okay?"

She gave a weak reply and did as I said.

"Okay, good. Now, do it again."

Her inhales and exhales were almost entirely drowned out by the noise of the bar, but I could just make out her weak voice as she said, "Okay. Done."

I looked at Mav and Cash. Cash's drunken grin had turned into a look of mild concern. Maverick jangled his keys at eye level and nodded toward the door.

"Do it again, Miss Charlotte. I'm on my way."

Chapter Fifteen

Feel Like This

Charlie

WAITING FOR RYDER WAS brutal.

Who'd have thought that so many people were out driving so late at night in such a small town, but I swear, at least five trucks passed by the long driveway to my sister's house while I waited. Each time, a trickle of hope filled me before cold loneliness descended once more at seeing those headlights pass right on by.

My breathing was still ragged, tears still slid down my cheeks, but I wasn't actively panicking like I had been in the kitchen. I still don't know how Cason hadn't woken up through my episode, but I was forever grateful he hadn't.

Small victories, I guess.

I'd been trying to do the breathing patterns Ryder coached me through on the phone, but either I was doing them wrong or it was the actual sound of his gravelly voice that calmed me.

I glanced at my phone once more. Fifteen minutes. How long had it taken us to get back to Sheldon's last night? Had something happened? He'd been at a bar; of that I was certain. Had he driven drunk and crashed? *Oh God.* My panicked thoughts sent prickles of dread along my skin and my heartrate racing once more. The cold air slicing through my lungs came out in shallow breaths.

Stop. This was stupid. Why was I such a mess? Why was everything setting me off? I'd managed to go five years without a single panic attack, and now I'd had more than I could count on one hand in two nights.

Get your shit together, Charlie.

But my stupid intrusive thoughts wouldn't shut the hell up. What if he'd hit a deer and wrecked his truck? It wasn't uncommon out here, especially just outside of town. Or worse…what if he decided not to come? No. He would have at least called. Right? *Right.* He was a gentleman. He'd call.

I looked at my home screen again, contemplating calling right then and there. *Where is he?*

The stirrings of another episode welled inside me, reminding me of those scenes in movies where the person was stuck in a car or something and water was rising, rising, rising with no way to get out. With each thought, with each passing second, that panic rose, icy and as terrifying as the water going higher and higher.

I sat on the top step of the porch, clutching my knees to my chest, trying to breathe as I rocked back and forth. It wasn't working anymore. Tears blurred my vision, and sound warped and morphed and made it seem like I was far away or underwater.

I can't do this. I can't do this. I—

A bright light pulled me from my thoughts. My gaze snapped open and hope gripped my heart. Gravel crunched beneath the truck tires as that light slowly rolled closer. He'd come. Why I'd been so terrified he wouldn't was dumb. Silly. But I couldn't help the thoughts that overtook me when this happened.

Wiping at my eyes, I stood up and leaned against the wooden railing. The truck stopped beside my rental, the diesel engine purring as it idled. I noticed movement behind the windshield, but couldn't make out what he was doing. The headlights drowned out almost everything. A moment later, the passenger door opened and a dark silhouette hopped out. He tipped his hat to the person driving, murmuring something I couldn't quite make out before closing the door. Then his boots were eating up the distance between us. The headlights glowed around him, making him look like some sort of guardian angel come to protect and rescue me.

Was it pathetic that I thought that? That he had so much power over me? That the minute I felt his presence, I immediately relaxed? At the very least, it was dangerous. Him having such a hold on me. But that sure as hell didn't stop me as I walked down the steps and launched into his arms. The scent of sandalwood, smoke, and leather filled my lungs as I breathed him in. That scent was like a drug. It had to be. Because, at that moment, I didn't care one bit. All my worries withered into a pile of ash as his strong arms slipped around me and held me against his warm, solid body.

"I'm sorry," I choked out.

He pulled away far enough to look down at me. Grabbing my chin with one hand, he tilted my face up so that my eyes met his. "For what? You ain't got nothin' to be sorry for."

I lowered my gaze, unable to hold his intense stare. Even in this state, I knew just how dangerous looking into those midnight eyes were. "Who dropped you off?" I asked.

"Mav." He still gripped my chin and held me against him. I knew I should pull out of his arms, but my mind and body were doing that annoying thing of not communicating again. "Him, Cash, and I were at the bar celebrating our wins."

Guilt settled like a stone in my stomach. "I'm sorry," I groaned. "That's the second night in a row I've dragged you away from your friends. They probably think I'm annoying as hell."

His lips tugged up in one corner and he shook his head. "Nah. We'd have left soon, anyway. Besides, this is more important."

"Why? Why would you come after the way I treated you tonight? You're being too nice."

"Mav is prone to panic attacks so I'm just used to tryin' to calm him down, I guess. As for comin' even after what you said…well, I guess you could say I'm stubborn." His lips curled up a bit more, and damn if it didn't make the ice around my heart melt a bit.

"I meant it…It won't work between us," I said, even as I clung to him. I realized that my breathing had evened out, my pulse had slowed. In his arms, the roar of doubt and sadness and panic had dulled to hushed whispers.

"I know," he replied, though his mouth still remained in that half smile.

Stubborn was right. Determination glimmered in his eyes, as bright as the stars above. I shook my head, his fingers falling away from my chin. A part of me admired that steely resolve, but this was a dangerous game. One that I didn't think my heart could take. "I mean it, Ryder."

"Yes, ma'am," he replied, releasing his hold on me completely. I shivered at the answering cold, hating that my body already yearned for his touch once more. He walked to the porch and sat on the top step, then held out a hand for me. And damn it, but I didn't have the will to resist. I slipped my hand into his calloused one and let him pull me down onto the step beside him. With his free hand, he pulled off his cowboy hat and laid it upside-down on the ground beside him then slid his hand through his hair. "You feelin' a bit better now?"

"A bit," I admitted. Since seeing those headlights coming down the drive, some of the anxiety writhing for dominance in me had calmed, like a cat curled up in a patch of sunlight.

He nodded and glanced over at me. "What brought it on?"

I blew out a breath and looked down at our joined hands. "It started out with my sister… It's her room, mostly. It just…it reminds me too much of her. I bought new covers, even took down some of the photos, but it still feels like her. Smells like her, too. And then, if that's bad enough, I feel like I'm stepping into her shoes or trying to take her place or something. Like—It's hard to explain. I just…I didn't think I'd be affected so much by a single room. The rest of the house is fine. But her room…I just, I can't deal with it, I guess."

"Have you thought about redoin' it? Maybe paintin' it or rearrangin' the furniture. Hell, maybe even buyin' new stuff?"

"I'm afraid it'll upset Cason." I looked back at the house, as if he'd walk out that front door any minute now.

"I get that, but this is just as much your house as it is his now. You gotta be comfortable in there too. Ain't no good livin' in a house that makes you feel like this." He gave my hand a soft squeeze. "Maybe try askin' him if he wants to help you redo the room. Maybe even offer to redo his as well. Y'all can go get stuff to decorate it together. Make it somethin' fun."

I honestly hadn't even thought of that. "That's a really good idea, actually. I'll have to talk to him about that tomorrow. Thank you."

He cast a sidelong glance at me, his lips hooking up into a smile. "You're welcome. You mentioned some other stuff on the phone. What else's on your mind?"

Tears pricked in my eyes and slid down my cheeks again. Not the fast-running, panicked tears that flooded from me during my episode a few minutes earlier. No, these were slow, unhurried, hot tears that seared me to my very soul. "The rodeo was way harder than I expected it to be," I admitted with a whisper.

"Because of me or your dad?"

I looked down at our joined hands once more, unable to see anything as I choked out, "Both."

Something warm tugged my chin, forcing my gaze in that direction. Not something, his free hand. He didn't speak, didn't say a word, but the guilt written plainly in the lines of his face broke my heart. He shouldn't feel guilty for doing something he loved. This was exactly why I hadn't wanted to say anything in the first place.

That guilt was all it took for the floodgates to snap wide open. My vision blurred further, quiet sobs fell from my lips, and my shoulders quaked. He pulled me into him, and even though I knew I should resist, I didn't. I was being selfish and giving mixed signals and making things so much harder than they needed to be, but since coming back here to Texas, he'd been the only person to make me feel safe. He was the only constant and calm in this crazy shit-storm that had become my life. So, call it selfish, or stupid, or both, but I didn't have the strength to stop him. Not tonight.

He let go of my chin and hand only for a moment before both of his calloused ones came up to cup my face. His thumbs scraped gently against my cheeks as he wiped at my tears. "You don't gotta talk about it if you don't want to, Miss Charlotte."

"No, it's okay." Maybe I needed to talk about it. Maybe once I did, I could make sense of my emotions. "I was there…the day he died. It happened so quickly, Sheldie and I didn't even know what was going on at first. I just remember seeing him lying there on the ground, not moving… Tonight, seeing you like that after your ride brought me back to that, I guess."

"I'm sorry," he offered.

That just made the tears roll faster. "No, you don't need to apologize. It's a total *me* problem, not a *you* problem. But, that's why I was acting so distant when I saw you there. I don't want to get into something with you and have my past get in the way." I sniffled. "Not that you necessarily even want to get into something…sorry, I'm just projecting now."

His lips quirked at the corners, making more of the ice around my heart crack and melt. "I think you know by now that I'd very much like to get into somethin' with you...but I can be patient."

"You don't get it, Ryder," I replied, my voice little more than a cracked whisper. "I don't know if it's something I'll ever be able to get over. I can't watch another person I love get hurt like that. And I don't want you to one day end up feeling like I'm making you choose between me and rodeoing."

"I wouldn't. I–"

I cut him off. "You don't know that. Besides, you don't even know me. What about me makes you want to take that risk? I appreciate and admire the persistence. I find it really attractive, not gonna lie. But I just...I don't understand why. Why are you so nice to me? So patient with me? What about me is so great that it's worth dropping your plans two nights in a row?"

"I honestly couldn't tell you, I'm just...drawn to you. From the minute I saw you last night I had this urge to talk to you. And once I talked to you, I found it just made me want to be around you more. I don't think at this point I could stay away even if I tried. It's like we're magnets."

My heart fluttered, some of the sadness giving way to the flicker of excitement that ignited in my chest. "I feel the same way. It's like...fate brought us together. But that's crazy. There's no such thing as fate or soulmates; this is the real world."

"Somethin's brought us together, Miss Charlotte. I wouldn't mind tryin' to figure out why." He still cupped my face, and I realized then how close our bodies were. Our faces. Our mouths. A couple inches and I could close the distance and feel those lips against mine once more.

God, I needed to get away. This man—this perfect, wonderful, kind, hot man—did dangerous things to my mind and heart. And even if he was optimistic about our potential, I'd always been more of a realist. People said a lot of things, made a lot of promises, but falling for Ryder would bring nothing but heartache for me. I knew it. "I just got out of a relationship. I don't know if I'm ready for another one."

He nodded, as if expecting I'd give some excuse. The confidence in his half smile, in his eyes, didn't dwindle or falter. "No one said this has gotta last forever."

"What do you mean?"

One of his hands drifted down from my face, along the corner of my jaw, until his fingers slid through my hair at the nape of my neck. "Ain't nothing wrong with, you know, calmin' the urge. Scratchin' the itch."

I grimaced at the phrase, my nose scrunching up. "I hate that analogy."

A soft chuckle rumbled up from his chest. "Alright, how about quenchin' that thirst? You know, like drinkin' an ice-cold drink on a hot summer day."

I couldn't stop the huff of laughter that bubbled up in me. "That's somehow even worse. I thought you cowboys were supposed to be smooth talkers."

A grin cut across his face as he shook his head and laughed softly. With the hand still cupped to my cheek, he dragged his thumb down my lip, his gaze never leaving mine. The fire burning in his eyes seared me to my very core. He leaned in. My eyes fluttered closed of their own accord. Anticipation thrummed through my veins. A small gasp escaped me as his lips grazed my ear. "This smooth enough, Miss Charlotte?" An answering shiver shot through me as I sat there helpless but to watch him pull back enough to look me in the eyes once more. "I want you, and I think you want me too. No one's saying we have to last years, or months, hell, even more than a week. All we need is one night, if you want."

Holy. Fucking. Shit. My breath hitched in my chest, and thank God I was sitting, or I think my legs would have turned to jelly right then and there. "God, you're perfect," I said, my voice more than a bit breathless as I shook my head, a smile forming on my lips. "You know, I'm half convinced that you're nothing more than a figment of my imagination to help me deal with this traumatic experience. Maybe I'll wake up in a minute or two, drunk on the couch, and realize this was all just a dream."

The corners of his mouth curled up. "Well, I don't know about perfect, Miss Charlotte, but I can guarantee you this ain't no dream."

And even though I knew he was telling the truth, a part of me still felt like this couldn't be real. *He* couldn't be real. The remaining walls of my resolve—however broken and pathetic they were—all but crumbled into rubble right then. God, I was such an idiot, but damn if I didn't want to kiss him again.

Reaching out with trembling fingers, I slid my hands over the planes of his broad chest, reveling in the warmth of him. "I take back what I said earlier. You do know how to make a girl swoon…but I shouldn't be surprised. Not when your name is literally Mister Wright."

Another chuckle escaped him; I felt it as it bubbled in his chest, absorbing into my hands pressed there. "Ah, there's my girl. The name puns are back…I thought I'd lost you there for a bit."

Well, if I wasn't a puddle of mush already, I was now. I was in trouble, so much trouble, but I couldn't seem to make myself care. What was so bad with a fling? A one-time hookup? Ryder was right. No one said we had to last forever, or even after tonight. He was single, I was single now, and we both wanted each other. Was it a little too soon after Cal? I'm sure plenty of people would think so, but fuck 'em. I'd kind of taken on the role of being the trainwreck disappointment of the family. Let people talk.

For the first time in far longer than I realized, I felt wanted and seen. I felt…treasured. And I was in no hurry to feel any different.

Even my mind had gone painfully quiet. The war between my head and my heart had died down, as if they'd come to a truce and were finally in agreement about wanting Ryder. Couldn't say I blamed them.

With newfound confidence, I slid my arms up around his neck, forcing us closer so that our mouths were but a breath apart. "Prove to me you're real, Ryder," I whispered against his lips.

Something shifted in him then. I can't quite explain it, only that I *felt* it. I felt it in the way he held me—though his grip didn't turn hard or rough, but instead urgent, wild. I felt it in his stare—now sharp and intense. His dark brown eyes had leached of color, looking like twin chunks of coal, burning with desire.

"Yes, ma'am," he murmured before capturing my mouth in a kiss that set my heart, my body, my soul on fire.

His mouth moved in slow, unhurried strokes that sent every nerve ending in my body trembling. I wanted—no, needed more. His lips left mine as he kissed the corner of my mouth, then up the line of my jaw. Little nips and kisses all the way to my ear, where he bit my earlobe gently. "Is this real enough for you, Miss Charlotte?" he asked, voice little more than a husky whisper.

The air in my lungs left in a whoosh as I clung to him. A breathy half laugh escaped me as I tilted my head, allowing better access to my neck. "I'm going to need more convincing."

His warm breath against my skin sent chills down my spine as a soft laugh escaped him. He tightened his hold on my hair, just as he led a path of kisses down my neck and to the base of my throat. "How 'bout this?" he murmured, nipping at my collarbone teasingly.

And as much as I loved how gentle he was, I didn't want gentle. I didn't want soft and sweet. Pulling back enough to look him dead in the eyes, I grabbed a fistful of his shirt and pulled him to me. "More," I replied, before claiming his mouth with mine.

Whatever timidness he'd shown a moment ago disappeared then. He took control easily, matching me passion for passion. Hunger for hunger. I don't know how, but one moment I'd been sitting beside him, the next, he'd pulled me into his lap. I straddled him as he stretched out on the porch steps, our lips somehow never breaking contact.

This was…this was heaven. It was like each touch, each stroke, each brush of his hands or tongue was perfectly designed to wreck me. Completely destroy me. And I didn't mind one bit.

Chapter Sixteen

She's Alright

Ryder

WELL, DAMN.

I hadn't expected that turn of events. Hadn't expected her to agree to a night with me. I'd wanted her to. Damn, I'd wanted her to, but a part of me still couldn't believe she'd been down for this. I wouldn't question it though, not when she sat in my lap, one arm wrapped around my neck, the other fisted in my shirt.

I reveled in her kisses, her touch. Her taste and scent. The way her soft curves fit in my hands like she'd been perfectly made for me. Everywhere she touched, I burned. Burned more than I ever had for anyone. What was it about her? Why was I so drawn to her?

She pulled away from me, breaking our kiss, but not before biting my bottom lip. A groan reverberated in my throat. Shit. Why'd she gotta do things like that? If all I had was one night with her, I wanted this to last every damn minute. Ain't no way I'd last if she kept that up.

"You wanna come in?" she asked, her voice sultry, breathy. I couldn't help but admire her. Sitting there, looming above me, with the porch light shining like a halo around her, she looked like some sort of angel. Her gray eyes were dark with desire, and the sadness had all but disappeared on her face. My hand drifted up to cup her cheek—it's like I needed to know she was real.

Did I want to come in? Of fucking course, I did. But should I? Probably not, though even that couldn't stop me. Not tonight. Not when she looked like some sort of fallen angel and smelled like lavender. She smelled like home.

Lifting her into my arms, I stood up. Her legs wrapped around my waist, her hands slipping into my hair. Her mouth found mine once more, the faint taste of whiskey still on her lips as she stoked the flames of my desire with every flick or stroke of that wicked tongue of hers. Damn, I was in trouble. *Ain't no turning back now.*

Not that I wanted to.

Stumbling up the steps, I moved across the porch and pressed her back to the wall. With one of my hands cupping her ass, my other went to her breast. A breathless, little moan escaped her, and I just about came undone.

Damn the fabric for stopping me from feeling her completely. *There'd be time*, I reminded myself. Time to touch, to kiss, every inch of her. If she'd let me.

Charlie arched into me and broke the kiss, her eyes meeting mine. "Is that a yes?" she asked, a smug smirk pulling on her lips.

It honestly took me a minute to realize I'd never answered her. "I thought in this case actions spoke louder than words," I said, sliding my hand over her chest up to cup the back of her head.

Her eyes flickered with need. "They do, but I still want to hear it."

"Then, yes, Miss Charlotte. I'd love to come in."

Our lips found each other again, and all sense of time and space left me as I lost myself in every bit of her. I don't know how we managed to make it into the house. I vaguely remember hearing the porch door slam shut after getting us through the doorway, but in the next minute, I was laying her down on the couch. She popped back up into a sitting position quickly, her eyes never leaving mine as she slipped her shirt over her head and tossed it to the floor.

Well, damn.

My heart skipped a beat, my body trembling with want, with need, as I drank every inch of her in. From the long red hair atop her pretty head, down to her white painted toes. Her sleeve of tattoos I'd seen last night weren't the only ones to grace her body. A bundle of beautifully drawn wildflowers spanned the space between her ribcage and waist on her right side, while her sternum boasted a gorgeous geometrical design that was partially obscured by her leopard print bra. She was all curves and soft, sun-kissed skin and ink…and I needed her. All of her.

The desire in her eyes dimmed, the sultry curve of her lips turning down into a worried frown the longer I stood there. "Do you…do you not like what you see?"

The doubt creeping into her voice, into her gaze, broke my damn heart. Someone put that doubt in her. The fact that she could even think I wouldn't like what I saw made anger stir in my chest.

And even though I wanted nothing more than to show her just how much I loved what I saw, I knew she needed to hear me say it. Sitting down beside her, I dragged her into my lap so she straddled me once more. No doubt, she could feel my hard-on, could feel how much she affected me.

I cupped her face in my hands, making sure to hold her gaze as I murmured, "I wasn't lyin' last night when I said you were gorgeous, Miss Charlotte. You're the prettiest damn thing I've ever seen. And I ain't just sayin' that."

It was true. She was beautiful—as if she'd been crafted specifically to bring me to my knees.

A soft smile blossomed on her lips, but doubt still lingered in her gaze.

"Let me show you just how much I like what I see." I pressed a kiss to her lips. It was slow, deep, but it held every bit of conviction I had in me. She might not believe me still, but I'd be damned if I wouldn't make her feel every bit as beautiful as she was. Her body melted into mine, little moans and breathy sighs escaping her now and then. It was music to my damn ears.

"Ryder," she whispered against my lips as her hand slid down my chest, down my stomach, before stopping atop my cock beneath my jeans.

I groaned. "Fuck." I slid one hand into her hair, the other falling to her breast once more, squeezing hard enough for another moan to fall from her lips. Her answering stroke against me sent a shiver down my spine.

"A-auntie Charlotte?"

I stilled at the soft, sleepy little voice coming from the hallway. Shit. I'd completely forgotten about the kid. In a lightning quick movement, Charlie launched off my lap, somehow grabbing her shirt off the floor and holding it to her chest.

"H-hey, bud? What–what's up?" she asked, her voice quaking.

I adjusted my jeans, trying anything to relieve the pressure of my lingering arousal.

Cason rubbed at his eyes sleepily, clutching a stuffed dinosaur plushie in one hand. "What's…going on? I…" He yawned. "I heard voices." He squinted through the dim room at me. "Is that…Mister Ryder?"

"Hiya, Cason. Your aunt and I…we were just…" Oh, shit. What the hell did I say? I glanced at Charlie questioningly, my heart racing. Though, for a completely different reason than a few minutes ago.

Charlie's deer in the headlight's gaze met mine before she looked at Cason. "We were um, looking for my uh…my earring. Yeah!" She grabbed gently at her ear lobe.

She hadn't been wearing earrings, but I found myself nodding. Kid didn't need to know that. "Right," I added as we shared a quick knowing look.

A hint of a smile tugged on her mouth. With far more confidence than a moment ago, she went on. "Yeah. My earring fell out and we were trying to find it."

"Oh, okay." Cason shrugged, rubbing at his eyes again.

"How about you go back to bed, bud? I'll be in there in a minute to tuck you in."

Cason nodded and called out, half turning back down the hallway, "Night, Mister Ryder."

"Night, bud."

As Cason retreated back to his room, I glanced over at Charlie. She slipped her shirt back on over her head before pegging me with her intense grey stare. A smile appeared on her lips, a hushed laugh bubbling out of her. "Oh my God!" She giggled. "I'm so embarrassed."

That smile and laugh were contagious. "Hey, at least you came up with a decent reason. I just…" I shook my head. "Froze."

"He's so tired, I bet he won't even remember waking up," she said with a half laugh as she stood up. "I gotta go put him back to bed. I'll be right back."

I nodded. "I'll be here."

Her lips quirked up before she leaned over and kissed me. It wasn't much, just a soft brush of our lips, but it set every inch of me on fire.

Damn.

I watched her walk down the hall with a lightness in her that hadn't been present when I'd first gotten here. I'd hoped that one night with her would be enough to tide me over. But waiting there on that couch, I knew I was fucked.

I didn't want one night with Charlie Evans.

I wanted more.

chapter seventeen

Blue

Charlie

I couldn't believe Cason caught Ryder and I hooking up. How could I have forgotten about him? Not that I'd actually forgotten he was here, but I hadn't expected him to wake up in the middle of the night. I'd have to be more careful in the future.

Future?

That gave me pause. Since when had this hookup turned into more than a one night fling? I'd already told Ryder numerous times it wouldn't work. I couldn't go back on that now without looking like a total idiot. No, it could only be one night. But I couldn't get out of my head just how perfect his kisses felt against my lips, or how I enjoyed entirely too much the way his rough hands scraped over my skin, sending little tingling waves throughout my body.

I still wanted him. Wanted him more now than I had earlier this evening. More than before I'd known he was a rodeo cowboy. *Well, fuck me.*

My mind and heart were back to waging war with each other again—my head trying to account for all the heartache and problems another night with him would cause. My heart wouldn't listen, though. It was like when you had too many voicemails in your mailbox, and couldn't even leave a message.

What the hell was I going to do?

Cason lay curled up in his bed by the time I walked into his room, eyes closed with his head on the pillow. "Goodnight, Auntie Charlotte," he mumbled, half asleep.

I tucked the covers around him and kissed his forehead. "Goodnight, bud. I'll see you in the morning, okay?"

He was back asleep by the time I closed his door.

I glanced down the dark hallway to Sheldon's room and a wave of guilt washed over me. Had Sheldon ever gotten caught hooking up with a guy? From the amount of photos of her and James throughout the house and her room, I doubted that. Great. So I hadn't even been in charge of Cason for a day and I'd already gotten caught bringing a guy back here. *God, I'm an idiot.* A selfish idiot.

I sighed and leaned against the closed door, fighting back a wave of tears. Why was I such a wreck? My heart, my brain...it's like they were stuck in overdrive and I couldn't get them to calm down. Taking a couple deep breaths, I walked quietly out into the living room.

Ryder still sat on the couch opposite the hallway, his face shadowed in the dim lighting. His dark gaze traveled up and down my body, whatever lust lingering there turning to concern as he took me in. God, was I that easy to read, or was he just really perceptive? I wouldn't be surprised if it was the former. Mama always said I wore my heart on my sleeve, and that's why I got walked all over.

I'd always hated how she made it out to be a bad thing. Since when was showing emotions bad?

Ryder didn't speak, just held a hand out to me, and I didn't have the willpower in me not to take it. He dragged me to the couch, into his arms. I melted into him, letting him hold me as I laid my head against his chest.

"He went down quickly." His voice was a hushed murmur against my hair.

I just nodded, feeling guilty for having him here, but also unwilling to let him leave. Which was stupid—I knew that—but I couldn't bring myself to stay away.

"What's wrong?"

I blew out a deep exhale and mumbled into his chest, "Am I a terrible person for what just happened?"

Ryder tensed beneath me and hooked a finger under my chin to force me to look at him. "What in the hell makes you think that?"

"I don't think Sheldon had been with anyone after James, and now the first night I have Cason, he finds me half naked, hooking up with you in the living room. I just...I feel bad. Like, I'm irresponsible or something."

Ryder's lips quirked up in the corners. "You ain't the first person to get caught by their kid, and you sure as hell won't be the last. That don't make you irresponsible. If Sheldon hadn't moved on, that's completely her business. You don't have to stop livin' your life just cuz you have a kid now."

The thought of Cason being mine was still crazy to me. But even if he wasn't my son, he was still my charge now. My kid to deal with. My nephew to raise.

Relief trickled through me at Ryder's words, but I couldn't completely get rid of that last bit of doubt. "I'm sorry that it kind of…ruined things," I said, my cheeks heating with embarrassment as I looked anywhere but at him.

He pressed a soft kiss to my lips—whisper soft. "That's quite alright, Miss Charlotte. It just means I have more reason to see you again."

I pulled away, my mouth falling into a frown. "Ryder, I—"

"I know, I know. You don't think it'll work."

"I *know* it won't work, Ryder." My heart panged at that. What kind of shit luck did I have to find the most perfect guy ever, only for him to have one hang up that I couldn't get past?

Ryder's hands moved to my shoulders before his finger tips grazed up and down my arms in slow, steady strokes. The motion was both soothing and seductive, sending wave after wave of tranquility through me, while also stoking the flames of my desire once more. God, it was like he'd been made to be my downfall.

I guess everyone had their achilles' heel. Their kryptonite. Ryder must have been mine.

"Tell me somethin'," he muttered, his piercing gaze holding me in place. "Do you want it to work?"

"What?"

He kissed me once more. One of those soft, sensual kisses that was filled with infinite promise and stole the air from my lungs. "Does a part of you want us to work?"

Did I want this?

I thought of the fierce attraction I had to him from the minute I started talking to him in Jack's. I thought of how he'd managed to be there for me emotionally, physically, mentally more in the last day than Cal had in nearly two years. I thought of how his presence soothed me, his touch set me aflame, and every word out of his mouth practically melted my heart.

Had I just gotten out of a relationship? Yes. Did that change the fact that a part of me, a forbidden, yet growing part of me, wanted to explore more with Ryder? Not a damn bit.

I was so incredibly fucked.

A smug smirk tugged on Ryder's lips, and though I hadn't said a word, it's like he'd read my mind. He didn't press the issue, though, instead just continued his soft, lazy strokes up and down my arms as he asked, "Tell me somethin' about you."

I scoffed at the random shift in conversation. "Like what?"

His face turned contemplative, his gaze moving past me before settling on me once more. "Why California?"

I settled into his lap a bit more. "Because my mama didn't want me to go there."

He chuckled. "Spiteful, aren't we?"

I shrugged. "I got a couple offers for cheer scholarships. California had been my least likely pick…until she and I got in a big fight.

We'd just found out Sheldon was pregnant, and Mama thought I should stay local so that I could help Sheldon. In fact, she tried to guilt me into taking a year off of school so I could be there for her."

His brows creased together, a frown forming on his face. "Really?"

I pursed my lips and nodded, thinking back to that fight. Anger and guilt stirred to life. "It was my breaking point with her. She'd always favored Sheldon over me. When she asked—no, demanded—that I stay to help out, as if my life or goals meant nothing, I just snapped. I was so done with never being enough. Always living in Sheldon's shadow. I hate confrontation, so I decided to remove myself from the equation. She couldn't fight with me if I was halfway across the country." I took a shuddering breath, looking at my hands in my lap. "Sheldon was disappointed, and that just about killed me. I know she wanted me to stay, but never would have asked that of me. It caused a rift between us for a bit, though."

"Shit, Charlie…" His words trailed off into nothingness.

My gaze snapped up to rest on his face. He'd only called me Charlie one other time. It somehow didn't sound right on his lips. Like it was too formal, which shouldn't make sense.

"Since when do you call me, Charlie?" The words came out before I could even process what I was saying.

"I thought you didn't like me calling you Charlotte?" His tone was light, a smug grin stretching across his face as his hands stilled on my shoulders before moving to my hands in my lap.

I pegged him with a playful glare. "Since when did that stop you?"

He laughed. "What would you like me to call you, darlin'?"

Damn him for making my heart flutter faster than butterfly wings. I flipped his hands over, running my fingers along the lines of his upturned palms, unable to meet his stare. But I could feel it. Holy God, did I feel it. "Miss Charlotte does sound nice," I admitted begrudgingly.

"Miss Charlotte it is, then," he murmured, pressing another kiss to my lips. Melting me even more.

I pulled away. "My turn now." He groaned, and I couldn't help but laugh. Typical man. Of course, he didn't want to talk about himself. "It's only fair for you to tell me something as well."

He loosed a dramatic sigh, leaning back against the couch cushions. God, he was gorgeous. Between the shoulder length black hair, confident smirk, and that dark gaze, I didn't stand a chance. I could get lost in the bottomless depths of his midnight stare. My eyes found the long, thin scar slicing across his cheek.

"Tell me how you got that…" I traced my fingertips across it. "Or wait, don't. Let me guess." I bit my lip. "Rodeoing?"

He shook his head, his lips drawing into a boyish grin, causing the scar to whiten as the skin stretched around it. "Nah. It's really stupid, actually."

"Tell me," I urged, cocking my head to the side.

He sucked his bottom lip into his mouth, and he rubbed at his forehead, a little chuckle escaping him. "You, uh…you ever heard of cowboy joustin'?"

I shook my head, even as a grin formed on my lips. "I'm guessing whatever it is, was stupid and got you into a whole lot of trouble."

He laughed. "Oh, so much. It was, uh, sometime during the summer Cash and I turned twenty-one. I wanna say Fourth of July."

"Oh God, it already sounds like a disaster."

Another laugh. "We were too drunk to ride the horses. Mav had already put a stop to that, but—" He rubbed at his forehead again, his cheeks pinkening a bit. I'd seen many things in my life, but I'd never forget how adorable it was to see him blushing for once. "Cash and I wanted to do somethin' stupid…so we, uh, decided to fire up a couple of his dad's four-wheelers and go out to one of the empty pastures. We played some version of Chicken, where we'd drive at each other and try to rope the other one before they did the same to us. Loser had to shotgun a beer."

I shook my head, trying and failing to suppress a laugh. "Idiots."

"Hey, we said we wanted to do somethin' stupid," Ryder defended with a smile. "That's about the dumbest shit I've done in my life."

"So, you crashed?"

Ryder's grin turned almost impish. "I honestly can't tell you what all happened, that's how damn drunk we were. I woke up in a hospital bed with damn near thirty stitches in my face."

My eyes widened, my mouth dropping open. "Oh my God. Ryder!"

He shrugged, that bashful smile still on his lips. "My dad was pissed. It was the same year he was runnin' for County Sheriff. He didn't want the bad PR that came with havin' a son who damn near killed himself being a drunken fool."

I'd forgotten his daddy was a Sheriff. In fact, I think most of the men in Ryder's family had been. Interesting that he hadn't followed in their footsteps. A part of me wanted to ask, but for whatever reason, I just couldn't bring the words to leave my lips. I settled on saying, "Well, it may have been stupid, but it does make you look like kind of a badass."

He frowned. "Only kind of?"

I laughed at his sudden seriousness and held my thumb and forefinger up about an inch apart. "Yeah, just a bit."

"Darlin', women dig scars," he all but purred as he leaned forward, his arms wrapping around my waist. Not going to lie, I enjoyed the feeling way too much to be acceptable, but in that moment I didn't care. Not one bit.

I rolled my eyes, even as my arms wrapped around his neck and I pressed a kiss to his lips. For a minute, I lost myself in him, letting go of every fear or worry in my heart and mind. When was the last time I'd felt so good? So…light?

He pulled away enough to kiss my forehead. "So, cheer scholarship? That's pretty impressive."

It was my turn to groan this time. "What's more impressive was how quickly I lost it."

"What happened?"

My gaze fell to my hands, once more in my lap, as I fiddled anxiously. "I hurt myself two days into cheer camp. Tore a whole bunch of ligaments and had to have surgery. Then I ended up having nerve damage, but I tried to push through it. I cheered for one event, but I couldn't walk for almost two weeks after that. After months of physical therapy that didn't help and a whole bunch of chronic nerve pain later, I just knew I wasn't going to be able to compete at the same level I had been." I sighed, disappointment welling inside me.

"Damn, I'm sorry. Does it still hurt you?"

I nodded. "Some days I'll have a flare up that's bad, but for the most part I can drown it out. It's just mildly annoying most days."

He frowned. "So you stayed out there even after losing the scholarship?"

"Yep. Mama told me to come home. That it was a sign I needed to come back and help Sheldon." I rolled my eyes. "I would have rather spent the rest of fucking forever paying off my student loans then go back. Not because of Sheldon," I added quickly. Not at all for that. "I just don't get along with my mother and I knew if I went back I'd never get to leave again."

"Is it really that bad here?" he asked, gaze curious. "Is California that much better?"

I sighed. How did I explain that it wasn't this place, but the way it felt? The memories it dug up. Every minute in this town brought back more and more of those same feelings I felt when I was growing up here—that my mother would forever rule my life and make me feel small, weak.

Not that California was much better, though, in the long run. Yes, I'd gotten my freedom, in a sense, but what had I done? Found myself another narcissistic bully to get trampled by.

"It's not the town. I guess I'm just worried that things will go back to the way they were now that I'm back. I don't like the way my mother treats me or how controlling she is, but I'm not good at standing up for myself." I sighed again, meeting his gaze. "That's like five questions you asked me, it's my turn."

A smile quirked his lips and he nodded. "Fair enough. Ask away."

"How come you aren't a sheriff like your daddy?"

Something shifted in him right then. It was subtle, so subtle most people likely wouldn't notice, but I did. I saw it in the way the light in his eyes dwindled and extinguished, like twin stars dying out. I saw it in the muscle feathering in his jaw as he clenched his teeth together. The way his posture, a moment ago relaxed and open, became hard, rigid. And yet despite all these subtle hints to the silent shift in him, his words remained even, calm. "That was always more my dad's dream than mine." He blew out a breath, leaning back against the couch.

Shit. I hadn't meant to ruin this moment. I'd truly been curious. "You don't have to—"

But he cut me off before I could finish. "I didn't mind the idea of bein' a sheriff. I'd always planned to apply." He rubbed a hand up and down my bare thigh absentmindedly. The movement more so soothing, calming, than sensual. His gaze glazed over as he focused on something beyond me, his voice a bit hollow as he went on. "But over the years, the more I rodeoed, the better I got. And the better I got, the more money I made, and I've just stuck with it since."

I bit my lip, contemplating asking another question or letting it go. Since seeing Ryder again, I hadn't seen this more serious and somber side of him. It was odd. But in the end, curiosity won out. "How'd your daddy take it?"

He huffed a bitter laugh, the sound humorless. "Oh, he was pissed. Still is, but he's gotten better over the years. Every once in a while, he'll bring it up and it'll start a fight—mostly during the holidays when family's around. But it is what it is."

I grabbed his hand on my thigh, stopping his lazy strokes, and curled my fingers in his. "I'm sorry. Parents and their stupid approval can be a real pain in the ass. What about your mother? Did she react the same as your daddy?"

The darkness in his gaze lightened a fraction, some of the tightness in his jaw disappearing. "My mom ain't the type to beat a dead horse. She was disappointed when I told them I wanted to rodeo instead, but she'll never be anything but supportive of me. She won't tell someone what they can and can't do." A ghost of a smile played on his lips. "Every now and then, though, I'll find a flyer with all the hiring information hanging on the refrigerator, with all the testing requirements and info all highlighted."

I smiled softly. "Subtle."

He finally met my gaze once more and tugged me to him, settling me into the crook of his arm. Releasing my hand, he slid his own up my neck and into my hair before placing a feather-soft kiss to my lips. "That's two questions. You got three left," he whispered against my lips.

His touch and kiss sent shivers through me, but even they couldn't stop the desire to know more about him from consuming my thoughts. There were so many things I could ask. So many things I wanted to know about that I'm sure he'd have no problem telling me. And yet, I couldn't stop myself from asking, "So, rodeoing, huh? That's the dream?"

He nodded. "Yep. I love it. Everythin' about it."

"What about when you're older? I mean you can't be riding bulls and wrestling steers forever."

The defiance that flickered to life in his stare spoke volumes of just how much he disagreed. "Darlin' the day I can't rodeo anymore, you might as well kill me."

A crushing weight settled on my chest, squeezing the air from my lungs. It shouldn't have upset me. Who the hell was I to judge him for what brought him happiness? Just because I couldn't deal with my own trauma, didn't mean Ryder had to feel the same way. I guess I just didn't understand. My whole life had been cheerleading up until I hurt myself, but the moment I realized that I'd have chronic pain for the rest of my life, I knew I was done. I gave it up and hadn't looked back since. How could Ryder be okay with risking his life every damn time he got into the saddle or on a bull's back?

Was it pride? Some thrill-seeking urge he needed to ease?

Maybe if Daddy was still here, I wouldn't feel this way. Or maybe he could explain it to me. But he'd died doing what Ryder did, and for what? The money he'd made was long gone by now, and the only reminder of his accomplishments were a few dusty boxes of old buckles, and some tack he'd won. Sure, his name in this town was legendary, but even as the years went on, he'd become just another face on the wall in Jack's.

"Aren't you worried about what you're going to do when you're too broken to ride? What about health insurance? A pension? Retirement? Aren't you worried at all?"

The muscle in his jaw feathered again, annoyance flickering to life in his coal black eyes. "What's your big dream, huh?" he asked, his voice turning defensive.

I opened my mouth to reply but no words came out. The thought hit me like a freight train. What was my dream? "I..." I sighed heavily, my breath leaving me in a loud whoosh. "I don't have one."

Ryder's gaze pegged me in place, his dark brows furrowing together. The defensiveness vanished, and straight disbelief seeped into the lines of his face, into his dark irises. "What do you mean?"

I shrugged and lowered my gaze, unable to hold his stare. "I don't know…the last time I had a dream was when I was a kid and wanted to be a vet. My mama told me I needed to have more realistic dreams. She'd made me feel so stupid for thinking I could ever reach for something so grand that I just…stopped dreaming." Sadness and anger waged war in my heart, causing my stomach to twist in uneasy knots. "It's why I got a degree in business. It might not be extravagant or even really what I want, but it also gives me a lot of options. I'm sure I'll find something one day that I enjoy. But for now, it's fine, you know?"

A frown pulled on Ryder's mouth as he shook his head. "No, Miss Charlotte. I don't. You're tellin' me, you're okay workin' some random job the rest of your life that you don't care about?"

An ember of annoyance sparked within me, but I kept the spark at bay. I gave a defensive shrug. "I'm sure I'll find something."

"Your mama really did a number on you, didn't she?" He dropped his head and shook it before meeting my gaze once more. Sadness swirled in the depths there, but also something else. Something like determination. "Will you do somethin' for me?"

What could he possibly want me to do? I bit my lip, but nodded. "Sure."

"I want you to close your eyes," he said, the words gentle.

A scowl formed on my lips, my brows furrowing together.

His lips twitched up into the ghost of a lopsided grin. "Just do it, please, Miss Charlotte."

With a deep exhale, I did as he said.

"I want you to imagine your life five, six, seven years from now. If you could be doin' anything you want, whatever job you want, any place you want, with whoever. What does that dream look like?" His deep, husky voice rolled over me like a soft summer breeze, soothing, relaxing.

What did I want? God, I didn't even know. I'd always been too afraid to dream, too afraid I'd never reach my goals or that my dream would be stolen from me, just like everything else I cared about in life—Daddy, cheerleading, Sheldon now.

I focused on Ryder's words. On what I wanted. And maybe it was the fact that his calloused hands had resumed their gentle strokes along my thigh, or that his gravelly voice just did something to my soul, but every time I thought of what I wanted years from now, all I could see was him.

And that terrified the hell out of me.

Chapter Eighteen

Broke Boy

Ryder

THE MORNING LIGHT PIERCED through the window, pale rays shining directly into my eyes. I squinted, a muffled groan escaping me as I scrubbed a hand down my face. Something shifted against my side and I glanced down at Charlie, who laid tucked into the crook of my arm. Dear Lord, she was beautiful. And peaceful. So damn peaceful, I didn't want to disturb her. She was all softness and curves and warmth, and a part of me wanted to stay there and watch her forever.

I didn't even remember falling asleep.

We'd talked for hours last night. About little things. Big things. Our likes and dislikes. Pet peeves, guilty pleasures. All the things that didn't seem important at all. But it was the little things that defined a person. And with every little secret or admission that came from her lips, I wanted more.

A noise drew my attention out to the front of the house. I'd recognize the sound of my truck anywhere. *Shit.* Mav must have come to pick me up. Trying not to jostle Charlie, I maneuvered her onto the couch. A little moan escaped her, and I worried she'd wake, but after running a hand over her soft hair and situating the blanket over her shoulder, she settled quickly. On silent feet, I rushed to the door, yanking it open just as Maverick stepped up onto the porch.

"Mornin', Sunshine." Amusement flickered in his jade eyes. "Did we have us a good night?"

"It ain't none of your damn business," I replied, slipping outside and pulling the door shut behind me. "Where's Cash?"

Before Maverick could answer, the horn on the truck sounded. *Damn it, Cash.* I was going to kill him. Guy couldn't go one damn minute without doing something stupid. Squinting at the truck, I could just make out Cash in the wind shield, leaning over from the passenger seat. He had his hangover sunglasses on. They blocked the most light.

"Did y'all go back to the bar last night?" I asked.

Mav nodded. "Not for long. They kicked us out of the bar. He punched the jukebox because it wouldn't stop playing Taylor Swift songs."

"I thought he liked Taylor Swift?" I waved to get Cash's attention. I didn't need him laying on that damn horn again.

"It was just Never Ever Getting Back Together playing over and over and over again. You know how Jack's has one of those jukeboxes you can control from your phone. Kelsea Karkula was there and…well you know how Kelsea feels about our Cash." Maverick shrugged.

Cash leaned on the horn and kept it down as he stared out the windshield directly at Maverick and I.

"He's going to wake the whole neighborhood up." I groaned, grabbing for my phone, only to realize I'd left it in the house. "What time is it?"

It couldn't be that late. The sun had just barely risen.

"We're two hours late for chorin'." Maverick's face turned red and he looked away.

"Fuck, its only six?" I wiped my face with a hand. The door opened and my stomach clenched. "I'm sorry to wake y—" I turned and stopped mid-sentence as my gaze fell on a sleepy-eyed Cason.

"Mr. Ryder?" Cason asked, scrubbing a hand down his face.

"Mornin', bud," I said, tousling his hair. "Sorry, if we woke you up. My buddy Cash is… well he ain't feelin' too good. We gotta get to work."

Cason frowned. "If he isn't feeling good, he needs breakfast."

"A cigarette and a blowjob, and the hair of the dog that bit me last night, more like."

Horror washed over me as I whirled to the owner of that foul fucking mouth. *Shit. Shit. Shit.* Cash half leaned, half laid on the wooden railing to the porch, his pink polarized hangover sunglasses covering most of his face.

How the hell had I not heard him get out of the truck? Onto the porch? I glanced over to Maverick, who just shrugged and said, "You know as well as I do, there's no controllin' him."

Cason gasped, drawing my attention. "You got bit by a dog?" Cason's voice shook with surprise.

I let out a breath I hadn't realized I'd been holding. *Thank God.* Thank God that was what he'd focused on.

"Cason this here's my best friend, Cash," I said, motioning at him against the railing. "And you already met Mister Maverick. We were just gonna head off to do chores. Would you mind tellin' your aunt that I'll call her a little later?"

"Aww stay!" Cason groaned. "I have Cinnamon Toast Crunch and Frosted Flakes and chocolate milk!"

"Fuck yeah!" Cash crowed, before I could even open my mouth to protest. "I'll take some chocolate milk, if I can't get head."

"Cash, shut up!" Maverick and I hissed at the exact same time. The last thing I needed was this poor kid to be influenced in any way by Cash. Charlie would kill me if anything Cash said rubbed off on him.

"We really need to get goin'," I insisted. "Mr. Mooney—that's Cash's dad—will get pretty mad if we're too much later."

"Eh, fuck it," Cash said, stumbling up the stairs onto the porch and toward the front door. Wrapping an arm around Cason's shoulders, he glanced back at me and said, "Kid said I could have some frosted flakes and chocolate milk."

With a giggle, Cason led him into the house. I speared a hand through my hair and groaned. Damn it all to hell. How was I going to explain this to Charlie? With a deep exhale, I pegged Maverick with a hard stare. "You brought him, you help me control him and get him out."

The dark-haired cowboy dipped his head, even as a ghost of a smile flickered to life on his lips.

With a sigh, I made my way into the house, Maverick hot on my heels. Cash and Cason shuffled around and slammed cupboards in the kitchen, even as Charlie still slept on the couch. How she still managed that was beyond me. Maybe, if I was lucky, she'd stay asleep till I could get Cash the fuck out of here.

Within minutes—seconds, actually—of him and Cason sitting down at the table, it looked like a bomb went off. Cash, in his half drunken stupor, decided the best way to make chocolate milk was to just pour the powder into the gallon jug.

"Kid would have probably done a better job than you, Mooney," Maverick said with an amused smirk as he sat down at the table and grabbed himself a bowl and the Frosted Flakes.

Cason hadn't stopped giggling from the moment he and Cash came into the house. He wore an ear-to-ear grin as he happily tried to pour himself a bowl of Cinnamon Toast Crunch.

I winced as nearly half the bag tumbled out into his bowl and all over the table. "Can y'all just shut the hell up?" I grumbled.

"Oooh! That's a penny, Mister Ryder!"

Well, shit.

"What's a penny?" Cash damn near shouted.

"Mama said it's not nice to cuss. Anytime someone says a bad word they have to put a penny in the swear jar."

Cash let out a braying laugh. "Well, that shit ain't gonna fly, little man. Ya know, there ain't nothin' wrong with a few cuss words.

Think of 'em like spices. The more spices, the spicier the food. The less, the more boring."

"Cash, shut the he–heck up!" I growled through clenched teeth. I swear, the minute we left here I was going to murder him. Absolutely fucking murder him.

Cash's lips pulled up into his award-winning shit-eating grin. The bastard still had his sunglasses on.

I looked at Maverick. "You gonna do anythin'?"

Maverick leveled me with an amused stare. "I will…after break-fast."

I fisted my hand and pressed it to my mouth. God, how I wanted to slam it against the damn table, but the thought of scaring Cason and waking up Charlie stopped me in my tracks. With a slow, steadying exhale, I forced myself to sit down. "You're an asshole, you know that?"

"Ooh! That's another penny!"

Maverick damn near choked on his cereal trying to hide his laugh.

With a shake of my head, I snatched up the Cinnamon Toast crunch and the last bowl off the table.

"Ryder? Cason? What the hell is going on?" Charlie's soft, sleepy voice froze me in place. My heart clenched, so damn hard I thought it might stop all together.

"Oooh!" Cash crowed. "That's another penny! Maverick, pay the kid."

Maverick dug a crumpled-up bill out of his pocket and handed it across the table to Cason. "I'm just goin' to give you a twenty. It'll get worse before it gets better."

Oh, fucking hell. I stifled a groan and whirled to face Charlie, only to be punched in the gut by the vision before me. Every time I didn't think she could get any prettier, she went and proved me wrong. Her hair was a wild mess, falling down her back and around her face in loose waves. Her gray eyes were puffy with sleep. I think this was my favorite look so far. One I wanted to see every morning, if I could.

The entire table had gone eerily quiet. I glanced over at Mav and Cash who both watched her as well. Appreciative looks on both of their faces. A pinprick of jealousy welled within me. "Umm Charlie, you know Maverick Holstrom, and do you remember Cash—"

"Mooney." Charlie's lips pulled up into an amused smirk. "Oh my God! It's been ages!"

"You remember me?" Cash pulled down his sunglasses and regarded her with a charming grin.

"How could I not? You somehow managed to round up three javelinas, numbered them one, two, and four, and set them loose in the main hallway at school."

Cash's bray of laughter damn near shook the house. "Shit! Remember that, Ryder?" He clapped a hand against the table.

A grin cracked my lips even as I shook my head and laughed. "How long were they looking for number three again?"

Charlie laughed, looking at me. "You were involved in that too?" She shook her head. "I'm sure your daddy was pissed."

"Oh, you don't even want to know," I replied. Pissed had been an understatement. He'd made me do community service all summer long, grounded me from rodeoing and damn near just about every-thing else fun I could think of. "It was worth it, though," I said, pouring some of the chocolate milk into my bowl. "Just to see the look on that old bat Principal Stevenson's face."

Charlie gave a nod, the smile on her face contagious. "She was the worst."

Even Mav agreed with a shake of his head as he silently ate his cereal. More relaxed than I'd seen him in a while.

Charlie came to stand at the foot of the table, her gaze still on Cash, a hint of a smile on her mouth. "Every guy in my grade wanted to be you, and every girl wanted to date you."

Cash's grin couldn't get any wider as he puffed his chest out like a damn rooster. Smacking the table once more, he all but shouted, "Everyone wants a piece of Big Daddy."

Maverick and I groaned at the same time. "Don't give him an excuse to have a bigger damn head than he already has," I grumbled.

Cash pulled down his glasses enough to wink at her. "It's nice to see you again, Miss Charlotte."

She dipped her head with a smile and took in the disaster before her. Spilled cereal, chocolate powder, and droplets of milk. We must have looked like a bunch of damn heathens.

"Breakfast of champions, eh?" Her gaze met mine, and I found the gray depths unreadable. The softness in her mouth, her body language, made me think she was fine, but her gaze still remained guarded. I gave her a sympathetic look, wishing like hell she could read my mind right then. I shouldn't have let Cash come in. Not that I hadn't tried, but I could have done more.

She moved closer to me, her leg brushing against mine from where she stood. I looked up at her once more and her answering half smirk told me all I needed to know. She wasn't mad. Surprised maybe—probably—but not mad. "Well, did you save any for me?"

The tension in the room dissolved as I got up and grabbed her a bowl. I lost track of time as all of us sat and laughed around the table. Cason absorbed every single word we said—bad and good—his eyes wide and an awed smile on his face. Charlie didn't even seem the least bit fazed by Cash's foul mouth or Maverick's silence. Everything seemed…natural. I couldn't help but think how easy and right it all felt. Which made no damn sense.

"Auntie Charlotte," Cason asked, "Mr. Cash needs a blowjob. Is there any way you could get him one?"

I coughed, my cheeks turning red. Oh sweet Jesus. Horror. Unbridled horror swept over me like a wave. Maverick spit chocolate milk all over the table.

Charlie gasped, her eyes bulging as she brought a hand to her lips. "Wh–what?" she squeaked out.

The only one unfazed was Cash. The fucking bastard. He chuckled, leaning back in his chair, fingers laced behind his head. He said with a shrug, "Well…How bout it? Can ya?"

I was up and out of my chair, grabbing Cash by the ear, like a flash of lightning. What a fucking idiot. Of all the dumbass shit to come out of his mouth, this was probably the stupidest. I smacked Maverick across the back of the head as I dragged a laughing, protesting Cash in my wake. I didn't need to glance back to make sure he followed, the sound of his deep chuckle and the chair pushing out were answer enough.

"I'm… Ms. Charlotte, I'm real sorry," I said, too embarrassed to meet her gaze. "He's… He's like a kid, you understand. I'm really sorry. We gotta get to the ranch and put some work in. Lea—leave the table, I'll be back later to clean up… *Without* Cash!" I didn't wait for a response, just shoved Cash out the door and down the porch steps.

Charlie's warm voice behind me gave me pause. "Bring him," she said with a laugh. "*Someone's* gotta pay for Cason's schooling, and the way y'all talk, he'll have his Bachelor's funded in no time."

Some tension in my heart eased, even if my blood still boiled from my best friend. I glanced back to find Charlie leaned against the doorway, Cason tucked against her side.

"Bye, Mister Ryder. Mister Maverick, and Mister Cash! Y'all come back now."

Charlie smiled and squeezed him to her side while waving at me, Mav, and Cash.

Cash shouted out a goodbye as I opened the back passenger door and all but threw him in. The blood and shame pumping through my veins wouldn't let me process exactly what he said. Mav tipped his hat and gave a wave before hopping in the passenger seat.

I walked around the front of my truck, a part of me wanting to get my ass out of there as fast as I could so I could lay into Cash—the fucking idiot. But seeing her standing on that porch, well… Even though I had no right, even though I didn't deserve to, I stormed up those steps and pressed a kiss to her lips.

I had no idea what we were after last night—hell, if she even wanted to be anything—but I did. And I needed her to know that.

"Bye, Miss Charlotte," I said, pulling away. I winked at Cason, tousling his dark hair. He grinned up at me. "See y'all around," I said, backpedaling down the porch.

Charlie pressed her fingers to her lips, trying and failing to hide a smile. "See you soon." It wasn't a question, but a statement. A promise. One I wholeheartedly intended to keep.

That kiss had me damn near skipping as I hurried to my truck, but the sound of Cash's braying laughter and goading the minute I opened the driver's side door brought me back down to reality.

Cash hooted from the back seat. "Well, shit, Ryder. What'd we leave for? She sure don't look too pissed."

"Just shut up and wave," I grumbled, pulling on my seat belt and giving an answering wave myself. Maverick did the same as I pulled out of the driveway. The minute we were on the main road, I glared back at Cash. "You *stupid* bastard! Why are you the way that you are?"

He wasn't even fazed. Not in the least. That shit-eating grin spread wider across his lips. "I don't know why your sorry ass is complainin', you should be thankin' me."

"And why's that?" I rolled my eyes, spearing a hand through my hair. "Shit! I left my hat!"

"Leave it," Mav said, his deep voice stopping me from turning around. Before I could even question, he went on. "Cash might be a rat bastard, but he is right that you should be thankin' him. Now you got another reason to see her."

I sucked in a deep breath, glaring back at Cash once more through my rearview mirror. He pulled down his sunglasses and winked at me. "You're welcome."

I exhaled loudly, some of the pent-up frustration dissolving as a smile cracked across my lips. "You're a pain in the ass."

Cash let out a crow of laughter. Even Maverick deigned to grace us with a full-fledged smile as we headed for the Mooney Ranch.

Just wait until I tell your dad that you're hungover." I gave Cash an evil grin via the rearview mirror.

"You wouldn't do that…" His grin faltered.

Chapter Nineteen

Damn Cold Vampires

Charlie

"So, is Mister Ryder your boyfriend *now*?" Cason asked as we cleaned up the dining room table.

I froze, nearly dropping one of the bowls onto the table. I chewed my lip a moment before meeting Cason's bright blue gaze. "Um… I'm not exactly sure." What the hell was I supposed to say? I'd told Ryder it was just a one-night thing, but that plan went to shit when I'd let him kiss me this morning. God, I was so screwed.

Cason paused in his haphazard cleaning, that is, if you could even really call it cleaning, but points to him for trying. More cereal crumbs fell onto the floor than into the trash can he attempted to wipe them into. Thank God for vacuums and brooms, I guess. "What do you mean you aren't sure?" he asked, cocking his head.

I sighed. Was I really trying to explain my love life to a five-year-old? Would he even understand? "Mister Ryder and I are…dating, I guess."

"What's that?" More crumbs on the floor.

I tried to hide my grimace as I finished plucking up all of the bowls and pouring out the little bit that was left of the chocolate milk. So much for cleaning the house two nights ago. "It's where you see someone and decide if you want to be boyfriend and girlfriend with them. It's like a…a practice test. Do you ever have those in school?"

His little nose scrunched up, his gaze turning contemplative, before giving me a slow nod. "Yeah. So, he's practicing to be your boyfriend?"

I huffed a laugh. "Something like that."

A smile split his lips. "Well, I like him. And Mister Maverick and Mister Cash too. Especially him, he's funny."

I let out a nervous laugh. Cash Mooney hadn't changed a bit. Just as wild now as he was back when we were kids. But dear Lord, that mouth on him. There weren't many things that could make me blush, but hearing Cason repeat those words so innocently… Oh. My. God. "Mister Cash is quite the character."

"Will we see them again soon?"

I glanced over at Ryder's hat on the hook by the front door. I'd almost stepped on it this morning after they'd left. I'd tried calling him, only to find that he'd left his phone here as well. Oh well, it gave me an excuse to see him. A little trickle of excitement welled in me at that. *You're walking a dangerous line.* One that I likely wouldn't recover from, but I couldn't deny the pull I had toward Ryder. I didn't need to make any decisions or commitments. I didn't need to dive head first into something new. But I *did* want to see him again. Of that I was certain.

"Auntie Charlotte?"

I shook my head to clear my thoughts. "What was that again?"

"Will we see Mister Ryder and his friends again?" he asked, placing the trashcan back in the kitchen.

I turned on the faucet and began washing the bowls. "I think so."

"Yay! Maybe later on today after church?"

My stomach flip flopped, and I whipped my head to find him standing in the center of the open kitchen. "Um...church?"

One of his brows rose in confusion. "Yeah. It's Sunday. Church is on Sunday."

I couldn't fight to hide a groan. I'd forgotten all about that little detail. I'd stopped going to church after a few failed attempts at finding a place in California. It had never really been my thing, anyway. The thought of going to church today...of being asked how Sheldon was doing—if they didn't already know, which would make that even worse—well, I just didn't want to deal with that today.

Sadness clutched at my chest, tightening and twisting my heart into painful knots. God, how had it only been two days? So much had happened. It felt both like forever had passed, and also no time at all. Would grief always be this weird? This constant push and pull of emotions? Being absolutely fine one minute, then in the next, having some random reminder of her pop into my brain and send me into a puddle of tears?

My gaze settled on Cason, who eyed me in silent question. Right, he'd been talking about church. "Oh, um...I um...I don't really go to church anymore, bud. But Grandma does, right? Maybe she could take you?"

Some of the light dimmed in his eyes, his face falling ever so slightly. "Oh. Yeah, okay. Sure." He sighed. "Can I go get ready then play in my room?"

Guilt bubbled to life, forcing a defeated sigh from my lungs, even as I nodded and said, "Sure, bud."

His head hung as he walked out of the kitchen, through the living room and down the hallway. I hadn't expected him to react that way. It was just church. I *never* wanted to go to church as a kid. But I wasn't Cason. If he liked church, that was great for him. I blew out a deep breath and turned off the faucet. Drying off my hands, I scrolled through my phone to find my mother's number.

"Oh, so you finally decided to check on me?" Her words dripped with venom, her tone sharp.

I rolled my eyes as I moved on to wiping down the dining table with disinfectant and a rag. "Good morning to you too, Mother. And I tried calling you three times yesterday. Your phone was off."

"It was dead," she snapped.

Another eyeroll. "Same difference. Anyway, how are you, Mama?" I already knew where this conversation was headed. I should never have called her, but that was a little too late now.

"My daughter just died, how do you think, Charlotte?"

Blood heated in my veins. I bit my lip damn near hard enough to draw blood just to stop myself from spouting off some snarky reply. Yes, she'd lost her daughter, but I'd lost my sister. We *both* were grieving. Though, I'm sure she'd try to say I couldn't possibly understand since I'd up and abandoned Sheldon five years ago and hadn't come back to visit since. I took a deep, calming breath in. No point in starting a war. I'd never win against her.

"I'm sorry, that was insensitive," I said on an exhale. "Do you need anything? Can I help out with anything?"

"It's fine. I'm fine. I know how to deal with grief, Charlotte."

Sure could have fooled me. I silently seethed, each second on the phone with her making my fuse shorter and shorter. "I'm sorry. Are you planning on going to church today?"

"Of course, and I expect you and Cason to be there as well." Her words rang with finality. I opened my mouth to argue, but it was like she could read my damn mind. "Or are you an atheist now? Buhdist? You Californians and all your *spirituality*. Back in my day…"

"Jesus Christ, Mama! I'm not an atheist! I'll go to fucking church!" I froze in place, my breath sawing in and out of my lungs like I'd just run a 5k. Why did she have to be such a pain in my ass? Why couldn't we have just one conversation without her being a burr in my side?

"*Charlotte Marie Evans* don't you dare speak the Lord's name in vain or cuss in my presence." It was a good thing she wasn't here. Her glacial glare would have been sharp enough to slice through bone. She'd have that ever-present frown she only ever seemed to aim my way on her lips, a look of pure disdain on her thin, sharp face.

My entire body trembled with unbridled fury, paralyzing me in place. Tears pricked in my eyes and threatened to slide down my cheeks. Thank God, she couldn't see them. She'd just use them against me. *Tears show weakness*, she liked to say. Drawing in on every last bit of calm I possessed, I said in a quiet, calm voice. "Cason and I will see you at church." I hung up before she could get another word off.

My heart thumped like a drum in my chest, echoing my footsteps as I stomped down the hall, on a warpath for Sheld—my—bedroom. Slipping out of my clothes, I hopped in the shower, praying like hell that it washed off some of my rage.

But it didn't.

CASON AND I PULLED up to the church with minutes to spare. Despite Cason excitedly rushing me once he found out I was going, I'd been dragging my feet. I wasn't looking forward to this. To the stares. The questions. The gossip. Because there *would* be gossip. That was the thing about small towns. There was always someone in someone's business…even if they had the best of intentions.

Walking up the front steps to the inner courtyard brought on a sense of dejavu'. How many times had I walked up these very stairs? Gone through those large, polished oak doors? A tremor went through me, making my legs feel like jelly, my weak ankle feeling as if it would snap like a toothpick beneath my heeled boots.

"Alright, bud," I said, glancing down at him by my side. "You know where to go?"

He gave me an enthusiastic nod before sprinting off to the right toward the Sunday school rooms. "Yep. See you later, Auntie Charlotte!"

The murals painted on the walls leading to the Sunday School rooms were still the same, though a bit more faded and cracked from the elements now. An animated image of Noah's arc.

I chewed my lip, standing frozen in place long after Cason had disappeared. My nerves were coiled tight, taut, like a rattlesnake about to strike. The church bells started to chime nine times, signaling the start of the service, and yet I still couldn't make my feet move. I tugged at my black crop top and situated my black, leather patterned leggings a little higher over my hips. Not like it would stop my mother from saying something about the inch and a half of my midriff that showed, but, well, I hadn't really packed for church before leaving California. At least she couldn't bitch about my tattoos. My gray cardigan covered those.

It's just church. Only an hour and a half of my time. I've got this….

Taking a couple calming breaths, I headed for the main building, hurrying through the oak doors before they closed them for the service. My anxiety spiked, the overwhelming feeling that everyone was staring at me so much that I almost, *almost* turned around and darted back out the doors. I had no idea where my mother was, but it didn't matter. I didn't have time to find her as the organ blared the familiar welcome hymn I recalled from my childhood. I slipped into the first free seat I could find. At least, it was close to the back exit. Maybe I could slip out at the end and grab Cason and leave without being bombarded by people.

The majority of the service went fine. A few hymns, an awkward 'say hello to your neighbor' game, a song or two from the choir, and then the main sermon from Pastor Stamper about grief, coincidentally. Or probably not coincidentally, since he likely knew about my sister because of Mama. But even that was fine.

"As some of you may already know, we lost one of our own just a couple days ago. Miss Sheldon was a shining light in this community and will be sorely missed. But may we rest easy knowing that she is at peace with our heavenly Father. I would like to take a moment, though, to call up her family, and uh, and pray for them in this hard time."

My stomach soured, and a wave of nausea settled over me like a sickness. Great. Just. Fucking. Great. Maybe when he meant family, he meant my mother. Maybe he hadn't recognized—

"Would Ms. Karen and Miss Charlotte please come up here so that I may put a hand on you and pray for God's mercy and healing during this difficult time in y'all's lives?"

Despite the queasiness and nausea, despite the fact that my boots suddenly felt like they were filled with lead, I stood up. Well, everyone sure as hell was staring at me now. There was no hiding. No getting out of this. My cheeks heated and my heart thumped so wildly I was honestly surprised no one heard it as I made my way down the center aisle. I couldn't get there quick enough. I felt like I was going the opposite way on one of those airport escalators. Despite the fact that my feet clomped against the floor of the church, that walk felt longer than anything I'd ever experienced. My mother already stood up next to Pastor Stamper, her eyes full of icy judgment as I headed for her.

And even though my anxiety made me want to literally shrivel up, curl into a ball, and rock myself into a soothing state, I couldn't help but fight the urge to roll my eyes as an ember of anger sparked like kindling to a fire at Mama's silent disdain.

Some things just never changed with that woman. I'd never win with her, so what was even the point of trying? Yet I was still doing it… I was here, wasn't I?

"Mama," I said quietly, dipping my head as I walked up onto the stage, coming to her side.

She gave me a tight smile, her lips hardly even moving as she replied, "Charlotte…interesting outfit choice." There was no denying her unapproving tone.

I flashed her what everyone else would think of as a welcoming smile, but from the way my mother's gaze narrowed, she took it as more of a challenge. "Now's not the time," I whispered, turning to Pastor Stamper.

"Miss Charlotte," he said with open arms. "It is lovely to see your smilin' face again. It's like a ray of light, leading us through the darkness of this difficult time."

And as uncomfortable as I was, as much as I didn't want to be here, I gave him a genuine smile. Pastor Stamper had always been kind. "Thank you, sir."

I didn't miss my mother's snarky huff from my side as Pastor Stamper asked that everyone bow their heads.

"Dear Heavenly Father, we come before You today in grief and in turmoil. We pray that You lift up this family into Your Grace and healing. We pray that You stay with them and comfort them as only You can. We ask that You help us to remember the kind, loving, selfless Sheldon, shining in her own grace and glory. We ask that You help us to heal this most grievous of wounds, and guide us through the fear and uncertainty of grief. We ask these things in Your Holy name. Amen."

"Amen," everyone echoed.

"Remember," Pastor Stamper placed a hand on each of our shoulders. "The church and the people of this fine town are here for you. You just tell us what you need and we will do everything we can. Be seated."

A s soon as the service was over, I excused myself from their side to go get Cason. There was no way I was staying for the Hour of Fellowship held in the courtyard after the service. No amount of free cookies and sweet tea could convince me to put myself through that torture. Maybe if I got out now, I could leave before too many people ambushed me with questions, condolences, and well wishes.

I didn't get even halfway across the courtyard before my mother's voice stopped me in my tracks. "Charlotte Marie."

I rolled my eyes and exhaled loudly through my nostrils before turning to look at her. She limped across the courtyard, her black cane smacking against the brick with each step. She refused to use her walker; stubborn woman wouldn't be caught dead looking *that* crippled. Appearance was everything to her, and anything short of perfection was a weakness. Hence the cane. She'd been using it for at least ten years, and the thing was as *extra* as she was. Black, polished wood, with a raven's head carved into the handle. Twin rubies glistened where the eyes should have been.

As she made her way towards me, I couldn't help but notice how much more Sheldon had taken after her in appearance than I had. They both had the same dark chocolate brown hair, though while Sheldon's had been long, Mama's was chopped into a severe lob that brushed against her collar bones. While Sheldon's eyes were bright and kind, Mama's were cold and cutting like ice. They had the same sharp features, from their jawlines to their cheekbones and noses.

And while at nearly seventy-six, she was still beautiful, I was happy I'd taken on more of Daddy's features.

No amount of pretty could hide an ugly heart.

"Mama." I dipped my head in acknowledgement.

"Where are you going?"

I glanced at the Sunday school room. *So close, yet so far.* "I was just going to grab Cason and head out."

Her lips drew down into a severe scowl as she limped to a stop before me. Even hunched over her cane she was a good few inches taller than me. "You're not staying for fellowship?"

"I wasn't planning to," I deadpanned.

"You absolutely *will* stay. People have been asking about you…have been wanting to see you. You owe it to them to stay." Her words held a layer of finality that made me feel like I was a kid again.

I wasn't a kid anymore though. Annoyance sparked in my veins. "I don't owe anything to anyone. I appreciate their concern and interest in seeing me, but I'm not really in the mood for it right now."

If looks could kill, I'd be dead. Ice cold rage flared in my mother's gaze, her sharp features somehow turning even sharper. "Oh don't be dramatic, Charlotte."

My blood boiled, that annoyance turning into fury. Dramatic? *I* was being dramatic? Me being upset and wanting to go home and grieve was dramatic? I opened my mouth to pop off some snarky reply, but a familiar, shrill voice cut through the courtyard.

"Oh, Karen!"

I let out a soft groan, to which my mother flashed me a scathing glare. Muriel Matthews, the Wicked Witch of West Texas and my mother's best friend, sauntered over to us.

My mother sent a tight-lipped smile her friend's way. "Muriel. Nice to see you."

Muriel clasped hands with her, big fat tears already rolling down her cheeks as she all but wailed, "I'm so sorry about Sheldon. You must be just devastated." They spent a moment or so exchanging teary eyed conversation before Muriel's beady stare landed on me. "Well, heaven above, I'm surprised you came back after all this time, Miss Charlotte." I didn't miss the accusation in her tone.

"Hello, Miss Muriel. Good seeing you again, I wish it was under better circumstances," I replied with a nod.

"It looks like you've been doing well in California."

I opened my mouth to respond, only for my mother to laugh over me. "I would say, those hips of hers are all filled out and then some." She glanced down at me, and even though a teasing smile pulled on her thin lips, it only made her appear colder.

Miss Muriel's eyes flicked up and down my body, and suddenly it was like I was sixteen again, being picked apart and judged and found completely inadequate. I'd always been curvy. Curvier than Mama, curvier than Sheldon. They'd gotten that tall, willowy build. I was much shorter, petite yet curvy. And while I was in shape and took pride in the way I looked, Mama always had a way of making my insecurities come out.

My hands drifted to my cardigan as I pulled it closed over my torso, blocking out my midriff from more scrutiny. *Thanks, Mama.*

And just like that, the courtyard flooded with people, a good majority of them making a beeline for us. And like a fire being fed kindling, the more attention my mother got, the more animated and livelier and bold she became, each word out of her mouth in regards to me stinging and stabbing harder and deeper than the last. I'd give her that she knew how to work a crowd, and that she knew just what to say to make me crumble.

Chapter Twenty

Mine, All Mine

Ryder

Cash, Mav, and I stood on the outskirts of the church court-yard. Charlie stood across the way next to her mother, a group of people gathered around and blocking her in. There was something different about her today. Something…reserved, unsure, dim. Yeah, dim was a good word. That girl, from the minute I'd seen her in Jack's again, had been like this shining beacon of light. So bright and open and welcoming, and I'd been nothing more than a moth drawn to her flame.

But today, that light was gone. All but extinguished. Her eyes were downcast most of the time, the smile on her face tight-lipped and forced. Even though I hadn't spoken to her, hadn't heard her speak, I guaranteed she sounded sad.

Even during her panic attacks over the last couple days, she'd still held a fire in her. A fighting spirit. This was different. I didn't like it.

"You gonna save her or just stare at her all day?" Mav's deep baritone pulled my attention away from Charlie. I glanced to him and Cash beside me. Cash's lips pulled up into a knowing smirk, while Maverick's scowl held a sense of concern.

"You notice how uncomfortable she is too?" I asked him.

He dipped his head once, but it was Cash who spoke. "Anyone with half a brain cell can see that, bud. She's got the Wicked Witch right there with her and her mama. I'd be uncomfortable too. I'd say she needs some savin'."

I'd noticed Miss Muriel Matthews there with them, that perpetual look of disdain lining the canyons of wrinkles on her face.

"Alright, I'll be ba—"

Cash had already stepped forward, his snakeskin boots eating up the distance between us and the group. He looked back over his shoulder at me, mouthing the words, *you owe me.*

"He does realize I've saved his ass more times than I can count, yes?" I mumbled to Mav.

"Eh, words, Ryder. We're in God's house."

Damn. I met Maverick's light gaze, a hint of a smile quirking on his lips. "A penny in the jar?"

That smile spread further as he, no doubt, thought of this morning. He nodded in Charlie's direction. "Let's go save your girl."

"A little preemptive, dontcha think?" I asked, even as my heart pounded at the possibility. I hadn't stopped thinking about her. Every minute, every damn second of the day was consumed with thoughts of her.

Maverick flashed me a knowing smile. "There's somethin' between y'all. I think even a blind man could see that."

Some of the tension eased within my heart. I'd been struggling to figure out the feelings writhing there. I'd never felt this way before.

Never wanted something so much—aside from winning buckles and titles. But I wanted Charlie. Wanted to get to know her more. Wanted to see her smile, hear her laugh. I wanted to hold her, touch her. If I closed my eyes, she was the first thing that came to mind. When I thought about what I wanted in months, years, even decades from now, I saw her.

I was probably an idiot for thinking all that, but I couldn't help it.

"Well, Miss Muriel Matthews!" Cash's church voice was more boyish than normal, sweet and innocent and curious, though still just as obnoxious. "Is that a new dress you have on? You know, that color purple really brings out your eyes!"

Muriel Matthews smiled. That woman hated just about everyone and everything on earth…except Cash Mooney and his father. She dipped her head in a demure smile, her eyes sparkling like Christmas lights.

"You know you've seen me in this dress before, Mister Mooney. You've complemented it before," she swooned.

"How the hell does he do it?" I muttered to myself, shaking my head.

"Ah!" Cash pointed at her and smiled. "Mr. Mooney's my father! Please, just call me Cash."

She reached out and rested her wrinkled hand on Cash's forearm. "Cash, then." She dipped her head.

"And is that Adeline Morris I see hiding back there?" Cash turned his grin on another of the little old ladies that had been crowding

Charlie. Now it was like she was invisible. They all quietly fought for his attention. I even spotted a few well-placed elbows fly out so they could get as close to him as they could manage. They all watched him and fawned over him… Except for Charlie's mother. She stood, staring pure hatred at Cash. His charms may not work on her, but he'd still distracted her.

"Now's our chance," I said to Maverick.

We skirted around the mass of people gathered in the courtyard, making our way up behind her. "Miss Charlotte," I murmured, tapping her shoulder gently.

She whirled around, her gray eyes locking with mine. "Hey. It's good to see you two." Relief rang in her words, but tension still clung to her.

I hated seeing that tension still there. I wanted it gone. Taking her by the arm, I led her away from the gaggle of grannies fighting for Cash's attention. Maverick dropped behind us. If anyone wanted to find us, they'd have to look through him.

"You look great today," I said, as we came to a stop behind a marble column.

Great was an understatement. She was beautiful, and even though it was positively indecent of me to do so in church, my gaze flicked up and down her body, admiring every inch of her.

Charlie smiled, but that sadness clung to her as she sighed and replied, "Thanks. But my mother has gone out of her way to mention three times now how much weight I've gained since moving to California…so, there's that."

What the hell? "That's fuckin' bullshit." The words were out before I could stop them.

"Words, Ryder!" Mavericks's voice was a low rumble, like rolling thunder.

"Cussing in church?" A smirk blossomed on Charlie's lips. "I'd say that's worth a little more than a penny."

I shrugged. "I don't care. You're perfect, Miss Charlotte. I need you to know that." I needed her to know that there wasn't a single thing wrong with her. That her curves were beautiful. She wasn't fat or heavy or out of shape in any way. But she also wasn't skin and bones. I'd never understand why people could be so horrible about weight, but I'd be damned if I didn't let her know just how gorgeous she was.

Charlie's cheeks flushed, and she tucked a stray piece of hair behind her ear. "Well, I don't know about perfect, but thank you." Her eyes met mine before flicking to Maverick and back again. "Did you guys get your chores done?"

Mav huffed from his spot by the column and turned back to watch Cash. A soft chuckle escaped me as I replied, "Chorin' ain't ever done...um, I uh, I want apologize again for this mornin'."

She waved a dismissive hand, a soft smile finally reaching her eyes. "Don't. Cason had an absolute blast. He hasn't stopped talking about you guys all morning."

"He seems like a good kid," Maverick chimed in.

Charlie nodded. "He really is."

"Don't let him around Cash then." I half laughed. No one could corrupt anyone quicker than fuckin' Cash.

Charlie's laugh was like a melody. "Cash is his favorite."

"Cash is everyone's favorite," Mav and I said at exactly the same time. We exchanged a look, both of us chuckling. It was true, though. Cash was funny, playful, and charming. If he wasn't breaking hearts, he was making people laugh.

Charlie's gaze clashed with mine, something in her eyes telling me without words that she had a favorite and it wasn't Cash. A shiver rippled through me.

"Speaking of Cason, I probably should go grab him from Sunday school. I've been trying for, like, the last ten minutes to get over there and leave."

Maverick's deep voice pulled my attention. "I'll go grab him for you. Y'all can stay here and talk a few more minutes."

"Oh, um…" Charlie's lips quirked up. "Thank you, Maverick."

He tipped his black cowboy hat to her and turned on his heel, walking away. I'd forever be grateful for him giving us a moment. Turns out, both my best friends were just as committed to me winning Charlie over as I was.

"Hey!" My stomach clenched at the sound of Cash's obnoxiously loud voice. "Which one of you just pinched my butt?"

The ladies giggled and covered their faces as he looked around, a huge, wide grin taking up his whole face.

"This is The Lord's house, I'll remind you." He winked at no one in particular. "We'd all better be on our best behavior."

"So," I said, shaking my head and turning back to her. "What do you have planned for today? Can I tempt y'all with dinner?"

Wariness flickered in her gaze. "I don't know, Ryder," she said with a sigh. "I don't think that's a good idea."

"And why not?" I asked, stepping closer to her, forcing her to look up at me. My fingers brushed against hers.

A sharp breath escaped her, her eyes flaring as she bit her lip. Another shiver went through me. "The more time we spend together, the harder it's going to be when this ends."

Another brush of our fingers. "Who says it has to end?"

Charlie blew out a loud exhale as she shook her head, an incredulous smile toying on her lips. "God, you're so stubborn and relentless."

I dipped my head, a sigh sliding out of my chest as I pulled my cowboy hat off—my backup, as I'd left that and my phone at Charlie's—and ran a hand through my hair before placing it back on my head. "I'm sorry, Miss Charlotte. I didn't mean to come on so strong. I know you just got out of a relationship… I just…well, I feel somethin' with you I ain't ever felt before."

Her cloudy gaze softened, one of the corners of her mouth drawing up as she wrapped an arm over her chest. "I feel it too." The words were little more than a whisper. "When I'm around you, I feel…safe. Secure. And that scares me."

Even though we were in the courtyard at church, even though at least a few dozen people stood around us and no doubt watched, it was like she and I were the only ones in the world. I slipped her hand in mine, my thumping heart easing just a bit when she didn't pull away. In fact, she squeezed back with just the slightest pressure.

I pulled her in closer, my dark eyes locked on her light ones as I said quietly, "I think the best opportunities in life should scare us a bit. I think that if you really want something…if it makes you happy, you should face it head on."

"Some would call that reckless."

"Darlin', I ride bulls for a livin'. Can't get much more reckless." The minute the words left my damn mouth, I knew they were the wrong ones. Shit.

She dropped my hand, her face turning into a mask of sadness. "Exactly. Which is why this won't work. Ryder…" her tone took on a pleading note. "I watched my daddy die rodeoing. I just… I can't go through that again."

"I ain't gonna die, Charlotte." How could I make her see? How could I convince her? I couldn't give up rodeoing, and I also didn't want to give up on her. Call it stupid, call it forward or reckless, but I knew…I just knew that letting her go would be the dumbest decision of my life.

Unshed tears hung like raindrops in her eyes. "You can't promise that," she choked out, crossing her arms over her torso. A protective stance, if I ever saw one. She looked just as sad and closed off as when I'd first walked over. *Great job, idiot.*

I blew out a frustrated breath and ran my tongue over my teeth. "You're right. I can't. But I can tell you this… I could give up rodeoin', get some bullshit suit and tie job, complete with a briefcase, even, and get hit by a car in the middle of a crosswalk on my way to the office. Hell, I could choke on a piece of steak, or die in a car crash… Literally anythin' can kill me. I ain't gonna stop livin' my life out of fear. If I die, if it's my time to go, well, then…I'll be damned if it ain't doin' somethin' I love."

Twin tears slid down her cheeks even as she huffed a laugh. "My daddy would have loved you."

"Please, Charlotte," I said, reaching a hand out only to drop it at the last second. Give me a—"

My words were interrupted by a woman's clipped, cool voice. "Charlotte."

Charlie and I both looked over at her mother approaching, Miss Muriel and a few other women in tow. My gaze flicked to Cash behind them, who gave me an apologetic shrug. Well, damn.

"Miss Evans, Miss Muriel, ladies." I dipped my head in acknowledgement before looking at Charlie. Any progress I'd made in the last few minutes might as well have been for nothing. Though she'd quickly wiped the tears from her eyes, her gaze was dark and guarded, her jaw clenched tight as she regarded her mother.

Miss Evans had always been a…closed off person. While her scowls were many, her smiles were few. With that glacial look in her eyes, it was no wonder why damn near half the town called her the *Ice Queen*. I shivered under the weight of that stare now. "Mr. Wright…I hear that congratulations are in order for your wins last night. I'm told your future looks pretty bright in the rodeo circuit." While her words were kind enough, they were laced with venom and disdain. And while I stood taller than her, the way she looked down her sharp nose, made me feel like she was looking down on me.

"Well ma'am, I qualified for Austin last night. That's a big show, where everyone's tryin' to get," I replied with a nod, tipping my hat in thanks. I suspected a trap, but I couldn't see where she could be going with this.

Her smile was as sweet as death and as warm as hellfire. "How charming. And then what? Start it all over again? My, my, you must be simply *swimming* in ribbons from all of your…*rodeo wins*."

"We don't really win ribbons, ma'am." I tipped my hat. She knew that.

"Buckles, ribbons…same thing, at the end of the day. I mean, you can't pay for hospital bills with a belt buckle."

Charlie stilled at my side even as her mother's gaze slid up and down me, assessing, leaving me feeling completely lacking in every way. Damn, is this what Charlie dealt with her whole life?

After a long moment, she moved on to her daughter, deeming me no longer important enough to talk to. "Charlotte," she said, a bite in her drawling voice. "How is your boyfriend?" She glanced back over her shoulder at her friends before settling her gaze back on me. "Charlotte's boyfriend is a *very* successful real estate agent in California. I wouldn't be surprised if he proposes by the end of the year. You know, I always told her, you can marry for love or money. But love doesn't make you rich, so you might as well marry someone who's got money." She laughed. "At least she listened to me about something."

I bit back a dark chuckle. So, she didn't like me being around Charlie. Looked like her daughter wasn't the only one who had a problem with rodeo cowboys. Message received, loud and clear.

Charlie's sugary-sweet voice drew my attention. "Actually," she said, the barest hint of a sadistic smile curling the corners of her mouth as she looked from me to her mother. "We broke up, Mama."

Charlie's mom glare turned colder than ice. "What happened?" While the words were innocent enough, there was a layer of anger in them. Anger for being made to look a fool. Her eyes flicked to me and my blood froze.

"Well, you know, there was the fact he was completely emotionally unavailable, self-centered, a total narcissist… I could go on and on." Charlie ticked the things off on her fingers as she spoke, all the while keeping that overly kind tone to her voice. Fury danced in her eyes.

Her mom might be like a cold winter—dangerous and deadly, but Charlie was wild and raging, like a summer storm. The storms in her eyes promised destruction. God damn, she was beautiful. I bit my lip to hide a smirk, pride trickling through me. I didn't know the details of her relationship with her mom, but I'd known it was rocky. This little interaction was enough to let me see just how strained it was. It was good to see her sticking up for herself.

Karen Evans sighed, her lips drawing into a thin line. "Well, how unfortunate."

Charlie gave a noncommittal shrug before turning to me. "Ryder," she said, her face drawn into a polite smile even as mischief danced in her eyes. "You left your hat and phone at my house. I have them in my car."

An eruption of hushed whispers and gasps traveled through Miss Evans and her friends—none louder than Miss Muriel. Not going to lie, even my breath left me in a whoosh.

Well damn, did she know what she just did? For someone who was hesitant to date me, she sure wasn't acting like it.

If looks could kill, Charlie would be dead. I would be dead. Hell, Cash might not even have been able to escape. Murder blazed in her mother's eyes. Her gaze flicked between Charlie and I. "So, you two are together now, then?"

My chest constricted, mouth popping open, though I didn't know what the hell to say. I glanced over at Charlie, but she wasn't looking at me. Her defiant stare warred with her mother's. She gave another nonchalant shrug, crossing her arms over her chest. "We're just getting to know each other."

Miss Muriel's shrill voice echoed through the group. "Is *that* what the kids call it nowadays?"

"I'd like to get to know Cash Mooney," one of the other ladies quipped, causing a chorus of quiet giggles to break out.

I bit back a response. Old witch never knew when to keep her mouth shut or mind her own business. The overwhelming urge to come to Charlie's defense welled up in me like a wave, but I held back. This was her battle, and I got the feeling she wouldn't appreciate the help. Not that she needed it.

She did take a small step toward me though, our fingers brushing for just a moment. I didn't miss her mother's gaze drop to our hands.

Miss Evans leveled us both with a scathing glare. "Well, good for you, Charlotte. I expect you and Cason at the house for dinner at six." There wasn't a single ounce of false kindness in her voice. In its place was a coldness I'd rarely felt from just tone. She looked down her nose at me, that scowl deepening the lines on her face with each passing second. "We have family matters to discuss, so no guests."

She didn't bother to say goodbye before turning on her heel and limping away on her cane. Miss Muriel glared down her hook nose at Charlie and I. She gave an indignant huff before following Miss Evans, along with the rest of their little group.

When they'd made it out of hearing range, Charlie let out a loud sigh. Her body trembled, her fingers shaking as she ran them through her hair. Tilting her head to the cloudy sky above, she let her eyelids flutter closed. "Well, that was fun," she said, finally recovering and setting her sights on me.

I couldn't help the soft chuckle that came out of me.

Her brows pulled together, a frown drawing on her mouth. "What's so funny?"

"So…we're dating now," I replied with a smirk.

"What?" She shook her head. "No, I didn't say that."

I cocked my head to the side, one of my brows quirking up. "You just told the biggest group of gossips that I stayed the night. The whole town's gonna know by the end of the day."

"By lunch, I'd say," Cash added, hands on his hips.

The weight of her actions settled over Charlie right before my eyes, seeping into her entire demeanor. "Oh my God, I was so selfish, I didn't even think about what that would do to your reputation." She ran a hand through her hair again, chewing her lip in worry. "I was just so angry at my mama and the way she was treating you and I just… I knew it would piss her off to have everyone talking about her tramp of a daughter. I'm…I'm sorry."

I wrapped an arm around her waist, pulling her in close. "I ain't worried about it, Miss Charlotte. My mom's gonna wanna meet you, but I can hold that off for a bit."

Worry flickered across her features, but she didn't pull out of my grip, so I'd take that as a win. "It looks like you got what you wanted," she said with a huff.

I frowned down at her. "What do you want, Charlotte? Tell me the truth."

She buried her face in my chest, nestling more into me. Her words came out muffled as she spoke, "I want you."

"I'm…gonna go find Maverick." Cash spun on his heel and sauntered away, shit-eating grin fixed in place.

Well, damn. A rush of pride and desire surged through me, sending a grin to my lips. I hooked a finger beneath her chin, tilting her face up to look at me. "I'm sorry, what was that? I couldn't hear you. Can you say that again?"

Her narrowed gaze held a playfulness to it as she pursed her lips to hide a smile. I laughed.

"I'm not saying it again," she replied, a smile finally gracing her lips.

I should have been mad. At least a part of me should have, knowing that really the only reason I was holding her right now was because she'd wanted to piss her mom off. But I wasn't. I was just happy she'd finally stopped fighting the pull we had toward one another. I'd take it slow, there wasn't any need to rush this. And I'd have to figure out how to get her more comfortable with me rodeoing, because that was going to be a point of contention. It already was.

But that was a problem for future me. One I had no intention of solving right now.

"Mister Ryder! Auntie Charlotte!"

Charlie and I pulled apart, my body instantly missing the warmth of her embrace. Cason came running up beside us, Maverick and Cash in tow. The latter two were whispering and both smiling like assholes. Well, the truck ride back to the ranch was going to be fun.

Charlie smiled down at Cason, enveloping him in a hug. "How was Sunday school, bud?"

"It was good!" He launched into an explanation of what they did during their David and Goliath lesson, flailing his hands and arms as he spoke animatedly. "Mister Cash and Mister Maverick invited us to lunch!"

"Oh, um…we have some errands to run, bud," Charlie replied, looking at Cason. "We probably should get going."

Cash waved a dismissive hand through the air. "So, what you're sayin' is you'll already be out. Let's all get lunch, then."

Charlie met my gaze, a silent question in her eyes. I smiled and grabbed her hand. "Come with us, Miss Charlotte. Please?"

She rolled her eyes even as she smiled. "Where are we even going, anyway?" she asked as I pulled her to my side.

"Well," Maverick started, "It's Sunday, so that means—"

"Texas Roadhouse, baby!" Cash crowed. Cason let out an answering shout of approval. We all smiled at that. Cash pulled down his glasses to appraise Cason. "Race ya to the truck, little man," he said before taking off through the courtyard. Cason's squeals of laughter followed close behind.

Charlie laughed at my side. "I don't know who is more of the child. Him or Cason."

"Cash," Mav and I both said in unison.

We ended up taking my truck after switching over Cason's car seat from Charlie's car to the backseat of my truck. He sat between Cash and Mav, while Charlie rode shotgun beside me. I snuck a glance over at her, a little rush going through me at the sight.

I'd gotten her. Not the way I'd wanted, but I'd gotten her all the same. Now I just needed to figure out how the hell to keep her from slipping through my fingers.

I DON'T KNOW WHAT part of me thought bringing Charlie and Cason along to Sunday lunch was a good idea, yet here we were. Cason brought up Star Wars on the drive and Cash and Mav had been bickering back and forth like an old married couple arguing over the weather. Cason was in heaven, and I'd found Charlie laughing a number of times now, but I couldn't help my nerves winding tighter and tighter with each passing second. The more Cash said, the more likely he'd say or do something offensive. Couldn't we just have one day? One fucking day without his crazy-ass bullshit?

Rolling into the parking lot, I put my truck in park. I glanced over my shoulder and pitted Cash with a withering glare, even as I referred to both him and Maverick as I spoke. "You're two grown ass men arguin' about Star Wars. Just, stop. We're goin' to have a nice lunch, and no one's gonna do anythin' stupid, right?"

I didn't want this turning into a whole Cash Mooney comedy hour. Because it would, it almost always did. I just wanted to enjoy spending time with Charlie and Cason.

"Right!" Cason piped in.

I nodded. "Good. Now let's go."

Charlie's hand came to rest on mine and I dragged my gaze to her. She offered me a soft, reassuring smile. Some of the pent up anxiety coursing through my veins like streaks of lightning fizzled out. Not all the way, but it was better than before. I took a deep breath and squeezed her hand in reassurance.

Cash's voice sent my nerves right back up to livewire status as I opened my driver's side door. "See, the problem is you're just going by the movies, you aren't—"

I turned back around and glared at Cash.

"I wasn't talkin' about Star Wars." Cash raised his arms in a guilty shrug, his lips crooking up into a familiar, mischievous smirk I knew all too well. "We're talking about something else now."

"If I hear you say one more, just, one more thing about Star Wars, I'm gonna make you sorry," I warned.

"Yeah?" He chuckled, a defiant look in his hazel eyes. "What could you do to me?"

"I'll tell your mom you were dancin' with Kelsea Karkula last night." One of my brows quirked up, a satisfied smirk of my own forming on my mouth, even as his turned into a thin line.

"That's a bald-faced lie!" Cash protested. "I wasn't dancin' with that crazy bitch!"

"Cash! Words," Maverick grumbled while getting out of the truck, even as Cason giggled.

"You know that, and I know that," I replied, meeting Cash's stare in the rearview once more. "But your mom'll believe me over you, any day of the week. Especially Sunday." My grin widened. I had the bastard now.

"If my mom thinks I'm back with Kelsea she'll lose her mind," Cash groaned.

I undid my seatbelt. "Exactly, now don't push me."

"Who is Kelsea Karkula? I don't recognize that name." Charlie asked as she slid out of the truck before coming around to my side.

"Is she your girlfriend?" Cason shouted from the car as Maverick helped him undo his straps on his carseat.

"Hell no." Cash grunted, closing his door and rolling his shoulders. "We dated off and on for a bit, but she was never my girlfriend."

"Did she fail the test?" Cason asked, his little nose scrunching up in question.

Charlie bit back a laugh as she settled at my side. I frowned down at her. What was Cason talking about?

"What test?" Cash said, voicing my thoughts aloud.

"The girlfriend-boyfriend test like Auntie Charlotte is giving Mr. Ryder," Cason explained.

"Cason! Hush!" Charlotte said with a huff of laughter, her gaze flicking to mine.

"Well, did I pass?" I asked, slipping an arm around her waist and pulling her to my side.

She rolled her eyes but a smile graced her lips. "Do you think you passed?"

Cash and Maverick shared an amused glance. My cheeks heated with all the attention. While I was nowhere near as shy as Mav, I didn't like having the spotlight on me all the time like fucking Cash. "Tell 'em 'bout Kelsea, Cash. Did she pass or fail?"

Cash laughed, sliding an arm around Cason's shoulder. "She sure did fuckin' fail. For future information, little man, givin' another cowboy a blowjob behind the bleachers while you're gettin' ready to ride a bronc is a surefire way to fail the girlfriend test!"

"Jesus Christ, Cash!" I yelled, dipping my head to hide the shame on my face. Charlie was going to kill me. Or better yet, leave. If this was a test, I was surely going to fail because of my dumbass best friend.

"Lords fuckin' name!" Maverick snapped, no longer able to hold back from cussing. I was impressed he'd managed for as long as he did.

Charlie laughed. Full on belly laughed, all the while shaking her head. "Dear God, Mooney. How the hell did your mama keep enough soap in the house to keep up with that mouth of yours?"

"Ooh, Auntie Charlotte you said hell! That's another penny!"

"What? Out of all the things said…" Charlie scoffed, her words drifting into nothingness. Cash snorted, buckling over to keep back from letting out his trademark laugh. Maverick couldn't hide the smile that formed on his lips. Oh to be a kid, at least Cason didn't register any of the bullshit Cash had said. I'd rather have him think hell was a cuss word than start asking what a blowjob was.

Maverick let out a soft chuckle as he pulled his wallet out of his pocket and pulled out two twenties before handing them to Cason. "Here, kid. Think this'll cover the swear jar for the day?"

Cason eyed the money like a kid in a candy store. He nodded, flashing a toothy grin. "Yes, sir, Mister Maverick."

CHARLIE AND CASON WENT off to the bathroom after the hostess seated us.

"What is the matter with you two?" I speared Cash and Maverick with a wild glare. "Can you please just let me have one fucking moment without you two cocking it all up?"

Maverick gave me a guilty shrug, while Cash's hazel stare held a mischievous edge to match his smile.

"You two behave yourselves or I'll kill you," I snapped.

Cash's grin pulled wider. "You'll kill us?"

"Dead." I nodded curtly.

Cason and Charlie returned—Charlie slipping in beside me, while Maverick helped maneuver Cason between him and Cash just as the waitress appeared at the end of our table, a pen and notepad in hand.

"Hi there, folks. What can I get y'all today?"

I didn't miss how Cash's eyes lit up when he saw her.

"Well, hello." He gave her his most charming smile. Her dark hair covered her name tag so he reached out a finger and brushed it aside.

"Savanah? That's a pretty name. I mean, it fits perfectly for a girl as pretty as you. My name is Cash but…well, uh, you can call me Big Daddy. Everyone does."

"Only he calls himself that." Maverick chimed in.

"What…what can I get y'all to drink today?" Savanah stammered, her cheeks pinkening as she bit back a shy smile.

Oh God. I groaned inwardly, fighting an eye roll. It's working. Whatever magic Cash had was working on this poor, unfortunate waitress.

"I'll take an Arnold Palmer, please," Charlie said with a polite smile, before looking at Cason. "And what about you, bud?"

"Lemonade, please!" he beamed.

Maverick and I both ordered Cokes.

"And you, sir?" Savanah turned her doe eyes on Cash. He just stared at her dreamily. "What did you want to drink? Sir?"

"He's waiting for you to call him Big Daddy," Cason supplied helpfully.

"Big…" She flushed bright red. "What did you want to drink…Big Daddy?"

"I was gonna get a sweet tea," Cash replied as if there'd been no interruption. "But I'm afraid with you here, that's just too much sweet. I'll take a water with lemon slices please. Thank you so much." He offered her that million dollar smile once more. The one he saved for all the pretty girls.

If he wasn't my best friend, I'd hate him. Hate him for how easily he could charm 'em and leave 'em. But ever since, well, ever since senior year, he'd given up on chivalry, and moved on to the art of heartbreaking.

"I'll…" She cleared her throat and collected herself. "I'll be right back with those drinks," she said with a dazzling smile aimed directly at Cash before walking away.

"What are you doin'?" I growled, leveling him with a warning glare.

The bastard laid his arms over the back of the booth, smirking at me the entire time. "I'm showin' Cason how to be nice to girls."

"Why?" Maverick and I asked at the same time.

Charlie let out a soft chuckle, whispering the words, "Oh, no."

Cash went on. "Well, if he wants to be like me—"

"He doesn't want to be like you," I almost shouted. This was going to end poorly. So damn poorly. "No one wants him to be like you."

"Now, the way I figure it…" Cash went on as if I hadn't said anything. "Kid's got four good choices."

"Here we go." Maverick leaned an elbow on the table and rubbed at his temple, as if he already had a headache. That made two of us.

"He can be like Maverick, here." Cash gestured at his cousin sitting on Cason's other side. "Severe, rule followin', no fun, mother goose. He can be like his Auntie Charlotte… Smart, brave, maybe a little too soft spoken, but as sweet as the day is long. He can be an asshole like Ryder. Or…he can be a cool, suave, handsome, witty, funny, charmin'—"

"Conceited, arrogant," Maverick interrupted.

"Incorrigible, irreverent, obnoxious," I added.

Charlie's soft, melodic voice drew our attention. "Audacious, cocky, pig headed."

"Number one cowboy like his Uncle Cash," Cash finished, unbothered by our interruptions. He squeezed Cason's shoulder. The little boy's smile was brighter than the sun.

"Now, he can learn to be like Maverick in one day. All he's gotta do is not be fun at all and ruin everyone else's fun by mindlessly followin' the rules. But to learn to be like Big Daddy… That's gonna take me some time." Cash dipped his head, mock humility on his face. "I'm willin' to teach him, though. I mean, someone has to."

I rolled my eyes even as Charlie bit back a laugh.

"So, Cason—" Cash turned to the boy. "Do you wanna be a rule followin', stick in the mud like Uncle Mav?" Cash shook his head. "Or do you want to be a chick-slayin', rodeo winnin' heartbreaker like your Uncle Cash?"

"Oh my God." I sighed, mimicking Maverick as I rubbed at my temples. "Shut up. Just fuckin' shut up."

Charlie leaned against me, laughter bubbling out of her as she patted my thigh reassuringly beneath the table.

"Don't listen to him," Maverick told Cason, his voice weary. "He's crazy."

"Like Billy Ray Cyrus is crazy? Like Patsy Cline was crazy?" Cash argued.

"What do they have to do with—"

"See, Cason." Cash cut me off. "People will always try and bring you down. Tell you, you can't touch the sun. Tell you, you can't get that cute waitress's number. Tell you, she won't go home with—"

"Watch it Cash, you're getting to be too much," Maverick warned.

"Stick with me, little man." Cash grinned, leaning back in his chair. "I'll teach you everything you need to know."

Cason was so damn screwed.

Chapter Twenty-One

The House That Built Me

CHARLIE

"CAL, STOP BEING A dick and making this harder than it has to be," I snapped from my end of the line.

God, he was infuriating. I hadn't wanted to call him, but I'd thought—crazy, right—that he could be a decent human being for two fucking second of his life and work with me on a way to get back my things. But surprise, surprise, that was too much for him.

"Making this harder than it has to be?" he snapped right back. "You're the one who broke up with me last night for some bullshit reason. Stop being so dramatic and come back here to work this out. I'm willing to take you back if you don't pull any of this shit again."

I rolled my eyes, biting my bottom lip so hard it almost drew blood. Dropping my head back, my eyes fluttered closed and I drew in a deep breath. How the hell had I been with him so long?

"The fact that you think gaslighting me is the way to get me back is exactly why we broke up. You know what…? I can't do this. I'll just…I'll figure it out myself. Don't call me ever again, asshole."

I hung up, ignoring the string of curses on the other end of the line. My pulse pounded in my ears, my heart hammering in my chest. My phone buzzed, his name flashing on the home screen, but I sent it to voicemail. Did he seriously just say all that to me? How had I not noticed how fucking toxic he was until now?

Tossing my phone onto my bed, I scrubbed my hands down my face, trying to center myself. Ryder, Cash, and Maverick were still here in the other room with Cason. I didn't want to be an absolute wreck when I went out there. At least Ryder wasn't like Cal. They couldn't be more different. I know I hadn't known Ryder long, but I *knew* he wouldn't treat me the way Cal did. That was for sure.

I sighed. Well, if Cal was going to be an unhelpful dick, I'd have to figure out getting my stuff back another way. Grabbing my phone, I started looking up moving companies.

I sunk onto the couch beside Ryder at a quarter after five. Ugh, I had to leave for Mama's in half an hour. Him, Maverick, Cash, and Cason lay sprawled out on one sofa or the other watching How to Train Your Dragon. A soft smile came to my lips. They were amazing with him. Not that my experience with kids was much to go off of, but from the happy look on Cason's face, he'd had fun. Ryder glanced over at me, a skeptical smile on his lips.

I kissed him softly. Crazy how such a small gesture could feel so second nature in such a short amount of time. Weren't you supposed to go through a somewhat awkward phase? There was nothing awkward about this. Ever since I'd announced to my mother we were dating, everything just felt so…natural with him. With all of them, really. Cash and Mav had settled into my life just as easily. And Cason's.

What if this didn't work out? The intrusive thought dulled some of the happiness inside of me. Was I stupid for getting into something so quickly with Ryder? If we broke up down the line, he wouldn't just be losing Ryder, he'd be losing Cash and Maverick as well.

My stomach clenched in knots. Ugh, why did I have to be such a Debbie Downer?

"You okay?" Ryder asked, running a hand up and down my thigh, his brows drawing together into a line.

"Yeah." I nodded and let out a sigh, deciding to keep my mouth shut about my fears about him and I and blame my mood on the other matter at hand. "I talked to Cal about him sending my things here, but that was pointless. So I spent the last twenty minutes on the phone with a moving company. It's going to cost a fucking fortune to get my stuff sent over, but I honestly don't really see any other way of getting it here."

"I can pay for it if you need." He gave my leg a reassuring squeeze.

"Thanks, but the money isn't really the issue. I'm just annoyed that I'm in this position to begin with." I blew out a heavy breath. "I was hoping Cal could be an adult for once and handle this amicably…apparently, I'm an idiot."

"He's causin' you problems?"

I nodded.

Ryder gave me another reassuring squeeze. "Well, hey, worse comes to worse, we make a little trip down there and get your stuff."

I huffed a laugh. "It would be more than a *little* trip. I couldn't ask you to do that with me."

"Did someone say road trip?" Cash all but shouted. "I'm *so* down!"

A laugh bubbled out of my throat as I looked between Ryder and him. "No offense, but I'm not sure I could be in the car with you for that long, Mooney."

The perpetual grin on his lips pulled wider. "Ah, you don't know what you're talkin' 'bout. I'm a good road trip buddy."

"Yeah," Maverick grumbled. "So good, we spent an entire damn day tryin' to find your ass when you went home with some girl and didn't tell us."

"Eh, it was honestly no big deal, Miss Charlotte." Cash grinned. "Mav just likes to bitch and moan."

"Cash, words!" Maverick scowled. I laughed. Of all the boys—all of us, actually—Maverick was the one who tried the hardest to stick to the no cussing rule. At least there was one responsible one in the group.

Cash just waved him off with a grin and a middle finger in the air. I buried my head in my hands, trying and failing to hide a laugh. Cason was so screwed. But honestly, for all these boys cussed, they were far kinder and responsible and good than Cal had ever been. Cason could learn a lot more from them than just a few cuss words.

I glanced down at my phone and sighed. "I hate to kick you all out, but Cason and I have to head to my mother's for family dinner."

"Aw, can't they come with us?" Cason pouted from his spot between Maverick and Cash.

"They can't, bud. Grandma said no guests tonight."

"But I don't want them to leave!" he replied, his pout turning to a full-fledged frown.

"I know. But we can see them later this week, okay?"

His blue eyes narrowed. "But I want them to go to Grandma's!" His little voice quaked with fury.

I rocked back at the explosion. I hadn't seen this side of him before. He hadn't even so much as raised his voice in the last two days. "Cason, they can't go to Grandma's. She told me earlier she just wants us there."

"But that's stupid! I don't want to go!" He stood up, crossing his arms over his chest with a harumph. "You can't make me!"

Anger of my own flared at his sudden defiance. Why was he so mad? Why was he lashing out now? I glanced between Cash, Maverick, and Ryder, trying to figure out what to do. How to react.

I stood up and took a few steps toward him before kneeling down so I was more at his eye level. "What's going on, bud?"

"I want them to come to Grandma's!" He dipped his head, glaring at me through furrowed brows.

"I understand that," I replied slowly, "But grandma said—"

"I don't care!" he shouted, stomping his foot.

I snapped, my anger getting the better of me. "That's it. Go to your room."

"No. I don't want–"

"*Now*, Cason!" I yelled right back.

He flinched, tears welling in his eyes before sliding down his cheeks. Without another word he sprinted for his bedroom, sobs trailing in his wake.

I watched him disappear into his room and slam the door behind him. My entire body trembled. With rage or embarrassment, I wasn't sure. But one thing was for certain: guilt gripped me and held me like a vice. I'd never dealt with anything like that, but whatever I'd done had been terribly, terribly wrong.

Tears pricked in my own eyes as I turned to look at Ryder and his friends. "What did I do wrong?"

Cash looked just as dumbstruck as me. Ryder offered me a sympathetic shrug. "I'd have probably reacted the same way," he said.

"He's a kid," Maverick said softly, his jade eyes meeting mine. "Kids have temper tantrums when they feel like they're not in control. Add to it, his mom just died. He might not show it, but he's hurtin'."

I tried and failed to bite back a sob, guilt growing and festering in my chest like an overgrown weed. "He's hurting and I just yelled at him." I wiped at the tears streaming down my face. "Great."

Ryder was there in an instant, offering silent support. Even Cash kept quiet.

Maverick offered me a sympathetic look. "This won't be the last time he lashes out. I did it a lot when my parents died, in the beginning."

His parents had died? How horrible. I could see how something like that would have shaped him into the quiet, reserved person he was now. Would Cason be like that? "What should I have done differently?" I asked. He might not have kids, but he'd been in Cason's shoes. So had I, but…well, Mama hadn't stood for this behavior. No matter how warranted it was. "What helped you?"

"You ever saddle break a young horse?" he asked seriously, the sudden shift in topic throwing me for a loop. I gave a slow shake of my head.

"See, their brain's still developin'. They can only handle so much. They have good days…and they have bad days." His voice was a soothing, quiet melody that calmed my nerves. "If you catch 'em on a bad day and try to get too much out of 'em…Well, they do that. They throw a tantrum. They don't understand why you're askin' 'em to do what you're askin' 'em to do. Cason doesn't understand why his mom just died… Them babies ain't upset you asked 'em to carry a saddle. They're upset because they're tired, scared, hungry, maybe sore. Cason ain't upset we can't go to your mom's house with you. He's run out of room in his little heart for emotions, and this is the straw that broke the camel's back."

He gave me a long, measuring look as if trying to decide whether to go on. I didn't say anything, not wanting to risk him stopping. This was the most I'd ever heard Maverick talk. And if the rest of his advice sounded as good as this, I didn't want to miss out on it.

"Cash's dad, Bad Mooney… He did this thing he liked to call takin' a break. It wasn't timeout, per se, but it gave me a chance to rein in my anger and feel like I was in control, while still makin' me deal with the consequences of my actions." Mav sat forward on the edge of the couch, placing his elbows on his knees and steepling his fingers. "I'd get sent to my room, but I was allowed to come out when I wanted to, on one condition. I had to be calm and respectful. If I came back out and gave attitude, I was sent right back to my room. It made me feel like I was in control, not him. And that was usually why the problem started anyway. My emotions would get too big, too loud, and I didn't know how to turn them off, how to control them. This gave me the opportunity to do it on my own. It took a while, but after a time, when I felt like I was gettin' out of control, I'd walk away and regulate my emotions somewhere away from everyone else until I was calm enough to be around others."

Maverick glanced at Cash and Ryder, the three of them sharing some knowing look I knew nothing about. "You can't force a young colt that's already made up his mind that today's gonna be a bad day, to have a good day. Sometimes, you gotta put 'em back in their stall and let 'em have their fit. They ain't gonna remember it tomorrow, long as you don't bring it up again. Or, you could have the fight with 'em and just know that everyone's gonna lose."

That made sense. I'd never broken horses, but I'd felt like that when Daddy died. So wild and angry and out of control with no idea how to express what I was feeling. No way of letting it out. Mama always just threatened to pull the disappointment card or spank us if we got out of hand. I wondered how differently things would have been had she been more willing to help me through my grief instead of bury it. But, out of sight out of mind, right?

"What happened when it didn't work?" I chewed my bottom lip. Not every time could have been a success. I'd been put in timeout and punished and still been defiant and fought back. I couldn't imagine this would work every single time.

"Sometimes my uncle would talk to me. I was a bit older than Cason, so I could understand a lot more, but sometimes just hearin' him talk would calm me down. Other times, he'd walk me through a breathin' exercise. Sometimes, I just needed someone to hold me. Physical touch can be soothing. Or other times, I just needed to do somethin' by myself that comforted me."

"Like, jerkin' off?" Cash asked with a shit-eating smirk.

Maverick's voice didn't change as he ignored Cash, but his eyes hardened a bit. "Like, whittlin', or lookin' for rocks that were shaped like animals."

I rolled my eyes at Cash even as a small smile bloomed, and met Maverick's stare, offering him a soft, genuine smile. "Thank you."

Maverick nodded in response.

The sobs coming from Cason's room had quieted a bit. Not entirely, but at least he didn't sound quite as upset. "I'll be right back," I said, heading towards the hall.

"Who's this talkative, introspective sumbitch, and where's my strong, silent type cousin?" Cash quipped as I left the room. "You're ruinin' the group dynamic. Ryder's supposed to be the one that says shit like that."

"Cash?" Ryder's voice held a layer of annoyance and finality to it. "Shut up."

I walked down the hallway, taking deep, steadying breaths to calm my racing heart. Would I just piss Cason off again by going and bothering him? Should I leave him for a while longer?

I knocked on the door. "Cason, can I come in?"

A muffled response I couldn't make out came from the other side of the door. I'd take that as a yes. Hesitantly, I turned the knob, easing into the room.

"Hi, bud. Can we talk?"

He sniffled into his pillow. "What?"

I sat on the edge of his bed. "I'm sorry for yelling at you. I shouldn't have done that. Will you forgive me?"

Another sniffle, then, "Yes."

"Wanna tell me what's wrong?" I asked, glancing at him.

He sat up slowly, wiping at his eyes. "I m–m–miss M–mama."

Tears slipped down my cheeks. "I know, bud. I do too."

"Mister Cash and Mister Maverick and Mister Ryder make me not so sad." The sorrow in his voice just about broke me.

"Oh, Cason…" I opened my arms and he launched into my embrace, both of us crying as we clung to one another. I understood exactly what he meant. Being around the boys today had been like a breath of fresh air. I was too busy laughing at Cash, enjoying Ryder's company, and Maverick's soothing presence to really be reminded of my circumstance. I'm sure it was similar for him.

"I'll tell you what."

"What?" he whispered, pulling back to look up at me with glassy eyes.

"Mister Ryder and his friends can't come to dinner tonight, but maybe if we ask really nicely, they can drive us there and pick us up."

A flash of excitement danced to life in his gaze.

"Does that sound good?"

He nodded, sniffling again. "Yeah."

I smiled and pressed a kiss to his forehead. "Okay, go ask them then."

Mama would be pissed, but technically she'd only said no guests at dinner. They wouldn't be staying for dinner.

The two of us walked back to Ryder, Cash, and Maverick.

I glanced down at Cason, who leaned against my leg. "Well, what did you want to ask them?"

"I know you can't come to dinner with us, but, um, well, maybe would you like to drive us there?" he asked shyly.

Cash nodded, a grin forming on his lips. Maverick just dipped his head once. Ryder took a step toward us, a questioning look in his eyes. "You think it's a good idea? Rilin' her like that?"

I shrugged. "That woman's always riled. There's no stopping you from dropping us off and picking us up. But if that's too much trouble for you all, I totally understand."

Cash came up and clapped Ryder on the back. "It ain't no trouble at all. Right, bud?"

Cason let out a little whoop of excitement.

"Come on, little man," Cash went on loudly—everything he did was loud, I'd quickly realized. "Race ya to the car?"

"You're on!" Cason squealed, already rushing for the door. They both tore across the living room, Cash crashing into the side of the door frame and making the entire house shake.

"Cash!" Maverick and Ryder yelled as one. But if Cash heard, he didn't respond. He and Cason just laughed and continued out the door and down the porch steps.

Maverick stood up with a sigh I felt in my bones. Though he couldn't be older than thirty, there was a sense of age to him that Cash and Ryder didn't possess. Like he'd seen things beyond his years. He was quieter than the other two. There was something guarded about him. But despite his quiet reservation, he possessed this calm, soothing kindness that I hadn't experienced with many people.

It was nice.

"I'm sorry about him, Miss Charlotte," he said, grabbing his cowboy hat off the hook by the door and placing it atop his head.

I just laughed and waved him off. "It's quite alright, Maverick."

He slipped out the door just as Ryder grabbed my hand and pulled me to him. "I just want you to know I think you handled that well. Better than I would've, that's for sure."

I blew out an exhale. "Really? I feel like I'm just bullshitting my way through this."

He kissed my forehead. "You're doin' great. Besides, when you get down to it, bullshit is what makes a farm work."

I melted into him, savoring the warmth of his body against mine, letting his calming touch ease some of the lingering nerves from mine and Cason's outburst. I'd never been in this type of position before. I barely even babysat as a teenager. Kids were not my forte, so that reassurance went a long way.

Meeting his gaze, I said softly, "Thank you. And thank you for driving us."

His next kiss brushed against my lips. "Anytime, Miss Charlotte."

A shiver went through me. I'd never get tired of him calling me that.

W ITH EACH MILE CLOSER we came to my mother's house, my nerves skyrocketed higher and higher, until I thought I might explode like a fourth of July fireworks finale. By the time we pulled into the driveway, my heart beat so wildly, so erratic, that I honestly was surprised I hadn't keeled over and died of a heart attack.

"The air conditioner broken in this piece of shit truck, Ryder?" Cash asked with a laugh. "Charlie girl's sweatin' like a two-dollar whore in church."

"Cash," Maverick growled. "Words!"

Cash just chuckled again.

The place looked exactly the same. Pale blue wooden siding with matching window shutters, and faded brick lining the bottom third of the house. The garden beds were tidy and in full bloom with blue-bonnets and yellow roses. Mama had always loved the smell of them best.

I let out a loud sigh as I undid my seat belt. It was just dinner. Just a couple of hours with her. It couldn't be that bad, right? I nearly scoffed at that blind optimism. My mother hadn't talked to me for more than ten minutes today and made me feel small and insignificant. That had been in public. There would be no audience for dinner, therefore no need for thinly veiled snark. Just her, me, and Cason.

God, I wished Ryder was joining us.

"Hey." His calloused hand scraped across mine as he drew my attention away from Mama's house. "You got this," he said, as if reading my thoughts.

I glanced over at him, pulling my lips into what I hoped was a confident smile. His brow furrowed. Guess I wasn't fooling anyone. "I'll text you close to when we're ready, if that's okay." God, I hated how small and weak my voice sounded. I hadn't even seen the woman yet and I was all but cowering.

He nodded and leaned over, giving me a soft kiss. "We'll be close. Call me if you need anythin'."

I nodded, wanting so badly to kiss him once more, but stopped myself. There was no rush. We weren't official… Just getting to know each other. Oh, who the hell was I kidding? I'd basically announced it to the entire town that we were together. There were no if, ands, or buts about it.

Fuck it. I brought my lips to his once more, savoring how safe and calm he made me feel…until Cash knocked on the passenger window with a knuckle. "Hey, can I have a goodbye kiss too?"

I nearly jumped out of my skin, my heart stopping altogether for a moment. When the hell had he, Maverick, and Cason gotten out?

"I'm gonna fuckin' murder him," Ryder murmured against my lips.

I laughed. "You might just break Cason's little heart if you do."

Ryder groaned, but warmth lined the corners of his smile. "Come on, your mom's at the front door."

It was my turn to groan as Ryder chuckled and hopped out of the truck before coming to my side and opening my door. And they said chivalry was dead. When was the last time Cal had ever done something like that for me? Actually, I don't think he ever had.

I thanked him, kissing him once more as I ignored Cash's loud whooping and Cason saying "ew" followed by a string of gagging sounds. I pulled away, rolling my eyes, sharing a sympathetic smile with Maverick.

My mother scowled from the front porch. With a sigh, I glanced down at Cason. "Come on, bud. Let's go see your grandma."

He gave a *yip* of excitement before hugging the three cowboys goodbye and darting along the brick walkway up to my mother. I shared one final look with Ryder before making my way towards the front door.

"Mama," I said after Cason disentangled himself from her hug and ran into the house. I didn't look back as Ryder's truck drove away. *No escaping now…* At least for a bit.

"Well, look at you, Charlotte Marie. You've really embraced being a buckle bunny haven't you?" She let out a bitter laugh. "Not just one cowboy, but three? Your Daddy would be so disappointed. And what a good example you're setting for Cason."

I fisted my hands at my side, my nostrils flaring as anger boiled over like water in a pot. "I am *not* a buckle bunny," I seethed.

"Well, you're sure acting like it. First, sleeping with that Wright boy, now this."

I squeezed my eyes closed, fighting the tears of anger threatening to spill down my cheeks. I wouldn't let her see me cry. Running my tongue over my teeth, I said in the most polite voice I could muster, "Not that it's any of your business, but I didn't sleep with him."

"Don't be ridiculous, you made it everyone's business the minute you said something this morning. And what are people supposed to think when they see you running around town with those three…*cowboys*." I'd never heard the word 'cowboys' said with such venom and vitriol.

I sighed. "I didn't come here to fight, Mama. Is there anything you need help with in getting dinner ready?"

"No, it's ready and on the table." Her gaze narrowed on me, but she didn't try to pick a fight any further.

Dinner was…awkward to say the least. Or, maybe it was just me? Cason and my mother seemed to have no problem chatting away about things. She was far nicer to him than she ever was to me growing up. He hadn't wanted pot roast, so she'd made him his own dinner of chicken nuggets and french fries, along with a bowl of mixed fruit. Had I not been a fan of dinner, she'd have just told me '*you get what you get*' and if I didn't like it, I could make myself dinner next time. At least she was good with him.

We made small talk. Well, I tried making small talk. Tried being the keyword. Anything I could do to fill the thick, tense silence as we ate. Why did she even bother having me over if it was clear she didn't want me here?

After dinner, Cason went off to play in the living room while I started on the dishes as Mama put away the leftovers.

Up to my arms in sudsy water and dishes, I said over my shoulder, "So, I was wondering if one day this week you wanted to come over and go through some of Sheldon's things with me? I'm going to figure out what I want to keep, and then I was thinking about donating it to the church. I know they used to give clothes and stuff to those in need. I figured Sheldon wou—"

"Absolutely not." Even without looking at her, I could hear the rage in her voice.

I braced myself for another fight, turning off the sink and grabbing a dish towel to dry my hands off.

"You are not giving away Sheldon's things! She just died. Or are you so quick to just get her out of her life and try to replace her?"

Ouch. Pain and rage and sadness and just about every negative emotion under the sun slammed into me like a hurricane. And even though I tried to hold them back, hot tears slid down my cheeks.

"I could never replace her, you've made *that* abundantly clear. But what the hell does trying to give her clothes away have to do with me trying to replace her? She's got drawers upon drawers of stuff I'm not going to wear. Instead of throwing it away, I'm a hundred percent positive Sheldon would rather me give them to someone who can put them to use." I wiped violently at my tears, glaring at the woman who'd raised me, before slapping the towel I still held down onto the countertop. "I didn't come here to fight with you. I'm packing up the things of hers I don't want. I'll bring them here once I'm done and you can do whatever the hell you want with them."

Her glacial stare was sharp enough to cut to the bone. "I honestly don't know why you're crying, Charlotte."

"Please, just let it go, Mama. I don't feel like Cason coming in and seeing us fighting."

"No one's fighting," she huffed. "Who said we're fighting?"

I sighed, turning away from her before she could see more tears leak down my cheeks. I hated that just a look from her sent me into a puddle of tears. I hated that her words cut so deep. I hated that no matter what, I would never be good enough. Because at the end of the day, I was the child she didn't want.

Postpartum really was a bitch, I guess. She'd had it bad with me. Maybe that's why I'd been such a daddy's girl. I had so many memories of spending time with him, but hardly any with Mama. Since I'd never had a kid, I didn't understand, but I know her postpartum had something to do with our relationship. That, and I wasn't perfect, sweet, obedient Sheldon…and never would be, to her dismay.

The kitchen descended into an icy silence, the only sound that of clinking pots and pans and the sink turning on and off. After rinsing off the last dish, I grabbed the towel once more and dried my hands off, pulling my phone out and sending a quick text to Ryder. I was tired of prolonging this dinner.

But before Cason and I could leave…

"So, we should probably talk about what all arrangements we need to make for Sheldon's memorial," I said, turning to lean against the countertop. My mother stilled, pausing before closing the fridge with a little too much force.

"There's no need," she replied, turning to look at me, mirroring my stance as she leaned against the opposing counter. Her hand went to her hip and she rubbed at it absentmindedly. Even though she'd never admit it, she was hurting. It lingered in her cold gaze; it pulled on the tightness in her face. Guilt settled in my stomach like stones. "Sheldon already had everything planned. The venue, food, invitations, everything. Everything's ready."

If I wasn't so emotionally raw, I might have laughed at that. Sheldon *would* be the one to plan her own funeral. She'd never been the type to leave much to chance. "Okay, so when do you want to set the date for?"

"I already did," my mother replied.

I froze, my mouth drawing into a thin line, my brows knitting together. "For when?"

"This Saturday."

My legs turned to jello, and thank God I leaned against the counter or I might have slid to the floor. She'd set the date without me? That white-hot anger returned, burning through my veins and every inch of me. "Why didn't you tell me?"

"I'm telling you now," she replied with a shrug.

I shook my head, biting my lip to try and quelch my rage. It didn't work. "First you didn't tell me Sheldon was sick. Then you waited until she was actively dying to call me and have me come back. Why in the hell would you fucking keep this from me?"

She rolled her eyes. "Oh, stop making this about you, Charlotte. Just like always."

"How am I making this about me?" I flinched even as I shouted. "All I'm asking for is to be included."

"Oh, so now you want to be included?" my mother snapped back. "You wanted nothing to do with this family up until a few days ago. Now, you care? Now you want to play the role of the loving sister, the doting aunt, the supportive child. Where were you all these years? Huh? Where were you, Charlotte?"

Her words were like a sledgehammer to the chest. My vision blurred as tears welled and rolled down my cheeks. It hurt to breathe. I couldn't think, couldn't speak. All I could do was stand there, trying and failing to catch my breath.

"I lost my daughter. My everything. So, stop being selfish. You're not the only one hurting."

"She may have been your daughter," I said, whisper-quiet, "but she was also my sister."

"A sister you abandoned when she needed you most." And with that, my mother grabbed her cane and limped out of the kitchen. Her voice drifted through the doorway from the living room beyond, a much happier tone to it as she talked to Cason.

I pressed a fist to my mouth, biting down as hard as I could without drawing blood. God, she knew how to cut me down. Knew how to make me feel small and stupid. And guilty. So fucking guilty. Because since coming back here, I'd been trying to make up for the fact that I *hadn't* been here.

Mama clearly hated me for leaving. I wondered if Sheldon had as well?

That guilt festering in my belly turned to fury. Downright, fiery fury that couldn't be contained. I didn't know what possessed me at that moment, but I stormed out of the kitchen after her. I was done. Done with the constant judgment. Done with the constant gaslighting. Done with every fucking word coming out of her mouth being used as a weapon. She was my mother. She was supposed to love me. Protect me. Not kick me down and beat me so that I couldn't get back up.

"It isn't my fault that Sheldon died!" I railed, all reason and logic abandoning me. "You can't keep making all of this *my* fault!"

"Jesus *Christ*, Charlotte, stop trying to make this about *you*!"

I reeled as if hit by a freight train. Mama never cussed or said the Lord's name in vain. Never.

"Lords fuckin' name!" Cason shouted from the couch.

My gaze snapped to him and a proud smile coated his face. Where had he heard—Oh, God…Maverick had said that earlier hadn't he?

My mother shot me a venomous glare as I spun on my heel to hide my expression from both of them—horror mixed with an almost insane glee as I fought not to laugh at the absurdity and perfect timing of Cason's Maverick impression. Of all three of them to copy, I would have expected it to be Cash. And poor Maverick had tried so hard all day not to cuss.

"I see," my mother said, her words clipped and tight. I whirled to face her again. "I see you're going to ruin his life, just like you've ruined yours."

Cason's voice trembled, and when I looked at him once more worry shone in his eyes. "Did I do something wrong? Am I in trouble? I was just saying what Mister Maverick said."

"No, bud." I jumped in to soothe him, sitting on the couch beside him and pulling him into my side. "You didn't do anything wrong. We just need to have a talk about when it is and isn't appropriate to repeat what you hear the boys say."

"The *boys*?" My mother scoffed. "If you want to go and waste your life away whoring around to those three, then so be it. But I won't let you ruin all the hard work that Sheldon put on that boy by filling his head with nonsense and turning him into some deadbeat, going-nowhere-in-life rodeo cowboy," she snapped, a grave coldness weighing down her words.

They rocked me to my core and stung like nothing I'd ever felt. I looked at Cason and breathed a sigh of relief. He hadn't understood what she'd said. The confused expression on his face said as much. But I had, and even though I knew she'd thought low of me, hearing her call me a whore…tears pricked in my eyes.

"Okay, Cason. Get ready to say goodbye to Grandma. It's almost time to go. Thanks for dinner, *Mother*." I turned on my heel before she could see the tears fall. I wasn't going to sit there and pretend like everything was okay, or better yet, sit in bitter silence.

God, I hoped Ryder got here soon.

CHAPTER TWENTY-TWO

One I Want

RYDER

CHARLIE ALREADY STOOD IN the driveway waiting as I pulled up.

"She don't look too happy," Maverick murmured from the backseat.

A knot formed in my chest. "No, she sure don't," I said with a sigh, putting the car in park. She turned back to the house, calling something, and Cason came running out happily. Her mom stood at the open doorway, a scowl on her face.

Charlie ushered Cason to the truck. Mav and I both hopped out, holding both passenger side doors open for them. I gave a wave to her mom, who just turned away and slammed the door.

I thought better than to ask how it went as I spied the tear stains streaking Charlie's cheeks. Her eyes were red-rimmed and puffy. Shit. She murmured a weak thanks before hopping up in and staring at her hands in her lap.

What the hell had happened?

I closed her door and went around to the driver's side and got in. Maverick helped Cason into his carseat. He didn't seem as glum as Charlie, but there was something sad in his eyes.

Pulling out of the driveway, I glanced over at Charlie and placed a tentative hand on hers. She didn't even react. Her long, copper curls fell around her face like a wall, blocking her off from me.

"What's wrong, Miss Charlotte?" Cash asked.

I met his sunglasses stare in the rearview mirror and gave a firm shake of my head. His shoulders rose into a guilty shrug.

"Nothing," Charlie replied, her voice a hoarse, broken whisper.

What the hell had her mother done?

I wanted to press. Damn, I wanted to, but I didn't think it would do any good. I just kept my hand on hers, letting Cash and Cason guide the conversation. When we pulled up to hers and Cason's place about ten minutes later, I told the boys to take Cason in the house while making Charlie stay back.

"Hey…hey, look at me, Charlotte?" I tilted her chin up gently, forcing her to meet my gaze when she refused. "You don't gotta tell me what happened, but what can I do to make it better?"

She crumbled against me, sobs escaping her. I wrapped her in my arms and ran my hand down her hair. "I don't…I don't know what I ever did to her to make her hate me so much."

"I doubt she hates you," I said softly, pressing a kiss to her head.

More quiet sobs. "You didn't hear what she had to say."

I pulled away enough to look down at her as I wiped tears from her cheeks. "I can't pretend to understand what you're goin' through. But I know she don't deserve your tears. She don't get to ruin your night when she ain't even here. Just…just piss on her."

She snorted, the ghost of a grin crooking her lips upward. "What the hell does that mean?"

I shrugged, a half laugh escaping me. "You know…like fuck 'em. Fuck givin' anyone the ability to hurt you. You don't like what they gotta say? Well piss on 'em? You don't like how they're treatin' you? Piss on 'em too."

She laughed, the sound bubbling out of her like a babbling brook. God, she was beautiful. "Why not just say fuck 'em? Piss on 'em sounds so…gross."

I shrugged. "I don't know, it just sounds worse."

Charlie laughed and sucked in a deep, trembling breath before blowing it out slowly. "I'm sorry," she muttered, her sad gaze meeting mine. "I'm such a fucking mess. This is the third night in a row you've had to come to my rescue and talk me down from a panic attack."

"I can think of far worse ways to occupy my time," I replied with a smirk.

A half laugh escaped her, her lips twitching upward at the corners. "You really are something else, Mister Wright."

My cheeks grew hot as a smile spread across my face, pride surging to life within me. I hadn't expected that from her, but hearing those words of approval on her lips made my heart damn near soar. I cupped her face in my hands and kissed her slow, steady. Unhurriedly.

"How're you feelin' now?" I whispered, pulling away to place a kiss on her forehead.

"Better. Not great, but definitely better. Thank you." Her gray eyes still held sadness in them, but they didn't look so desolate now. Another surge of pride went through me at that. I'd done that. I'd made the storm in her eyes break.

"Good. Now, let's go check on them boys. Lord knows what trouble they're causin'."

She laughed, nestling into my side as we walked up the porch steps. "Cason said, 'Lord's fuckin' name' in front of my mother tonight."

I stopped in my tracks. "What?"

She turned to me, a smile on her lips. "Yeah, the delivery was perfect. His voice even dipped low and everything. I always thought he'd repeat something you or Cash said, especially Cash. But, nope. He said that."

I intertwined our fingers together and kissed her before pulling her towards the front porch. "Don't tell, Mav. He might just die of disappointment. He was tryin' so damn hard not to say somethin' today."

"Don't worry. I won't."

Chapter Twenty-Three

Someday

Charlie

THE REST OF THE night had been quiet since the boys left. Not going to lie, I missed the chaos that came with them being around. You'd think that the craziness would only make me more anxious, with everything going on, but it was oddly comforting. It was a distraction from the shitshow my life had become. Sheldon's death still hung like a storm cloud threatening showers at any moment, and my mother's words…

I bit back tears as I got Cason's clothes set out on his bed while he took a bath.

I still couldn't believe she'd said all that. Actually, I could. That's what was so fucked up about all of this. I'd thought that leaving would change things, but it didn't. I hadn't resolved the situation, I'd just prolonged it. Like a bandaid over a bullet hole, me leaving had been pointless. Mama hadn't changed, and I hadn't learned to stick up for myself.

"Auntie Charlotte!" Cason shouted from the bath, drawing me from my thoughts.

"Yeah, bud?" I called out.

"Have you, um…have you gotten my lunch ready for tomorrow yet?" His voice grew in volume as he walked into the room, wrapped up in a dinosaur towel.

My brow furrowed. Why would I make him—*Oh.* School. I'd completely forgotten about school. Fuck, where did he even go to school? Was it the same one Sheldon and I had gone to? There were a couple in town, I didn't want to just assume.

"Um, no, not yet. Did you have any special requests?" I asked, moving to the doorway so I could let him change.

"Do you think I could have lunch at school? They have spaghetti on Mondays."

"Of course," I called, closing the door.

He opened the door excitedly a few minutes later. "Really? Mama never let me get hot lunch."

I shrugged and nodded. I didn't mind. It was one less thing I needed to get ready tonight or tomorrow morning. "Yeah, it's no problem, bud." I met his soft blue gaze. "You sure you want to go to school tomorrow? I completely get it if you need a bit more time at home."

He shook his head. "I want to see my friends."

I nodded. I understood that. He wanted a distraction as much as I did. "Okay. Well, if it gets to be too much tomorrow, just let me know, okay? I won't be mad if you want to come home."

He nodded.

T URNS OUT, SCHOOL *HAD* been too much for him. Not even by noon I'd gotten the call. Honestly, though, I completely understood. I wouldn't have been able to make it either. I remembered how hard the first few weeks after Daddy's death had been for me at school. I'd just wanted things to go back to normal. Wanted to see my friends, and be distracted. But everyone went out of their way to bring it up. The condolences and the questions and the tears and words of encouragement had just been too much. I'd asked Mama to stay home for a couple extra days, to which she'd said no. Shocker.

I'd been waiting for this call all morning. The minute I heard the school nurse mention he'd been crying all morning, I just said I was on my way and hung up. Mama might have made me stay at school, but I wasn't Mama. And I'd be damned if I made Cason stay there and suffer through all of his negative emotions.

"**H**EY, BUD," I SAID, walking into the main office at my old elementary school. God, nothing had changed. The same linoleum floors. Same flickering halogen lights. The main office was decorated with St. Patrick's day decorations, the student's little leprechaun traps on display. A little black cauldron with a pot of chocolate gold sat on the main counter. I may or may not have snagged a couple gold coins, because, why not? Who in their right mind could resist chocolate?

Cason barely met my gaze, his eyes puffy and red-rimmed. My heart broke. "Hi, Auntie Charlotte," he whispered.

I gave him a big hug before signing him out with the receptionist and leading him out to my rental. He got into the car without a word, buckling himself in, tears streaming down his cheeks.

"Hey, you okay?" I asked, glancing at him in the rearview mirror.

He broke down then, little sobs wracking his body as he crumpled in on himself. "I'm… I'm sorry," he wailed, drawing out the *s*.

I turned around fully to face him. "Oh, Cason," I soothed, "What're you sorry for?"

"F-for m-making you c-c-come g-get m-m-me," he said through his tears, the words barely intelligible through all the crying.

I sighed, sadness gripping me so thoroughly it hurt to breathe. "Come here, bud." I urged him into the front seat and then my lap. It was uncomfortable and a tight squeeze, but I didn't mind. Wrapping my arms around him, I held him for a few long, silent moments, letting him cry and cry and cry. I cried too.

"Don't feel like you need to apologize for needing to call me. I'm always gonna be here. I'm always just a call away," I said, pressing a kiss to his head as I rocked him back and forth.

He sniffled and nodded in response.

"What do you wanna do, bud? You wanna go home? Maybe watch a movie and eat junk food?"

He shook his head.

"Wanna go to the zoo?" It'd be a bit of a drive, but that didn't matter. I'd drive to Houston for the day if he wanted. But he shook his head no a second time. "You hungry?" I asked.

A muffled, "No."

I wondered what Ryder was doing. What did he even do for a living anyway? He had to do more than just rodeoing. "Hold on…I have an idea," I said, pulling my phone out and looking up Ryder's number.

Cason sniffled as I pressed on Ryder's name and listened for the dial tone. *Please, don't be working,\. Please, don't be—*

"Hello, Miss Charlotte?"

"Hey. Are you busy right now?" I met Cason's question stare. "Cason would really like to ride a horse."

I wish I had my camera ready for the smile that lit up his face like the dawn of a new day.

THE MOONEY RANCH WAS gorgeous. A simple, yet impressive gate face greeted us as we turned off the county road and down the long driveway lined with weeping willows and green pastures beyond. A large two-story, flagstone house with a green metal roof was settled back at the end of the drive on the left; the dirt road continued on to the right. A large red barn and three small, matching houses rested around a massive arena. And then beyond that, more pastures upon pastures of grassland. And cows. lots of cows. I'd forgotten Cash's daddy was a cattle rancher.

I recognized Ryder's truck among a couple others by the barn and parked. "You ready, bud?" I asked, turning back to meet Cason's gaze.

His eyes weren't on mine, though. They were glued to the arena, where Ryder, Cash, and Maverick rode on horseback.

Cason all but clawed at his carseat straps, the excitement on his face fully replacing any lingering sadness. I laughed as I got out and opened the door for him, nearly falling over as he launched passed me and raced for the arena.

"Cason, wait!" I called, trailing after him. But it was no use, he was already in the process of climbing the pipe-stall railing.

"Do it again!" A harsh voice slashed through the dry air. "If I wanted to see a buncha idiots trippin' over themselves, I'd go watch the cows chase the feed truck around. Set up and do it again!"

My gaze settled on a man in a dusty old cowboy hat who sat on top of the arena fence about twenty feet from Cason. He watched Ryder, Maverick and Cash ride.

"Miss Charlotte!" Ryder called, whipping his cowboy hat off his head and offering me an awkward bow. God, he looked good. Like, really fucking good. What was it about a guy in a t-shirt, cowboy hat, and a good pair of jeans that just hit so hard? His white shirt made his tan skin look sunkissed and bronze in the sunlight. "You came."

"That's what she said!" Cash shouted across the arena.

I laughed and shook my head, coming to a stop beside Cason. Ryder trotted over to meet us.

"How could I resist an invitation from a handsome cowboy?" I smiled, climbing up the first rail of pipe-stall so I could see over the top. Ryder came to a stop beside us.

"And that handsome cowboy was Big Daddy!" Cash crowed from the arena.

"Shut up and get your head in the game," the man sitting on the fence grumped. "I ain't gonna watch you three idiots embarrass me like that at another damn rodeo. It started here, and it ends here."

Ryder leaned over and kissed me, which earned a whoop from Cash. I bit my lip as he pulled away, my cheeks heating. I hated how easy this felt. It made me scared, even as butterflies fluttered in my chest wildly.

"Come on, I'll introduce you." Ryder jerked his head to indicate the man on the fence.

"Oh, um, you sure? He seems kinda pissed," I all but whispered, eying the man warily. "We don't want to be a bother."

"No bother," Ryder insisted, before nodding at the older cowboy. "Hey, Bad. This here's Miss Charlotte and her nephew. Miss Charlotte, this here's Bad Mooney, Cash's dad."

The man Ryder called Bad jumped down off the fence. He doffed his cowboy hat and strode forward, offering me his hand. "You can call me Clint, or Mister Mooney, if it pleases ya," the man said. "Pretty much only these boys call me Bad anymore."

Bad Mooney had short, curly hair the color of wheat ready for harvest, and thoughtful, hazel eyes the same color as Cash's, only his didn't hold the perpetual mischief in them that his son's did. And, unlike his son, his mouth was set in a forever scowl. I'd be surprised if he even knew how to smile. His tan face looked like old leather and his bottom teeth were stained from chewing tobacco. Looked like chewing ran in the family. But despite that, and his age, he had a certain charm to him. In his prime, I bet he was just as attractive as Cash.

"Charlie," I said with a smile as I shook his hand, unsurprised at his vice-like grip. "You can call me Charlie."

"And who's this?" Mister Mooney asked, looking down at Cason. "Wait a minute, I remember you. Your mama was Ms. Sheldon, right? Yeah, I seen y'all around town a few times. Casey, right?"

"C-Cason, sir," he replied with a nod.

Mister Mooney dipped his head and held out his hand. "How are you doin', son?"

"Good, sir," Cason replied, glancing between Mister Mooney's extended arm and me.

"Don't be shy." I nudged him gently, nodding at Mister Mooney.

Cason eyed his hand for a second longer before giving it a good, strong shake.

"He's alright." Mister Mooney waved away my concern, his gravelly voice rising and falling to a rhythm all its own. "Maverick's pretty shy too."

I looked out to the arena and found the boys huddled together on their horses, talking and laughing. Well, Cash and Mav were laughing. Ryder was shaking his head, even as a smile lit up his face.

It was interesting. Maverick seemed like a completely different person here. The usual harsh lines on his face had all but smoothed, and there was a lightness to him that he normally lacked. I wouldn't say he was as carefree as Cash, but then, I don't think I'd ever met anyone quite as carefree as him.

"I don't remember saying we was done!" Mister Mooney hollered as he spotted the boys talking. "Excuse me, ma'am, son... I got three knuckleheads needin' to be knocked together."

Mister Mooney climbed back up and resumed his perch on the top railing as he laid into the boys. "Spread that stupid out a little bit before one of them horses goes lame. I didn't drag ya out here in the sun so y'all could socialize, I brought ya out here to work! Ryder, get out of the way. Maverick, Cash, get your asses back in that box. Maverick if you miss one more Goddamn time, I'm gonna lose my mind out here. Cash, you're supposed to remove your head from out of your ass *before* you get on the horse!"

"That's a lot of bad words," Cason said with a gasp, looking up at me with a guilty smile on his lips.

"That's just the way cowboys talk," Ryder said, riding up to the fence again as he watched Maverick and Cash back their horses into the chute.

"Maybe cowboys shouldn't talk *so much*," I joked, flashing a smirk Ryder's way. We were all going to go broke from adding money into the swear jar. At this point, it was pointless.

He just laughed and shook his head. "Miss Charlotte, you'd have better luck changin' the color of the sky, than changin' the way that man talks. Old Bad Mooney's got a temper, but he's taught us just about everythin' we know 'bout horses."

"I thought I told you to warm that roan nag up." Bad Mooney grimaced as Cash's horse tried to rear up in the chute.

"I *did* warm him up!" Cash called back. "He's just ready, is all."

Mister Mooney grunted. "We'll see how ready he is. Goodie, open the chute."

A man I hadn't noticed before hauled on a rope, causing the chute to fly open, and a steer came barreling out like a bat out of hell. Right behind him thundered Cash and Maverick as they swung their ropes over their heads. Maverick caught the steer, dallied up and turned it so Cash could rope the heels. The whole thing was over in a moment, and Cash cheered in triumph.

Roping had always been a favorite of mine to watch. The stakes weren't so life and death—it just felt safer. And it was always interesting to see how well the duos worked together. Cash and Maverick worked well. Really, well. I started to clap, but the sound died as Mister Mooney's voice boomed across the arena.

"What are you celebratin', ya idiot? That steer took ya halfway down the arena. I'm not gettin' y'all ready for some jackpot roping where everyone's so drunk, they couldn't catch the ground if they fell on it. This is *Austin*. And you assholes barely qualified for it. If that Howell kid hadn't missed his heel loop, I bet y'all wouldn't be so damn happy. Now do y'all want to go to Austin and win some money, or are ya more interested in gettin' your peckers wet? Cuz if that's the case, y'all can get off them horses now."

"Auntie Charlotte, what does he mean?"

A huff of laughter escaped me as I hid my face in my hands. Oh, sweet Jesus…this kid was doomed. Positively doomed. I could just see the calls from the principal now. "Nothing, bud. He's just saying the boys need to focus more."

"Do it again," Mister Mooney said.

Cason and I watched as Cash and Maverick backed their horses up again.

There was a shift in the air this time, so small that I might not have noticed it if I weren't paying attention.

They both still smiled, still acted like they hadn't a care in the world. But something was different. There was a sharp focus in Maverick's eyes as he tensed, waiting for the chute to open. Cash was silent, except for his ear-to-ear grin, which could probably be heard in the next county.

"This is it," Mister Mooney told them. "Get ya some money."

The chute opened and the horses exploded out of the box right behind the steer. I hadn't even realized Maverick had already thrown his loop as it wrapped around the steer's horns. He turned the cow and ran it right into Cash's heel loop.

It had started and ended so quickly. I still was processing it as Mister Mooney's voice sliced through the air once more.

"There ya go!" Mister Mooney called, sounding an awful lot like his son. "See? What did I tell ya? You can do a lot better once you get your head out of your ass!"

"Big Daddy's in the house!" Cash shouted. I shook my head. His happiness was infectious. There was just something so lively, so entertaining about Cash, you couldn't help but laugh around him. Whether it was at him or with him, it didn't matter. He was a performer. Through and through.

"What about you, son?" Mister Mooney looked down at Cason from his perch atop the rail. "You want to chase one out of the chute?"

"Oh, I don't think he's ready for that yet," I answered quickly, looking down at Cason. But his eyes were glued to the arena. A little piece of me died right then because I knew that look. My daddy had that look. Cash and Mav and Ryder…they all had it too.

"Don't worry, we'll work up to it," Mister Mooney said in a much nicer tone than he'd used with any of the boys. His hazel gaze appraised me.

I blew out a breath. Was I really going to keep him from riding? After a moment I dipped my head in a nod.

"Well, how about it?" Bad Mooney quirked an eyebrow at Cason. "You wanna learn?"

"Yes, please!" Cason shouted, glancing at me for approval.

I smiled, even though my heart raced in my chest.

"Don't worry." Ryder soothed from atop his horse, as if reading my thoughts. "Bad knows what he's doin'. Everythin' will be fine. We won't let anythin' happen to him."

I bit my lip, blowing out a shaky breath. I'd set myself up for this. I'd known the minute Cason saw Ryder and the boys riding he'd want to be just like them. He already did. *It's just riding. There's nothing wrong with riding horses.*

"Maverick!" Bad called out. "You mind getting Peckerhead out of the barn and throwing Cash's old ropin' saddle on him? We got a kid here wants to ride his first horse."

"Peckerhead?" I chuckled, glancing at Ryder. "Jesus Christ, I see where Cash gets his mouth from."

He shrugged and let out a laugh. "It's just a nickname. His real name's Black'n'Decker, and he's a good boy."

Mine and Ryder's definitions of good had to be vastly different as the stocky, black gelding came prancing out of the barn with a bad attitude and an adorable little saddle on his back. Etched into the stirrups were the words 'Cash Mooney Pee Wee Roping Champion'. Black'n'Decker's head damn near touched the clouds, it was so high—I was not going to call the thing Peckerhead—and his tail swished angrily as he snorted at any and everything.

Great. Cason was going to die. I took a deep breath, worry seeping into my bones.

"Jesus." Mister Mooney chuckled. "When's the last time anybody got ol' Peckerhead out of his stall?"

"We got him out last week for that Thompson girl to ride," Maverick answered. "He's a little high."

"Ya *think*?" Mister Mooney laughed.

"I… I don't think this is a good idea," I said, glancing at Ryder and then Mister Mooney. I didn't mind Cason riding…but *that* horse?

"It's no trouble," Mister Mooney said with a dismissive wave of his hand. "He just needs some groundwork, that's all. Maverick, get him ready. You wanna lunge him or ride him?"

Maverick looked at the horse as he let out an ear shattering neigh that got the attention of every horse on the property. "I'll lunge him," Maverick said with a tight smile as he led the horse into the arena.

As Cash's dad interacted with Cason, some of the worry in my gut started to dissipate. With each new thing Maverick did with the horse, Mister Mooney explained to Cason what he was doing and why, as well as telling him what every little thing the horse did meant. It didn't take long before the black gelding calmed down as Maverick worked him on a long line.

It was no wonder Maverick had given such good advice the other day. He truly had a way with animals. There was something so calm, so melodic about the way he moved and interacted with them. After watching him for a few moments, I realized my nerves had even started to ease.

Ryder's deep, gravelly voice pulled my attention. "Mav ain't the best rider, but he's good at gettin' 'em to calm down."

"He's got a gentle soul," Mister Mooney added from his spot atop the fence. "A gentle soul and a thick skull. Maverick, turn him around!"

Maverick stopped the horse…somehow. I hadn't seen him do anything. Black'N'Decker stopped, turned, and trotted off in the other direction. Sitting here, leaning on the pipe-stall, I felt like I was a kid again, watching my daddy ride. The nostalgia of it made me happy, but sadness weighed on me still.

"Think he's ready?" Mister Mooney asked Ryder.

"The horse is, the cowboy's aunt looks like she's still a little fresh." Ryder nodded at me.

I gave him a weak smile. "I'm sorry. This is just…it's hard. I don't want him getting hurt."

He cupped my cheek; I leaned into the touch on instinct. "Do you trust me, Miss Charlotte?" Ryder asked, smile fading.

I bit my lip, meeting his dark gaze. It swirled with a seriousness I hadn't seen from him before. "I… Yeah. Yeah, I do."

It was true. I might be crazy. Actually, I knew I was crazy, but I trusted him to keep Cason safe.

"Well, I trust Bad. With my life. He won't let Cason get hurt. I promise."

"**B**OY MUST HAVE BEEN born on a horse," Mister Mooney said, looking over at me as Maverick and Cason led Black'N'Decker back to the barn. Ryder followed along, his horse in tow.

"I honestly don't think he's ever been on one before," I admitted with a shake of my head. Sheldon hadn't been much of a rider to begin with, and she'd never mentioned anything about Cason riding over the years. Pride and worry warred within me. Mostly, pride though.

Mister Mooney nodded. "Some people are born with a natural seat. An affinity for horses. Cason's one of them people."

"What about me, Pa?" Cash asked, swinging his rope lazily. "Was I born with it too?"

"You were born with your head up your ass and no intent on movin' it. First time we put you on a horse you cried so hard you pissed your pants." Mister Mooney shot back with a wicked grin.

I snorted, unable to hide my laughter.

"That ain't true, Miss Charlotte." Cash's smile faltered.

"It's true," his father insisted. "And he's still got his head up his ass, and he still wets his pants when he rides, though for different reasons now."

Cash laughed and spurred his horse across the arena, and off toward the barn. I shook my head, looking at his father.

"Your son is…" I began.

"A pain in my ass, that's what. But, deep down…really damn deep, he's a good kid. Cason's a good kid too. And this is good for him. Y'all are welcome to come out and ride any time. Got plenty of horses."

"I appreciate that. Cason seems to love it."

"And what about you?" He gave me a knowing look. "I saw ya over there grippin' that pipe-stall like it personally offended ya."

I bit my lip and blew out a breath before lifting my shoulders into a shrug. "My daddy was a steer wrestler. You might have known him, or heard of him, at least. Will Evans?"

Something rippled across Mister Mooney's features. All of his harsh lines softened just a bit. "Well, damn. Everythin' makes a lot more sense now."

I didn't know what to say, so I just nodded. Cason ran over from the barn, Maverick and Ryder in tow.

"Auntie Charlotte, Auntie Charlotte, Uncle Maverick said he was gonna make us dinner. Can we stay? Can we? He said he'd teach me how to grill a *steak*!"

I couldn't help but smile as Cason ran circles around me. His enthusiasm was intoxicating.

"You sure that's what you want?" I asked.

"Yes! Please! Please! Please!" Cason stopped in his tracks to beam at me.

"Well…alright," I said with a grin, my eyes settling on Ryder. "I guess we're staying for dinner."

"Yeehaw!" Cason shouted, bounding off with Maverick toward the main house.

Ryder's grin was bright enough to rival the sun as he wrapped an arm around my waist. "Hey, come here a minute."

My hands slid up the planes of his rock-hard stomach to rest on his chest. "Hm?" I asked, looking up into his dark eyes. If his smile was brighter than the sun, his eyes were darker than the midnight sky. A sky I wanted so badly to get lost in.

I was crazy. Positively crazy for enabling this relationship. But my mind had lost the war to my heart a while ago. Honestly, I don't even think it really had a chance. Worry still knotted and twisted in my gut though, when I thought about him rodeoing. It was so easy to forget when he wasn't actively doing it. In moments like this, everything felt so perfect.

And that was terrifying.

His smile died, his eyes narrowing at the corners slightly. With one arm still wrapped firmly around me, caging me to his chest, he tilted my chin up with his free hand, forcing my gaze to meet his. "What's wrong?"

God, he was a mind reader. Or I was just an open book when it came to my emotions. Probably the latter.

I chewed my lip. "I'm scared."

"Of what?" His hand on my chin slid along my jaw until he cupped the side of my neck. His touch sent shivers through me, chasing away some of the worry.

"Of all of it. Cason riding. Us dating. You rodeoing. I'm terrified, Ryder. Absolutely fucking terrified."

Ryder took a deep breath, his thumb brushing along the edge of my jaw in slow, soothing strokes. I should have pulled away, but his touch was like a drug. I wanted it. No, I needed it.

"I can't tell you that I ain't ever gonna get hurt, but I can tell you that I'll be smart. I ain't gonna be reckless—well, too reckless." His mouth crooked up in the corner. "As for us datin', I ain't in no rush. We can take this as slow as you like. I'm in it for the long haul."

Okay, worry officially extinguished. Any resolve left in me melted right then and there, like an ice cream on a hot summer day. He knew just the right words to say, the right things to do. He wasn't perfect. No one was, but God, he was really damn close.

With a boldness I wasn't used to, I slid my hands up his chest and around his neck. I grabbed his hat in one hand and pulled it off, while sliding my other through his soft, dark waves. Leaning up on tiptoe, I dragged his mouth down to mine.

His hand on my neck tightened just the barest bit so he could press himself harder to me. As if I might float away if he didn't hold me in place. I felt the same way. I didn't stop even as Cash whooped and hollered, but the sound of Mister Mooney's chuckle froze me in place.

"Don't stop on my account," he said, walking past us, a smirk on his lips.

Ryder pulled back enough to press his forehead to mine, a husky laugh escaping him. "I wasn't expectin' that," he murmured.

I giggled. "Me neither."

Chapter Twenty-Four

The Outskirts

Ryder

CHARLIE AND I WALKED hand in hand toward the main house. I'd contemplated dragging her into the empty bunkhouse…I wanted her, needed her so damn badly. Maybe if Cason weren't here, I would have, but I resisted. How the hell I had was still a bit beyond me.

I'd told her I was in no rush. That I'd take it slow. I wouldn't make myself look like a liar now.

She'd admitted she was scared. Terrified, even. I hadn't mentioned I was too. But for completely different reasons. I didn't believe in love at first sight. I'd never been the type to fall easily like Cash. But my heart also wasn't as closed off and guarded as Maverick's. I'd never met anyone I wanted to bring home to my mom and dad. I'd had a couple more serious relationships, but none that lasted more than a year. I'd always been more focused on rodeoing.

Charlie Evans threatened everything I knew. Because if I wasn't careful, I'd offer her everything I had to give. I just hoped if it came down to that, it would be enough to keep her.

I snuck a sidelong glance at her beside me, her long copper curls waving down her back and brushing against her exposed waist.

She seemed to live in black crop tops and leggings, which was completely fine with me. They showed off her glorious curves well.

A god-awful noise came ahead of us, breaking my trance. Charlie let out a laugh that left me feeling lighter. "Is Cash always so loud?" she asked.

I chuckled, rolling my eyes. "Always."

I led her around the side of the house and into the gated backyard. Maverick and Cash stood before a firepit situated in the middle of the nicely manicured lawn. Red and white lawn chairs sat in opposing order in a neat circle around the pit—Bad sitting in one as he smoked his pipe—while a pathway of pea gravel led from the concrete slab just outside the back porch, all the way around the firepit. Twinkle lights hung across the entire yard—from one side of the fence to the other.

Charlie's voice held a sense of awe to it. "Wow, it's so pretty!"

I nodded, though I wasn't focused on the yard. I was focused on her. I kept my mouth shut though. Lord fuckin' knew if I said something as corny as that, Cash and Mav would never shut the hell up about it.

"Auntie Charlotte! Mister Ryder!" Cason came running across the yard from his spot beside Cash and Mav, Dutch hot on his heels.

"Hey, bud." I grinned down at him, ruffling up his hair. "You and Dutch havin' fun?"

He flashed me a wide grin and nodded, before looking at his aunt. "Uncle Maverick gave me forty bucks for the swear jar!"

I laughed as Charlie hid her face in her hands, a chuckle of disbelief escaping her as she glanced over at Maverick. "You all do know that the point of the swear jar is to *not* swear…right?"

Maverick's usually stoic face pulled up into a smirk. "Miss Charlotte, if I'm correct, I've heard you swear more than a time or two."

Charlie opened her mouth to reply but then blew out a loud sigh and rolled her eyes with a smile. "Oh, fuck it. Keep giving him money. That better cover my swearing as well," she said, grinning.

Maverick dipped his cowboy hat at her and offered a wink before fixing his gaze back on the firepit.

"You do got quite a mouth on you, Miss Charlotte," I said, pulling her to my side.

She laughed. "Shut up."

"Well, damn. I was expectin' a better comeback than that." Cash grinned.

"I'm trying to be a good example." She looked down at Cason who glanced back and forth between us, a happy little smile on his face.

Cash chuckled. "Yeah, cuz fuck it is so much better than shut up." He grabbed a beer from a cooler beside the firepit and tossed it to me. I caught it and offered it to Charlie.

She grimaced, her lip curling up. "No thanks. I don't like beer, but really? Pabst Blue Ribbon? Might as well be drinking piss water."

"How do you know what piss water tastes like?" I asked with a smirk.

She huffed a laugh and rolled her eyes.

We settled around the firepit, the flame's warmth welcome as the clouds rolled in on a crisp wind. I slid into one of the seats, Charlie perching on the arm of the chair.

"That's too much salt," Cash said from his spot beside Mav. Fucker practically hovered over his shoulder—a feat as Mav was a good four or so inches taller. Cash always liked to mess with his cousin when it came to cooking. Mainly because Maverick was all about control, a complete perfectionist, while Cash was…well he was complete chaos. Through and through.

Maverick turned and glowered, clicking the tongs at him. "Shut up."

"I'm tellin' ya, it's too much salt!" Cash insisted, waving his hands so wildly he almost spilled beer on Cason who'd ambled over to watch. "If you want to teach him right—"

"It's steak," Maverick snapped. "You can't *have* too much salt."

"You're gonna overcook 'em." Cash shook his head, looking back at Charlie and I with a shit-eating grin.

I shook my head. Mav was gonna kill him.

"Will you shut up? You do what *you* do—"

"Drink!" Cash interrupted, saluting with his beer.

"And let me do what *I* do," Maverick finished with a pointed look.

Cash let out his trademark laugh. I winced at the sound. How such an unholy thing could come out of such a decent looking man was beyond me. And yet, he scored women in spite of that horrible, god-awful laugh. "Which is overcook and oversalt steak," he said, clapping Maverick on the shoulder.

"How do ya like your steak cooked, Miss Charlotte?" Mav asked, ignoring his cousin.

"Oh, um…medium rare for me. Well done for Cason."

I stilled and looked up at her. Mav and Cash froze in place as well. Even Bad lifted his gaze from the flames to stare at her.

Charlie frowned and glanced at everyone, worry etching across her features. "What?"

Maverick's voice cut through the silence. "Ma'am, I have *no* problem, whatsoever, cooking for everybody." He gave her a solemn look. "But I will not…*cannot* bring myself to cook a steak well done. I just…I can't do it."

"Ryder will cook 'em for her." Cash's mischievous grin settled on me.

Bad Mooney laughed from his chair, grabbing his pipe and blowing out a thick cloud of smoke. "Last time Ryder Wright tried to cook anythin', he burnt up his daddy's nice new Exiss livin' quarter trailer… Didn't ya, boy?" Mister Mooney said with an evil grin.

"What?" Charlie laughed, her gaze meeting mine.

My cheeks heated. "We don't talk about that," I muttered.

"Are ya still grounded?" Cash mocked.

"I'm *here*, ain't I?" I snapped, flipping him off. That earned a loud, braying laugh from my best friend.

Cash's grin couldn't get any wider as he pressed his beer to his lips and took a drink. "Oooh, looks like you struck a nerve there, Pa."

"Yeah?" Bad chuckled. "Well, he ain't gonna do *shit* to me. I figure if I keep pissin' him off, he'll take it out on you."

Charlie's laugh drifted around the firepit. "You're really that bad at cooking?"

I huffed a laugh, shaking my head. "Let's just say, I ain't the best."

She blew out a loud sigh even as a smile lit up her face. "Well, damn. I see a lot of fast food in our future, because I suck at cooking too."

Our future. Something tightened in my chest, similar to the familiar thrill I got from rodeoing. I don't even think she noticed what she'd said, and she might not have meant anything by it, but I hadn't missed it, nonetheless. I pulled her fully into my lap, earning a giggle from her, before tilting her chin towards me. I kissed her then, unable to behave any longer.

I didn't care that Mav and Bad laughed, or that Cash and Cason made obnoxious kissing noises. All that mattered, all I needed in that moment, was her.

Damn, I was so fucked…but I couldn't bring myself to care.

Mrs. Mooney's drawl from the back porch had me pulling away. "How are those steaks coming, Mav? Oh—Ryder Wright, where are your manners? Were you plannin' on introducin' me to…"

"Miss Charlotte, this is Violet Mooney. Cash's mom. Mrs. Mooney, this here is Cason's aunt, Miss Charlotte," I said, clearing my throat, not quite meeting Mrs. Mooney's intense brown gaze. Mrs. Mooney was both the sweetest and most terrifying woman I'd ever met. She'd give you the shirt right off your back, but shoot you if you threatened what was hers.

Charlie stood up quickly, stepping toward Cash's mom as she strode across the yard, a big salad bowl in her arms. Holding out a hand, Charlie said a bit shakily, "Uh, hi. I, uh…it's actually Charlie. Charlie Evans."

Mrs. Mooney's face softened. "My condolences, my dear. We're happy to have y'all for dinner tonight."

Charlie smiled. "Thank you. Is there anything I can help with?"

"Actually, would ya mind tossin' this salad?"

"No problem." Charlie nodded, grabbing the salad bowl and moseying over to the outdoor table already set for dinner.

"Mav, sweetheart, how are them steaks comin'?" Mrs. Mooney asked.

"Well…" Maverick scratched at his chin. "*Ours* are almost done… But I guess this one's gotta cook another hour or so."

"*Hour?*" Mrs. Mooney quirked an eyebrow.

"Miss Charlotte said Cason eats his steak well done," Cash supplied helpfully.

"Oh no, honey, we don't do that here." Mrs. Mooney looked back at Charlie with genuine concern. "Has the boy never had a real steak before? My goodness. Maverick, medium well, please. That's bad enough."

"Well then, I guess steaks are done!" Maverick announced with pride.

Chapter Twenty-Five

What Was I Thinking

Charlie

Ryder and I followed an over-excited Cason as he barreled out the front door and down the steps, chasing after Dutch. I was stuffed, exhausted, and my face hurt from laughing so much. I couldn't even remember the last time I'd just sat and laughed until my stomach hurt, but these cowboys were hysterical. Fucking hysterical.

"Thank you for having us over today," I said, turning to wrap my arms around Ryder's neck.

I still wasn't able to get over just how kind and hospitable he was. They all were, actually. Cash's family had just welcomed us into the fold as if we'd always been a part of their lives. And the way they all interacted with Cason. God, it made my heart nearly burst with happiness.

"Aw shit. It was my pleasure." Cash sighed as he threw his arm over my shoulder, knocking me out of Ryder's grip. Dear Lord, for a guy as fit as him, he sure weighed a ton. But that probably had something to do with him being sloppy drunk. How he stood upright was an absolute mystery. He'd eaten three steaks and drank six beers in the course of dinner. Not to mention the couple he'd had when we were outside. I didn't know which was affecting him the most at this point: The beer or meat.

Ryder chuckled and rolled his eyes before offering me an apologetic grin.

Maverick's smooth, deep baritone boomed through the cold night air. "All you did was drink. I cooked all the steaks and your mom made everythin' else."

"And I did a damn good job, if I do say so myself." Cash slipped his arm off of me and laughed. "The night's young, boys! Let's go find some buckle bunnies!"

"You don't need buckle bunnies. We got chorin' in the mornin'. You need three aspirin and some sleep." Maverick's brows furrowed.

Ryder was right, Maverick was a mother hen. But then, someone had to be the responsible one in the group. Cash was too reckless and attractive to be anything but irresponsible, and Ryder was too laid back to be the one in charge. Which left poor Maverick to take care of everyone.

Ryder grabbed me and pulled me to him, and even though he hadn't said anything yet, I was already dreading the goodbye that would no doubt come from his lips.

A gravelly tone made me nearly jump out of my skin. "He's right about the night bein' young." I hadn't even noticed that Mister Mooney had followed us outside. "I ain't ready to go to bed just yet. Y'all wanna do somethin' stupid?"

Cason turned to me, his mouth pulled up into a hopeful smile. "Can we stay?"

I pursed my lips. "We can't, bud. You have school tomorrow."

Some of the light left his eyes, his face tightening with anxiety. My heart broke for him. I understood. He had to go back to school at some point, but was it really so bad for him to miss another day? He was in kindergarten after all.

I met Maverick's soft gaze. Of everyone here, he had the most sage advice. "What do you think?"

Maverick's face turned thoughtful. He offered me a shrug. "Everyone's different. I didn't do well being in a classroom after my family passed. Aunt Violet homeschooled me 'til my senior year."

I thought, for the second time that day, of how my mother had forced me to go back to school after Daddy died. And maybe it was just to spite her, but I found myself sighing and meeting Cason's still hopeful gaze. "Okay, you can stay home tomorrow on the condition that you try to go to school on Wednesday."

I wouldn't make him stay like my mama had, but I didn't want to seem like a total push-over either.

His grin pulled almost as wide as Cash's. "Yeehaw!"

I rolled my eyes with a laugh and looked up at Ryder. "Hope you guys are okay with us tagging along."

A soft kiss to my lips was answer enough. After a moment, he pulled away, glancing at Cash. The smiles that twisted on their handsome faces were pure mischief.

Maverick groaned. "Y'all are gonna get me in trouble, aren't ya?"

FIFTEEN MINUTES LATER, I sat with Cason and Dutch on the tailgate of Cash's old pickup truck. If you could even call it that. I still wasn't even sure how the thing ran. It was scratched and dented and the bumper was missing, along with both side mirrors. The front windshield was cracked and covered in mud and what I could only assume was cow shit, and the driver side door was completely gone. Just gone.

Somehow, by the grace of God or just dumb luck, the thing ran.

We were out in the middle of a field, no one but cows around for at least a mile. Ryder and Cash faced one another on a pair of four wheelers. Cash's dad sat in an old lawn chair with a cooler full of Coors next to him and his pipe in hand.

"Alright!" Mister Mooney called out. "Y'all know the rules. Three runs. Highest score wins. Loser of each round shotguns a beer. Y'all ready for some cowboy joustin'?"

"Oh, dear God." I rubbed at my forehead and glanced back at Maverick, who stood on top of the truck so he could see better. "Isn't this how Ryder got a face full of stitches?"

Maverick raised his shoulders in a sheepish shrug. "What can I say, Miss Charlie? They're idiots."

I huffed a laugh. Idiots was right.

"Ryder, ready?" Mister Mooney asked. Ryder revved the quad.

My heart hammered in my chest. This was almost as bad as the rodeo. What idiots did this for fun?

"Cash, you ready, boy?"

"Big Daddy's always ready!"

"Go!"

My hand came to rest on my mouth as I bit back my anxiety. Sweet Jesus, if he got hurt…

Ryder and Cash hit the throttle and raced towards each other, both struggling to get their play ropes up and swinging. As they passed by, they threw their loops at one another—Cash's sailing off into the night, while Ryder's settled firmly around Cash's shoulders.

"Oh shit!" Cash shouted just before he was yanked off of the four-wheeler and fell, tumbling to the ground.

My stomach twisted in knots as I watched him roll to a stop, but in true Mooney fashion, he sat up, that infectious grin on his face.

He really was attractive. I understand why he got girls so easily. With caramel brown hair, hazel eyes, and a forever five o' clock shadow lining his jaw, he was easy on the eyes. But it was his personality that was the real ringer. Confident, charming, didn't take himself too seriously… He could charm the skirt off a nun.

Thankfully, I'd never really been one for the himbo type. Asshole had apparently been more my type, at least from my previous track record. But that all changed with Ryder.

Cash crowed as he stood up and plucked the rope off him.

"You guys are crazy!" I shouted. "Someone's gonna get hurt."

"Just my pride." Cash laughed as he dusted himself off. "And my shoulder—" He gripped his shoulder and rolled his arm in a windmill motion, grimacing slightly. "I landed on my shoulder."

"That better not be your ropin' arm!" Maverick grumbled from behind me. At least someone else shared my concern.

"Here." Mister Mooney threw Cash a beer. "It'll make you feel better. Go on, don't be a wuss; get that medicine up in ya."

Cash shot-gunned the beer as Maverick jumped down and strode over, fussing over his shoulder. Cash swatted him away after finishing his beer. "I'm *fine*, mama."

"Think you can handle two more rounds?" Ryder asked as he rode by, a triumphant grin on his face. He winked at me as he went past.

God. How could his smile just melt the worry within me? With a smile like sunshine, and kisses sweeter than fucking pie…I'd never need to go to therapy again.

"Big Daddy's just gettin' warmed up." Cash shoved a still fussing Maverick off him and climbed back onto his quad. "Let's do it again!"

Maverick had joined in a few rounds later. Well, he'd been bullied more like. Cash and Ryder had nagged him until he'd thrown his hands up in the air with an annoyed shout and all but threw Cash off his four-wheeler.

Cason had curled into my side, his eyelids heavy despite having the time of his life. Dutch laid beside him, her head in his lap. I glanced at my phone. It was only about 8:45, but we'd need to leave soon.

Maverick and Ryder squared off for the championship run. Both Cash and Mister Mooney had been eliminated, each claiming it was the other's fault. It had nothing to do with the cooler full of beer they'd consumed, apparently. Ryder was buzzed. Definitely not drunk, but there was a glassy look to his eyes and a perpetual smirk on his lips. Mav was the only one sober, having not drank a single drop of alcohol. I wondered why he didn't drink.

Though some of my nerves had calmed down, worry roiled in my gut this round.

"Now," Mister Mooney called, standing on shaky legs in the field. "Pay a-damn-tention to what your doin'! If we get anymore head-on collisions, you idiots forfeit and I win."

"Why do *you* win?" Cash cried from his spot beside me. Well, more like half on top of me. Cason all but dozed against my left side, while Cash sat on my right, his arm loosely wrapped around my shoulder. Every movement he made sent me jostling this way and that.

"Because they're *my* four-wheelers, asshole. That's why. Now, get ready!" Mister Mooney shouted from his spot in the center of the field.

Before anyone could say anything else, a noise like thunder boomed and echoed through the night. Was that… dear God, was that a gunshot?

Mister Mooney's eyes widened, and even from a distance, I noticed a flicker of fear cross his face. "Uh-oh," he said, downing the rest of his beer.

Maverick killed the engine and sat down heavily, tilting his head up to the sky. "I knew it. I knew y'all was gonna get me in trouble."

"If she asks, this was Ryder's idea." Mister Mooney chuckled as he stumbled over to us, picking up beer cans and shoving them back in the cooler. Even Cash had the sense to hop down and clean up as well. Ryder and Mav drove the four-wheelers over and hopped off.

"What was that?" Cason asked, suddenly wide awake, his worried gaze meeting mine.

"Was that a gunshot?" I asked, my brows furrowed as I looked at Ryder. Dutch had hopped off the tailgate and ran to his side.

"Oh yeah!" Cash guffawed. "That was Lorena, alright."

"Lorena?" I frowned. "Who's Lorena?"

"My ma calls her gun Lorena." Cash downed the rest of his beer too. "After Lorena Bobbit."

"Why would she—" It took me a moment, but I got it a moment later. "Oh…"

"I don't get it," Cason whined sleepily. "Why did Mrs. Mooney name her gun?"

I ran a hand over his head, pushing his dark hair off his forehead. "Never mind, bud. Just don't worry about it now."

"She's never used it for that," Mister Mooney slurred. "It's just the threat of it, ya know?"

A big diesel engine roared and the nicest truck I'd ever seen rolled into the field before us.

"Should we run?" Ryder groaned, looking at Maverick, Cash, and Mister Mooney.

"You can't run fast enough, boy." Mister Mooney chuckled. "Best to just stand your ground and take whatever she hands out."

The truck stopped, and a moment later Mrs. Mooney got out. Her silver hair was in curlers. The pink robe wrapped around her plump body had the words 'Jesus loves me' embroidered on it. Fuzzy pink slippers shaped like cowboy boots adorned her feet. In the crook of her left arm rested a brown and white chihuahua, while dangling in her left hand was a long-barreled revolver.

"Now," she said, surveying the scene. "Who wants to tell me what exactly is goin' on out here? And mind you, don't lie. Y'all woke Lorena up and she's pissed."

"Ma, we was just practicin'—"

"Nope." She cut Cash off. "You're done. Maverick?"

"Well ma'am, there's a section of fence that—"

"Mmm-mm." She shook her head. "What did I say about lyin'? Ryder, you got anything?"

He shook his head and held his hands up. "I plead the fifth, ma'am."

"Well, you're smarter than your friends at any rate." She frowned. "Mister Mooney?"

"We was just being stupid, Violet. That's all. Havin' the kid around made us all feel like boys again. We just wanted him to have a good time." Mister Mooney took his cowboy hat off and held it out in front of him.

"Alright." Violet Mooney shook her head and looked up to the sky. "Lord, give me the strength to deal with the boneheads you done put in my life. Praise be."

She looked at me, pegging me in place with her brown gaze. "Miss Charlotte, I wanna tell you somethin'. If you're plannin' on takin' up with any of these cowboys, there's somethin' you oughta know. Whatever age they are emotionally when you find 'em…that's what age they stay. You remember that before you go and do some damn fool thing like accept a ring from one of 'em."

My gaze met Ryder's on instinct, a flush coming to my cheeks. Did I want to end up marrying Ryder? Why was I even thinking that? That was beyond a bit preemptive. And also, what poor timing. There were more pressing issues. Like the fact Cash's mother stood in an open field with a gun in her hands.

I found myself nodding. "Yes, ma'am."

"Alright now." Mrs. Mooney grunted. "Cash, get your ass back to the bunkhouse and get in bed. I don't want to hear any hootin', hollerin', *or* carryin' on from you tonight, or I'll ship you off to some cattle ranch in Kansas."

"Ah, but Ma, it's *early*." Cash whined, sounding more like a kid than a twenty-seven-year-old. "There's plenty of time for some hollerin'. At least some hootin'."

"You got chores in the mornin'." She reminded him. "Bed. Now."

"Aww," Cash groaned. "Goodnight, everybody. Big Daddy'll see ya in the mornin'."

Mrs. Mooney's hard gaze met Maverick's. I didn't miss how the dark-haired cowboy seemed to lose a couple inches on him as he cowered before his aunt. "Maverick, I'm surprised at you. You're supposed to be the responsible one."

He refused to meet her gaze as he mumbled, "Sorry, ma'am."

"Someone could have gotten hurt."

"Sorry ma'am."

"You and Ryder get those four-wheelers put up, then get back to the bunkhouse, and, if y'all are smart, you'll lock all the doors and windows and turn your phones off. Cash already has you in hot water, no reason to let him get you in any more trouble tonight."

Maverick nodded. "I'm sorry, Aunt Violet."

"And you two—" Mrs. Mooney gestured at me and Cason. "Y'all don't live here, so I can't tell ya what to do, but if ya wake me, my dog, or my gun up again, that won't protect ya much. I suggest y'all get home and get that little boy in bed before he does somethin' stupid like decide to be a cowboy. And miss Charlie, if you'd be a dear and take Cash's truck back to the bunkhouse?" Mrs. Mooney asked.

I nodded. "Yes ma'am."

"Bad Mooney." Mrs. Mooney turned her attention to her husband. "I don't even know what to do with you. You get in my truck and if ya get any mud on my floor mats, you're gonna have to suck up your chewin' tobacco with a *straw*!"

"Yes ma'am," Mister Mooney said around a wry grin.

As he walked past me to his wife's truck, he reached out and placed his hand on my shoulder. "I hope ya had a good time. Y'all are welcome back whenever you want." He got in the truck and waited for his wife. With a final hard look at us all, Mrs. Mooney turned around and stomped back to the truck before driving away.

Mama had always been scary, but Mrs. Mooney…dear Lord. I'd have to remember to never piss that woman off.

"You promise you won't let him drive you home, Miss Charlie?" Maverick asked me, drawing my attention. There was an edge to his voice, a half wild look in his eyes. The planes of his brutally handsome face were lined with worry.

I frowned. Why was he so distraught?

"You won't let Ryder drive you, right? He's had a lot to drink."

"Jesus, Mav. I ain't gonna drive drunk." Ryder shook his head even as he clapped a hand on Mav's shoulder. He gave it a reassuring squeeze. "Let's just get these four-wheelers put away."

"I didn't drink anything so I'm good to drive myself and Cason. I really need to get him to bed, anyway. I'm afraid if I let him sleep here, he'll never leave," I said, hoping my answer gave Maverick a little relief.

"Just promise me you won't let him drive, okay?" Maverick's insistence made her heart ache. What had happened to him?

I nodded. "I promise, Maverick."

Ryder sighed, turning to look at me. "You better hurry and get that old truck started. Cash took off walkin' in the wrong direction. If he keeps goin' that way, he'll end up in east pasture and pass out in a thorn tree."

"If he don't drown in the water tank," Maverick added with a huff of laughter.

I laughed, grateful for the ease in tension. Worry still lingered in Maverick's heavy stare, but at least he was acting more like himself.

"I'll go pick him up and take him home." I sighed. "Man, no one told me how much work cowboys are."

"Miss Charlie…" Maverick wiped at his forehead with his sleeve, pushing up the brim of his hat. "You have no idea."

"T

HANK YOU FOR TONIGHT." I leaned into him as we walked to my rental. Ryder carried a sleeping Cason in his arms. Poor kid just couldn't hang.

"Of course…sorry, I can't drive you home. I feel bad makin' you head back alone this late."

"It's fine. I just wish the night didn't have to end." We came to a stop before my car and I opened the back passenger door so he could slide Cason into his carseat. "You, um…you could stay the night," I said, my words hopeful.

His back stilled before he turned to look at me—fire blazed in his eyes. "What?"

I lowered my gaze, unable to meet his intense stare as I crossed an arm over my chest, rubbing my hand up and down my opposite one. I didn't want tonight to end. Didn't want to go home. I didn't even care if we hooked up or just hung out on the couch again talking 'til we fell asleep. I just didn't want to leave him. Call it foolish, call it selfish, but I craved the calm he brought with his presence.

"Sorry, too soon? I mean, you've stayed before, but that was different. I was having panic attacks, and, well, it's probably a bad—"

Ryder pulled me to him, an arm caging around my waist as he tilted my face up. My breath caught in my throat, my heart beating like a war drum. His deep, gravelly voice sent shivers down my spine as he spoke. "I want nothin' more than to go home with you, Miss Charlotte. But I don't think I can behave myself. Not after tonight. You sure you want that?"

Yes. God, yes, I did. I wanted all of him. Every. Damn. Inch. But something in me, the logical part of me, urged me to wait. There was no rush to this. I'd just gotten out of a relationship, and the last thing I wanted was anyone thinking that Ryder was a rebound.

Because he wasn't. There wasn't a scenario in this world that made Cal the better man than Ryder.

Besides, wasn't the anticipation half the thrill? Shoving down my desire, I pressed a soft kiss to his lips. "I do…but I also want to savor every moment of it—" I glanced at Cason, still sleeping in his carseat. "I don't want any distractions."

His lips crooked upward for just a moment before he kissed me. It was soft and sensual and had my toes curling as his hand drifted from my chin to slide into my hair. When he finally pulled away, my legs were like jello, my breathing shallow and labored.

Had I made a mistake? Maybe I should just say fuck it and have him come home anyway. What was the likelihood Cason would wake up again and interrupt us?

"You're a tease," I murmured against his lips.

He chuckled, pegging me with an intense look. "No, darlin', you're the tease. Lookin' as good as you do."

I rolled my eyes, unused to the compliments. When was the last time Cal had complimented me? If anything, he'd always been more like Mama, constantly nagging me about the way I looked, what I wore. If I gained a couple pounds, he'd have something to say, if I lost weight, same thing.

Ryder didn't make me feel anything other than beautiful.

After a final goodbye kiss—okay, a couple more— I buckled up a still sleeping Cason and left Ryder standing there waving goodbye. As I drove down the tree-lined drive, I couldn't help but think I was completely and totally fucked.

I had no self-control.

How the hell was I going to do this? I'd fallen for Ryder, in spite of him being a rodeo cowboy. I just hoped he didn't trample my heart the way that bull had trampled him.

CHAPTER TWENTY-SIX

Runnin' Outta Moonlight

RYDER

As the days went by, one thing became painfully clear. Charlie Evans had consumed me. Body, mind, and soul.

From the minute I woke up, 'til the moment I went to sleep, my thoughts were always on her. And if I wasn't thinking about her, it was only because I was with her.

It both amazed and terrified me how easily she'd fit into my life. Everything just felt… easy with her.

I wasn't about to question the *how* or *why*, I was just happy to have her.

Pulling my cowboy hat off, I wiped the sweat off my brow with the back of my arm. Damn, I wasn't ready for this heat in March. At least the truck's AC felt nice. I put my hat back on and grabbed my phone, pressing on Charlie's name when I pulled up my calls.

She answered on the second ring.

"Hey. How are you?" Relief rang in her voice. I didn't miss the layer of sadness wrapped up in it, though. Something bothered her. Understandable with her sister's memorial tomorrow.

"A lot better now that I'm talkin' to you."

Her words, full of warmth, were soft melody I could listen to forever. "That was so incredibly corny. Did Cash teach you that one?"

I barked out a laugh in response. "Oh, come on, it wasn't *that* bad."

"It was," she replied with a giggled huff.

"And how are you doin', Miss Charlotte?"

"Okay, now that I'm talking to you," she teased, faking my accent. It was funny, for someone who grew up here, her accent was all but gone. And the one she faked was god-awful. But it had me grinning from ear to ear nonetheless.

"Now, I *know* I don't sound that bad when I talk."

Another giggle through the line. I heard water turn on and the clinking of dishes in the background.

"How're you doin'?" I asked again. "Really?"

There was a loud sigh on the other end, the sound of the water turning off, and a long moment of still silence. "Um…kinda shitty."

"Wanna talk?" I asked, as I turned onto the main road.

"I just… I'm worried about tomorrow." Her voice shook, trembled. "I have this horrible feeling that Mama is gonna do or say something, because, well…because she can." She went quiet for a few moments, but I heard the near silent sobs through the phone. "And, well…I'm frustrated. I understand why Sheldon wanted to plan her own funeral, but—but I was looking forward to—well, not looking forward to, but… But I wanted to do *something* for her. I…" Her words dissolved into another few moments of silence. I heard a door click shut, and then a muffled sound, almost like she was sliding her back down the door.

I waited for her to talk, not daring to interrupt her. If she wanted to cry, she could cry. My heart clenched, frustration rippling through me that I wasn't there to ease the hurt.

"When Daddy died—" Her voice cracked. "I found it…I found that helping Sheldon get the funeral arrangements ready was…c-cathartic. It gave me closure. I didn't get that this time." A broken sob escaped her, followed by erratic breathing.

Shit. "I'm here, Miss Charlotte. If you needa cry, cry."

She did, all the while I silently cursed myself for still being at least half hour out of town. This hadn't gone at all like I'd planned.

I offered her sweet nothings, words of reassurance, but mostly I just let her cry, all the while reminding her to breathe when the sobs got too broken, too heavy. It seemed to work, and after a few moments she sniffled and said, "I'm sorry."

"For what? For feelin'? For missin' your sister? Don't ever apologize for that. I'm glad you feel safe enough to fall apart with me. I just wish I was there to do more."

Another sniffle. "Ryder, you do more than enough for me. Just your voice alone helps so much." Sadness still hung in her words, but some of that familiar lightness had returned. "What're you doing right now?"

"Drivin' back to the ranch. What about you?"

"Not much. I'm trying to tidy up… Cason's playing on his iPad. I gotta figure out what to do for dinner. Wanna come over?"

I grinned. "I gotta better idea."

"Oh, and what's that?"

"You and I are gonna go on a date."

A huff of laughter on her end. "I guess I can call my mother and see if she can watch—"

"I already got it covered," I interrupted. "Cason's gonna have a pizza party with Uncle Mav and Funcle Cash."

She laughed, sounding more like herself by the minute. "Are you sure about that? Cash babysitting sounds absolutely terrifying."

I chuckled. "Ah, Cash's good with kids…mainly cuz he is one. But Mav won't let anything bad happen to Cason. I'd trust him with my life."

Charlie laughed once more. "Okay. When are you coming?"

The immature, Cash-like part of me bit back a response to that, like *that's what she said*. "How's forty-five minutes sound? Think you'll be ready by then?"

She scoffed. "Well, that depends on where we're going. What should I wear?"

Just the anticipation of seeing what outfit she came up with had my heart racing and a smile tugging on my lips. "Wear whatever you want, Miss Charlotte."

I could practically hear her eye roll as she let out an annoyed sigh. "I'm serious. Is it somewhere casual? Fancy? Do I need to dig up some heels, or should I wear boots? Tennies?"

"I mean it. You could wear a trash bag and still be the prettiest girl in the room."

She laughed, damn near all of the sadness gone from her. *Good.* "Well, thank you. That's still incredibly unhelpful, though."

"You're welcome."

"Rude," she teased. "Well, I better go get ready and stress over what the hell to wear. Should I tell Cason, or do you want it to be a surprise?"

"I'm sorry," I replied with a chuckle. "And it's up to you. I say, surprise him."

She let out a dramatic sigh. "You're forgiven. And okay, surprise it is. See you soon."

"Bye, Miss Charlotte."

I was still grinning like a damn fool when I pulled up to the Mooney Ranch. I headed for the bunkhouse, a nice, welcome aroma greeting me as I opened the door. Mav hovered over the stove while Cash lounged in one of the empty recliners before a large TV mounted to the wall. The Cowboy channel blared from the speakers.

"Hey! It's the man of the hour!" Cash crowed from his perch. "You get all your shit done?"

"Yeah, no thanks to your lazy ass," I said, making my way over to Maverick.

"Hey! I've been busy helpin' Mav."

I grunted, pulling my ball cap off and shaking my head as I shared a look with Mav. He pegged Cash with a scathing glare and went back to cooking.

"Sure looks like it," I replied.

Cash chuckled, pressing his beer to his lips. "What? It's called moral support. He cooks, while I drink and tell him he's doin' a good job."

Another laugh escaped me as Mav shouted from the kitchen. "You've been doin' a piss poor job of that, dipshit."

The two bickered back and forth and I shook my head, a smile on my lips. "I'm gonna clean up. Mav, how's the food lookin'?"

"Fifteen minutes," he called out.

Perfect, had just enough time to shower and shave. Giving him a thumbs up, I disappeared into the bathroom to wash up.

CHAPTER TWENTY-SEVEN

Settle Me Down

CHARLIE

I'D JUST SLIPPED INTO my black boots when Ryder's truck rumbled up the driveway. Cason's door crashed open, sending the whole house shaking as a loud whoop left him.

"Mister Ryder's here!"

I smiled at the pure excitement in his tone as I glanced at the mirror in the corner of my room. After Ryder's less than helpful insight on what to wear tonight, I'd opted for a mix of nice and casual. A lightweight, sleeveless black patterned high-low dress—since this Texas heat was already getting to me. Besides adding some foundation, eyeshadow, and mascara to the mix, I'd not done much different than my normal look.

Hopefully it was dressy enough if we went out, but simple enough in case it was something as casual as going to dinner in town. Oh god. Was he taking me to dinner at his parent's house? My stomach did a somersault and my pulse raced.

Fuck. Would he really take me to meet them so quickly? Oh God, I didn't know. I blew out a breath. Too late to worry about that now. Not waiting another moment, I forced my feet one in front of the other and walked down the hallway. The front door was wide open, thanks to Cason, and I almost spouted off something like *'were you born in a barn?'* or something else   Mama would holler. That thought alone stopped me from saying anything. I'd be damned if I became anything like her.

I walked out the door and closed it behind me. A loud whistle echoed through the trees surrounding the house. "Well damn, Charlie girl." I'd recognize Cash's familiar voice anywhere.

I rolled my eyes and bit back a smile as I turned to them at the foot of the porch. Cash and Mav were there, Maverick holding four boxes of pizza, and Cash two six packs of beer. But my gaze snapped to Ryder's like a magnet.

How was it that he could look so damn hot in a black t-shirt, cowboy hat, and jeans? It should be a sin. But his casual outfit made me instantly feel overdressed. Maybe this was too fancy?

"Is it too much?" I asked. "It's too much. I'm gonna go change." I was already turning toward the door when his voice sliced through the air like a cracking whip.

"No!" Did I sense desperation hidden in there somewhere? I paused, looking down at him. "No," he repeated, his boots echoing off the wooden steps as he ate up the distance between us and pulled me into his arms. "Please, don't change."

I shivered beneath his unrelenting gaze. Those dark depths were like endless pools I could drown in. "Okay," I managed to get out in a breathless whisper.

He clutched my chin and kissed me. "Damn, you're perfect."

I laughed softly and smiled against his lips. "I could say the same about you."

Cash hollered from down in the driveway. "Yeah, boy! Get some!"

Ryder groaned, leaning his forehead to mine.

"He's *your* best friend." I smirked before pulling out of his grip and grabbing his hand. Leading him down the steps, I made my way over to the boys and Cason.

"You're going to stay with Uncle Mav and Uncle Cash, okay?"

Cason nodded emphatically, a wide grin lighting up his face and highlighting his freckles.

"I want you on your best behavior," I said, pegging him with a hard stare, before sliding my gaze to Cash. "All of you. And you better not give him any of that beer, Mooney."

Cash's shit-eating grin said behaving was the last thing he had on his mind. Dear God, I hoped Ryder was right about leaving Cason with them. "You wound me, Charlie girl. I'd never give alcohol to a minor."

I laughed, shaking my head. "I mean it. Not a drop."

"Yes, ma'am," he replied with a mock salute.

I looked to Maverick, offering him a sympathetic smile. "You sure you got this?"

His jade eyes shone with fierce determination, the harsh lines of his face severe and serious. "I won't let nothin' happen, Miss Charlie. You have my word." He tipped his hat to me.

Some of the anxiety eased in my chest. I could trust Maverick. Of that I was certain.

Blowing out a breath, I nodded and squeezed Ryder's hand before turning to look at him. "Ready?"

"**Y**OU'RE SERIOUSLY NOT GOING to tell me where we're going?" I asked for at least the dozenth time.

Ryder glanced at me. The corner of his mouth tugged up into a lopsided grin, as if he was enjoying this way too damn much. I wanted to be annoyed; I generally hated surprises—they only ever seemed to give me anxiety over anything else—but there was something so ridiculously attractive about the confidence he exuded right now. Sitting there in the driver's seat, one hand on the steering wheel, one hand on my thigh…he could probably ask anything of me at that moment, and I'd say yes. Wholeheartedly, emphatically yes.

"We're almost there." He smirked. I shook my head and growled, earning a chuckle from him. "Did you just growl at me?"

I laughed. "Yes! The anticipation is killing me. I hate not knowing what's going on."

He gave my thigh a reassuring squeeze and nodded at a dirt road coming up on our right. "We ain't far."

He turned down the road before putting the car in park just off to the side. What the hell?

"Um… Ryder?" What were we doing out in the middle of nowhere?

He pulled out a red handkerchief. "You gotta wear this the rest of the way."

I scoffed. "What?"

He shrugged. "You wanna find out where we're goin' or not?"

I cast a playful glare his way and rolled my eyes. "Okay, put it on."

The smile on his face sent tremors of excitement through me. I hated how easily he made me melt. It's like I had no willpower against him. None. He leaned over, gently tying the blindfold behind my head. That familiar sandalwood and leather scent drifted to me, melting me even more.

"Why are you doing all of this for me?" My voice was little more than a trembling whisper as darkness descended upon me.

I wasn't expecting his lips to brush against my own. Desire ignited low in my belly. Fuck, he knew just what he was doing.

"There gotta be a reason, Miss Charlotte?" he asked, his tone somehow deeper and more gravelly than a moment ago. Or was that simply because my other senses were heightened now that my vision was gone?

What the hell did I possibly say to that? I just let out a disbelieving laugh, a thrill rushing through me when his mouth captured mine in a kiss once more.

I don't know how long we drove down the dirt road, but every second felt like a lifetime. With each curve or dip, with each bump, my nerves wound tighter and tighter until I was so on edge that I was honestly surprised I hadn't combusted yet.

"Don't take the blindfold off yet, Miss Charlotte," he said, his tone somehow soft and stern at the same time as he put the truck in park and opened up his door before hopping out.

God, I wanted to peek so bad. Where were we? I huffed. What would one quick glance hurt? No, I'd been good all this time, I'd find out soon enough. But dear Jesus, this anxiety was going to kill me. I tapped my foot impatiently against the floorboards, even going so far as to sit on my hands so I wouldn't touch the blindfold.

Just when I thought I couldn't take it any longer, just when I was about to rip the blindfold off and say fuck it, my door opened, a gust of warm air dancing across my skin. "Alright, you ready, darlin'?"

A shiver went through me. I didn't trust my voice not to break, so I just bit my lip and nodded. In the next instant, he pulled me out of the car and into his arms, slowly sliding me to the ground. I gasped as I felt his hard cock brush against me. Glad to see how much I affected him, because he'd sure as fuck affected me.

A low growl rumbled from his chest. "Careful, Miss Charlotte. Do that again, and I may not be able to behave."

My lips pulled into a grin. "Is that a promise?"

Still blindfolded, he kissed me. Hard and brutal and unrelenting. With one hand wrapped around me, his other hand drifted from my waist, up along my side, before his fingers brushed beneath the swell of my breast.

All of the air left my lungs in a whoosh, my knees going weak. God, I wanted him. From the moment he'd come over and talked to me at Jack's, I'd wanted him. I didn't even care at this point if he rodeoed. Not when his touch felt like fire and his kisses were like a drug.

I pulled my blindfold off, sliding one arm up around his neck, while dancing my fingers across his torso with my other hand. Nipping at his bottom lip, I stole some of the control from him.

His breath hitched, and a swell of satisfaction rose up in me, ratcheting my desire even higher. He pulled away first, breaking the kiss to rest his forehead against mine. His ragged breath fanned against my cheeks as he blew out a shaky exhale. "Damn, Miss Charlotte."

My answering laugh was husky, sultry.

Ryder cupped my face in his hands, a ghost of a smile lighting up his features. "Come on. As much as I want you, right here, right fuckin' now, I want you to see this first."

My body cried out for him, yearning for his scorching touch, but I nodded. I wanted to see where we were too. Letting him turn me away from the truck, I took in our surroundings.

My hands flew up to cover my mouth, a gasp escaping me. We stood about twenty yards from a river beside a large jacaranda tree, its purple blossoms blanketing the earth. But the pretty scenery wasn't the focus of my attention. No, beneath the tree was the most Pinterest-worthy setup I'd ever seen. Blankets and pillows were arranged around a cooler and a couple trays that had lit candles on them.

My chest tightened—so much it hurt to breathe.

No one had ever done something like this for me. Never.

"Ryder," I choked out.

"You like it?"

Noting the tremor of worry in his voice, I turned to look at him, letting out a disbelieving laugh. How could he even doubt himself? I pressed my hands to his chest, to his face, to his arms.

His dark gaze narrowed, brows furrowing together in confusion. \"What're you doin'?"

I leaned up on tiptoe and pressed a soft kiss to his lips. "Making sure you're real."

He huffed a laugh, a confused look still on his face. "What do you mean?"

"You're perfect, Ryder," I breathed, wrapping my arms around his neck. "Absolutely, fucking perfect. I didn't even think men like you existed outside of books."

His brows knit tighter even as his arms wrapped around me. "I just wanted to show you I was thinkin' about you. Show you how much I cared."

If I hadn't fallen for him already, I would have then. He was so earnest and kind and thoughtful. There was no more war within me. I wanted him. Needed him in my life. In just a week, he'd picked up and healed more of the broken pieces of my shattered soul than anyone else in my life ever had.

He was everything a cowboy should be. And he was mine.

I pressed a soft kiss to his mouth and pulled out of his grip, grabbing his hand and leading him forward. "Come on."

CHAPTER TWENTY-EIGHT

No Time Soon

RYDER

M Y HEART WAS PLAYING dangerous games with me tonight.

Between how carefree, vulnerable, and open Charlie was being, and that dress—damn, that dress—my heart didn't stand a chance. She sat across from me, knees tucked under her, as she pressed her stainless-steel tumbler full of Cash's infamous sangria to her lips. That shit was a hangover in a cup, but she didn't seem to mind. A soft smile toyed on her mouth, amusement and desire swirling in her stormy eyes as they settled on me.

"I still can't believe you did all this…and that the boys helped you."

I took a sip of beer and shrugged. "Mav helped, Cash drank…but I didn't have to do much convincin'. They like you. Cason, too."

"We don't deserve you guys," she replied with a shake of her head, grabbing a honey buttered biscuit and taking a bite. Her eyelids fluttered closed, a satisfied little moan escaping her. "Remind me to ask Maverick if he will be my personal chef. Like, seriously. I can't believe how good everything is."

I barked out a laugh. "He'd probably agree to it. He's the best cook I know, second maybe to Mrs. Mooney."

"I'll fucking say," she said around another bite.

I grinned, my cheeks hurting from how much I'd been doing it tonight. But I couldn't help it. Something was different about Charlie. There was a lightness to her I'd never seen. It's like whatever storm she'd been fighting had broken.

This was the real her—foul mouthed, a bit sarcastic, and full of laughter—and Lord help me, but I think I loved her.

Which was crazy and stupid and didn't make no damn sense, but I'd no other words to describe exactly how I felt. Not that I'd tell her. Not yet. She'd only recently stopped having that deer-in-the-head-lights look whenever the mention of rodeos came up. I wouldn't go and say something as stupid as being in love with her. I didn't want to scare her away.

Charlie's head cocked to the side, a coy smile toying on her lips. "What are you thinking, cowboy?"

"I'm thinkin' how much I love you in black." I nodded at her dress, taking another sip of my beer.

Her laugh danced on the wind, her smile rivaling the sunset. "Good. Because it's basically the color of ninety-eight percent of my wardrobe." Her gray eyes settled on me. "You look pretty damn good in black too."

My cheeks warmed as I pressed my beer to my lips. I wasn't used to compliments being aimed back at me like that.

She took another sip of her drink, glancing down at the river before looking back at me. "I dare you to jump in."

A laugh escaped me, and I shrugged, setting my beer aside as I pushed up into a stand. "Done." I pulled my hat off and placed it upside down on the blanket before shucking off my shirt. I didn't miss Charlie's hungry gaze on me, taking me in. I shivered under her stare as I pulled off my boots, then my jeans, until I stood in only my boxer briefs.

"You gonna join me," I said, nodding at her.

She huffed a disbelieving laugh, leaning back on her elbows, settling herself onto the blankets more. "Absolutely not. I'll just sit right here and enjoy the view."

"Oh darlin'…" I laughed, running a hand through my hair as I stalked toward her. The smile on her lips died as I picked her up easily in my arms. "It wasn't a question."

She squealed, kicking and flailing halfheartedly in my grasp, cussing up a storm and pleading for me to put her down.

"You might as well stop fightin', Miss Charlotte."

Her storm cloud gaze met mine and she stilled in my arms. "Okay, okay. Fine. Just…just let me take my dress off?"

I eyed her suspiciously for a moment, a smirk on my lips. "You try runnin', I will chase. If I go in, you're goin' too."

She glanced around, as if that very thought had crossed her mind, and sighed. "Fine. You can put me down now."

I obliged. The minute her feet hit the ground she was in motion, trying to dart away like a spooked deer. I laughed, caging her to me. Her back pressed against my front, my arms like iron bands around her waist.

"Damn it!" She wriggled and writhed to no avail.

With another chuckle, I leaned down and pressed a kiss to her neck, just below her ear. "Stop fightin' it darlin'."

She stilled at that, the fight leaving her. My grip on her loosened, so that I no longer caged her to me. My hands drifted down her waist to graze against her hips, before traveling back up, up, up toward the swell of her breast. All of the tension melted away from her, her body leaning into my touch.

I kissed a path down her neck to her collarbone, and a little breathy moan escaped her. I smiled against her skin at the sound.

One of her arms drifted up to wrap around my neck, her fingers knotting in my hair, causing her back to arch against me. I cupped her breast and was rewarded with another moan. Fuck, I wanted her. Wanted her so damn bad I contemplated just laying her down on the blanket right here, right now. Water be damned. But there was no reason to rush this. No distractions. No interruptions. Just her and I.

Continuing a trail of nips and caresses back up her neck and along her jawline, I slowly slid the fabric of her dress up over her curves. She pulled away from me long enough to lift the dress above her head and toss it haphazardly onto the blankets.

Charlie turned to face me, a mischievous smirk quirking her lips and fire dancing in her eyes. She wore only a lacy, black bra and matching underwear—her tattoos on full display. How I wanted to trace every line and curve of them. Especially that sternum tattoo.

There'd be time for that. We were just getting started and I had no intention of stopping any time soon.

"Well? We getting in or what?" One of her brows rose in question.

I grinned, swooping her up over my shoulder, her answering laughter drawing me under her spell like a sailor to a siren song.

CHAPTER TWENTY-NINE

Skinny Dippin'

CHARLIE

I DON'T THINK I'D ever been so turned on by a man in my life.

Ryder Wright was perfection. Complete and utter perfection. And I couldn't get enough of him. I didn't even mind that the water was absolutely freezing. Okay, that might have been a bit of an exaggeration. I didn't mind *that* much.

I'd fought like hell the minute my toes hit the water, but he'd dunked me in anyway. At least he held me now, his strong arms banded around me, offering me some warmth as we sat in the water.

The sound of crickets chirping and water lapping at the shore and the small wooden dock created a song of the night. The dying sun reflected off the water, sparkling like a thousand diamonds. It was all so perfect it didn't quite feel real. Like I'd somehow stepped into a romance novel or a country love song—however corny that sounded.

"What're ya thinkin', darlin'?"

A shiver went through me that didn't have to do with the water. I liked him calling me darlin' almost as much as I liked the way Miss Charlotte sounded on his lips. Almost.

I settled my gaze on him, admiring the muscles in his shoulders rippling with the smallest of movements. He was even more cut than I'd thought. A sculpted chest and abs, strong arms; he even had that "v" at his hips. But what enchanted me more than that, was the raised brand right over his heart.

I traced my fingertips over the three letters burned into his flesh. "What's this?" I asked, noting the M, R, and C.

His lips quirked up, the scar on his face whitening just a bit. "It's mine, Cash, and Mav's brand for when we open up our ranch."

"Really? Tell me about it?"

Ryder held me to him as we moved in slow, lazy circles in the center of the river. His gaze traveled beyond me as he spoke. "We're gonna start up a breedin' operation for buckin' bulls, as well as raisin' and trainin' performance horses. There's a property just outside of town that we've been lookin' at. We've got just about enough saved up between the three of us to make it happen if we play our cards right."

Hope blossomed in my chest. Why hadn't he told me about this before? Maybe I wouldn't have been so worried about rodeoing. If this was the ultimate goal, maybe once he'd achieved it, he wouldn't need to wrestle steer or ride bulls anymore. Wouldn't need to risk his life every weekend. I could deal with him training and breaking babies. "That's a great idea. Do you guys have a name in mind?"

He nodded. "Our initials sound out merc. So, we were thinkin' Mercenary Ranch."

"I like that."

"Glad you approve," he replied, a ghost of a smile on his lips as he kissed me softly.

I twirled my fingers through his dark hair, brushing against his shoulders. "Why brands over tattoos? Wasn't it more painful?"

Ryder shrugged. "The idea was to get it tattooed. After we'd come up with the logo a couple years ago, I bought us a branding iron to hang up in the bunkhouse as, like, a manifestation, or whatever you wanna call it. One night, Cash and I were piss drunk, and Cash had the bright idea for us to brand it on us." He shook his head, chuckling. "The ultimate manifestation."

I laughed, trailing my fingers over the scarred flesh. "I can't believe Maverick let you guys do that."

Ryder laughed, the sound like a song I could listen to forever. "He's learned that there's just some battles that ain't worth fightin'."

I huffed a laugh. "Poor Mav."

Ryder's lips curled upward, but he didn't respond. We descended into silence for a few moments. A calm, soothing kind where we just enjoyed one another's quiet company.

When I'd left here five years ago, I swore I'd never come back. But now, I couldn't imagine leaving. Was I crazy? Was I falling too fast? Probably yes for both, but right here, right now, wrapped up in Ryder's arms, I'd never felt more comfortable. More at peace. More at home.

With a newfound boldness I'd only felt with him, I kissed him. Slow, unhurried, but not any less intense. I put every bit of desire into that kiss. Let him know without words just what I wanted.

Ryder's hold on me changed as he pressed me to him a little tighter, his touch going from relaxed to possessive. When he broke the kiss, his eyes had darkened somehow, gobbling up any lingering light in them. The change was subtle, but welcome.

"What're you thinking?" I asked, my words breathless.

"I'm thinkin' how much I want you," he replied, cupping the back of my head.

I wrapped my legs around his torso, my arms snaking around his neck. "Oh yeah?" I pressed the softest kiss to his lips. Just the whisper of one. A teasing touch that sent every muscle in his body taut. "How much?" I murmured, my voice dipping low and seductive.

The laugh that rumbled out of his chest filled me with desire. "Oh, Miss Charlotte…if I were to tell you all the ways I want you, we'd be here for hours."

One of my hands drifted down along the curve of his neck and over his chest, my fingers tracing his brand before skimming down, down, down over his abs and to the waistband of his boxer briefs. I went lower still, my hand brushing against his erection. His hissed response sent a ripple of excitement through me.

No more waiting. No more teasing. No more talking. I wanted him. Wanted him so badly it hurt to breathe.

"Show me, then, Ryder." I gripped his cock and whispered against his lips, "Show me what you want to do."

Ryder cupped the back of my head and drew me in close, his lips clashing with mine.

My heart fluttered in my chest at the possessive edge to his touch, his kiss. I opened my mouth to him, letting his tongue flick against mine as he waded through the water and toward the shore. I didn't pull away as he walked up the embankment, or as he leaned down and laid me on the blanket. His lips moved against mine in a perfect rhythm, as if he'd been specifically made for me.

Maybe he was.

If soulmates were such a thing, I'd bet good money he was mine.

That thought alone should have stopped the lust pooling low in my belly, but not tonight. No, there was no stopping tonight.

Ryder broke the kiss and leaned back on his knees, his breathing just as ragged as mine as he gazed down at me. With the broken rays of sunlight peeking through the jacaranda tree, he looked like some fallen angel come to earth. He even had the wings tattooed on his back, which I'd noticed earlier, leading across his shoulders and down the backside of his arms. My own personal guardian angel.

"Fuck, you're gorgeous," he all but purred.

A coy smile danced across my lips as I reached a hand up around his neck and dragged his mouth back down to mine. "So are you," I murmured.

He chuckled, pressing an answering kiss to my mouth, before lazily traveling to the corner of my lips, tracing along the line of my jaw. He trailed lower and lower, down my neck, along the curve where my shoulder and collarbone met, his teeth nipping gently.

His kisses were like lightning, sizzling through me and ratcheting up the desire within. I shivered under his electrifying touch, earning another chuckle from him. He settled one hand right on my hip, his thumb toying at the fabric of my underwear, even as his mouth descended lower still, brushing over the swell of my breast. Anticipation writhed within me, coiling tight like a snake poised to strike. He went lower still, his mouth moving toward my sternum. A gasp fell from my lips as his tongue darted across my tattoo there.

Was he…? Oh, dear God, he was tracing it with his tongue. A little whine went through me as another shudder made me shiver beneath him.

My fingers knotted in his damp hair. "God, you're a tease," I breathed.

He looked up at me with eyes burning hotter than coals and the sexiest smirk on his lips. "Want me to stop, Miss Charlotte?" he asked, just as his hand dipped beneath the fabric of my underwear, dangerously close to my core.

"Oh please, fuck, no," I growled, my head falling back against the blankets.

His smirk pulled wider as his hand danced lower and lower. He leaned down and pressed a feather-soft kiss to my lips. "Yes, Miss Charlotte."

Leave it to him to make manners fucking sexy. But holy hell, he somehow did. My hands tightened in his hair as I dragged his mouth back to mine for another soul-scorching kiss.

I moaned against his lips as Ryder's fingers finally brushed against my core, sending a shudder crashing through me. I lost all sense of time, of space, of sound as he worked his seductive magic.

He slid a finger inside me, and I failed to bite back a moan as my back arched against him. A satisfied rumble erupted from his chest that just about undid me completely. Each stroke, each kiss, each nip sending me higher and higher.

I was close. So fucking close. Teetering right on the edge of an orgasm.

Closing my eyes, I dipped my head back to the blankets once more, reveling in the feel of his soft caresses against my skin. My breath hitched in my throat as he pulled my bra down enough to expose my nipple. And then his mouth was on me, tongue teasing the sensitive peak, sending me full throttle towards the edge. A whimper escaped me, my hands sliding over his shoulders before I pressed my fingertips to his flesh. His answering groan of approval, followed by a second finger added to my core, was all I needed.

My orgasm thrashed through me like a streak of lightning. Sizzling and scorching in its intensity. I cried out Ryder's name, squeezing my eyes shut as my body shuddered and writhed beneath him. Wave upon wave of pleasure coursed through me, sending my nerves into overdrive. All the while, he continued stroking, continued caressing me.

When I'd finally come down from that ledge, when my limbs felt like jello and every nerve ending in my body seemed more like a livewire than anything else, I finally opened my eyes, finding Ryder's hungry gaze on me.

That's all it took. One look from those midnight eyes and my desire sparked back to life. If that's what he was capable of with his hands and mouth, Lord fucking knew what he could do with his cock. And I was ready to find out.

Leaning up to press a rough kiss to his lips, I whispered, "Fuck me."

Something ignited in his eyes, almost like surprise, maybe, his body going rigid beneath my touch. "Yes…" holding himself up above me, he grabbed with a free hand for his discarded clothes. "Let me just…Fuck… Where the hell is it?"

Sitting up, I watched Ryder go from calm, cool, and collected to a frenzy of chaos as he tried to find a condom, no doubt. It was the only explanation. A smile quirked on my lips at the sight. So, some things did rattle him. Good. I'm glad it was me that had.

"Ryder…*Ryder*," I called, reaching a hand out towards him.

He paused, his questioning gaze meeting mine as he sat back on his haunches. "I could have sworn I brought—"

I reached behind me and unclasped my bra, tossing it to the side. "Fuck the condom."

Whatever restraint he still possessed vanished, a look of pure, undiluted determination blazing in his eyes. A shiver of anticipation went through me and I bit my lip.

That was his undoing.

CHAPTER THIRTY

Thunder and The Rain

RYDER

WELL, DAMN.

I didn't think I could possibly want Charlie any more, but there she went, proving me wrong yet again.

Biting back a groan, I grabbed the back of her head and dragged her mouth to mine. "You've got such a dirty mouth, Miss Charlotte," I said against her lips.

Her head fell back and she exposed her neck to me, a laugh bubbling out of her. "You know you love it."

Clutching her chin and drawing her gaze back to mine, I used my free hand to slide her lace underwear down over her hips. "Damn, right, I do."

There was something about such filthy words coming out of that pretty mouth of hers that just sent me over the edge.

Still kissing me, she helped shimmy out of the fabric before her hands fumbled at the waistband of my briefs, repeating the process until my cock sprang free. She grasped it, and that just about did me in.

Fuck. A ripple of pleasure jerked through me, her touch like fire searing me to my soul. I groaned as her hand glided up and down my cock.

A husky little laugh escaped her as she broke the kiss, leaning back to meet my gaze with her dark, stormy one. The smile on her lips was one of pure confidence. Of a woman who knew what she wanted and just how to get it.

I knew I sounded like a broken record, but I'd never seen her more beautiful.

With one hand still around my cock, the other sliding into my hair, she laid back against the blankets, dragging me down with her, guiding me to her entrance.

"Fuck me, Ryder." Her words were a command. One I was happy to oblige.

I slid inside her, a shiver traversing the length of my spine as her head fell back, her eyes fluttering closed. "Yes," she hissed.

That half-whispered word spurred my body into motion, and I set up a slow, steady rhythm as I took in every inch of her. From the way her long coppery hair splayed around her, reminding me of the sunset at my back. Or the way she bit her bottom lip and fisted the blankets at her sides, so tight her knuckles turned white. To the way her dark tattoos contrasted her flawless, freckle-dusted skin.

I pressed a kiss to her jaw, one of my hands sliding in her hair, while I grabbed the back of her thigh and hiked her leg up against my side, thrusting myself into her. She moved against me, hips rocking against mine with just as much intensity, sending me higher and higher.

Dear Lord, she felt good. So damn good.

Charlie's hands slid up my sides and over the backs of my shoulders, her touch scorching. Wherever she touched me, I swear I burned. Burned brighter than the fucking sun. How was it this good with her? This…intense? Everything she did—every kiss, ever sound, every damn look she gave me—just about made me come undone. I'd always prided myself on patience, on restraint, but damn…it's like she'd been made to bring me to my knees.

Her mouth met mine once more, the kiss intense, insistent, wild. And when she finally pulled away, her hot breath fanning my cheeks, she whispered, "More."

Fuck.

I nearly came right then and there. Hiking her leg up higher, I thrust into her, my hips moving quicker, faster, harder. Her cries and moans drowned out all other sound, the most tantalizing symphony I'd ever heard.

"Fuck, Charlotte." Each pump of my hips sent me closer and closer to the edge, the flames of my desire burning so bright and hot I thought I might explode.

The satisfied purr that left her sent a shudder through me. "Say it again."

Her breathing turned ragged, her gaze glassy, and when her eyes met mine, I knew without needing to ask just how close she was. Gripping her hair just a little tighter and keeping her thigh to my side, I leaned down and whispered in her ear, "Come for me, Charlotte."

Her fingernails dug into my shoulders, and I hissed as she raked them down my back. But the pain blended with the pleasure, shooting a thrill of adrenaline through my veins.

I pumped into her, over and over and over, each thrust harder than the last, and as she shattered apart on my cock, my own release rocked my very senses, blurring my vision as I came.

Right then I knew I was fucked. Ruined. She was it. There would be no other. No one who'd even compare to her. I'd been with plenty of girls—more than I cared to admit—but not a single one had come close to her. And after tonight, I didn't think I'd ever want anyone else.

Charlie Evans was it for me.

It wasn't until I'd slid out of her and collapsed at her side, settling her into my arms, that I'd realized I'd come inside of her. Fuck. What if…?

I voiced the concern aloud, my chest constricting as I anticipated her anger. But when her eyes met mine, not an ounce of it shone.

She rested her chin atop my chest, her fingers drawing lazy patterns over the planes of my stomach. "It's okay, Ryder. I'm on birth control."

Relief trickled through me, but not enough to wash away the lingering worry. I'd been stupid. Stupid and rash. Even Cash—the dumb idiot—remembered to use a condom. I was glad she was on birth control, but even that wasn't fool-proof.

I ran a hand through her hair, my brows drawing together. "I'm sorry."

Pulling her hair over one shoulder, she leaned to press a soft kiss to my lips. "Don't be. I loved every single minute of it." I pushed up on my elbows, before reaching out to cup her cheek. She leaned into the touch. "I did too, darlin'."

I did too.

BY THE TIME WE headed back to Charlie's, it was nearly midnight. We'd laid naked on the blankets, talking and eating cookies Maverick made before making love as the moon rose and the stars and fireflies came out to dance across the dark sky.

It couldn't have turned out more perfect.

But with each mile away from the river, my nerves wound tighter and tighter. I couldn't exactly explain why. Maybe it was that a part of me still expected her to pick up and run off at the first chance of trouble. We hadn't talked about rodeo stuff in a while, but next weekend was Austin. What if she couldn't handle what I did? What if she was never able to get over that trauma?

I hoped she could. Dear Lord, I hoped she could.

I'd never wanted something to work so badly. How had my life changed so quickly in just a few short days? How did Charlie have such a strong hold on me? Not that I was complaining. The more time I spent around her, the more I was convinced she was made for me. It's the only thing that made sense.

And I'd be damned if I let her slip through my fingers.

I glanced over at her in the passenger's seat—her feet curled up beneath her, those copper curls a wild mess from drying naturally, and her black dress strap falling off her shoulder. She met my gaze and bit her lip before offering me a coy smile.

That's all it took. One damn look and I was burning hotter than a damn bonfire. I had half a mind to pull over and drag her into the backseat and lay her down in that moment. The glint in her eye led me to believe she wanted the same.

Fuck. I fought the blazing need stirring within me and grabbed her hand, dragging it to my mouth as I pressed a soft kiss to her knuckles. It'd have to do for now.

We'd tempted fate enough tonight. I'd never found the condom. Not that either of us had really tried. There was something both thrilling and terrifying about that. I didn't know the first thing about being a father…probably wouldn't make a very good one, and I had no idea what her thoughts were on parenthood. She already had her hands full with Cason, though. The last thing either of us needed was a baby. But not gonna lie, a part of me—a small, forbidden part of me—imagined how drop-dead gorgeous she'd be carrying my child.

A streak of desire sizzled through me. *Nope. Shut it down.*

Charlie's perfectly manicured brows drew into a deep "v" on her forehead, a frown pursing her lips. "What're you thinking?"

I kissed her knuckles once more and settled our hands on the center console, training my gaze ahead as I spoke. "I'm glad you agreed to tonight."

She smiled. "I am too. A part of me doesn't want it to end."

She had no damn idea. I huffed a laugh. "You're preachin' to the choir, Miss Charlotte."

"How much do you wanna bet Cason's still up when we get home?" Charlie asked, her tone light.

I chuckled. "Oh, I don't need to bet. I *know* he'll be awake, especially if Cash is involved."

"Hopefully he isn't too tired tomorrow at the memorial. That's just what I need, Mama complaining to me about Cason not acting properly."

Guilt settled over the desire, extinguishing it like water over a flame. Shit. "I'm sorry. I should have gotten you home earlier."

"Don't be. I'm glad for tonight," Charlie said, her stormy gaze settling on me. I turned to meet her stare, braving the risk of taking my eyes off the road. Despite a hint of sadness on her face, she looked happier than I'd ever seen her. "I'm glad I got to spend time with you."

I offered her a soft smile and looked at the road once more. "I'm just happy to have gotten you all alone for once."

Her laughter eased the tension winding my nerves tighter. "Me too."

THE LIGHTS WERE STILL on in the living room as we pulled up the drive. Turning the truck off, I hurried around to her side and helped her out, savoring the way her body moved against mine as she slid out of the truck. Cupping her face in my hands, I kissed her long and hard. I didn't know when the next time we'd get a night like this was. I needed just one more kiss. One more touch to tide me over in the meantime.

She wrapped her arms around my neck, leaning into it, taking everything I had to give her. When she pulled away, her words were breathy, low, seductive. "Can we just stay in your truck for the rest of forever?"

I pressed one final kiss to her lips. "There'll be plenty more nights like tonight, Miss Charlotte," I murmured, pulling out of her grasp while grabbing hold of one of her hands. I led her up the gravel drive, up the stairs and across the porch. She bent down and grabbed the key from beneath the welcome mat before jamming it into the lock.

"Well, here it goes," she huffed, twisting the doorknob and opening the door.

Dear Lord, the place was a mess. Pillows and couch cushions and blankets littered every inch of the living room. The boxes of pizza lay opened and abandoned on the dining table. At least a six pack's worth of beer cans lined the granite countertop in the kitchen. The TV blared the ending credits of one of the Star Wars movies, while Cash was passed out on the larger couch. My stomach twisted in knots, anticipation getting the best of me.

"Whoa." Charlie's voice held a sense of awe or horror to it—I couldn't quite tell. "This place looks like a bomb went off."

I frowned, scanning the room for Cason and Mav. I voiced the thought aloud, concern knotting my nerves tighter once more.

"Maybe they're in Cason's room?" Charlie shrugged, tiptoeing through the area, avoiding the pillow fort directly in the middle.

That made sense, especially if Cason was tired and Mav was trying to put him down. But a quick search in the room left both Charlie and I frowning. Where the hell was Mav? Charlie checked her room and the other bathroom, while I took the guest bathroom and front closet.

She walked down the hallway toward where I stood in the living room. "Anything?"

"Nope. You?" I asked, chastising myself instantly. She wouldn't have asked had she found them.

Charlie shook her head, worry swirling to life in her gaze. "Do you think Maverick would take Cason anywhere?"

I shook my head. "No. He didn't have a car, and both your rental and your sister's truck are still here."

It didn't make any sense. Maverick was the most reliable, responsible person I knew. I could count on him with anything. Everything. So, where the hell was he?

The living room erupted into chaos.

Twin battle cries rang through the air, followed by a flurry of motion. Before I could even comprehend exactly what was going on, Charlie and I were assaulted by a barrage of Nerf bullets.

I turned and hunched over, trying to protect Charlie as best I could. "What the hell?"

She shrieked before a string of giggles escaped her. "Cason?"

Sure enough, Cason and Maverick materialized from within the pillow fort, felt dinosaur masks hiding their faces. Blankets fell from around their shoulders.

"Ha ha! We got you guys!" Cason's confident shout drowned out most of the noise from the TV. "Were you scared?"

Charlie laughed again and I looked to Maverick as he pulled off his mask. The widest, most genuine grin coated his face—the sight so foreign it stopped me in my boots. None of the weight he usually wore around seemed to hold him down.

"So scared," Charlie grinned, hugging Cason as he launched into her arms.

Maverick came up beside me, and I nodded at the mask dangling in his grasp. "Looks like y'all had fun."

He rubbed the back of his neck with his free hand, a sheepish grin on his lips. "We did."

"What happened to Cash?"

"Fell asleep watching Return of the Jedi. Cason thought we should leave him be while we cooked up a plan to scare y'all."

"You should've seen your faces!" Cason grinned, before letting out a big yawn.

Charlie huffed a laugh. "Alright, bud. It's *way* past your bedtime. Can you say goodnight to Uncle Mav and Uncle Ryder?"

"Yeah, we should probably get Cash and head out," I replied, wishing like hell we didn't have to.

"Aw, but why?" Cason groaned.

Charlie turned to look at me. "It *is* late," she said with a shrug. "And Cash is already passed out. You guys could stay…if you wanted." Her gray eyes held an ember of longing in them. "Mav can stay on the top bunk in Cason's room or the couch."

Well, damn.

I wanted nothing more than to spend the night in her bed, with her in my arms. I looked at Mav, sharing a silent look with him.

His lips curved up into the ghost of a knowing grin as he dipped his head. "That's fine by me."

Cason let out a whoop of excitement that left me and Maverick laughing, but when my gaze met Charlie's, a shiver went through me.

Maybe the night wasn't over after all.

Chapter Thirty-One

Wreckage

Charlie

I HAD TO GIVE it to Sheldon. She knew how to pick a venue. She'd opted out of doing it at a funeral home or a church, thank God, and chosen a ranch just outside of town that used to be where Mama and Daddy would take us as kids to go pick wild flowers and berries for a small charge. Looked like they'd made a few upgrades since then. They'd transformed the place into an event venue for all sorts of occasions. Lavender fields sprawled just about as far as I could see, the gentle scent soothing as I breathed it in.

The memorial went off without a hitch, surprisingly. But I guess that was the beauty of having it all planned out ahead of time. I think just about every single adult in town was there. Where Sheldon had come up with the money for such an extravagant event was beyond me.

Pastor Stamper's eulogy had been lengthy, but kind-hearted. Layla's speech had left me in tears. Cason's had broken me so thoroughly it took me a moment to recover for my speech.

The way his little voice broke on those last four words… "I miss you, Mommy." My heart shattered at that, grief pounding into me so hard that it hurt to breathe.

I'd struggled with finding the words I wanted to say over the past week. It'd been so bad that I'd ended up giving up. They all seemed hollow, rehearsed, fake. The words that flowed from me today were straight from the heart.

I hoped Sheldon approved, or at the very least, appreciated it. Everyone else seemed to like it—well, aside from Mama.

Speaking of her, *surprise, surprise*, she hadn't said anything. She'd walked up to the wooden arch covered in lavender and sunflowers, all but ripped the mic from my hands, looked at the crowd, let out a sob, and dropped the mic at my feet.

Maybe I was callous, maybe I was being too hard on her, but I couldn't stop the burning rage that scorched a fiery path through me. She'd been like this for Daddy's funeral too. I didn't doubt that she was hurting—Sheldon was the clear favorite of the two of us. Mama and my sister had always been much closer, they'd shared a bond her and I never would…but, I just…I hated that she couldn't say *anything.*

I guess we all grieved in different ways. Who was I to say how she should react? But it didn't stop the anger, no matter how hard I tried to push it down.

When the speeches were done, the memorial switched to a lighter atmosphere. Catered food was brought out and everyone was urged to come up and share a happy memory with Sheldon. It wasn't surprising that the line was about a mile long. Sheldon had been a shining beacon of light and hope, whose kindness was far reaching.

Ryder hadn't left my side since after my speech—actually, Maverick and Cash hadn't either come to think of it. I was grateful for their presence. Cash had thankfully toned down some of the obnoxiousness, settling on his charming self. Maverick was stoic and quiet as usual, but I appreciated his silent support.

Cason had run off with Jace, the two of them so jacked up on sugar from eating way too many of the most delicious cake pops I'd ever tasted. At least he seemed happy. I had no idea how today was going to go for him. I'm sure tonight there'd be some tears, but for now, he was okay. And that's all that mattered to me.

"How're you doin'?" Ryder's husky voice in my ear and soothing touch around my waist sent a shiver through me.

I leaned into him, savoring the warmth, the steadiness of him. The calm to my storm. Glancing up to meet his dark stare, I offered a soft smile and a shrug. "I'm not sure," I answered honestly.

So many emotions bombarded me, one right after the other. I couldn't sort through them all. Sad and a bit broken from her loss, but also happy to see that she touched so many people. Soul tired from trying to keep it together. Guilt for not having done more. And also anger and bitterness at my mother.

Ryder turned me to face him and pressed a soft kiss to my forehead, running his hands up and down my shoulders in gentle, lazy strokes. "I'm here for you, darlin'."

I caught my mother sneaking a dark look my way, no doubt for witnessing such blatant affection between Ryder and I. I didn't care. Let her glare, let her silently seethe.

Ryder's gaze followed mine, and I felt him shiver beneath me. "She really don't like me, does she?"

I sighed, turning away from her. "It's not you, it's what you represent. If you were a sheriff, or anything else really, she'd be all but over the moon."

He huffed. "Now I see why you hate rodeoin' so much."

I sighed, pressing a hand to his chest. "I don't *hate* rodeoing. I'm scared of what can happen. Now, Mama? Yeah, she hates them. Always has. I remember them fighting over it a lot when I was little. She never wanted Daddy to go. Always wanted him to find a safer job. One that was more stable and steady."

Cash's cocky voice drew my attention. "Ah, shit. I can change her mind real quick. She just needs to take a ride with Big Daddy."

Maverick and Ryder simultaneously groaned. A gasp escaped me as I leaned over and smacked Cash's shoulder playfully. "Dear God, Mooney, if she hears you, she'll kill you."

"Nah…not once she has a piece of this." He gestured to himself, puffing out his chest like a rooster.

I rolled my eyes and shook my head. No one was a match for my mother. She always found a way to cut deeper, sharper, harder than anyone I'd ever met.

Maverick's low voice pulled my gaze. "Charmin' as you think you are, I'm afraid I have to agree with Miss Charlie. She'd eat you alive, bud."

Cash looked to Ryder for some shred of support, but Ryder just shrugged, offering him a guilty grin. "Sorry, man. That woman would eat you alive, spit you out, and use your bones for toothpicks."

A huff of laughter fell from my lips as I nodded. "He's right, Mooney. Save your efforts for someone else."

Cash grumbled out something unintelligible under his breath, but I didn't have time to make any sense of it. A soft, feminine voice rang out from behind me. "Ryder, how come I have to hear from Miss Muriel that you're dating someone?"

I turned, coming face to face with a pretty, middle-age woman with long raven-colored hair braided down her back in a single plait. She had a deep, coppery skin tone that contrasted well to the ornate pieces of turquoise she wore around her neck and wrists. Her eyes were like twin pools of the blackest night. I'd know who she was from those eyes alone.

My heart clenched in my chest, a trickle of panic coiling tight in my stomach. Ryder's mother. And, Oh god, not just Ryder's mother, but his father as well. Even without the Sheriff uniform on, Ryder's father had this…air about him. He was a man who commanded respect with nothing more than his presence.

And while Ryder definitely had some of his mother in him, the resemblance between father and son was uncanny. Panic welled in me like a rising tide as I snuck a quick glance up at Ryder.

He didn't meet my gaze as he spoke, but he did pull me a little tighter to his side. "Mom, Dad, this is Charlie Evans," he said, his rough voice soothing some of the anxiety in me. He glanced down, finally meeting my gaze. "Miss Charlotte, these are my parents... Lorraine and Stroker Wright."

I nearly choked on a laugh. *No way.* There was no. Fucking. Way his father's name was Stroker Wright. I hid my laughter with a smile and held out my hand. "Hello there, Mister and Mrs. Wright. Thank you for coming today. It's nice to officially meet you."

Ryder's mother offered me a soft, sad smile and nodded her head. "We're very sorry for your loss. And you can call me Lori. Lorainne was my great aunt's name." Her voice was melodic, nearly as soothing as the scent of lavender that floated on the breeze. She looked between Ryder and I, and while I knew her mind raced and she was silently assessing what to say, I didn't feel any judgement. At least, none compared to my mother.

"So, what brought you two together? How long has this been going on?" Lori pressed a hand to her lips and let out a soft chuckle. "I'm sorry. I just...I have so many questions. Ryder hasn't had a girlfriend...in...well, a very long time."

Ryder's father spoke for the first time then, his voice deep, yet also smooth like silk. A shiver traversed my spine when his hard, amber gaze slid over me before landing on Ryder. "You finally thinkin' of settlin' down, huh?"

Ryder tensed. When I flicked a quick glance up at him, his stony gaze was trained on his father. His jaw feathered as he clenched it shut. I'd noticed when he was really focused or frustrated, he did this thing where he jutted his bottom jaw out slightly. He did it now. Dear God, he was pissed. And while Mister Wright hadn't been anywhere near as cold or judgy as my mother, I understood Ryder's anger from our past conversations. I leaned into Ryder and weaved my fingers through his before giving them a reassuring squeeze.

When he finally spoke to his parents, I didn't miss the warning in his voice. "Mom, Dad…maybe now's not the time for all these questions. Today ain't about that."

Lori's face fell into a mask of guilt before she aimed an apologetic smile my way. "Oh, right. I'm so sorry. Y'all should come over for dinner this weekend then!" She'd looked at her husband, then back at me. "We'd love to learn more about you, Charlotte. Ryder tends to be very…secretive with his girlfriends."

I opened my mouth to reply, but Ryder cut me off. "Can't this weekend. I got Austin, remember?" There was an edge to his voice I'd never heard before. A guarded expression in his gaze, on his face, that I wasn't used to. My heart went out to him. I knew what it felt like to be in his shoes.

Lori nodded, her lips pulling up into a smile. "Oh, how could I have forgotten? Maybe after it's done?"

Ryder nodded, and I took the opportunity to speak. "That sounds lovely. Thank you so much for the invite."

Her lips pulled wider. "We should probably get going, but I look forward to getting to know you more."

Mister Wright met my gaze one last time. "Yes, I'm looking forward to it."

I couldn't help but feel like the next time I saw them would be more of an interrogation than anything else, but I smiled anyway and thanked them for coming. When they'd left, I pulled out of Ryder's grip, an impish smile tugging on my lips.

"Your dad's name is Stroker Wright? Like…stroke her right?" I erupted into a fit of immature giggles.

The unfamiliar darkness coating Ryder's features withered away like ash in the next instant, a smirk quirking in the corner of his mouth. "It ain't like that. My grandparents named him after a character from a novel from the seventies."

"Oh, *sure*," I replied with a chuckle. "It has nothing to do with that amazing little innuendo."

Ryder raised his hands in an innocent gesture. "Hey, that's what they told me."

I looked at Mav and Cash, who'd been surprisingly quiet since Ryder's parents' arrival. "What do you guys think? Does that sound like a bunch of bullshit? There's no way that Stroker came from a book."

Cash's lips pulled up into a familiar, mischievous grin. "Well, it depends what kinda book…"

I burst out laughing so hard I doubled over. Maverick even joined me with a deep chuckle. But my confidence shattered as Cash hooked an arm around my shoulders. "Speakin' of Wright, Charlie girl… how'd our boy perform last night?"

My cheeks heated—burned actually. In fact, I wouldn't be surprised if someone had lit a match inside me and coated me in kerosene. My mouth popped open and closed like a fucking fish, fumbling for something to say. My gaze landed on Ryder's, the midnight depths dancing with amusement. That smirk widened on his lips, forcing his scar to whiten on his cheek.

"Dear God, Mooney!" I finally got out as I spun out of his grip and landed a playful slap to his shoulder. "You're fucking horrible!"

Cash's hands came up in a plea for peace, his laughter infectious. Even Maverick laughed. Not just one of his low chuckles. There was real mirth in the deep baritone of his laugh.

"Well, did he live up to his namesake?" Maverick asked, surprising the hell out of me.

"Maverick!" I pegged him with a wide stare. "You too?" Of all of them, I expected him to be the most respectable. But I guess boys would be boys in some cases. He just shrugged, laughing some more.

I shook my head and giggled. "I'm not the type to kiss and tell."

"Aw! Come on," Cash replied. "It's a simple question, really. We know y'all have been headin' that way for a while now."

Placing my hands on my hips, I looked Ryder. "You gonna stop them?" I tried to keep my voice stern, serious, even as a smile flitted across my lips.

"Alright, alright. Leave the poor girl alone." Ryder waved them off and pulled me in close. His lips brushed against my ear, his voice a low, husky whisper. "Well, did I, Miss Charlotte?"

Even now, in the middle of a public place, with people all around and looking at us, desire ignited in me like a sparkler. It took everything in me to not wrap my arms around his neck, crush my body to his, and kiss him till my lungs screamed for air.

I settled for a single kiss. Intense in its simplicity.

When Ryder broke the kiss, he pulled away only enough to look down at me and brush my hair off my face before cupping my cheeks. "You did good today, darlin'. I'm proud of you."

His words both warmed and froze me in place. A perfect paradox. For in that moment, I remembered why all these people were here—who today was about. This wasn't just some party. This wasn't a wedding or a baby shower. Today was about Sheldon. No matter how pretty the venue was. No matter how delicious the food, or extravagant the party, this was a memorial. And for a minute, I'd forgotten.

God, was I really acting like this at my sister's memorial? Guilt washed through me so thoroughly I thought I might lose my balance.

An invisible force seared in my back, right between my shoulder blades. I recognized that feeling from the years and years of judgement I'd received. Mama's gaze was like a laser, scorching in its intensity. I pulled out of Ryder's grip, turning slowly to meet it clear across the way. Her accusatory glare was cold and sharp enough that it cut to the bone. The pure loathing in her eyes told me everything I needed to know.

I was terrible. A terrible sister. A terrible daughter…. And I would never live it down.

CHAPTER THIRTY-TWO

More Surprised Than Me

RYDER

I WASN'T ONE TO usually get nervous. In fact, I'd always been the one everyone turned to in a panic. Always the one able to keep a level-head. But Saturday morning I was a jittery, anxious fool. Between the first round of Austin in just a few hours and Charlie's ebbing and flowing grief, I was wound tight and ready to explode.

She'd gone back and forth over the last six days between seeming perfectly fine, to falling apart at the slightest provocation. I'd never lost anyone before, not really, but I could only imagine the toll it would take emotionally. Then add in the rodeo, and well, I guess it was no wonder she was a wreck.

She didn't stay down for long though; I'd give her that. She was strong. She never came apart when Cason was around, or when he lashed out for any number of reasons. She always waited til he was gone or asleep, letting the sobs consume her for a few moments before wiping her tears away and going about her business.

"What are you doin'?" A rough, brusque voice drew me from my thoughts.

I whipped around to find Bad Mooney framed in the doorway of the trailer, demolishing a bag of Skittles. What the hell *had* I been doin'? I glanced around the coffin-like space of the trailer's tack room trying to remember why I'd come in here.

"Just makin' sure I got everythin' I need." Not really a lie, I guess. Why had I come *here,* specifically?

Bad's hazel eyes narrowed in suspicion. "You okay, boy?" he asked, shoveling a handful of Skittles into his mouth and chomping on them as if they owed him money.

"I'm fine." I frowned. "Are you supposed to be eating those?" I reached towards the bag to try and snag one. Mrs. Mooney had put him on rations—according to him—after finding out he was pre-diabetic. Bad hadn't had any plans on changing his life now, though, at nearly seventy years old.

His brows furrowed as he snatched the candy away from me. "Never you mind what I'm supposed or ain't supposed to be doin', boy. If you're done jerkin' off or whatever it is, you want to get the hell out of there so we can get goin'?" His gaze was hard, unreadable. Typical Bad Mooney.

"It's Cash that jerks off before a rodeo." I flashed him a smile I didn't feel. Not when it felt like a freight train sat on my chest.

"Cash jerks off before he does *anything.*" Bad chuckled, rolling his eyes. "Even jerks off before he jerks off. Smartest thing he does… But I ain't askin' about Cash, I'm askin' about you."

I couldn't help but laugh at that. "I assure you, I ain't jerkin' off in here," I said, trying to push past him out the doorway, but he didn't move.

"Didn't think you was. What's wrong?" One of his brows rose in question, disappearing beneath the brim of his cowboy hat.

"Nothing's wrong!" I felt my cheeks flush as my temper surged…for some reason. What was I doing? Snapping at Bad Mooney was like trying to fight a lightning storm with a golf club—you looked stupid and you were probably going to die. "Just nervous is all."

"You don't *get* nervous," he pointed out, completely unfazed by my outburst, even going so far as to lean against the doorframe.

"That's right." I nodded, as if to prove my point. "So, I guess it's nothing."

Tell that to my head…my heart though. Charlie had agreed to come to Austin, she'd wanted to even. To my complete and utter surprise. And while I was excited as hell to have her here with me, I knew she was nervous, and I wished like hell I could figure out a way to ease her fears.

"It's somethin' alright." He grunted around a mouthful of Skittles. "And that somethin's got a pretty face and an armful of tattoos."

"So? What if I don't want to talk about it?" I snapped again. "Private stuff."

"Ain't no private stuff in a rodeo arena." His tan, weathered face was passive still, but a storm brewed in his eyes. "Everyone can see everythin' all the time. 'Specially if they know what they're lookin' at."

I pulled off my ball cap and ran a hand through my hair. Fuck. Was it that damn obvious? Maybe…probably, but Bad always had a way of knowing when something was up. I sucked in a deep breath and sighed. "I don't know what to do or say to make her feel better about this."

He didn't play dumb or make a joke. He just stared at me like a cow dog starin' down a herd of Herefords. "Can't make her feel better," he grumbled before turning away, leaving me standing, mouth agape in the trailer.

I frowned, his words striking a chord of annoyance within me. Damn him and his vague fucking riddles. "What does that mean?" I demanded, stepping out into the sunlight.

He didn't stop as he called over his shoulder with a shrug, "Means you can't make her feel better."

I fisted a hand at my side, running my tongue over my teeth even as I glared at his back as he walked away. "So, what do I do?" I finally called after him.

"Win the fuckin' rodeo," he called over his shoulder.

"What does that have to do with Charlie?" I shouted, raising my arms up in a questioning gesture before letting them fall to my sides in defeat.

Lost. I never felt so damn lost in my life. It's like I was adrift at sea. No land in sight. I'd never been more sure about two things in my life than I was about rodeoing and Charlie Evans. But trying to bring them together…? It was like fire and ice. Kerosene and a lighter.

Bad spun on his heel and covered the distance between us with deceptive speed. The bastard was old, but he was fast. He got right in my face and stared me down. Eye to eye like a cuttin' horse. "What's Charlie got to do with you winnin' tomorrow?" he asked, his breath smelling like a rainbow.

"Nothin'." I shook my head, frustration snaking through my muscles until they clenched tightly. A muscle in my jaw ticked as I ground out, "What's your point?"

"She can't ride those bulls for ya. Can't take down them steers. Can't warm up your horse, can't make sure your gear's good to go. All she can do is watch you ride and pray and cheer for you louder than anyone else. And you can't tell her how to feel about you ridin'. Can't do nothin' but show her how good you are, be understandin' when she gets scared, and always come back home to her."

"What if that ain't enough?" I huffed. "What if she can't get over it? What if she tries to leave?"

"Then you make a choice." He shrugged. "Rodeo or the girl."

"Why can't I have both?" I bunched my hat up in my hands, curling the bill in on itself as anger rippled through me. Fuck. I wanted to hit something. *Something* to ease the sense of helplessness I felt. I hated this. Absolutely fucking hated this feeling.

I was pretty handy. There weren't many things I couldn't fix. But this…I didn't know what the hell to do. And it ate at me.

"Which is more important?" Bad asked, his hazel eyes pinning me in place.

I ground my teeth together. "They're both important. The Rodeo's now, she's the future."

"So put your cowboy hat on straight, put your fuckin' chaps on, and get your head in the game. Win this shit so you're one step closer to that ranch you boys are always on about. Or scratch. Quit. Those are your options." He took a step back and regarded me.

"I ain't scratchin'...and I ain't gonna let her go." I took a deep breath, letting all of my pent-up anger out on the exhale. Bad was right. There wasn't a thing I could say to ease her fears. "That only leaves one thing to do."

A smug grin sliced the old man's lips as he nodded. "Win the whole. Fucking. Thing." He emptied the Skittles into his mouth, continuing to grin around them like a schoolboy. "Go get Cash and Mav and let's get this shit goin'."

"I wanted some of those Skittles," I replied with a mock frown as we walked toward the show barn.

"Grow up," he growled. "Candy's for champions. And I already won all my buckles. It's game time."

He left me standing there, whistling some old cowboy tune as he stalked away. Bad was right, there was nothing I could say to change Charlie's mind...but I could show her.

I looked to the trailer tack room once more, determined to figure out what I'd been looking for. It hit me like a lightbulb turning on. My gear bag. *That's right.* Grabbing it quickly, I made my way back over toward the stalls where mine, Cash, and Maverick's horses were being kept.

CHARLIE AND CASON WERE in the process of brushing out Boone, while Maverick and Cash worked on readying their own horses. I couldn't help but watch her for a moment in awe. Everything about this had to be terrifying for her. Knowing what she was getting Boone ready for. Knowing that I was competing in the same event her dad had. And despite that terror, despite what she'd seen and been through, she was here, supporting me. Helping me.

She'd mentioned a lot in the last few days how she didn't deserve me, but that was a lie. It was the other way around.

As if sensing my presence, she turned, that storm cloud gaze landing on me. Her brows furrowed as she paused in brushing out my horse's tail. "You okay?" she asked.

I summoned a smile to my lips, but from the way her gaze narrowed, it hadn't been convincing. She placed a hand on her hip, tilting her head to the side. "What's wrong?"

I ignored Maverick and Cash's gazes aimed at us. Even Cason poked his head around the front of Boone's chest to see what was going on. I strode over to Charlie and drew her into my arms for a moment. "Nothin', Miss Charlotte. Y'all didn't need to get ready Boone for me."

She shrugged, snaking an arm around my neck. "We didn't know where you were, and Mav and Cash were getting their horses ready so we figured we'd just help."

I kissed her softly, hoping, praying that she understood just how much it meant to me. I'd never had a girlfriend be involved in anything behind the scenes of my rodeoing.

This was new. This was nice. This was terrifying. How perfect it all seemed. She was like a missing puzzle piece. Fitting in perfectly to my life. Everything about this—the feel of her in my arms, the sight of her and Cason being here… It was perfect. Nothing had ever felt so right.

And I was terrified to mess that up.

Despite Bad's words, a trickle of fear shot through me, spearing straight for my heart.

Charlie pulled away and looked up at me, her eyes searching. "Are you sure you're okay?"

I cupped her face in my calloused hands, reveling in the feel of her soft warmth. Leaning my forehead against hers, I nodded. "I am now."

"Can I get a good luck kiss too, Charlie girl?" Cash called from a stall over.

I sighed heavily, turning to glare at him. He pulled his polarized sunglasses—neon blue today—down to wink at me, his trademark grin on his lips.

Charlie laughed and flipped him off, her black manicured nails glinting in the dim barn lighting.

Cash's grin somehow pulled wider, a bellow of laughter escaping him. Even Maverick grinned from his spot beside Black Betty. "Don't tempt me with a good time!" Cash warned.

"Ooh!" Cason's little voice drew my gaze. "Auntie Charlotte, that's not nice to flip people off!"

Charlie's mouth popped open, a little gasp escaping her. "But he…what?" Her words fell away into nothingness before she sighed. "I give up."

"Yeah, you tell her, little dude!" Cash said, moving to grab his saddle pad and place it on Playboy's back.

I shook my head, a genuine smile drawing on my lips. "You're an idiot," I huffed. I looked down at Charlie again and stole one more kiss before letting her go.

I buried the fear, the worry, deep within me. There was no room for it. Not tonight.

With newfound confidence, I started tacking up Boone.

CHAPTER THIRTY-THREE

Cause He's A Cowboy

CHARLIE

BEING AT THE RODEO grounds, doing all the behind-the-scenes things, was like taking a step back in time. I'd always begged Daddy to bring me along, to which he'd happily oblige. Watching the boys warm up their horses, stretch and check their gear, and suit up was both oddly comforting and terrifying.

I hated that every moment here watching Ryder was tainted with my haunted past. I hated that I couldn't enjoy this fully. Because a part of me—a larger part than I anticipated—loved this. Loved everything about the rodeo and what it stood for. I especially loved how happy Cason was. I don't think he'd stopped grinning since he'd woken up this morning in the RV with Maverick, Cash, Ryder, and I.

And yet, despite the happiness clawing for dominance in my chest, fear roiled and reared its ugly head at every turn. I'd not missed the way Ryder looked when he'd first come into the barn. Haunted. Haunted and worried. I didn't need to guess too hard to know he was worried about me. Here he was, the one competing, the one risking his life, and his main concern was me.

I felt so guilty for how insecure I was. But I wouldn't be. Not anymore. I *had* to get over this. I *had* to deal with this trauma. I *had* to heal from it. Ten years was far past time.

And Ryder meant too much to me to let him go because of this.

I owed it to him to at least try. After everything he'd done for me…it was the least I could do.

Cason and I sat at the picnic table outside the group of trailers and RVs we were staying in. Mr. Mooney smoked his pipe in a camping chair a few feet away, his boots propped up on the edge of the table. He'd traded his stained white t-shirt and holey jeans for a red long-sleeved dress shirt with an embroidered design on it claiming him the PRCA Champion of 1995 for the Saddle Bronc event. His black starched Wrangler jeans were the same color as his felt hat, a hawk feather tucked into the ornate leather hatband. And gleaming from his waist was one of his prize buckles shined to perfection.

Amazing what difference clothes could make. Dressed up like this, it was no surprise that him and Cash were father and son. The attractive resemblance was there.

I glanced up as the RV door to my left creaked open, finding Mrs. Mooney dressed up in a flashy western ensemble. It was no wonder where Cash got his over-the-top fashion tendencies. Mrs. Mooney wore a turquoise and black rhinestone accented western shirt and black high-waisted Wranglers tucked into black and turquoise ac-cented cowboy boots. Atop her head sat a bright turquoise cowboy hat, obsidian and…you guessed it, turquoise stones glistening from the hatband. Looped around her hips was a blue and black leather gun belt bedecked in more matching rhinestones, her revolver tucked into the holster on her right hip. Slung over her left shoulder was a small dog purse, her little chihuahua, Bodacious, trembling from his equally bedecked carrier.

"Dear Lord, Violet," Mr. Mooney grumbled, nearly choking on a plume of smoke. "You're not wearin' that gun in there."

Mrs. Mooney's lips pulled up into a smirk, her eyes twinkling. "Oh, don't be such a baby, it ain't loaded. It just matched perfectly."

I bit back a laugh. Mrs. Mooney and her guns…and that dog. I'd quickly learned she never went anywhere without either of them.

Looking over at the second RV for yet the umpteenth time, I sighed. We only had thirty minutes until the opening ceremony. What the hell were the boys doing? And how was it that Mrs. Mooney and I were ready before them?

I huffed. *And they said girls took forever to get ready.*

"Where are them boys?" Mrs. Mooney said with a scowl.

"Probably circle jerkin'," Mr. Mooney chuckled.

My eyes bulged, and I choked on the air in my lungs as I fell into a coughing fit.

Mrs. Mooney smacked the back of her husband's head, nearly tipping his hat clean off. "Clint Mooney, you watch your mouth! There are children present," she said, her voice ringing with violence. Mr. Mooney grumbled something back at her, but Cason's words drowned out whatever it was.

"Auntie Charlotte, what's circle–"

"I'm—" I dissolved into another fit of coughs "—gonna check on the boys."

Dear God. Mr. Mooney was just as bad as his son. If there was ever a doubt of them being related, just listen to the way they talked. They were just as foulmouthed and crass as the other.

I'd finally stopped coughing by the time I reached the steps of the RV. It burst open with none other than Cash, himself, first.

"Woo! Big Daddy's ready to rodeo!" He descended the three steps with his thumbs tucked into his belt loops. I took a step back, my mouth popping open as I took him in… In all his untamed, rhinestone glory.

Cash Mooney literally sparkled. Rhinestones… There were so. Many. Damn. Rhinestones. On his highlighter blue shirt, on his matching chaps, even down to his turquoise hat band on his white felt hat. He was more glitzed up than a damn rodeo queen. Probably prettier too, if I was being honest. Despite his obnoxious attire, there was no ignoring how attractive he was. And with that charming grin on his lips and a devilish look in his eyes…I felt bad for whatever woman he met tonight. They'd never stand a chance.

Ryder came next, with Maverick in tow—the two of them looking much more toned down than their bedazzled best friend with their black shirts and matching felt hats. But Ryder's chaps were mostly white with black and red fringe, while Mav's were all black. They both wore gleaming belt buckles as well. I couldn't read what they said, but there was no doubt at all that they'd won them. Those were prize buckles if I'd ever seen them. All of the spurs clinked as they moved.

"How is it that I'm ready before all three of you?" I asked, crossing my arms over my chest. "I had to curl my hair, do my makeup, *and* get Cason ready in the time it took you three to finish up."

Cash's suave, buttery smooth voice caught my attention. "Ya can't rush beauty, Charlie girl."

I rolled my eyes before turning back to Ryder. "We have thirty minutes…no, less now, to get over to the opening ceremony. We need to go."

Ryder's lips curled up into a ghost of a smirk. The worry in his gaze had vanished, only a quiet confidence glowing in the dark depths. Everything about him was relaxed as he winked at me. "Don't worry, Miss Charlotte. We're almost ready."

I cocked my head to the side. "Almost?"

His lips tugged wider and he revealed a box from behind his back I hadn't noticed. He pressed a quick kiss to my forehead before moving past me and toward Cason. He, Cash, and Maverick all stopped before him, Ryder handing him the box and saying, "A cowboy ain't nothin' without his hat."

Cason let out an excited whoop, and my heart constricted, tears springing to life in my eyes. Ryder did the honors of crouching down to settle the hat onto Cason's head. I clutched a hand over my chest, my lips pulling up into a smile.

Cason looked adorable in his little white straw hat, the grin on his face positively infectious as he turned to me. "Auntie Charlotte, does it look good?"

I beamed, closing the distance to him and the boys. "You're the most handsomest cowboy I've ever seen."

"Hey!" Cash grumped. "What about me?"

"You don't need a bigger head than you already have, Mooney. You might float away altogether," I replied with a wink aimed his way.

He shrugged and let out a chuckle.

Ryder snagged my attention, pulling me into his arms. "I thought I was the most handsome," he whispered, the sound a husky rumble in my ear.

"Is someone feeling insecure?" I grinned up at him.

"Maybe." He smirked.

I leaned up on tiptoe and kissed him, answering without words. Pulling away, I said, "Come on, we're going to be late."

I DON'T KNOW WHAT was different about tonight's rodeo from the previous one. Maybe it was the fact that Mr. and Mrs.

Mooney were here, helping me feel grounded and comfortable, or maybe it was the fact that I'd just fallen *that* hard for Ryder, but my anxiety didn't grip me quite so hard tonight.

Oh, it was still there. Creeping beneath the surface, slithering lazily around my heart, my stomach, but it didn't constrict or squeeze the very breath from my lungs. At least not yet.

After the opening ceremony, Cash had gone first in the Bareback Bronc event and won second place with his score. From the way Mr. Mooney talked to the boys at the ranch, I'd have thought he'd have had more to say to Cash after his run, but he'd just nodded as he passed by us and said, '*there's always tomorrow.*'

My nerves started winding tighter as they announced the Steer Wrestling event. I paced in the box we sat in right up against the arena—a perk of coming with the Mooneys. Cason shoveled popcorn into his mouth, eyes glued to the chutes as they loaded the first steer into it. I couldn't even think about eating right now. Not as I watched the first rider ready himself and his horse in the box.

"You keep walkin' like that, and you're gonna walk a hole in the floor, girl." Mr. Mooney's gruff voice drew my gaze for but a second.

Blowing out a sigh, I came to a stop and settled my arms on top of the highest rail of pipe-stall. "Sorry," I grumbled. "I can't sit still."

Boots shuffled against the metal ground of the box, and a moment later Mr. Mooney came to my side, mirroring my stance. He smelled like aftershave, leather, and the sweet smell of tobacco. He started talking then. Not about anything in particular. He mostly just commentated on every little thing the riders were doing with each run. Why they scored the way they did, why they were penalized points. Whether or not it was a shit steer or a shit run from the rider. He just…talked. Which was oddly soothing. By the time Ryder's name was called out by the announcer, my heart didn't thump so wildly in my chest.

Ryder made his way into the box atop Boone, his face a mask of pure concentration. His gaze met mine for a brief moment. I sucked in a deep breath, trying to get some air in my lungs, and offered him what I hoped was a reassuring smile. The sound of my blood rushing through my ears nearly drowned out Mr. Mooney's voice, but still he talked, for which I was eternally grateful.

The chute opened with the slamming of metal, and then that steer tore off across the arena, Ryder and Boone right on its heels. Where we stood was so close, I could feel each of Boone's hoof beats; they reverberated through every inch of me, through my very soul. Ryder came up on the steer's side and then he was sliding out of the saddle, his arms wrapping around the cow's horns.

My chest constricted, all of the air leaving me. I gripped Mr. Mooney's arm on instinct, squeezing, squeezing, squeezing. He continued his hushed rambling, even as he patted my hand with his weathered, calloused one. Ryder landed, his boots digging into the deep dirt of the arena as he and the steer came to a halt.

Everything was clean up until then.

But for whatever reason, the steer just wouldn't go down. It fought and struggled against Ryder. It was only a matter of seconds, but those few seconds felt like a lifetime. By the time he got the cow to the ground and settled, the buzzer sounded at twelve seconds.

A crap run, but at least he had a time. Three of the other guys didn't even score.

Ryder got up, retrieving his hat that had fallen off at some point, anger permeating from him so thick and hot I could practically feel it. Fury blazed in his eyes as he brushed off his hat and slammed it on his head before grabbing Boone, who stood waiting nearby.

"He looks pissed," I said.

Mr. Mooney let out a deep sigh and shook his head. "Yep… He don't do too well with losing."

I understood. I hated losing too. At least for me, when I'd lost in competitions at cheer, it was a collective loss as a team. Ryder didn't have that luxury.

His anger stayed with him throughout the rest of the events. Throughout Team Roping, where Cash and Maverick came in first for the event. Even as Bull Riding was announced, I could see clear across the arena how his silent fury ate at him.

I'd started pacing again the minute they began loading bulls into the chutes.

"Boy's fuckin' up already," Mr. Mooney grumbled at my side once more. He'd remained standing the duration of the events. Right by my side to ease any fears. The last person I expected to be accommodating or reassuring was Mr. Mooney. I still half expected him to tell me to suck it up or get out of the arena.

"How so?" I asked. "Because he's angry?"

Mr. Mooney nodded. "He don't know when to let shit go. That's the problem with him doing two events. If he fucks up in one, he typically fucks up in the other."

"Clint, words!" Mrs. Mooney growled from her seat a couple feet away from us. Cason sat beside her, feeding Bodacious stray pieces of popcorn. The three-pound chihuahua only seemed to like him and Mrs. Mooney. He wouldn't even let me near him. I couldn't say I was too sad about it.

Mr. Mooney just shrugged and chuckled before fixing his hazel gaze back on the arena.

"You probably think I'm ridiculous, don't you?" I asked, needing to fill the silent void that descended over me despite the music blaring from the speaker system and the crowd's constant chatter as the final event was readied.

Mr. Mooney turned to look at me. "Why?"

"For being so nervous…so anxious."

Mr. Mooney shrugged again without glancing my way. "We all deal with shit differently. Just look at the boys losing, for example. Ryder gets quiet, gets angry. He don't like feeling out of control. Cash…well, when Cash loses, he goes absolutely ballistic. It's like a damn bomb went off. But once the initial explosion's over, he fizzles out quick and is back to his dumbass self. Maverick…Maverick just might deal with loss the best of all…poor kid. When he loses, he becomes more determined. He's reflective, finds out what he did wrong then fixes the behavior and pushes through."

"So, you're saying be like Maverick?" I glanced over at him.

Mr. Mooney's eyes crinkled in the corners, accentuating his crow's feet, his lips pulling up into the smallest, softest smile as he let out a low chuckle. "Everyone could learn somethin' from that boy, if they only took the time to watch and listen." He turned to face me more fully. "But I ain't sayin' that. Everyone's different. No one's gone through your shit but you. Run your own race. Worry 'bout yourself and conquering your own demons."

I blew out a breath and faced the arena again. Mr. Mooney might have the foulest mouth I'd ever heard, but he was wise. I wondered if Daddy would have been like him. My heart squeezed in my chest. I missed him. I wished I could talk to him. Would he like Ryder? *Probably*.

I shook the thoughts from my mind. Why was I doing this to myself?

"What happened to Maverick?" I asked, watching the chutes as cowboys bustled around between the pipe-stall. I spotted Cash amongst the fray first—at least those rhinestones were good for something—then found Ryder and Maverick soon after.

"That ain't my story to tell." Mr. Mooney's words rang with finality. As if to punctuate it, the announcer's voice blared through the speakers, introducing the first rider.

He and I fell into the same rhythm as the Steer Wrestling event. He provided a constant stream of conversation. Nothing that required me to answer back, though I managed to ask a couple questions about a rider's score now and then.

Ryder was the last of the competitors to go in the first round. And while my heart hammered in my ribcage, so hard I was surprised I hadn't cracked a damn rib, I felt a rush of excitement as he settled onto the bull's back in the chute. The beast thrashed around behind the gate as he got ready.

I sucked in a shaky breath. I wasn't the most religious person, but I'd be lying if I said I didn't pray like hell that nothing happened to him. Time and sound seemed to stop and fade when that gate burst open. It was like watching him through a slow-motion lens. Each buck or spin or shake of the bull felt like an eternity, the seconds ticking by at an impossibly slow rate.

My hand found Mr. Mooney's arm once more as I tried to focus on my breathing. I was terrified, completely petrified for Ryder, but even I couldn't help but watch him in awe. The way he rode, the way he moved... He was impressive. Beyond impressive, really. And yet I couldn't quiet that little, intrusive voice in the back of my mind whispering his demise.

Don't let him get hurt. Don't let him get hurt. Don't let him get—

The blaring buzzer brought everything—sound, speed—rushing back to normal. He let go of the bull rope, managing to slip off the bull's back while still landing on his feet. He ripped off his hat and held it in the air, his dark gaze settling on mine.

My heart fluttered in my ribcage for a completely different reason than a few moments ago. God, he was hot. And talented. And he was mine.

A swell of pride surged through me…and with that hope. Maybe I *could* do this. Maybe we could make this work. No… We *would* make this work. I cared about him too much to let him go. Would all nights be as good as this? No, likely not. But I wouldn't focus on the what ifs or the could be's. It had to be just the here and now. One day at a time. One rodeo at a time.

A squeal of excitement escaped me as I squeezed Mr. Mooney's arm. "He did it!" I cheered.

Mr. Mooney nodded, a satisfied smirk toying on his lips. "Well, damn. Kid proved me wrong."

Chapter Thirty-Four

No Cure

Ryder

THAT RIDE SHOULD HAVE been cause for celebration. That, and the fact Charlie had flung herself into my arms the minute the rodeo had ended and whispered, '*I'm so fucking proud of you,*' should have been enough to rid me of my shit mood. But despite all that, despite the fact I was about four beers in, my blood boiled at the mere thought of my shitty run.

Still in my rodeo getup, I sulked in one of the chairs between the RV's. No one else seemed to share in my misery. Why would they? Cash won an event and got second in the other. Maverick had done excellent, as always. Sure, I'd gotten top standing for the night in Bull Riding, but that damn run. I'd have probably been better off scratching at that point. *Twelve seconds.*

I pressed my beer to my lips once more, glaring at the ground as I ignored everyone's blissful happiness. Something snaked around my waist before pulling tight, nearly knocking my drink out of my hand.

"Uncle Ryder, come play!"

I whipped around in my seat, gaze landing on Cason holding a play rope in his hands. Cash and Mr. Mooney laughed from behind him. Maverick stood off to the side with Charlie, both of them smiling and talking quietly.

"God damn it, Cason!" I snapped on instinct, surging up out of my chair.

Fear and uncertainty flashed in his big blue eyes. He shrank back against Cash, tears brewing like a storm on the horizon. My anger shattered into a million pieces as guilt replaced it.

Charlie stomped over to me, her gaze hard, angry. "Um, no. Do *not* be mean to him just because you're pissed off."

I sighed, tilting my head up to the sky and pinching the bridge of my nose. "I know," I mumbled. "I'm sorry."

"Don't tell me." She huffed, placing a hand on her hip as she pointed Cason's way with the other. "Tell him."

I nodded and moved to stand before Cason, half hiding behind Cash. "Hey, bud."

Cason sniffled and struggled to meet my stare. "I'm s-sorry for upsetting y-y-you."

My chest squeezed. Well, damn. With a sigh, I placed a hand on his shoulder. "No, no. You don't need to apologize, bud. I'm the one who needs to. I'm just upset and snapped. I'm sorry."

Another sniffle. "But you won. Why are you mad?"

I blew out a breath and shrugged. How could I explain to him and make him understand? Make him see that it didn't matter if I won in one event. I needed to be perfect. Nothing else was acceptable. Growing up, my dad always said, '*If you're gonna do something, you give it your all. More than your all. Nothing's worth doing half-assed.*'

He already didn't want me rodeoing, so the only way I could justify doing this was to go out and perform perfectly. Anything short of that wasn't acceptable. Not in my book.

But Cason wouldn't understand that…he was five. I forced my lips up into a soft smile. "I just wish I would have done better."

He surprised the hell out of me by wrapping his arms around my neck. "It's okay, Uncle Ryder. You'll get it tomorrow night."

"Thanks, bud." I gave him a reassuring squeeze back, guilt still roaring in my ears.

I needed to get out of here. I'd yelled at him for nothing. For being a kid. No one needed my shit attitude. Best to just leave and let everyone else enjoy the rest of the night. Standing, I looked at Cash and Mav, before settling on Charlie. Her gaze still swirled with uncertainty, but the anger was gone at least.

"I think I'm gonna head out for a bit. Need to clear my head," I said, ignoring the tightness in my chest snaking its way around my heart. She'd come all the way up here to be with me, and here I was, going off on my own.

Charlie was nothing if not stubborn. One of her delicate brows rose, her gaze flickering with silent challenge. She crossed her arms over her chest, and God, if I weren't in such a shit mood, I'd pull her behind one of the trailers right then and there. "The fuck you are," she countered, pegging me in place with her scalding stare.

"I'll be fine. I ain't dumb enough to drive," I replied.

She frowned. "What're you gonna do? Ride Boone down to the bar?" she huffed a bitter laugh.

I smirked. I'd done that once… Not here, but Cash and I had done it back in town on more than one occasion. "I'll walk. The bar ain't that far."

Charlie rolled her eyes but sighed after a minute. "If that's what you need to do, then fine."

I bit back a laugh. I wasn't an idiot. It was most assuredly *not* fine, but between the alcohol and my mood, I didn't want to stick around and end up getting in a fight.

I walked over to her and kissed her forehead. "I'm sorry, Miss Charlotte. Just give me some time, okay? I don't wanna fight."

The rage fizzled out in her stare, her stance, even as worry took its place. "Ryder…" My name was little more than a defeated whisper on her lips.

I wanted nothing more than to reassure her. To ease her worries. To be her stronghold like I had over this last week. But I couldn't. Not right now. "I'm sorry," I murmured against her forehead before walking away.

I didn't turn back or meet anyone's gazes, not wanting to see the disappointment lingering there. Hanging my head low, I stalked for the nearest bar.

CHAPTER THIRTY-FIVE

Trouble

CHARLIE

"WE'RE NOT JUST GOING to let him go off on his own, right?" I asked once Ryder had disappeared into the night.

Cash settled into the chair Ryder had just vacated, stretching himself out while smacking his can of chew against his palm. "Eh, he'll be fine," he huffed, pinching a piece of tobacco out of the can before tucking it into his bottom lip.

Of course, Cash wouldn't have a worry in the world. I turned to Maverick beside me, my brow raising in question.

"He's always like this after a loss," he replied, rubbing the back of his neck with a hand. "Just give him some time to cool down. We'll go get him in a bit."

I frowned but let out a sigh. "Okay. I'm gonna go get Cason ready for bed."

"Aw, come on, Auntie Charlotte!" Cason muttered, coming to stand before me. "I'm not even—" His words broke off into a yawn. "—tired."

I smirked. "Sure, you aren't, bud. It's been a long day, and it's *far* past your bedtime."

He hung his head, kicking at the dirt beneath his boots as he grumbled something unintelligible under his breath. I looked at Maverick. "Make sure Ryder gets back safe, please?"

As much as I wanted to go with them, I couldn't leave Cason in the RV alone. At least it wasn't just Cash going to bring him back. I trusted Mav. He dipped his head, his light eyes holding a silent promise.

Mr. Mooney cleared his throat, reminding me of his presence. He had a way of blending into the background to the point I forgot he was even there. "Violet and I'll watch him. He can sleep on the fold-out couch."

I frowned. "Oh, I couldn't ask that of—"

He cut me off. "You didn't ask, I offered. Go find that boy of yours and knock some damn sense into him." He looked at Cason. "What say you to some of Mrs. Mooney's infamous hot cocoa and *Tombstone?*"

"What's that?" Cason asked.

"You're about to find out," Mr. Mooney winked, clapping Cason softly on the shoulder. He glanced up at me. "As long as that's alright with you and your aunt."

I smiled. "It's fine with me." Meeting Cason's gaze, I asked, "What about you, bud?"

His little face turned contemplative for a moment, but from the twinkle in his eye, I already knew his answer before he nodded.

"Alright, let's go get you showered real quick and into your pajamas, then you can go hang with Mr. and Mrs. Mooney, okay?"

Cason let out a whoop and raced for our RV.

THERE WASN'T ANYTHING PARTICULARLY special about the bar as we walked through the door. The same typical dim lighting, an overabundance of neon signs, loud music, and a couple pool tables. It was busy, which was unsurprising for a Saturday night, especially with the rodeo. But despite the crowd of people in varying stages of inebriation, my gaze found Ryder easily enough.

He sat in the middle of the bar, straight ahead of Mav, Cash, and me. He couldn't see me, but, boy, could I sure see him…and the gorgeous blonde bombshell sitting way too damn close to him, smiling as he talked.

A flare of possessive rage blazed to life in my chest.

Really? He'd said he needed some time to cool down, not flirt with a new girl. Reason warred with my emotions, the logical side of me begging the impulsive, anxious part to slow down and read the signs. Like the fact that while she was angled toward him—he remained seated straight ahead, his gaze not so much as flicking to her for a second as she talked. Or the fact that he tensed every time she placed a hand on his shoulder or arm. But I'd had a couple swigs of Cash's pre-game juice, as he liked to call it. I quickly realized it was just homemade apple pie moonshine. It smelled God-awful, but I had to admit, it was pretty damn good.

"Who the fuck is that?" I asked, the impulsive, slightly buzzed side of me winning that little battle. I didn't look at Cash or Maverick as I spoke, my heated gaze glued to Ryder and the woman at his side.

"Charlie it's not—" Maverick started, but Cash cut him off with a chuckle.

"No, let her go," Cash replied. "I want to see this play out."

I frowned and met his stare—he still wore his damn sunglasses. His lips pulled up into a mischievous grin. "What do you mean, Mooney?"

He held his hands up in a placating gesture. "Nothing, Charlie girl. I'm just looking forward to watching this play out, is all."

I should have known right then and there that something was up, but I was too angry and buzzed to care. Pushing my bangs back off my face, I let out a deep breath and strode for the bar, slipping into the free spot to Ryder's right. Placing a hand on his arm resting against the bar, I said in a low, clipped tone, "Ryder, what are you doing?"

His dark gaze met mine, wild terror shining in the depths. He stilled beneath my touch, his mouth popping open and closed once, twice, three times. But it wasn't him who spoke.

"Sweetheart, you best be on your way. He ain't in the mood for no buckle bunny." The blonde's voice was a mixture of smooth and smoky, the perfect bedroom voice. I bet the pretty bitch smoked cigarettes to get it to sound like that. *Wow, judgy much?* I didn't know this girl from Eve, but she'd struck a nerve.

Ryder spoke for the first time since my arrival, two words escaping him in a hushed whisper. "Oh fuck."

"I'm not a fucking. Buckle. Bunny," I ground out. My jaw hurt from how tightly I clenched my teeth together.

Her turquoise gaze danced with challenge, her pouty, bowtie lips pulling up into a smirk as she looked me up and down. "Coulda fooled me, sweetheart."

Every logical, people-pleasing, go-with-the-flow nerve ending in my body screamed at me to back down from this woman, even as I tilted my chin up, meeting her violent stare. "Stop calling me sweetheart. And, by the way, who the hell are you to be saying what he is or isn't in the mood for?"

"I'm his friend. So, you better back up, *sweetheart*, cuz I got a bad temper, and he's got a girlfriend," she replied, that confident smirk curling into a feral grin.

If I was completely sober, I'd have been terrified of her. She was the type of girl I always dreamed of being. Confident, dangerous, the fuck-around-and-find-out type. But between my rage, the alcohol, and the fact that Ryder still hadn't managed to say anything in my defense, I almost welcomed a fight. *No more of Cash's moonshine.* That shit was dangerous.

"I *am* his girlfriend, dipshit," I snapped, crossing my arms over my chest. Two warm presences appeared at my back. Cash and Mav—I didn't need to turn around to check.

Had I just imagined it, or did her gaze flicker for just a moment? "You're his girlfriend?"

I glared at Ryder. "Are you going to introduce me, or do I have to do that myself?"

He offered me a pleading look, but I didn't care. Removing his hat to run a hand through his hair and replace it atop his head, he let out a deep sigh. "Cheyenne Harris, this is Charlie Evans, my girlfriend. Charlie…meet Cheyenne. She's a friend of mine. She's here competin' in the rodeo."

Cheyenne's eyes widened, the fire leaving her even as the confidence remained. A ghost of a grin pulled on her lips. "Well, shit," she said, letting out a low, smoky laugh as she playfully smacked Ryder's left arm. "Why'd you let me go on like that? Now I feel like a damn idiot."

Ryder mumbled something under his breath, but it was drowned out by Cash's braying laugh.

I turned to glare at him. "You knew?"

He threw his hands up once more, wheezing with laughter. I moved on to Maverick, who offered me a guilty shrug. "I *did* try to tell you."

Blowing out a breath, I wiped a hand across my face. He did. It was the only thing keeping me from being angry at him as well. These dumb cowboys and their lack of communication. I moved behind Ryder, meeting Cheyenne's stare. "I'm sorry…I saw him and you together—which, this might be weird, but you're gorgeous, by the way—and I just…" I shrugged and sighed loudly. "I got territorial."

She moved to mirror me, a dazzling, genuine smile lighting up her face. I hadn't been lying, she was beautiful. Maybe a few inches taller than my five-foot frame, with a coke bottle figure and the prettiest blonde hair I'd ever seen—the color you saw scrolling through Instagram or Pinterest for summer hair inspiration. "You're a fiery thing. I think we're gonna get along real well."

I huffed a laugh.

Her gaze moved to the cowboys at my back. Something shifted in her then. The fire returned, that confident smirk holding a predatory grace about it. "Howdy, Cash… and hello, Maverick."

I didn't miss the way those gemstone eyes of hers flicked up and down the dark-haired cowboy's body or the way her voice dipped just a bit lower when she said his name. I didn't need to worry about her at all. She wasn't after my cowboy, or Cash, for that matter. She wanted Maverick.

And Maverick—poor, sweet, innocent, oblivious Maverick—didn't have a damn clue. Or maybe he did and he just wasn't interested. I couldn't tell with him. He kept so much of his emotions wrapped up tight. I was typically good at reading people—okay, well, minus tonight— but I couldn't ever fully read him.

"Well, now that everyone's here, let's party! Bartender!" Cheyenne whistled, drawing damn near everyone's attention in the bar. "A round of whiskey for me and my friends here, please." She winked at him for good measure, before her sights set on Maverick once more. "Who's up for a game of pool?"

After a round of shots—Maverick, as usual, kindly refused—he, Cheyenne, and Cash made their way to one of the empty pool tables. Ryder made no move to join them though, so I stayed behind.

My emotions were all over the place, thanks to the shot and moonshine. Why had he not said anything to Cheyenne when I'd first come over? Why had he let me go on like that, making a fool of myself—acting all territorial and possessive? Even though I knew there was nothing going on between him and Cheyenne—it was obvious with the way she simped for Mav—I couldn't help but be just a bit jealous. I'd wanted to be the one to make him feel better. Wanted to be the one who brought him out of whatever darkness he was fighting.

"She seems like a wild time," I said from Ryder's side, unsure of what to say.

He'd gone right back to sulking after everyone left, gaze fixed ahead at the wall of bottles lining the mirror-backed shelves. He didn't respond, only nodded.

I frowned. "What's wrong?"

"Nothing."

My gaze narrowed, and I turned to face him more fully. "Talk to me."

"Ain't in a talkin' mood, Charlie."

I stilled, white-hot anger bubbling to life in me. He had *not* just called me that. "You didn't seem to have a problem talking to Cheyenne." I regretted how low I'd gone the moment the words left my lips, but there was no taking them back now.

He pegged me with an incredulous stare for a long moment, before turning back toward the bar top. He pressed his beer to his lips and muttered, "Jealous?"

I almost said no. Almost tried to turn it around on him, but then I thought of all the fights Cal and I got into. They always started from a lack of communication. Both of us being too stubborn and not wanting to admit our faults. So, despite the fact that every inch of me seethed at how Ryder was trying to shut me out, I took a deep breath and sighed. "Yes, actually," I admitted, "I am. I'm jealous that she was the first one to make you genuinely smile tonight. I'm jealous that she got to spend time alone with you, be there for you." I sighed. "It probably seems petty and childish, but I wanted to be the one who turned your night around."

"I didn't come here looking for her. She saw me and came over to say hi." He still wouldn't look my way—which annoyed the hell out of me. It felt too eerily familiar. Too much like the start of the fights I had with Cal. I hated comparing the two of them, but, well…he wasn't really giving me an option.

"I'm not upset about that anymore," I said, pressing a hand to his arm. "I'm sorry for the way I acted. Tell me what I can do."

Ryder finally glanced my way, his eyes meeting mine for the briefest moment. They were dark and desolate, like twin black holes of nothingness. No emotion, no light, just…nothing. He heaved a deep breath, and for a moment I thought I'd gotten through to him. But then he turned forward once more. "Go with Cash and Maverick, Charlie. I ain't good company tonight."

"Damn you, Ryder!" I hissed, my anger skyrocketing once more. "What did I fucking say about calling me that? You want to be alone? Fine. You want to drink yourself stupid, be my fucking guest. But tell me one thing, at least…" My chest rose and fell in heavy, angry breaths as I stood beside him, a part of me surprised he didn't turn to ash under my scalding gaze. "Why are you so set on being miserable? So, you got a shitty score in *one* event…you still won in the other. And it's not like you scratched in steer wrestling. You've got nine more days of rodeoing to make up for that twelve-second run." He flinched at the mention of his time, but I continued on. "You and I both know that the notoriety, the money, is in bull riding, the event you fucking won in…so why are you acting like it's the end of the world?"

"Because I could have done better!" he growled, surging to stand over me, his cold, dark gaze pinning me in place. Fury—icy deep-rooted fury—lined the planes of his handsome face. "I *should* have done better."

Under normal circumstances, I'd have cowered, shut down completely, and gone to cry in the bathroom, but not tonight. My own anger, white-hot to his ice-cold, bubbled up to clash with his. "Yeah, you could have. But you didn't. So, what's sitting here, being miserable, going to do to change that?"

"Nothing," he ground out.

I placed my hands on my hips, glowering up at him as he glared back at me. "Exactly. So, stop sulking, finish your beer, hang out with us, and kick ass tomorrow to make up for today's loss."

Something shifted in his gaze for the briefest moment. My heart squeezed with hope. Yes, I'd finally gotten through to him. He removed his hat once more, running a hand through his midnight waves. But as he placed the hat back on his head, that defiant set of his jaw remained. "It ain't that simple."

I growled—legit growled at him—as I threw my hands up in the air. "You know what…? Fine. You want to sulk? Sulk." I started to walk away, but turned on my heel, pegging him with a hard glare. "You know, on the chance of sounding selfish, it took a lot for me to get through tonight, but I did it. For you. Because I care about you, because I wanted to be there and support you the way you have so fiercely supported me. I understand not wanting to lose. I understand being angry. But I don't understand why you're being a sore loser and pushing me away."

My chest squeezed, but I pushed the emotions down, down, down as I stomped off toward Cash, Mav, and Cheyenne. I probably sounded like a bitch—no, there was no probably about it—and I wouldn't be surprised if he called it off after how I'd reacted, but I couldn't bring myself to care.

chapter thirty-six

Drop

Ryder

I BLEW OUT A frustrated breath and clenched my hand in a fist as I settled back onto my barstool and watched Charlie walk away.

Damn. That hadn't gone at all like I'd thought. I hadn't meant to piss her off. Hadn't meant to make her feel insecure or jealous. I didn't want to be angry, but telling me to stop being mad was like expecting a snowstorm in the middle of a Texas summer. It just wasn't possible. It's why I'd wanted to be alone in the first place. I couldn't turn it off like the flip of a switch how Cash did. I couldn't just use it as fuel to make me more determined and resilient like Maverick. I just needed time to be mad. Time to ride that wave of self-loathing and fury until the storm died down and I could think straight. But now, not only was I still pissed about that damn run, I was pissed at the situation I was in with Charlie.

My head shouted at me to listen to her words, to chase after her and make things right, but pride was a stubborn thing. Between my anger and the half dozen beers I'd had, along with that shot of whiskey, I had no doubt my foolish pride would win out.

As I nurtured a seventh beer, my gaze kept drifting to the pool tables. It seemed Charlie and Cheyenne hit it off well enough despite that heated introduction. The two chatted easily between their turns at pool, all the while dancing and singing to the music playing from the speakers. Cash joined in as well; Maverick even seemed to be enjoying himself as he positively wrecked everyone he played pool against.

A part of me, a growing part, wanted to go over there. Charlie was right. Why was I wasting my night away alone when I could be hanging out with them? But remnants of my anger still gripped me like a vice. So stubbornly, I settled my gaze on my beer bottle, letting myself stew.

AN HOUR LATER, MAVERICK made his way toward me, Cash in tow.

"Alright," he said, his deep voice cutting through the noise of the bar. "What's goin' on?"

My head and vision swam, my words slurring slightly as I replied, "You know this is how I get. Why can't y'all just leave me be?"

Annoyance swelled in my chest. First, Charlie nagging me, and now, Maverick. I already knew I'd hear it from Bad tomorrow morning as well. Why couldn't they just leave me alone?

Maverick leveled me with a hard stare. "Because this ain't just about you anymore. You're part of something bigger than yourself now. You've got her to worry about, and she may not look like it, but she's hurtin' and worried about you. So, stop bein' selfish."

Anger rippled through me like a flash of lightning, thanks to the alcohol. "Selfish?" I growled. "That's why I came here so that she wouldn't have to see this part of me. But instead, you—" I pointed a finger at him and then at Cash "—and this asshole brought her here and set me up to look like a damn fool. You're lucky Cheyenne didn't start brawlin' with her right then and there."

Cash finally spoke up, stealing my half-drunk beer and draining it dry. "As bat-shit crazy as Cheyenne is, my bet woulda been on our Charlie girl."

I rolled my eyes but couldn't help but agree. The look in her eyes when Cheyenne called her a buckle bunny promised death. And yet, now the two of them acted like long-lost best friends.

I looked at Maverick, sighing under the weight of his stare. "My head's not in a good place right now," I tried to reason.

"And you think hers is? She's been on an emotional roller coaster all night long. Watchin' you ride, watchin' you snap at Cason and leave her in a cloud of dust. Then comin' here to find you talkin' to some girl she don't know. And even after she apologizes and tries to make it right, you still push her away."

"Jesus, Mav. Whose fuckin' side are you on?" I snapped, pushing up to stand toe to toe with him. He was taller than me by a good four inches, but I didn't care. Rage boiled in my veins.

He didn't bat an eye. "It ain't about sides, Ryder. Y'all are both hurtin'. Instead of bein' miserable apart, be the bigger person and go make her night before someone else tries to."

Cash chuckled beside me, pulling down his sunglasses. "Looks like someone's already tryin' to."

My gaze snapped to the pool tables. Charlie leaned against one, her pool cue in hand, as a guy made his way up to her. My vision went red, adrenaline and anger pumping through me at an alarming rate.

"Ah, hell." Maverick blew out a breath. "Ryder, don't do anythin' stupid. You can't win if you're in jail."

"Jesus, who said anythin' about jail, Mav?" Cash chuckled. "Ain't nothin' wrong with a little tussle."

I barely heard anything through the blood pounding in my ears. Not Maverick and Cash bickering, not the din of the bar, not the music playing in the background. My boots ate up the distance between Charlie and me.

Her eyes widened as I came to her side, pulling her against me and angling myself between her and the guy. "How can I help you, friend?" I growled out.

God, I seemed like a possessive asshole, but I didn't care. No one was stealing her from me. Charlie was mine until she wanted otherwise, and even then, I'd fight like hell to keep her.

"What're you doing?" Charlie snapped, her gaze flickering with anger.

The guy glanced between the two of us, face set in a scowl. "Is this guy botherin' you, darlin'?" he asked.

"She ain't your darlin', bud. Now I don't want a fight, but if you don't leave, I ain't afraid to throw hands."

The guy's chest puffed up at that, challenge settling over his features. He opened his mouth—likely to spout off some bullshit—but Charlie stopped him. "He's right. I'm not your darlin', and you should leave."

The guy threw one last glare my way before storming off. I turned to Charlie, grabbing her by the hand and dragging her into the hallway leading to the bathrooms, hoping for some semblance of privacy. I was half surprised she followed. Fury still danced in her eyes.

"What the fuck was that about?" she hissed, tearing out of my grip the moment we were alone. The lighting was dimmer in here, the music slightly quieter in the secluded space.

"So, just cuz we had a misunderstandin' earlier, you decided to go tit for tat? Flirtin' with some random dude just to piss me off?" A low blow, but, fuck, I was drunk and pissed.

She glared up at me, leaning against the wall as she crossed her arms over her chest. "Maybe if you'd have come over earlier, instead of sulking like a sore fucking loser, we could have avoided that all together."

I clenched my teeth so hard a muscle feathered in my jaw. "So, me bein' upset justifies you to flirt with some knock-off cowboy?"

Her lips pulled up into a devilish smirk, one of her brows rising defiantly. "Jealous, Ryder?" she asked, throwing the question right back at me.

God, she was fucking hot. Cruel, wicked, and entirely too beautiful. I fisted a hand before placing it against the wall above her head, even as I wrapped an arm around her waist with my free hand and dragged her against me. I dipped my head to meet hers, her hot breath feathering against my cheeks. She smelled of whiskey, vanilla, and lavender.

Just like that, my fury faded, and in its place came scorching desire. No, *need.* I needed Charlie Evans. Needed her like the air inside my lungs.

"Yes," I ground out. "Yes, I was fuckin' jealous."

Her gaze flicked down to my mouth then back up to my eyes. She bit her lip, and a growl rumbled out from deep in my throat. "Show me, Ryder." One of her hands pressed to my chest, the other sliding up around my neck. "Show me."

Our mouths met as we clashed against one another. It wasn't gentle or slow like the night of our date. No, this kiss held anger, frustration, pent-up desire, and passion.

At that moment, meeting me stroke for stroke, touch for touch, I realized she was made for me. She had to be. God, I wanted her. Right here, right now. I wanted every inch of her.

I hadn't gotten to tell her how gorgeous she looked tonight in her low-cut black dress that showed off all of her glorious curves. Curves I wanted to trace with my hands, my tongue. I wanted to kiss every damn inch of her. "God, you're fuckin' beautiful," I breathed, finally breaking the kiss enough to rest my forehead against hers.

A little hum of approval escaped her, making me all the more hard for her. Fuck. Why the hell were we so far from the damn fairgrounds? As if reading my mind, she whispered, "I want you, Ryder."

I groaned and pumped my fist against the wall above her head in frustration. Dear Lord, I wanted her too. Pressing another kiss to her lips, I dragged my hand at her waist along the curve of her torso and up over the swell of her breast.

She hissed, arching into the touch. "Fuck."

"That's exactly what I wanna do to you, darlin'," I murmured against her lips.

Her breath hitched a moment, a little gasp escaping her. With her arm still wrapped around my neck, her hand on my chest slithered lower, lower, lower, until her fingertips dipped below my shirt and toyed at my pant line. She wasn't making this easy, that's for sure. I had half a mind to take her right here in the hall.

The door to the bathroom opened with a slam, jolting Charlie and I back to reality. "Oops!" A woman squeaked, offering us a sheepish smile as she refused to meet our stares. "Sorry!" She half ran out of the hallway toward the bar.

Charlie let out a groan when we were alone once more, tipping her head back to the wall. "Why'd she have to interrupt us?"

My blood still sang for her despite the interruption. In fact, with her head tilted back like that, the sexy curve of her neck was on display. I leaned in and trailed a path of kisses from her collarbone to her jaw. Maybe it was the alcohol or the pent-up anger-turned-desire, but I found myself whispering in her ear, "Ain't nothin' stoppin' us from hookin' up in the bathroom."

A throaty laugh fell from her lips, sending a shiver down my spine, ramping up my need tenfold. Her stormy gaze met mine, mischief and lust flashing like strikes of lightning. "As much as I want you, Ryder Wright, I'm not drunk enough to fuck you in the bathroom."

Damn, I loved that filthy mouth of hers. I chuckled and kissed the spot just below her ear. "Wanna head back to the fairgrounds?"

She claimed my mouth in a kiss that set fire to every inch of me. When she pulled away, she captured my bottom lip between her teeth, giving it a playful nip before letting go.

My cock jumped. "I'll take that as a yes," I managed to get out.

Her answering grin had me dragging her out of the hallway, past a smirking Maverick and a shouting Cash, and out the front door of the bar.

Chapter Thirty-Seven

Wine Into Water

CHARLIE

BY THE TIME WE reached the fairgrounds, my lungs burned, but adrenaline and pure desire drove me forward. Ryder held my hand tightly, as if afraid to let go. I felt the same.

As we came upon the rows of trailers and RVs, I veered toward ours. Not the one with Mr. And Mrs. Mooney in it, thank God, but the second RV that was technically Cash's.

Ryder stopped me though.

"But what about—"

"Cash and Mav'll be back soon. You really want to get caught by either of them? We'll *never* live that shit down."

I giggled at that, some of my buzz still lingering, though nowhere near what it was at the bar. It kept me warm in the brisk, night air though, so that was nice. "So where are we going?" I asked as he led me onward.

We weaved our way toward his horse trailer, coming to a stop before the door to the tack room. He grabbed a small set of keys out of his pocket and unlocked the door before holding it open for me. "It ain't fancy, but it'll do."

I bit my lip and let him help me up the giant step into it. He followed after, flicking on the dim overhead light. He'd barely closed the door when I dragged him to me, pressing my mouth to his. After everything that had happened tonight, I needed this. Needed to feel him pressed against me. In me.

A rumble of approval fractured in his chest as he slowly pushed me back against the wall of the trailer, all the while kissing me. My lungs seared in my chest, desperate to come up for air, but it was a pain I savored. Relished. Something possessive and predatory lingered in his touch, making me want him all the more. I liked this angry side of Ryder.

Pinning me to the wall, he ground himself against me, and I let out a little moan of approval, dipping my head back. "More," I whispered as he trailed kisses and nips along my jawline and neck.

"Someone's demanding," he murmured, gently biting my earlobe as he placed a balled fist to the wall behind me, even as he held me firmly to him. The way we stood, he both caged me in but also held himself back. Ever the gentleman even while taking charge.

His hand around my waist snaked along my hips and up to my breast before he dipped a hand beneath the low-cut fabric. His callouses scraped against my skin, sending a shiver through me as he cupped my breast and kneaded gently.

I moaned again, arching into him. God, he felt amazing. His kisses and touch were like a drug. And like a junkie, I needed more. All of him. Everything he was willing to give.

I slid a hand down his chest, along the planes of his chiseled stomach, before settling on his belt buckle. I undid it hastily, my other hand joining as I worked at his button and zipper next.

"Fuck, Charlotte," He hissed under his breath as my hand dipped under his jeans and boxer briefs to settle over his cock.

I stroked him up and down, reveling in the way every inch of him had tensed beneath my touch. Maybe it was the alcohol, but the power I'd felt in that moment…I'd never felt anything like it before. His lips dragged across my chest until he captured my nipple in his mouth.

I hummed, biting my lower lip before tilting his chin up with a free hand to meet my stare. "Fuck me, Ryder."

His midnight eyes ignited like galaxies exploding. And then his hands were around my waist, dipping below my dress and tugging down my underwear as I shoved his pants further down so his cock sprang free. Lifting me in his arms and pressing me against the wall once more, he settled his cock at my entrance. I was ready. Waiting. Wanting.

His mouth captured mine in a searing kiss, a clashing of tongues and teeth, as he slid his cock inside me. "Oh, fuck," I groaned, letting my head fall back as he started up a slow, smooth rhythm.

"Careful, darlin'," he whispered in my ear, his breath hot against my neck. "You better be quiet…don't want no one comin' to investigate."

God, he felt good. So. Fucking. Good as I rode his cock. But still, I wanted more. No. *Needed* more. After the rollercoaster of emotions

I'd gone through tonight, the residual nerves still lingered, coiled tight but with nowhere to go. This…this helped. But I needed more of him.

A husky laugh fell from my lips as I wrapped my arms around his neck and met his coal-black stare. "Make me."

Something flickered in his stare, his pace faltering for only a moment. "Charlotte?" My name was little more than a hushed question on his lips.

I flipped his hat off his head, my fingers snagging in his hair as I drew his mouth to mine. Cash's moonshine really was doing a number on me. Fuck. I'd never felt so confident. So alive. So comfortable in my skin. So, I was just as surprised as Ryder as two unbidden words fell from my lips. "Choke me."

He stilled in me all together, his wide-eyed gaze meeting mine. "W-what?"

I slid my hands over the planes of his chest undoing the snaps of his shirt buttons to expose his torso. My fingers brushed over the raised flesh of his brand before I pressed a kiss to his mouth once more. "Choke me, Ryder," I whispered against his lips.

For a moment, I almost thought he wouldn't do it. He hadn't pumped his hips inside me, hadn't so much as moved an inch. It was like my words froze him in place. Fear blossomed in my chest, doubt creeping in like vines of ivy. I opened my mouth to…to what? To take back what I'd said, tell him never mind… But it was like a switch went off in him.

Ryder's gaze settled on me—scorching, positively scorching in its intensity. He moved inside me once more, his thrusts harder, wilder, faster. And along with the feel of his cock, came the most glorious pressure against my neck.

I gasped at the feeling as blissful helplessness crashed through me, sending me higher and higher. Each stroke, each labored breath from my lungs stoking the flames of my desire until I burnt so bright, so hot, I knew it was only a matter of time until I exploded.

"Like this, Charlotte?" His voice was little more than a breathy growl in my ear, his hand still gripped around my neck as he pounded into me, making the entire trailer shake.

A little whine escaped me. "More."

His breath hitched even as he kept his fast, punishing pace. His fingers tensed around my throat, though he didn't grip tighter. Those dark eyes of his burned into me, a silent question lingering in the depths.

A ripple of frustration speared through me at his hesitance. I was so close. So. Fucking. Close. Rocking on a precipice, waiting to shatter into a million pieces. Wrapping my fingers around his wrist, I put more pressure on my neck, blocking the air from my lungs more thoroughly. "More," I managed to get out on a strained breath.

A groan escaped him, severing any semblance of control he possessed. He thrust into me, brutal in his intensity, and I matched him stroke for stroke. His grip on my throat tightened, enough that my vision blurred around the edges and sound began to fade into the background.

I broke apart then, my orgasm crashing into me harder than a wave on the shore. It rocked through me so thoroughly I saw stars, a strangled, choked scream escaping me. He released his hold, pressing his forehead to mine as he thrust himself into me once, twice, a third time, before his own release took him, my name a ground-out groan on his lips.

My chest rose and fell in heavy gasps as I urged air into my screaming lungs. My arms wrapped around his neck, and for a long moment, we remained just as we were. Heads pressed together, him still inside me.

As my desire ebbed away like leaves on the wind, a sense of calm I'd never experienced settled around me like a warm blanket, wrapping me in its soft embrace. I'd never felt like this before. Never felt so satisfied, so wanted, so…so loved.

Was this what love felt like?

I'd thought I'd felt it over the years, but maybe I'd been wrong. Because this…this feeling I felt in Ryder's arms…I'd never shared this with another soul in my life.

That thought alone should have scared me.

And yet, in the following minutes—as we righted our clothes, walked back to the RV, and crawled onto the fold-out couch we were sharing—I realized something.

I just might be in love with Ryder Wright.

Chapter Thirty-Eight

Sun To Me

Ryder

I woke with the dawn. As always. I didn't need an alarm clock anymore to get me up. My body had grown so accustomed to it, that it woke me up on instinct. Charlie slept soundly tucked against my side, her body turned away from me. As much as I didn't want to leave her, I needed to get up. Needed to feed Boone and clean his stall. Work him a bit.

I slipped out of bed and rifled through my bag, pulling on fresh clothes. She didn't even move or stir. In the waning darkness, she looked like a beautiful, slumbering angel. My lips pulled up into a ghost of a grin. She hadn't been angelic last night…but holy hell, I'd loved every damn second of it.

Sure, I was apprehensive at the start. I'd never done something like that before, never had someone ask me to do that. But there wasn't much I wouldn't give that woman. She'd possessed me, body and soul. And I'd give her the world if it made her happy. If it made her shatter apart on top of me like she had last night.

Damn. I needed to stop. Stop thinking about her like that or else I'd be dragging her ass out of bed and back to the trailer for round two. Pushing the desire down, I pressed a kiss to her forehead and left, hoping she stayed asleep. As much as I wanted every moment of my day to be filled up with Charlie Evans, I needed this time to myself. To focus. Reorient myself and get ready for tonight's rodeo.

Black Betty wasn't in her stall when I came into the barn. It wasn't surprising though; Mav was always the first to get up. Even earlier than me. I'd be surprised if he even slept at all. Cash wouldn't be up until Mav dragged his ass out of bed, so, for now, I was alone. Boone already chewed on a flake of alfalfa, no doubt thanks to Maverick, so I grabbed a rake and began cleaning his stall.

A lingering headache pulsed across my forehead, but I did my best to ignore it. A couple ibuprofen and some water would help. That or a beer to get rid of the hangover.

I was just finishing up Boone's stall, when Bad's voice cut through the barn. The sweet smell of tobacco lingered in his wake as he spoke around his pipe. "Hey, Dickhead." He came to rest his arms on Boone's stall.

"Mornin', Bad." I nodded, running a hand down Boone's neck.

"Hey, I wanted to tell you somethin'." His gruff voice held a grave note to it.

My blood froze and I stopped what I was doing to look at him. Literally nothing good came from him starting off like that.

"Oh, yeah?" I kept my tone neutral, meeting his gaze. "What's that?" My mind raced, trying to guess what he was after. Probably going to lecture me about last night. How I needed to get my head out of my ass or something.

"If y'all go out at night to check on the horses or whatever, you need to be careful."

Relief flooded through me. Thank God, I didn't want to dwell on last night anymore. Well, not that part of it. "Why's that? What happened?"

"Well, you know how Violet likes to feed them horses at all hours? Seven, eight times a day?" He took a deep drag on his pipe. "Well, I came out last night around, oh, eleven, twelve 'o clock…was on my way to the barn when I heard somethin'."

My heart raced, my stomach clenching in knots. Oh, shit. Had he…he couldn't have. "What did you hear?" I asked, careful to keep the worry out of my voice. If he heard Charlie and I…*fuck*. I didn't even want to think of the shit he'd give me. I'd never live it down.

"God damn raccoons," Bad replied with a shake of his head.

"Raccoons?" Some of the tension left me as I met his stare.

"Yeah, you gotta be careful with those lil' fuckers." Bad nodded. "They may look cute, but they'll tear a chunk outta ya, faster than Maverick's stupid mare. I'd hate for Cason or Charlie to get bit by one. Think they got rabies…" He shrugged. "Just somethin' to watch out for." He pushed off from the stall and turned to walk away.

I stood dumbfounded, staring after him. Was he serious? He couldn't be. Bad didn't give a damn about some cat-sized trash pandas. What the hell was he getting at?

"Especially these raccoons." Bad turned back, revealing a full-on shit-eating Mooney grin. "Real violent ones. One of 'em was chokin' the other, and ya know what? She was asking for more."

Well, shit.

My cheeks burned, no, blazed with heat. He knew. He fucking knew. And I was so damn screwed. Bad finding out was almost worse than getting caught by my dad. I blew out a breath and rubbed the back of my neck. "Don't tell Cash," I pleaded.

Bad just chuckled and reached over to pet Playboy in his stall. "She help you get your head outta your ass?" Bad asked, ignoring the question.

A wave of anxiety settled around me. Shit, this didn't bode well. But instead of focusing on that, I settled my thoughts on Charlie. How her touch, her kisses, had dulled the rage and consumed me with a burning desire. We hadn't talked about last night yet, but I needed to.

I'd been an ass. I'd been selfish. She tried to be there for me and I'd pushed her away. Not only that, but I'd completely ignored the fact that she'd watched every second of that rodeo, front and center, and made it through for me. I hadn't even gotten to tell her how proud I was of her for that. Or how grateful I was.

"Yeah," I finally replied to Bad, "she did. Took a bit, but she did."

He nodded, puffing on his pipe once more. "She's a good girl. Bit too uptight, but I s'pose bein' round you, Mav, and that dumbass kid of mine will help loosen her up."

A smile cracked on my lips. Charlie was everything I wanted and more. And I wouldn't let her slip through my fingers, that was a promise.

B Y THE TIME I got back to the RV, Maverick stood before the barbeque, cooking up sausage, bacon, and some potato and egg concoction. Charlie sat on the picnic table facing him as she sipped on something from one of Mrs. Mooney's Pioneer Woman mugs.

"Better be careful with that," I said with a chuckle, grabbing an energy drink from the cooler and cracking it open. "Mrs. Mooney will hunt you down if you break one of her mugs."

Charlie smiled as she took another sip. "Oh, I know. She told me, like, three times already. But Maverick said not to use any of the cups in your guys' trailer. Something about Cash using all them as spitters."

I came up and kissed her before sitting at her side. "Mrs. Mooney's hot cocoa?" I asked.

She nodded, taking another sip. "Not much of a coffee drinker. I can't stand the taste." She glanced at Maverick with a mixture of awe and horror as he drank from his stainless-steel mug.

Even I couldn't muster up the willpower to drink coffee black like Mav did. Caffeine was fuel, but it still had to taste good. Maverick just smirked, taking another large sip from his cup. Charlie laughed and glanced over at me. "Heart attack in a can?"

I chuckled and shrugged. "At least it's sugar-free."

Her grin was bright enough to chase away any worry…until Bad opened the RV door and strolled over to us. Cason was hot on his heels, still in his dinosaur pajamas paired with his cowboy boots and hat.

"Well, you're quite the sight, bud," Charlie said with a laugh.

Cason barreled over to us and hugged her. "Morning, Auntie Charlotte." He glanced at me and wrapped his arms around my waist. "Hi, Uncle Ryder."

I winked at him. "Mornin', bud."

Bad's voice cracked through the space like a bullwhip. "Mornin' everyone." His hazel gaze flicked to Charlie, then settled on me. He hid a smirk behind his coffee mug as he took a sip.

I fought to keep my heart rate calm.

"Where's Uncle Cash?" Cason exclaimed, grabbing the play rope off the back of a camping chair. He set himself up to rope the plastic cow head stuck into a bale of hay.

I looked to Mav, who shrugged. "He was gone when I got back from feedin' this mornin'."

"Yeah, he left while I was getting ready," Charlie added. "He said he had to go get something and would be back soon."

My frown deepened. Where the hell had he gone? He wasn't the type to wake up early, and certainly not the type to go out and do something of his own volition before noon, unless it was church or his latest fling.

Maverick's voice drew my stare. "Breakfast's ready."

After grabbing paper plates and utensils, we all settled around the table—well, minus Cash, who still hadn't shown. Thank God, though. I don't think I could deal with his usual antics, as well as Bad's knowing grin pegging me in place every time I caught his gaze. I don't think I'd ever eaten a meal so quickly, trying as hard as I could to get out of there before he inevitably said something. Because it *was* inevitable. I just hoped it didn't happen around Charlie.

I stood from the table, heading for the trashcan when Cash appeared between the RVs. To my surprise, Cheyenne followed him, her red Australian Cattle Dog hot on her heels. My brows furrowed. Why were they together? Cash had shot his shot with her before and she'd turned him down. Everyone knew she'd wanted Maverick from the moment she'd laid eyes on him—well, everyone except Mav.

"Where have you been?" I asked him, coming to stand by Charlie.

Cash's lips pulled up into an easy grin. "I had some errands to run." Even though I couldn't see his eyes through the pink polarized sunglasses he wore, I knew, just fucking knew, they danced with mischief.

"Errands?" I arched an eyebrow.

"Errands." He nodded, hefting up an offensively purple gift bag clutched in his right hand. "I got a present for Charlie Girl."

Bad groaned under his breath. "Oh, shit."

"For the last time, Clint…*words*," Violet scolded.

"Oh shit, what?" I asked, narrowing my eyes at Bad, before looking to Cheyenne for a clue. She offered nothing but a sickly sweet smile. I didn't like this. Apprehension roiled in my gut, making me regret the plate of food I'd just eaten.

"A gift?" Charlie lit up, glancing between me and Cash. "For me? Why?"

"Well—" Cash sounded out of breath like he often did just before unleashing one of the punch lines to his awful jokes. The apprehension thickened to dread. "I saw this, and thought of you."

Charlie's brow furrowed even as she went to him and accepted the bag. "There has to be a reason. People don't just give gifts like that."

"No reason," Cash insisted with another grin. "I just like…doing things like that."

Bad coughed into his coffee mug suspiciously, as if he were trying to keep from laughing. What was going on? My heart pounded as Charlie pulled a t-shirt out of the bag.

"A shirt?" She offered a questioning smile to Cash.

My nerves wound tighter and tighter as Bad asked, "What's it say on it, there?" His light gaze shone. I didn't like that. Not one damn bit.

Charlie unfolded the black shirt and started to read aloud.

"No wait!" I protested, dread tightening my vocal cords as I spotted one of the bright pink words.

"Choke…me…Daddy? Choke me, Daddy? Choke…" The color drained from Charlie's face as she turned to stare at me in horror. "You *told* him?"

She looked like she'd seen a ghost, pure panic shining in her gray eyes. I nearly choked on my own saliva. He didn't. No, he fucking didn't. I offered Charlie a pleading look before leveling Cash with the most wrathful stare I could muster.

"Nah! Ryder didn't tell me—" Cash's words dissolved into his obnoxious braying laughter as he bent over from convulsing so hard. "My dad did."

Charlie and I both shot wild glances at Bad.

"You told Cash!" we both exclaimed at the same time.

I'd known. I'd known Bad would pull some bullshit, but I hadn't expected this. This was beyond what I could even fathom.

"Well, I ain't gonna tell nobody else." Bad wheezed around his guffawing laughter, spilling coffee all over everything.

"This isn't appropriate. For breakfast. Or kids. Or anything, really." Violet shot up from the table, collected her dog, and placed a controlling hand on Cason's shoulder. "Come on, honey. Let's go watch some cartoons."

"Ryder!" Charlie shouted, pure, unbridled rage lining her face. She trembled, whether from embarrassment or fury, I wasn't sure. Guilt cut me to my core. Well, shit. I'd finally made things right with her only to have things fucked once more.

"Bad!" I shook as I leveled an accusing finger at the old fool.

"Cash!" he insisted, quaking with laughter.

Cheyenne's cheerful, smoky voice joined the fray. "Cheyenne!"

Maverick let out a deep sigh and wiped a tired hand over his face.

"Well, don't worry, Charlie girl." Cash chuckled as he unbuttoned his blue and white flannel shirt. No...no, no, no. There couldn't be more. But to my horror, with a flourish, Cash whipped his flannel off, revealing black lettering that read: *Choke me, Momma.*

"Good Lord, Cash." Violet sighed as she ushered Cason into the RV.

I thought Bad was going to have a heart attack, his laughs breaking off into a coughing fit. Maverick just shook his head. I didn't miss the hint of a grin on his mouth, though. Bastard.

"What does 'choke me' mean?" Cason's little voice rang out as Violet hauled him into the RV. Oh, Lord. Charlie was going to kill me. Poor Cason...*poor her*. Shame filled me.

"It means my son stopped maturing around seven years old," she grumped as she guided Cason over the threshold and slammed the door shut.

Before the silence could even settle in, Maverick downed the rest of his coffee and shot to his feet. "This is awkward," he said, offering me a guilty look. "I'm goin' to do some chores."

Cheyenne was quick to add, "I'll go with you."

Whether Maverick wanted it or not, Cheyenne and her cattle dog fell in step with him.

A window on the RV whooshed open. "Clint Mooney, in here, now!" Violet's tone left no room for arguing.

"Damn it, Cash." Bad's laughter died immediately, though the amusement remained in his eyes. "You got *me* in trouble."

"Give her hell." Cash grinned, his pink shirt burning my eyes. I was going to murder him. Absolutely fucking murder him for what he'd done.

"Ryder—" Bad grunted as he got up. "When you kick his ass, punch him in the throat a couple times for me."

"I'll be comin' for *you* next," I warned with a glower aimed his way.

"You can't scare me." Bad chuckled. "I gotta go in this here RV with the Devil's little sister. What are *you* gonna do, hit me? That woman cooks all my food."

Bad disappeared, leaving Charlie, Cash, and I around the table.

Cash sat down and helped himself to breakfast. "Did Maverick make bacon?"

I growled, my fists curling at my sides. "Get the fuck outta here, Cash." He didn't move an inch, even proceeded to reach for a bacon slice. "Cash, I swear, if you wanna compete tonight, you best get your fuckin' ass outta here. I ain't warnin' you again."

He sobered then. Not completely, but that shit-eating grin faltered and fell enough to let me know he knew he'd fucked up.

"I'm…gonna go," he said quickly, snagging the plate of sausage and bacon before disappearing between the RVs once more.

Charlie's still panicked gaze met mine for the briefest moment before she shot for our RV.

"Charlotte, wait!" I called, moving toward her, but she'd already slammed the door. I wrenched it open, finding her pacing the aisle of the space, her hands on her head, the gift bag and shirt discarded on the made-up couch.

"Charlotte," I breathed, pulling my hat off and spearing my fingers through my hair. "Are you okay?"

She paused in her pacing, facing away from me. She dipped her head back, her long, fiery waves brushing her hips as her shoulders quaked.

Well, shit. Was she crying? *Dear Lord, please don't let her be crying.* I still couldn't believe Cash and Bad had the time to pull some ridiculous fucking stunt like that off. How had Cash even managed to get those shirts made?

She let out a deep breath and turned to me, unshed tears shining in her eyes. "I…I don't know whether to crawl under a rock and die of humiliation or applaud Mooney for how fucking brilliant of a prank that was." She knotted her hands in her hair on either side of her temple and let out a disbelieving laugh, before meeting my gaze. "How did they find out?"

The weight of her stare nearly sent my knees buckling. I rubbed the back of my neck and sighed. "Bad came out this mornin' when I was cleanin' stalls and said he heard us last night. I figured he'd mention somethin' to Cash and Mav, but I didn't think it would escalate like that. I…" I smacked my ball cap against the table, a frustrated growl escaping me. "I'm sorry, Miss Charlotte. I really am."

I hung my head, unable to meet her stormy gaze. I couldn't read it, or the way she stood there. I'd understand if she was pissed at me. I'd honestly even understand if she was done. After last night and now this…hell, I'd be pretty done with the bullshit. But to my complete and total surprise, she made her way to me and pressed her palms to my chest.

"Why are you apologizing?" Her voice was quiet, soft. I glanced at her, my brows knitting together in question. She went on before I could offer a response. "You didn't tell Bad or Cash. You can't control what they do. Not even Mrs. Mooney can at the end of the day. Those two are wild, feral." She let out a loud sigh. "Am I embarrassed? Fuck yeah. But at the end of the day, I should have been more careful with what I said last night."

"I should have—"

"Should have what?" she asked. "Should have told me to be quiet? That's about all you could have done." A smile toyed on her lips as one of her hands slid up to cup the side of my neck. "Would I have preferred your friends and Mr. and Mrs. Mooney to *not* know my kinks…? Yeah. But I don't blame you, and I don't regret what we did last night. Do you?"

"No," I shot back quickly, cupping her face in both my hands. "God, no. I loved every damn second of it."

She leaned up on tiptoe and pressed her lips to mine. "Good." Pulling away, she moved to the couch and took off her sweatshirt and shirt, revealing a red lace bra.

Desire flared to life even as confusion warred within me. "Charlotte…as much as I'd love to go round two, you really think that's a good idea right now?" I wanted her, God, did I want her, but knowing my damn luck, Cason, or worse, Cash, would come bursting in.

Charlie's lips pulled up into a mischievous smirk as she grabbed the black t-shirt and slid it on. "Cash made this with the complete intention of me not wearing it—" She paused, concentrating on tying the end of it into a knot, cropping the shirt at the waist. "I'm not giving him the satisfaction of thinking he and Mr. Mooney won."

A rush of pride swelled in my chest. "Dear Lord, I love you," I said, pulling her into my arms. I immediately froze, the rush of blood thrumming in my ears drowning out all sound. Oh, shit. Shit, shit, shit. Had I said that aloud?

"I um… I'm sorry. I…I gotta go—" The heat in the RV rose to an unbearably hot temperature. I released my hold on Charlie, unable to meet her stare as I turned and bolted for the door.

"Ryder!"

I didn't turn around as a blast of cold morning air hit me, nor as I all but ran for the barn. I had to get away. Had to clear my head.

Fuck. I'd told her I loved her. One damn week and I'd professed my love to her. To be honest, I'd fallen for her the night of the first rodeo. The moment I'd seen her there, I knew I wanted a shot at forever with her. But she wouldn't believe that.

Well…looks like today's gonna be fun.

CHAPTER THIRTY-NINE

Til You Can't

CHARLIE

HE SAID HE LOVED me.

Excitement, disbelief, and unbridled happiness overwhelmed me so thoroughly as he pulled me against him that I couldn't even function properly. But before I could say anything, before I could even fully meet his gaze, he'd been backpedaling, stammering, and rushing out the trailer.

I heaved a sigh, watching Ryder from the door as he stalked toward the barn. I could chase after him, but then what? Was I really ready to tell him I felt the same? I mean, to be honest, it wasn't really a hard question to answer. I wasn't the type of person who felt there was a time limit on saying things like that. Some things were beyond our control, and love was one of them.

I did love him. I might be a crazy, damn fool, but I did. It should have scared me, a part of it still did, but fighting the feelings I had for Ryder was as impossible as breathing underwater. But what if he hadn't meant to say that?

Obviously, he didn't *mean* to, or else he wouldn't have tucked tail and run afterwards. Maybe it was just one of those little slip ups that weren't as big as they seemed. A Freudian slip, or whatever it was called. Would I look like a fool if I told him I loved him back?

Don't make a big deal about it.

Pushing thoughts of Ryder aside, I settled my attention on the other matter at hand—finding Cash. But first, I needed to check on Cason.

I strode for the Mooney's RV and knocked on the door. Violet opened it, her eyes widening as a gasp escaped her. "Miss Charlie, you are *not* wearin' that shirt!"

I shrugged as I stepped into the open space, finding Cason on the couch still in his pajamas beside Bad, who looked more like a recently scolded schoolkid than a wild, reckless cowboy. But his light gaze filled with mirth as it landed on my shirt, his lips drawing up in the corners. "Well, shit. You're really gonna wear it?"

I settled my hands on my hips. "I'm not giving him the satisfaction of thinking he won… either of you, really."

Violet gave Bad a fearsome look that promised violence before turning to face me, pride warming her eyes and softening the planes of her face. "Good on you, Miss Charlie."

"Is anyone going to tell me what that means?" Cason asked, crossing his arms over his chest.

Mr. Mooney nudged him in the side with an elbow. "Don't worry, kid. I'll tell ya later."

"You most certainly will *not,* Clint!"

I grinned and looked at Cason. "You ready to go find the boys, bud?"

Cason's shout of excitement was answer enough.

CASON AND I RAN into Cheyenne as we meandered across the fairgrounds. We'd tried the barn first, but neither Ryder, Cash, or Maverick were there.

"Have you tried the trailer?" Cheyenne said, "Maybe they're gettin' their tack set up."

"So, what roll did you have to play in this?" I asked, pointing down at my shirt as we made our way toward the trailer. Cason trotted ahead of us, tossing a ball to Cheyenne's red heeler, Brandy.

Cheyenne had the decency to look embarrassed as she offered me an apologetic smile. "I got a Cricut machine to make and sell fun little shirts and cups when I ain't rodeoin'. He wouldn't leave til I made him one." She sighed. "I'm sorry."

I waved her off. "Don't be."

"You're takin' it like a champ. Not gonna lie, I ain't even sure I'd wear that around."

My lips drew up into a satisfied grin at that. This girl oozed confidence, so the fact that she might not even have the courage to wear this said a lot. Or did that just make me stupid? I probably didn't want to know the answer.

Her turquoise gaze flicked to me, a devilish glint in her eyes. "So, are the rumors true?"

I frowned. "What rumors?"

"About Ryder… does he really know how to…*ride her right?*"

My grin spread wider as I thought of last night. "Wouldn't you like to know."

"Alright, keep your secrets," she replied with an answering grin.

I laughed, setting my gaze ahead as I asked, "So, you're into Mav?"

Cheyenne groaned. "Is it that obvious?"

I lifted my hand and pinched my forefinger and thumb together so that only a sliver of space remained between them. "Just a bit," I replied with another laugh.

She chuckled. "I swear, I can't read him at all. Sometimes I feel like we're connectin', and then other times it's like I don't even exist."

"I've never met anyone like him," I admitted as we turned a corner and Ryder's truck and trailer came into view.

Sure enough, the boys were there. Cash, Mav, and Ryder were going through their tack, cleaning and oiling it to perfection. Cash wore his flannel once more; I wondered if he'd taken off the pink shirt or if he still had it on beneath. *Only one way to find out.*

Cheyenne hummed at my side and said softly, "He's different. Closed off. Maybe that's why I'm so into him."

"Uncle Ryder, Uncle Mav!" Cason shouted as he darted for them. "Uncle Cash!"

The three cowboys waved him over, a grin bright enough to light up a stadium gracing Cash's lips. My heart warmed as Cason all but hurled himself into the cowboy's arms. "Hey, little man!"

The way they included him… It couldn't always be fun having to drag along a kid—I was still getting used to it—but they never let him feel unwelcome. They'd make great dads one day, even Mooney, despite how wild and crass he was.

I didn't get to answer Cheyenne as I heard Cash's loud, obnoxious laugh. "Well, shit!" he shouted. "You're actually wearin' it."

"And miss a chance to show off free advertising for Cheyenne's business?" I replied with a smirk, stopping before them.

Cash's grin didn't falter. "That's my Charlie girl. Always knew I liked you."

I shook my head, even as a grin of my own stretched across my face. "I'm a bit sad you're not wearing yours. I was hoping we could be twins."

Cash pulled his sunglasses—neon pink again today—down, challenge burning in his hazel irises. He winked at me and began unbuttoning his flannel, revealing his bright shirt beneath.

Maverick's usually harsh features softened, one of those rare, genuine smiles gracing his lips. I couldn't see his eyes from beneath his dark aviator sunglasses, but I wouldn't be surprised if they danced with laughter. Ryder met my gaze, his face unreadable, especially with his Raybans on.

I wanted to talk to him, needed to talk to him, but not here. Not with everyone around. Instead, I settled on a smile, hoping, praying it would be enough for now.

THE DAY WORE ON, my nerves growing with each passing moment that Ryder and I didn't talk. It wasn't like last night, when he'd sulked and alienated himself. This was different. He held my hand, even kissed me at random little moments, he talked and interacted fine enough with everyone, but he never let us have a moment for just *us*. He wasn't ignoring me, not fully, but he certainly was making it hard to talk to him.

At first, I'd settled on just letting it go. I hadn't even planned on saying anything about our little conversation this morning, but with each passing second this…awkward tension grew between us. I hated it. Absolutely hated it. We'd never been awkward, not even the first night. How could three small words make such a difference?

Before I knew it, everyone was ready for the rodeo. Mr. and Mrs. Mooney had already taken Cason to their box seats, but I lingered behind with Ryder and the boys in the barn as they did a final inspection on their horses and themselves.

"Alright…final check," Maverick called out. I couldn't hold back a smirk as Ryder and Cash lined up before him and he did a full once-over of them, straightening their collars, wiping a fleck of lint or dirt off their felt hats… He was meticulous in his inspection. Ryder didn't complain about it, but after a few moments, Cash began fidgeting, batting a hand at Maverick.

"It's fine, *mama*," Cash grumbled, begrudgingly, handing over his sunglasses to his cousin.

Maverick continued to fuss, and I took the moment to approach Ryder, who busied himself with his bull rope before slinging it over his shoulder. "Good luck tonight," I said, pressing a hand to his back.

He turned, dark eyes unreadable as he dipped his mouth to mine and kissed me. "Thanks," he replied.

God, you could cut the tension with a knife. *Okay, that's it…* I couldn't deal with this anymore. He couldn't go out and compete like this. He was distracted, completely coming apart at the seams, and I wouldn't be the reason for him doing poorly. I couldn't do anything to help him during the rodeo itself, but I could help ease his worries now. "Ryder. We need to talk."

Something flickered in his eyes, all of the tension leaving him in the next instant only to be replaced by defeat. It shone in his gaze, settling over every inch of him. Ryder blew out a deep breath. "Can it wait, Charlotte?"

Was he really this messed up by it? My heart squeezed. I should have said something sooner.

"No." I reached up to press a hand to his cheek, running my thumb along his freshly shaven jawline, ignoring the way he'd stilled beneath me. I leaned up and kissed him, slow, unhurried, as if no one else was in the barn. "I love you," I whispered against his lips as I pulled away.

His eyes ignited like a supernova. Like a thousand stars exploding against a midnight sky. "Charlotte, I—"

I touched a finger to his lips, shushing him. "No. Don't say anything," I said. Partly because I didn't want him to feel forced to say it back, and partly because I couldn't bear to hear that he hadn't actually meant it. "I don't know if it was just a slip-up this morning, or if you actually do feel that way, but I do. I love you, Ryder Wright…and I want you to know that. Now, go kick some ass and win."

Ryder's face lit up, the most brilliant smile pulling on his lips. God, he was fucking gorgeous… And as his mouth met mine once more, he told me everything I needed to know without saying a damn word. My body melted into his touch as he stole the air from my lungs.

"Maverick…" Cash's voice, oddly gentle and tender, floated on the air.

"What?" Annoyance lent weight to Maverick's world-weary voice.

"I…I love you."

I heard boots scuffling across the ground and Maverick snap, "Get the fuck off me."

More scuffling. "Come get your good luck kiss," Cash laughed.

Maverick grunted. "Eat shit and die."

"Kiss me first."

I broke the kiss, rolling my eyes even as a huff of laughter escaped me. Ryder's smile was warm enough to chase away any of the lingering darkness and worry within me. Gripping my chin between his thumb and forefinger, he pressed a feather-soft kiss to my lips, his whispered words sending a shiver down my spine.

"I love you, Charlotte Evans…and I'm goin' to marry you one day."

Laughter bubbled out of my chest, even as the thought stirred something low in my belly. "Worry about winning the rodeo first, cowboy."

CHAPTER FORTY

Somethin's Gonna Kill Me

RYDER

MY PULSE RACED, MY heart dancing behind my ribcage as I readied myself to hop in the shoot atop my bull's back. He was a mean sonofabitch, ornery as hell as he snorted and thrashed against the metal. But it didn't slow the adrenaline pumping through my veins.

Tonight, was the night. I could feel it. After that damn near perfect run in Steer Wrestling, after Cash and Mav's wins—both together and individually—it was shaping up to be a good Sunday night. My gaze flicked to the Mooneys' box seats, finding Charlie leaning against the railing beside Bad, eyes trained on me.

A rush went through me at the thought of earlier. I hadn't stopped grinning most of the night—probably looked like a damn fool, but I didn't care. Funny how three little words could have such an effect on someone.

Holding her gaze for a moment longer, I finally dipped my head toward the sound of my name.

"Ready, Ryder?" Maverick asked, his deep voice a boom in my ear.

I met his serious gaze and nodded, pulling myself over the pipe-stall and into the bull's chute. Cash and Mav, along with a couple other cowboys, helped me get my rigging set up and tightened as I settled on the bull's back.

Breathe.

I forced air into my lungs, slow, deep breaths meant to calm, as that rope tightened and tightened around my hand.

Cash gripped my shoulder, shouting over the music and the crowd, "Get some, bud."

I nodded and settled my gaze ahead, right between the bull's horns.

Time went differently on a bull's back. A few seconds felt like an eternity. The sound of the arena vanished, my vision sharpened, and every muscle in my body tensed. For just a few moments, it was like I was in my own world. The only two things existing were me and that bull.

Breathe.

Right as I settled into that zone of focus, the bull surged forward, thrashing against the chute. Hands from all around reached in to grab me, haul me up before the bull could do any damage, but it was too late. Pain ignited in my right knee. Enough to send a string of curses from my lips.

Push through. You got this.

"You okay?" Mav shouted over the cacophony around us.

I nodded as the bull settled once more, ignoring the pain as I lowered back onto its back. There was no way in hell I was scratching.

Not tonight. Not ever. Pain I could deal with, but wounded pride? No.

Be smart. Breathe. Focus. I could do this. I had to do this.

Settling atop the bull's back once more, I desperately tried to bring back that sense of calm I'd fallen so deep into moments before. It was there, lingering on the outskirts, so close I could nearly touch it.

It would have to be good enough.

With a shout that I was ready and a nod, the gate slammed open. My left arm gripped the bull rope, my right flying up over my head, a shot of adrenaline pumping through every inch of me, drowning out the pain screaming in my knee. Each buck, each turn or twist or spin, reverberated through my bones, my soul.

This was who I was. What I was born to do.

Everything slowed down, quieted, until all I could hear was the sound of the bull's breath and mine, the leather of my chaps moving as I rose and fell to a rhythm created by the beast beneath me.

Funny how something so fast could feel so slow in the moment. The sound of the buzzer cut through the pocket of calm I'd found myself in, bringing every sense screaming back to life in me—sight, sound, touch, smell, taste. I struggled to pull my hand from the bull rope as my weight shifted. For the briefest moment, my gaze met Charlie's. How I was able to find her so swiftly in a stadium full of people while on a bull's back was beyond me. But there she was.

That single moment was all it took.

Time sped up then, everything happening so fast I could barely process it. One moment I was leaning back as the bull bucked, the next slamming forward, my face connecting with his horns. Pain followed, excruciating for but a moment before…

Nothing.

Chapter Forty-One

Stand By Me

Charlie

EVERYTHING HAD BEEN GOING great. Too great. That should have been the telltale sign. But between mine and Ryder's little moment in the barn, and with the way they'd all performed tonight, it felt like nothing could go wrong.

By the time they'd announced Bull Riding, I was ready. Excited even.

I met his gaze across the arena, Cash and Mav both dutifully at his side. I put every ounce of love and hope and faith into that look, hoping, praying he understood just how much I believed in him.

Crazy that so much had changed in such a short time, but love was a funny thing, I guess. If this made him happy, if this brought him joy, well, then…I had no choice but to get on board. It still scared the hell out of me. My nerves were wound tighter than a corkscrew, but Bad's calming presence helped.

"Folks, we have our next contestant, Ryder Wright, ridin' Rock-crusher! This bull may be small, but, man, he's quick and mean."

With a final nod my way, Ryder looked to Mav and climbed over the pipe-stall into the bull chute.

"Kid's got this," Bad said at my side.

I nodded and let out a deep breath.

Cason, on my left, hugged my thigh. "He's gonna do great, Auntie Charlotte."

I smiled down at him. "He is, bud."

Please, let him be okay.

Forcing my breath to stay even, I trained my gaze back on Ryder just as the bull decided to spook and thrash in the chute. Even the sound of the music blaring from the speakers couldn't drown out the shout of pain I heard, causing the blood to drain from my face and a sense of dread to skitter down my spine. Goosebumps prickled along my skin.

Ryder.

My hand shot to squeeze Bad's arm.

"He's okay. That shit happens all the time. He—" But the rest of his words were drowned out by the commentator's voice. "Told y'all this bull was mean."

I watched the chute, my breath quickening, my lungs searing. *Please, let him be okay. Let him be okay. Let him—*

The gate flung open, and Rockcrusher tore out of the shoot, Ryder atop him. "Don't blink y'all. Rockcrusher's faster than you think! But that Ryder Wright—" his voice tapered off as sound and space all seemed to blur. All I could focus on was Ryder.

I didn't know hardly anything about what all went into determining a score, but he was flawless. Perfection. He made it look easy. Each dip and rise, each spin or buck. It looked as effortless as breathing.

He was magnificent.

The buzzer went off. Time and sound sped up, like a song being fast-forwarded, and with it, a surge of relief. It crashed over me, soothing my fears and worries.

Thank God.

Somehow, some way, Ryder's gaze met mine. How he managed to find me in the chaos was impressive, but like a magnet, we were drawn to each other. I managed a smile, pressing a hand to my lips. It was then I felt the tears. Not of terror, but happiness.

Pure, unbridled happiness.

But then everything went to hell.

He struggled to get off the bull. Rockcrusher bucked—high. So damn high I was surprised he managed to land on his front two feet. As he came down, Ryder's body rocked forward, colliding with his horns. I screamed, at least I think I did, but no sound came out. Or maybe it did, but the blood rushing through my ears drowned out all the noise.

He must have been knocked unconscious. It's the only thing to explain the lack of movement from him. I swear, I could feel every pull and tug of his arm as the bull continued to buck and spin. Panic trembled through me, paralyzing me in place. Finally, after what felt like an eternity of flailing, Ryder fell to the dirt.

Get up. Get up. Get up!

But he didn't.

My hands cupped my mouth, and a gut-wrenching sob escaped me.

No.

No, this couldn't be happening. He'd done so well. He'd made his ride.

I went numb, wholly, entirely numb, a sense of Déjà vu settling around me. All the while, a voice, hauntingly similar to my mother's, whispered in my mind, *I told you. Cowboys will do worse than break your heart.*

The bullfighters managed to distract Rockcrusher and send him out of the arena, all the while, Ryder remained motionless on the ground. A blur of pink drew my attention—Cash tore across the arena, skidding to a stop beside Ryder, Mav not even a step behind. They both kneeled beside him as a medic team rushed out with a stretcher and a large first aid kit.

"What's happening? Is he breathing? Bad. What's going on? Bad?" My voice broke, the words raw and choked out.

Mr. Mooney's face replaced my view of the arena. He clutched my arms, a wild look in his eyes despite his calm, yet urgent tone. "Charlie…Charlie. *Charlotte!* Breathe."

Tears stung in my eyes, the vision of him blurring before me. "Is he… Ryder. I need—" It's like I'd forgotten how to talk. A rambling of words escaped me, but nothing made sense. My brain had stopped functioning, overridden with crippling fear.

"Breathe," Mr. Mooney repeated. "He's alive, but I need you to breathe."

"H-how do y-you know?" How had he even understood me? The words were little more than broken sobs.

Fierce determination blazed in his green-gold irises. "Because Cash and Mav would be burnin' down this whole damn arena if he was dead." He pushed my hair back off my face, the palm of his hand glistening with my tears as he pulled it away. "Now, breathe."

That spurred me into motion, and I forced a deep, cold breath of air into my lungs.

"Good. Another." His harsh, gravelly voice grounded me.

I tried to look beyond him, to reassure myself that Ryder was truly alive. But Mr. Mooney shifted and shook his head with a single, curt nod. "No. Not yet. You focus on me. I'll tell you when you're ready to see him."

More hot tears slid down my cheeks, but I nodded, obeying Mr. Mooney's commands, inhaling and exhaling at his prompting. Terror still clutched at my heart, but by the time he released his hold on me, I was pretty sure I could form a simple sentence.

Mr. Mooney moved aside just as the medics loaded Ryder up onto the stretcher. Maverick walked with them even as Cash bolted across the arena for us. "He's breathin', but unconscious. They're gonna take him to the hospital to evaluate him." A grave seriousness rang in Cash's voice as he reached for my hand through the railing. "He's okay, Charlie girl. He's okay."

Tears still streamed down my cheeks. I couldn't help but feel the words were just as much for him as they were for me. "Is Mav going in the ambulance with him?"

He nodded.

I swallowed the lump in my throat and nodded. "Maverick will make sure he's okay."

Cash squeezed my hand. "I'll drive you to the hospital."

Mr. Mooney's voice cracked like thunder beside me. "No, I'll drive." He looked at Mrs. Mooney. "Violet, you take Cason back to the RV—"

A little wail left Cason. Oh, God. He'd seen all this. I turned to find him curled up in a seat behind me, Mrs. Mooney at his side, trying and failing to console him. He rocked back and forth, his face buried in his hands.

I darted for him, coming to kneel in front of his seat. Gripping his shoulders gently, I said in the calmest, most soothing voice I could muster, "Hey, hey, Cason, it's okay, bud. It's okay. I'm here."

He launched into my arms, his breathing as ragged as mine. Maybe even more, actually. "Is Uncle R-Ryder g-g-going to b-be o-k-kay?"

Dear God, I hoped so. I blew out a breath, and with a certainty I sure as hell didn't feel, I nodded. "Yes."

He had to be. I couldn't, *wouldn't,* lose him.

"Please, don't leave me." Cason's words were broken, strangled.

I squeezed him tight and looked to Mr. Mooney. I couldn't leave Cason. Not when he was terrified. Mr. Mooney nodded, and let out a loud sigh. "Alright. All of us'll go."

THE NEXT FEW HOURS were little more than a blur. Not that there was much to do other than sit in the ER waiting room and wait. Wait. Wait.

Maverick and Mr. Mooney were the calmest. Mav might even have had him beat in that department. Cash surprised me, though. I'd expected him to bring that comedic relief we always could depend upon, but it's like he'd suddenly learned how to read the room. I almost wished he'd pipe in with something completely inappropriate just to ease the tension. He was a good distraction for Cason though. The two had set up some of Cason's coloring books and his iPad, and were watching episodes of Bluey while they quietly colored. Mrs. Mooney fiddled with her knitting needles, her fingers working furiously as she knit in silence. Every now and then she'd level the receptionist with a scathing glare that could have seared flesh.

I'd thought for a few tense minutes when we'd first arrived that they'd kick Mrs. Mooney out of the ER altogether when they'd seen little Bodacious in his carrier slung on Mrs. Mooney's shoulder.

"Ma'am, I'm sorry. But only service dogs are allowed in the hospital."

"He *is* a service dog," Mrs. Mooney replied.

The young receptionist rolled her eyes, a sneer on her lips. "Can you provide documentation?"

Mrs. Mooney spouted off a whole string of laws and curses, educating the poor girl about service animal law. I don't know if it was the threat of a lawsuit or the fact Mrs. Mooney looked and seemed damn near batshit crazy, but the woman finally conceded.

After a couple hours of no answers and only more unanswered questions, a female doctor finally came out, calling out for Ryder's family. It was a tie between Mav, Cash, and I, with Mr. Mooney following close behind, as we hurried to the doctor's side.

"He's stable, but unconscious for the moment. We just got his results back from X-ray and MRI. He's in rough shape. Broken eye socket, some fractured ribs, and a partial tear to his right meniscus tendon. There's a lot of swelling around his eye that we're most concerned about. We'd like to keep him overnight for observation."

Dear God. Hearing the laundry list of injuries made my stomach queasy.

"Can we see him?" I asked, my tone just a step above pleading.

The doctor nodded. "Only two guests per room at a time. I can take the first two back now."

Guilt warred in my chest as I turned to look at Cash and Mav. Both of them looked just as worried as me. And they were his best friends. They deserved to go first. "You guys go back first. I'll wait."

Maverick was the first to protest, his face as stern as his deep voice. "No, Miss Charlie. You go."

"No, I—" I shook my head. "You two are his best friends."

"You need to see him more than we do," Cash said, his hand surprisingly gentle as it settled on my shoulder. "You needa see he's alright."

I blew out a deep breath, but it did little to quell the guilt. Fighting them would be futile though. They were too stubborn.

"Mr. Mooney?" I asked, meeting his somber gaze.

I didn't even have to ask him if he'd come with me, it's like he'd read my mind. "Of course."

I hated hospitals, I realized. And yet, I'd been to two in just as many weeks. The smell of antiseptic stung my nose, the overwhelming amount of white too harsh on my eyes. I hated that for how quiet they were, there was constant sound and movement. Beeping machines, sheets about as soft as cardboard scraping and shifting with each patient, hushed murmurs from doctors, patients, and their family members.

Ryder's room was dim as the doctor opened the door. Tears already burned in my eyes. What state was he going to be in? How much pain? Would he still be asleep or awake? What the hell did I even say to him? I was such a jumbled mess.

Mr. Mooney's calloused hand engulfed my small one as he met my gaze. He took a slow, deliberately deep breath, and I knew without words he wanted me to do the same.

Inhaling a lungful of cool air, I exhaled and took a step into the hospital room.

Seeing Ryder lying motionless in the bed stirred up a wave of memories that threatened to swallow me whole. My mind instantly went back to being in the ICU with Sheldon.

He's not dying. But it's like my brain and my heart just couldn't understand that. Tears hung in my eyes, the lump in my throat so dense and thick that it was a miracle I managed to breathe around it.

Mr. Mooney pulled me into the room, thank God, or I may have just stood out there trying to find the courage to cross the threshold. We came to a stop at the foot of the bed, where he released my hand. I got my first good look at Ryder, my gut churning at the sight of his poor face. Bruises—black and indigo—covered most of the left side, his cheek and eye swollen shut.

Bad took a seat in the chair tucked against the wall on the right of his bed, while I stood paralyzed before it. I knew he wasn't dying. I knew he was okay. In the grand scheme of things, he'd come out a lot better than I could have hoped for. So much better. So why was I a sobbing, inconsolable mess?

"Charlotte…?" The sound of his familiar, gravelly tone was like a salve to my soul.

Tears slid down my cheeks as I met his midnight eyes—well, one, since the other was swollen shut. A choked sob escaped me as I wiped furiously at my cheeks and blew out a breath. "You scared the shit out of me, you know that?" I choked out, half laughing, half crying.

A weak chuckle escaped him, which turned into a cough, then a pained groan—God, his poor ribs—but a ghost of a smile danced on his lips. "It's good to hear your voice," he murmured, the words slurred from the pain meds, no doubt. "You look beautiful, as always."

I sniffled, a huffed laugh escaping me. Of course, even half-conscious he'd be chivalrous enough to comment on how pretty I was. He truly was Mr. Right.

"Before your dumb ass gets all sappy, just know I'm here too," Mr. Mooney grumbled from his chair.

My lips tugged up and I moved to the recliner on the left side of the bed, scooching it as close as possible so I could reach for Ryder's hand.

"What all happened, Bad?" Ryder asked, knitting his fingers through mine.

Mr. Mooney recounted what happened, dredging up all of the emotions and images. It tightened my stomach in knots, making my pulse race just at the thought.

Ryder's brow furrowed, anger flickering in his good eye. "So, what's the damage?"

Mr. Mooney went on to tell him that as well. Some of the anger evaporated from Ryder, not all, but enough that his jaw had unclenched and he didn't look like he wanted to murder someone. "How long you think I'll be out?"

"Depends…we'll know more tomorrow," Bad replied. I didn't miss how vague the answer was. Neither did Ryder for that matter, but he let it go.

Mr. Mooney left after about ten minutes, mentioning he'd have one of the boys come back. It was just an excuse to give us a moment of privacy, I was sure, but it was definitely appreciated.

"So, you still love me?" Ryder asked when we were alone once more.

My lips curved up at the corners. "Of course. Why would you think differently?"

"Just makin' sure," he replied, squeezing my hand. The little half smile on his lips drew down into a frown after a moment, his voice turning grave. "I'm sorry, Charlotte."

"For what?"

"For makin' you watch that."

"Ryder…" I let out a sigh. "You didn't make me watch anything. I wanted to be there. I wanted to watch you ride. I'm just happy it wasn't worse."

Something flickered in his gaze, like guilt maybe, but in the next instant it was gone, and the half smile was back—at least the medicine seemed to be helping him. "How bad do I look, honestly?"

There was a vulnerability in his voice I hadn't expected. Did he really think I'd care about some swelling and bruises? Squeezing his hand, I stood up and leaned over the bed. I brushed my lips against his, feather-soft, before pulling back to trace my fingers over his scar on the good side of his face. With my lips cocking up into a smirk, I whispered, "I'd fuck you."

The answering flame that flickered to life in his eyes made my smirk widen. "Don't tempt me, darlin'—"

I huffed a laugh, even as I continued to trace his scar. "Ryder Wright, you've got broken ribs, a broken face, and a torn knee. You're—"

"Partially…partially torn," he pointed out, some of that smooth confidence coming back. He was still hurting, it lingered along the chiseled planes of his face. My heart panged at that.

I shook my head and kissed him gently once more. "Get better first, cowboy. There'll be enough time for that later."

Chapter Forty-Two

Dear Rodeo

Ryder

Cash and Mav replaced Charlie not too long later. While I didn't want her to go, a tidal wave of relief crashed over me when the two of them walked into the room. Their spurs clinked against the floors as they made their way to my bedside and a little pang of sadness coiled tight in my gut. How long would I be out for? The doctor hadn't been back around to tell me the damage yet. Just Bad and Charlie.

When would be the next time I wore my spurs?

I didn't want to think about that. Didn't want to dwell on it for the moment. Ignoring the stabbing pain in my side, I propped myself up a bit more. "Hey, guys."

Maverick offered me a small smile, but Cash…fuck, it's like all the light had left him. His hazel eyes were dull, the usual cheerful lines of his face filled with worry. He plopped into the recliner Charlie had been in.

"How're you feelin'?" Mav asked.

"Like I got hit by a fuckin' bus," I admitted with a sigh.

He huffed. "Yeah, you hit that bull pretty hard."

"Did they give me a score?" I asked. I had to know. I had to know what it'd been.

"A ninety-three point three."

I dropped my head back to the pillow, a groan escaping me at the movement. It took me a minute to regain my breathing, trying to force air down my throat and into my lungs without bothering my ribs. A good score. A great score, even. And I didn't even get to celebrate it.

Helpless fury welled within me.

I hated this feeling. Being stuck in a hospital bed, pain meds pumping through my veins making me feel tired and groggy. Even now, my eyelids felt heavy. But if I looked too tired, they'd leave me. I wasn't ready to be alone with my thoughts. Not yet.

I looked at Cash. "You've been awful quiet. It ain't like you."

Cash just shrugged. "Not much use in bein' happy right now."

"Well, I mean…you could argue that me not bein' dead is cause for celebration," I replied, my lips quirking up.

But Cash didn't smile. Didn't so much as react. Serious Cash was my least favorite. He made Maverick's dour moods seem like sunshine and rainbows. They were few and far between, but, man, when they hit, it was like a hurricane, devastating in its destruction.

He finally settled his light gaze on me, a seriousness burning in the depths that I rarely saw. "You scared the hell out of us," he murmured. I didn't need him to admit that this was more about him.

I sighed. "I know."

Cash shook his head. "No, you don't. That was…it was scary to watch. I'm startin' to understand our Charlie girl."

Annoyance stirred to life, my gaze narrowing on him and sending a ripple of pain as the pressure around my left eye changed. It pounded and pulsed. "So now you're sayin' you don't want me rodeoin'?"

"No," Cash snapped back quickly. "I'm just sayin' I get her bein' scared, is all. Am I not allowed to worry 'bout you?"

Some of the anger dwindled at that. I never took into account how a serious injury might affect both Cash and Mav. Cash had his fair share of crazy spills, each one terrifying to watch. But I couldn't hold back the defensive note to my voice as I replied, "You've never acted like this before? What's goin' on?"

"You and I both know that tear in your knee happened before you even rode." Flames flickered in his eyes, his anger finally boiling to the surface.

So that's what he was pissed about? I narrowed my gaze on him. "Yeah, so?"

"So, you were already hurt," Cash countered. "You're lucky you came out with the injuries you did."

"You're tellin' me I should have just scratched?" The thought alone made me hot. I didn't scratch. Ever. Call it stubborn, call it foolish pride, I didn't care. I'd never scratched and I never would.

"Fuck, I don't know," Cash all but shouted, pursing his lips together. It accentuated the lump of chew tucked into his bottom lip. "It scared me, Ryder. Is that what you want to hear? You scared me. Seein' you on the ground, not movin', I didn't know what all that bull had done to you. I didn't know if you'd ever fuckin' walk again."

I struggled to swallow past the lump forming in my throat. For a long moment, we sat there, staring the other down, all the while Maverick loomed over us like a silent sentinel. Watching, waiting to intervene if necessary. Cash's chest rose and fell in deep, labored breaths, a wild look in his eyes.

The remaining fire snuffed out of me, like a flame doused with water. "I'm sorry," I whispered, shame gnawing at me.

Cash let out a loud sigh before spitting into his spit cup. "Nah, I'm sorry. You got enough shit to deal with. Ain't no use in me bitchin' and moanin' about what could have been."

Maverick's deep tone drew both our gazes. "It was one hell of a ride though."

My lips drew up into a lopsided grin even as Cash nodded. At least we could agree on that.

I AWOKE TO PAIN. Loads of pain. Just about every damn inch of me hurt. Where the hell was I? I blinked my eyes open, well only my right eye. Pain radiated around my left, the pressure pushing on my cheek, nose, and eye socket enough to make me clench my teeth.

The hospital room filled my field of vision, dark but for the dim nightlight that cast the front half of the room in warm, orange light. In the recliner beside my bed, Charlie slept, curled up beneath a blanket.

A part of me couldn't believe she was here. After what happened, I half expected her to have decided this was too much and just leave altogether. The fact that she'd stayed, the fact that she was here, right by my side…I didn't have the words to describe how grateful I was.

I didn't deserve her. That was for damn sure.

My face hurt, but I think the ribs were the worst right now. Every breath, every tiny movement sent pain rippling through me, forcing the air from my lungs. I watched her in silence; it was the only way to ignore the agony. I couldn't bear the thought of waking her.

Guilt gripped me like a vice. She shouldn't have to spend her night wrapped in a thin hospital blanket, making sure I was okay. She deserved so much more than that. And I wanted to be the one to give it to her. But…but rodeoing was who I was. It was as natural as breathing. I couldn't imagine a life not doing it. I was okay this time, but there'd be more injuries. There always were. Would she stay through it all? Or would she get tired after a while?

I must have fallen asleep at some point because next thing I knew light shone through the window, little flecks of lint and dust swirling in the air, reminding me of glitter. Hushed murmurs drew my gaze.

"Ah, kid's awake." I'd recognize that gruff voice anywhere.

Bad Mooney offered me a nod before looking back at the doctor from yesterday. Charlie stood silent at his side, her gaze flicking to mine. The doctor walked over to my bed. "Mr. Wright, how're you feeling?"

I pushed myself up into more of a sitting position, wincing as pain lanced across my ribs, knocking the air out of me. "I've been better, ma'am."

"On a scale of one to ten? Ten being the worst pain you've ever been in. How bad would you say your pain is in your eye?"

I always hated this question. It didn't mean anything. Pain was subjective. I shrugged, wincing once more. "I don't know. Like a four or five?"

She frowned, her manicured brows drawing together in a line. "Really?"

"Should it be more?" I asked.

"Everyone's threshold for pain is different," the doctor replied. "But there's extensive swelling to your eye, and from the X-Ray, a good portion of your inferior wall is damaged. I'd expect a higher number. Not to mention your other injuries."

I shrugged. "I mean, it hurts like hell, but I'm alive. So it can't be that bad, can it?"

She huffed a laugh. "I forget how you bull riders are. Let me try to explain this better. I'm scheduling you for surgery in a week from now to repair your eye socket. I'd like to get as much of the swelling down in the meantime before we go in and try to reconstruct the damaged bone."

Fuck. Disappointment flickered to life in my chest, the muscles in my jaw tightening. "Can I still compete?"

"Mr. Wright…" The doctor shook her head, an incredulous look filling her eyes. "No. Absolutely not."

I spied Charlie's disbelieving look from behind the doctor, but I chose to ignore it. "How long will I be out for?" I asked, setting my sights on the doctor once more.

"Well, for the eye surgery, at least two to three weeks. That's not even taking into account the broken ribs or the meniscus tear. I'd advise no strenuous activity for at least four to six weeks for the ribs. I'm going to get you set up with an orthopedic surgeon to get his opinion on what course of action he wants to take with your knee. Until then, I want you on crutches."

And just like that, all my hopes came crashing down. Austin was out of the picture now. Fury welled inside me. I fisted my hands beneath the blankets. I wanted to throw something. Hit something. Wreck this damn room. But I couldn't. I couldn't even fucking walk right now.

I tried to suck in a deep breath, only to fall into a coughing fit, my ribs screeching in pain from the movement. Laying my head back against the pillows, a wave of defeat pummeled into me. With a broken sigh, I nodded. I didn't know what to do, what to say. A lump formed in my throat, my eyes stinging with unshed tears of rage.

"I'm sorry, Mr. Wright. I'll get the paperwork started to get you discharged, and we'll have scheduling contact you about a surgery date."

I muttered a thanks, and then she was gone.

The smell of lavender and vanilla filled my nose—Charlie. "Hey." The word was hesitant, timid as she came to the bedside.

"I just…I think I need a minute," I replied, unable to look at her.

I saw her nod through my periphery. "I'm going to go call Mrs. Mooney and check on Cason. Be back in a bit. Love you," she whispered before walking out of the room.

My gaze flicked to her as she left, Bad pausing at the door behind her. He opened his mouth as if to say something but shook his head instead. Then he left me there, feeling more alone and helpless than ever.

Chapter Forty-Three

If I Were The Devil

Charlie

IT WAS SAFE TO say that Ryder was the worst patient I'd ever seen. The crutches hadn't even lasted a week.

I walked into the house, a slew of groceries in hand, to find Ryder limping around the kitchen, grabbing himself something to eat from the fridge.

"What the hell are you doing?" I asked, rage coiling tight in my belly.

He turned to me, guilt written all over his face like a kid caught stealing candy. He straightened, a hiss escaping him as he ran a hand through his hair. "I was hungry."

I swear… There was stubborn, and then there was Ryder. Sucking in a deep breath, I stifled the urge to roll my eyes.

I glanced over at Cason, who shared an equally guilty look on his face, before turning my scalding gaze back on Ryder. "You agreed that you'd let Cason help you."

"He was in the bathroom," Ryder argued, still standing in the middle of the kitchen.

"He sure doesn't look like he is now! Also, why are you still up? Go sit down before you hurt yourself."

Ryder grumbled something under his breath, but I couldn't hear him. God, he was so stubborn.

Talk about testing a relationship. On the drive home from the hospital, we'd discussed where he'd stay to recover. I'd offered for Cason and me to stay in the bunkhouse with him and the boys, but all three cowboys had adamantly refused. Which left us with the option of him staying here. Don't get me wrong, falling asleep in his arms every night and him being the first thing I woke up to every morning was something I didn't think I'd ever get tired of. But, sweet Jesus, I hadn't expected how frustrating it would be to get used to living with someone as well as taking care of them while they were hurt.

We stared each other down for a long moment until he finally conceded. Not before grabbing the whole box of Cinnamon Toast Crunch though. I watched him for a long moment, first hobbling over to the couch and then struggling and wincing as he situated his leg on a mountain of pillows. Cason flashed him an apologetic look, to which Ryder answered with a ruffle of his hair.

I blew out a sigh, taking my armful of groceries into the kitchen. Was I crazy for having a guy I'd only been dating for such a short time live here? Probably. Did I care? Not really. It made sense for someone to help take care of him. Cash and Mav had their work on the ranch, then to add in taking care of Ryder… I still hadn't gotten a job yet, so it worked out. And it's not like I'd be taking care of him forever. I had enough money saved up to not have to worry about that for a bit, at least. Besides, I liked taking care of him. It was frustrating at times, like right now, but like a dragon hoarding its gold, I'd revel in any moment I could muster with that man.

After finishing putting my things away, I grabbed an ice pack and a Monster and took it over to the couch. "Peace offering?" I asked, stopping before him, blocking his view of one of Cason's TV shows.

Something glimmered in his gaze, a lightness I hadn't seen in the dark depths since we'd left the hospital. He'd been a shell of himself these past few days. There, but not. I couldn't even imagine what he was going through. My heart squeezed with hope at the flicker of his usual self surfacing. He pulled me into his arms, settling me atop his lap.

"Ryder!" I hissed, fully aware of how he spasmed in pain from my body brushing against his ribs.

He just waved me off after recovering. "I'm fine, Charlotte," he murmured, breath labored.

My jaw tightened, and I shook my head, pegging him with a hard stare. His lips quirked up, a flicker of playfulness warming his gaze. It was good to see that again. I blew out a breath, all of the annoyance leaving me. "I'm sorry for being such a nag."

He cupped the back of my head, pulling me in for a kiss. "You ain't a nag. Fussy, that's for damn sure, but you ain't a nag."

I huffed a laugh, leaning my forehead against his. "I'm just worried."

He pressed a kiss to my forehead. "I know. And I know I don't make this easy."

"You said it, not me," I chuckled.

"Thank you, for all you're doin'." He tucked a piece of hair behind my ear, his thumb grazing my cheek, sending a spear of desire straight to my heart.

"Um…are you two going to kiss again?" Cason's voice in my ear nearly made me jump out of my skin.

Ryder groaned at my sudden movement, buckling against me. Guilt gripped me, worry washing away the lighter feelings there just a moment ago. "Oh my God. I'm so sorry!"

It took him a minute to recover—each second ratcheting up my nerves higher and higher. How was it that he was so quiet? The amount of times I'd forgotten he was there… A secondary wave of guilt settled over me. And shame. A lot of fucking shame. I'd been so absorbed in Ryder that I'd completely forgotten about Cason.

I disentangled myself from Ryder's embrace, unable to meet either his or Cason's stares. "I'm going to go take a shower and get ready to go. Cason, you should probably get your overnight bag ready for Grandma's."

"Aw, but why can't I go with you guys to Uncle Ryder's surgery?" he groaned, a pout drawing on his face.

"Because you can't miss that much school, bud."

He let his arms go limp at his sides and tilted his head skyward, a loud sigh escaping him. I readied myself for a meltdown. The stance, the defiant look in his eyes…they were telltale signs of his that he was about to go off like a bomb.

But before I could diffuse the situation, Ryder's voice drew Cason's attention. "Hey, bud. How 'bout we make a deal?"

Cason leveled Ryder with a questioning look.

"When I get back this Tuesday, I'll make sure your Uncle Cash, Uncle Mav, and I are there to pick you up from school."

Cason's blue eyes lightened like the sky after a thunderstorm. "Can you guys take me riding too?"

"We'll talk to Uncle Mav and Cash about that, bud," I cut in before Ryder could try and sneak in a way to get himself on the back of a horse again. Before I knew it, he'd be trying to get on a bull. The thought alone terrified me, but I pushed it aside. I wasn't going to worry about rodeoing right now. We had quite a few weeks until that topic needed to be brought back up. "Uncle Ryder won't be riding anything for a little bit."

It was Ryder's turn to groan as he mimicked a similar head tilt to Cason. I just shrugged, returning my gaze to Cason. "Does that sound like a plan?"

He tapped a finger to his chin once, twice, three times, before finally offering me an emphatic nod. "Deal."

I nodded, grateful to have diffused that situation. "Good. Now go get ready."

RYDER AND I PULLED up to my mother's house in his truck. He'd all but begged me to drive, to which I'd hesitantly agreed, under the condition that once we left my mother's, I'd drive. It hadn't gone as smoothly as the situation with Cason, but I'd managed to get my way in the end, so I'd take my wins where I could.

Worry gnawed at me as I helped Cason grab his things, and we walked to the front door. Mama had been surprisingly understanding of Cason staying with her for the next couple days so I could take Ryder up to Austin for his surgery. I couldn't help but wonder why. Understanding or agreeable just weren't two words I'd ever use to describe the woman.

Each step toward the front door felt like another second ticking down on a bomb, only when this one exploded, I didn't know exactly what damaging effects it would have. All I knew was that there *would* be some. I was certain of it.

"Hi, Grandma!" Cason chirped as she opened the door and he barreled into her, giving her a hug.

"Cason! Careful," I said, not missing the way my mother winced or the sharp intake of her breath. "Hi, Mama."

Pain shone in her icy eyes, but she held herself up tall, looking down her thin nose at me. "Charlotte. How's Ryder? Is he doing alright?"

Her curiosity struck me by surprise. What was the hidden agenda? Why was she concerned? She couldn't *actually* care about him. So why did she sound sincere? "He's doing okay. I left him in the car so he didn't have to get out. Too much movement bothers his injuries."

She nodded, gaze flicking to the truck for a moment then back to me. "Why don't you come in for a moment? Cason, there's a bowl of Lucky Charms and strawberries on the dining table for you."

Cason squealed even as I bit my lip. "Oh, um…" I glanced back at Ryder, offering up a single finger to let him know I'd be out in a minute. He nodded, and I met mother's stare once more. "Okay, sure."

Tension, thick enough to cut with a knife, filled the living room as we made our way into the house. My mother limped over to her recliner and sat in it while I took a seat on the couch, trying to ignore my pulse pounding in my ears. What did she want to talk about? Her gaze gave nothing away, as usual. Was she going to yell at me for taking Ryder? Try to guilt trip me into leaving him?

Her gaze settled behind me, and I turned, finding one of the only photos of her and my father on the wall. They were so young. Probably younger than me. Some unreadable emotion settled around her as I turned to her, but I couldn't make out what it was.

"That was taken the day we met," she said softly, the normal bite in her voice all but absent. My brows furrowed, but I didn't dare say anything. I just sat there, poised on the edge of the couch, my left leg bouncing nervously.

"It was the summer of '91. I was there with some friends. He'd just won the Steer Wrestling event with a record-breaking run and thrown his hat into the crowd. I caught it—" A ghost of a smile curved her lips. "It's like there was magic in that hat, pulling me under his spell the moment I picked it up. When I found him after to return it, that was it. I took one look at him up close, and I was his. He asked if he could buy me a drink, and I never left after that." She huffed. "People say love at first sight doesn't exist, but I have no other way to describe it."

My heart panged, even as my nerves wound tighter in my chest. I'd never seen her like this before. Never heard her talk of Daddy this way. For as long as I could remember, she'd only ever talked about him with cold bitterness.

"We went on the road together, bouncing from rodeo to rodeo. It was a whole group of cowboys. They welcomed me into the fold like I'd always been a part of their lives." That ghost of a smile pulled just the tiniest bit wider. "We had fun. Lots of fun." As the next words rolled off her tongue, her gaze hardened a fraction. "They always talked about starting up a ranch together… About the big *dream*. Bucking horses, at the time. They'd designated roles, created the brand and name. They talked about it so much, I couldn't help but believe in it."

My stomach knotted as I thought of Ryder's brand. The boys talked about the dream all the time—they had the name, the brand. Was this just a thing that cowboys did? Was their idea something that would die out as the years went by? I shook off the thought. *No.* Ryder, Cash, and Mav were too close to drift apart. To let that idea die.

Was she trying to scare me? It wouldn't work. I believed in Ryder. He was more prideful and stubborn than anyone I'd met in my life, save for my mother. He was too determined. If anyone could make it happen, he would.

She went on before I could question what this had to do with anything or where this was going. There was a lesson in here somewhere. A point to all of this uncharacteristic talking. But I still couldn't figure out what it was.

"The dream died shortly after your sister was born. We settled down here—traveling cross-country wasn't the best while raising a baby—and your father started becoming a bit more choosy about the rodeos he partook in. His friends went on their way, drifting on the wind."

A flicker of annoyance stirred like an ember to kindling. Cash and Mav would never leave Ryder. They were thick as thieves. They were brothers. Was this some roundabout way of trying to make sure I didn't get pregnant? Of scaring me into not being in a relationship with him? My fingers curled into fists at my sides. "Ryder, Cash, and Mav are nothing like Daddy's friends."

Her mouth drew upward, a cold, smug smile flitting across her lips. "I never said they were."

I bit back a snarky reply, not wanting to give her the satisfaction of starting a fight. Sucking in a deep breath, I forced the fire in my soul to wither to ashes. "Where are you going with this, Mama?"

Her voice still held that overly calm tone as she spoke. "For a while, everything was perfect. I was convinced your father had finally found something far more important than rodeoing. He had you and Sheldon. But, especially, *you*." Something shifted in her gaze, the glacial depths hardening into fractals of ice even as her voice remained the same. "Even when I got diagnosed with R. A., your father refused to give up rodeoing, but I thought for a moment he'd give it up for *you*. To be there for *you*. Oh sure, he loved Sheldon, but *you* were his world. If anyone could make him realize his dream was right in front of him, it was you."

Accusation shone in her eyes. The weight of her stare so heavy, it crushed the breath from my lungs. Was she really blaming my father's death on me now too?

Tears burned in my eyes as I narrowed my gaze on her. "Get to the point, Mama," I ground out.

My mother leaned forward, all pretenses of sincerity gone. "Let me put it plainly, Charlotte. Horses will be horses. Pigs will be pigs... And cowboys will always be cowboys. Rodeoing is their one true love. Are you ready for that? Are you ready to always be second best? To watch your children—if you're stupid enough to have them with him—be second best?"

My breath left me, my jaw clenched so tight pain pulsed through it. "You're just saying this bullshit to scare me."

She laughed, the sound bitter, dark, and cold. "You're a fool, Charlotte. A damn fool. You couldn't save your father, what makes you think you can save this boy. You will *never* be enough."

The words hit me harder than a sledgehammer to the gut. Harder than a freight train to the heart. My lungs screamed for air, but I couldn't breathe, couldn't think. I just sat there, paralyzed in place. Something dropped into my lap—a tear, I realized— my leggings absorbing the water. Another tear followed. And another. And another.

My vision blurred. So, that was the lesson. *Message received loud and clear.* I blew out a trembling breath, forcing myself to rise on legs like jello. I wiped furiously at the tears leaking down my cheeks. Settling my gaze on her, I said quietly, "You didn't need to go to such extravagant lengths to reiterate just how much you hate me, Mama, but thank you for story time."

My mother rolled her eyes. "I'm trying to prevent you from making the same mistakes I did. Trying to show you the path you're walking and how it will end. Do you want to be like me, Charlotte?"

"I. Will. *Never.* Be. Like. You," I bit out. "And Ryder isn't Daddy."

She waved a dismissive hand in the air. "They're all the same. That's what I'm trying to tell you. You think you can change them, tame them, but they're wilder than any horse. They can't be broken, they're too stubborn, proud."

I wiped my tears. I wouldn't let her make me feel small and stupid. "Too stubborn and proud?" I huffed bitterly, a sneer drawing on my lips. "Sure you aren't talking about yourself, Mama?"

"Oh, stop being dramatic, Char—"

"No, you're the one being dramatic. You dragged me inside here, wove some grand, old tale, only to say what you've been telling me my entire life. That I'll never be good enough. Well, thanks, Mama… You know what? I think I'll just take Cason after all."

Some of the ice melted in her gaze, doubt and worry creeping along the weathered planes of her face. "No. *Do not* take him away from me."

I wanted to. A selfish, angry part of me wanted to. But that wasn't fair to Cason. From what I'd seen of their interactions, she truly did love him and treated him well. Until she did something or said something to him horrible enough to justify never seeing her again, I wouldn't keep him from her.

Leveling her with the hardest stare I could muster through my tears, I hissed under my breath, "If I find out you've been shit-talking Ryder, Cash, or Maverick to Cason, it'll be the last time you see him. You can hate them all you want, but they've been *so* good to him, and I won't let you poison him against them."

I stormed off before she would get in a word. Cason wasn't at the table when I entered the dining room, he'd gone off to the guest bedroom to play with his toys. "Hey, bud. I'm gonna go, okay?"

He nodded, coming to hug my side. "Are you and Grandma fighting again?"

I sighed. *No use in lying to him.* "Yeah, bud."

"Why?" His eyes dimmed with sadness.

Running a hand through his hair, I replied, "Your grandma and I don't see eye to eye on a lot of things."

"What does that mean?"

"It means we don't agree. But that has nothing to do with you, okay? It'll be alright. I hope you have fun with Grandma. Ryder and

I will Facetime you tonight from the hotel, okay?" I bent down and pulled him into a hug.

He clutched me back for a long moment. "Love you, Auntie Charlotte."

"Love you too, bud."

I WALKED OUT OF my mother's house like a bat out of hell. Rage danced in my veins, my skin stiff from the tears staining my cheeks. Ryder still hadn't moved to the passenger seat, which only fueled my fury. Why was it that everyone I loved had to be stubborn as hell?

I stalked over to the driver side and wrenched open the door.

"Hey, you okay?" He frowned.

"No, I'm not. Now move over, I said I was driving."

"Are you su—"

"Now, Ryder." My voice dipped low.

He threw his hands up in a placating gesture, sliding slowly out of the truck. Every second I spent in this fucking driveway was too long. My blood boiled at the mere thought of being so close to that wretched woman. I needed to be as far away from her as possible.

I knew I was being rude, mean, and callous, but it took everything in me not to fall apart. It was either wrath or tears, and Mama didn't deserve my tears. She didn't deserve my anger either, really, but anger sure felt a hell of a lot better than crying.

It wasn't until we'd gotten out of town and on the highway that my heart rate had begun to calm.

Ryder's calloused hand settled on my thigh. "Talk to me, Charlotte." His voice, soft yet stern, forced words to my lips.

"Piss on her," I growled.

I didn't even realize I was crying at first. I kept turning on the fucking windshield wipers, thinking it was raining. But nope, just me being a hot mess, unable to control my emotions.

I don't remember Ryder telling me to pull off the road. I don't remember even listening, or how I ended up facing towards him, his hands cupping my cheeks, his black gaze pleading as he begged me to talk to him. But there I was in park, hazard lights blinking, sobs wracking my body so thoroughly I thought I might pass out.

"What the hell happened?" he breathed, concern ringing in his gravelly voice.

Could I tell him what my mother said? I *should*. I wanted to, but part of me just couldn't bear uttering the words again. It was already bad enough that they lived in my head, replaying like a broken fucking record over and over and over.

Besides, what good would it do? He'd reassure me that he wasn't going to do any of that. That whatever happened between my parents was their own story. That we had our own, and we controlled the narrative. Ryder didn't need this right now, anyways. Didn't need to carry my worry as well as his own into tomorrow's surgery.

He'd been strong for me through so many moments already. He'd held me together and let me fall apart in his arms… It was my turn to be that safe haven for him.

Mama wasn't going to ruin that.

Pressing a firm, desperate kiss to his lips, I let myself get lost in the feel of him for a single, long moment before pulling away. "Nothing, Ryder," I whispered against his lips. "Not anymore."

His brows furrowed, worry still clinging to his gaze but he didn't press. For which I was forever grateful.

Chapter Forty-Four

Truck Bed

Ryder

Four weeks. Four weeks since my accident. Three weeks since my surgery. My eye socket still bothered me by the end of the day, but for the most part, it was easy enough to ignore. The bruising would stay for a bit, but I didn't mind. The knee was more temperamental. Physical therapy was helping—some days it felt almost back to normal, then the slightest tweak damn near brought tears to my eyes.

The ribs were the worst though. I'd had broken ribs before, more times than I could count, but I always forgot what a pain in the ass they were. Everything hurt them. Breathing, laughing, working out, sleeping. All of it.

The only good thing to come out of this was moving in with Charlie. There'd been some bumps and curves to navigate, hell, we were still navigating them, but, damn, I loved waking up to her every morning, holding her in my arms every night. She could be a bit overbearing on occasion, but overall, she'd been such a blessing. One I'd never tire of.

Sweat dripped down my face as I went through my daily workout in the gym the boys and I had built on the back of the bunkhouse.

The number of modifications I'd had to make just to work out was ridiculous, but I'd be damned if I wasn't ready to ride the minute I got the okay from the doctors.

The door slammed open, so loud it drowned out my music. I flinched on instinct, my ribs barking in agony, and I growled out a whole string of curses.

Cash whistled, spurs clinking against the ground as he walked. "Damn, look at you go! Told you, you didn't even need this shit." Maverick moved like a shadow in his wake, his spurs joining in the chorus, his gaze positively murderous.

Steadying my breathing, I sat up, placing my elbows on my knees. "What's up?"

Cash grinned and tossed me something. I grimaced as I stretched my arm up to catch it, before glancing down to inspect the small clear vial. Banamine. Horse-grade anti-inflammatories. I met his hazel gaze—he'd taken off his glasses. "I thought you didn't want me takin' this shit."

"Yeah, well, I hate seein' you all depressed even more. Not even Charlie girl's wily charms are helpin' keep you calm at this point."

I rolled the bottle of NSAIDs in my palm, a war stirring in my chest. The logical part of me, that sounded a lot like Charlie's voice in my head, screamed at me to give it back. That taking horse-grade pain meds was a dangerous, stupid path to go down. But the other part of me, the wild, reckless part that longed to compete once more, all but drowned out the other half.

I wouldn't take it all the time. This shit was a lot more potent than my Norco. It was only for certain times, like riding, and practicing on bulls. And as soon as my side didn't feel like it was on fire, as soon as I could hold air in my lungs without buckling over in pain, I'd stop.

That was a promise.

I blew out a pained breath and nodded, my gaze meeting Cash's. "Well, let's get to work boys. I'm back."

Cash whooped, clapping his hands together. Maverick just scowled at me as I slowly pushed myself into a stand, my body pulsing with pain.

"I don't like this," he warned, his jade eyes pegging me with anger and concern.

I swallowed past the lump in my throat, lowering my gaze. I hated disappointing him, but I didn't know what else to do. I couldn't be out too long. I couldn't let my standings fall too much. Austin was a bust, and there weren't too many large rodeos until Cheyenne in the summer. It would be a busy next couple months of rodeoing if all went well. I needed to be on my A game.

"I'm sorry, Mav," I all but whispered, moving past him.

He turned with me, his deep voice sending a tremor down my spine. "She's gonna kill you when she finds out. Or leave. You really want that?"

I ran a hand through my sweat-soaked hair, biting back a wince. He was right. She'd be pissed if she found out I was doing this.

"You gonna tell her?" I asked. I wouldn't blame him if he did. I wouldn't be mad. But in the end, it still wouldn't stop me.

Maverick blew out a deep, sharp breath through his nostrils. "You're a fuckin' idiot," he huffed.

I nodded. "I know. I'm sorry."

Cash's crow of excitement pulled my gaze. "Let's get you on a bull!"

CHAPTER FORTY-FIVE

Fixin' To Break

CHARLIE

CASON AND I PULLED up to the Mooney ranch a quarter past four.

"You ready for your lesson today, bud?" I asked.

We'd settled into a routine of coming here almost every day. Ryder would head over a few hours earlier so he could have some time to himself and hang with the boys, then we'd go home after Cason rode. It worked out well, and Cason absolutely loved getting to spend so much time with the three of them, and Bad.

"Yep! I wonder who'll be giving me my lesson today," he mused, as I put the car in park and we got out.

I looked to the arena, some commotion going on at the opposite end. Probably Cash and Mav working cows or something.

I glanced around for Ryder. He wasn't there to greet me like normal. My brow furrowed. Okay, odd. Bad's shouts rose on the wind, but they were too far away to make out the words.

"What's going on?" Cason asked.

I shrugged, a little ember of worry flickering to life in me. "I don't know. Let's go see."

Gravel crunched beneath our feet as we started walking. My gaze remained fixed on the arena, trying to make out what the hell was going on. Where the hell was Ryder? He knew we were coming.

Cash's familiar bray of laughter should have been reassuring—at least they were here—but it only filled me with more worry. Dread. Because followed by that obnoxious laugh, was a string of words that turned the blood in my veins to ice. "Yeah, Ryder. Get some."

I tore off towards the other side of the arena just in time to climb up the pipe-stall and find Ryder in the practice bull chute.

My heart clenched, fear gripping it so painfully tight that my vision blurred at the edges. I opened my mouth to scream out his name, but no sound came out. I was helpless to watch as the gate slammed open and he went flying out the chute atop a brindle bull's back.

He rocked and twisted and anticipated the bull's moves, making it look so fucking easy. How was he doing this? We'd had to stop fooling around last night because of how much he hurt. But now he was riding a bull?

How?

Bad's voice echoed as he shouted for Ryder to get off. Ryder slipped his hand free and toppled to the ground. My heart stopped, completely stopped as flashes of Austin fluttered across my mind. But he didn't stay on the ground, to my relief. He popped up, a shout of pure undiluted joy escaping him, the grin on his face wider than Cash's trademark one.

The bull, having lost his rider, stopped bucking and stood in the middle of the arena while the boys whooped and celebrated.

"You. Fucking. Idiot!" I clambered over the other side of the railing to stomp through the deep sand toward Ryder.

"Oh shit!" Cash at least had the decency to sound surprised from his spot behind the chute.

Ryder's dark gaze landed on me, happiness turning to plain guilt in an instant. "Charlotte, I–"

"What the hell are you doing?" I seethed, coming to a stop before him.

He tried to draw me in close, his fingers cupping my cheeks for the briefest moment to try and calm me, no doubt, but I wasn't having it. I thrust him off, amazed that the shove only caused him a mild wince. Nothing like when we'd fucked last night. Nothing like when he sneezed or coughed, or, hell, even breathed. How the hell was this possible?

It was only when his fingers brushed my skin that I realized I was crying, my cheeks slick with white-hot tears. His dark gaze shone with regret, guilt, sorrow as he dipped his head in shame, pulling off his hat to run a hand through his hair. "I uh…I took some Banamine."

"You *what?*" I shouted, noticing two figures making a beeline toward me from the left, and another from my right. "Are you really fucking telling me that you're doing drugs now?"

"No! Charlotte! It ain't like that!" His words held a pleading note to it.

Anger, sadness, concern, and complete disbelief slammed into me, each emotion more intense and discombobulating than the last. "Then what the hell is it like, Ryder? Because I'm failing to understand why you felt like taking horse pain meds was the fucking answer."

"They're just NSAIDs, Charlie girl," Cash chimed in, finally coming to a stop at my side.

"Cash, shut the fuck up!" Maverick, Ryder, and I all managed to say in unison.

If I weren't so pissed—no, not even pissed, *livid*—then I'd have laughed. As it was, I just glared at him. "Was this your idea?" I snapped.

He threw up his hands. "I didn't tell him to do shit." I don't know why, but for some reason, I believed him.

My gaze settled on Maverick next. "And you?" I couldn't believe that he'd let this happen unless they bullied him into it.

Maverick didn't react to my biting tone. Understanding and sadness hung in his eyes. "You already know the answer, Miss Charlie."

"It was me." Mr. Mooney's words cut to the bone. "I gave it to him, and I told him to take it."

I whirled to him. "What?" I asked through a broken sob. "Why?"

"It's just somethin' our kind does, Charlie. He told me he needed to ride again and this was the way to do it. It ain't a routine thing, just a way to manage the pain in extenuating circumstances… Like today," he replied with a shrug. There was no shame on his weathered face, or in his hazel eyes. He spoke as if this happened all the time. Maybe it did.

A large shape moved into my peripheral vision and I turned to see the bull trying to sniff Maverick.

"Cash, put that fucking bull back in the pen," Mr. Mooney growled.

Maverick swatted at the bull as it tried to eat his shirt.

"Are we safe?" I asked, gesturing to the bull.

"Pilate's just our practice bull." Mr. Mooney waved away my concern. "He ain't like those headhunters the stock guys have. He's just annoying."

I shook my head, tears dripping down my cheeks, down my neck. I sniffled and wiped angrily at my face, settling a scathing glare back on Ryder. "Are you so fucking eager to hurt yourself again that you thought you'd speed it up by doing some stupid bullshit like this?" When he didn't respond, when he couldn't even have the decency to look me in the eye, I let out an angry huff. "I'm done, Ryder. I'm fucking done."

"Auntie Charlotte?" A warm weight settled against my side.

All of the rage left me as my gaze dipped to Cason. In its place, defeat. Heaps and heaps of crushing defeat. He'd seen all of this.

"Yes, Cason?" I choked out.

"Why are you yelling?" His words trembled as he spoke.

I glared at Ryder as a reply fell from my lips. "What Mister Ryder did was incredibly dangerous because he's still hurt. He scared me.

Very badly. And he did something very wrong. He was selfish. And stupid. And he's lucky he didn't hurt himself."

Ryder flinched, his guilt written into every dip and crevice of his handsome face. God, I hated him right now. Hated that even while angry, I couldn't help but be drawn to him.

"Are…are we not going to see him anymore?" Cason asked.

I shook, struggling to calm my breathing, trying not to break apart further in front of everyone. Gaze settling on Maverick, I managed to murmur, "Maverick, will you and Cash take Cason to go tack up Black-N-Decker for his lesson? Ryder and I need to speak alone."

"Yes, ma'am." He tipped his hat to me.

Cason tugged on my arm. "Auntie Charlotte—"

"It's okay, bud," I said, squeezing him to my side.

"Come on, little man," Cash said, ushering Cason along. He met my gaze, guilt written plainly on his face. "Don't go too hard on him, Charlie girl."

It took everything in me not to shout at Cash. Go easy on Ryder? He'd felt taking Banamine was a good idea. If he was going to be stupid, he better be tough. But before I could snap off some nasty remark, he and Maverick led Cason toward the barn.

"Put that fuckin' bull away!" Mr. Mooney reminded them as they left. I whirled to face Ryder, pausing as Mr. Mooney stepped into my path. "Charlie," he began.

I held up a trembling hand. "Mr. Mooney, with all due respect, I think you've said enough at this point."

I'd never seen him look so taken aback. He didn't try to press, though that wasn't entirely surprising. He simply blew out a deep breath, dipped his head once, and turned to Ryder. "You tell her the truth. I gave you that shit and put you up to it. Don't try to be noble and take the blame." He gave me one last look over his shoulder and walked away. "I guess *I'll* put the fuckin' bull away! Come on, dickhead, let's go," he yelled at the bull grazing at the far end of the arena now.

Ryder's sheepish gaze found mine, desperation and regret glimmering like stars against a midnight sky. "Charlotte—"

"You told me you'd be smart. That you wouldn't be reckless. This…" I waved a hand through the air. "This is why I didn't want to date you, Ryder."

And with that, I walked away, trudging through the sand.

I'd barely gotten to the arena gate when Ryder's hand caged around my wrist. Not tight enough to hurt, but firm enough to tell me he wasn't letting me go without a fight. I spun to face him, finding white-hot anger lining his gaze. "Now, hold on a damn minute, Charlie. You may have been hesitant to date me, but I ain't the one who announced to half of town that we were together."

Blinding fury of my own flashed through me. "This isn't about that! This is about you self-dosing yourself with horse-grade pain meds just so you could try and get yourself killed, Ryder! Are you so fucking eager to die?"

A muscle feathered along his jaw, his teeth clenching together. I prepared myself for the explosion—it's what Cal always did. The yelling would come next. Then the gaslighting. But I wasn't prepared for the quietness with which he spoke. "I shouldn't have done it. I knew it was wrong and stupid, but—" His words broke off, unshed tears hanging in his eyes like starlight. He blew out a breath and shook his head. "This is my life, Charlotte. This is—*was*—all I had. For so long this was all I had, I don't know how to just walk away from it. This is how I make a living. What am I supposed to do?"

The desperation in his broken voice all but doused the anger burning through my veins. But I clung to that last ember that hadn't withered to ash. "Not this. Not drugs. What was even the point of going to the doctor's if you're not going to listen to them? How you're able to walk around without crutches is still baffling to me. A feat of pure fucking stubbornness, I'm sure," I spat out before my throat closed up, tears rolling down my cheeks once more. I let out a deep, broken breath. "This…" My voice trembled. "I expected this of Cash. But not you."

His head dipped, and he pulled off his hat to spear his fingers through his hair. He glanced up at me. "I know. I promise I won't do it again. I swear it."

Was I stupid for wanting to believe him? Probably, but I wanted to.

"I can't watch you die," I choked out, burying my face in my hands. My heart pounded in my chest, hard enough to crack a rib.

His arms enveloped me as he pulled me into his warm embrace. And despite how angry and hurt and worried I was, his familiar scent soothed my soul. God, I loved him. And that was the problem, wasn't it?

Was Mama right? This was what she was warning me about all along. That rodeoing would always come first. Over me, over his health.

I pulled out of his grip, sniffling as I met his pleading stare. "What if you'd gotten more hurt, Ryder? Better yet, what happens when that Banamine wears off? You think you were hurting this morning, I'll be surprised if you can even walk tonight."

"I know, I wasn't thinking. I—"

"That's for damn, fucking sure." I traced gently over the lines of the still healing bruise beneath his eye, the skin still black and blue and yellow. The lengths he went to for this sport. "Are you still taking the meds the doctor gave you?"

"Yes, ma'am." He nodded.

"And how do they mix with the Banamine?" I demanded.

He rocked back, he hadn't even thought about that part. *Of course not.*

"I…I don't know. Honest. I think it's fine."

"You *think*?" I shook my head. "I don't know if I can do this, Ryder."

The color drained from his face, his black eyes turning desolate. "Please, Charlotte. I—"

"I love you…more than I should. But I don't know if I can do this. I can't be in a relationship with someone I don't trust."

"No, please. You can trust me. You know you can. What do I need to do? Want me to pour the rest of it out? Give it to Bad or Maverick? What do I gotta do to keep you?" I'd never heard him beg before. Never wanted to hear it again. This absolutely broke my heart.

Give up rodeoing. The traitorous little thought danced through my mind, sounding eerily like my mother's voice. I squeezed my eyes shut, tears leaking through. I couldn't ask that of him. I *wouldn't* ask that of him. I wasn't my mother, nor would I ever be. Did him rodeoing terrify me? Yes, absolutely. But he loved it, and even today, seeing so much joy on his face was reason enough why I'd never force him to choose.

Maybe it was foolishness, maybe it was the petty part of me that wanted to prove my mother wrong, or maybe it was both, but I found myself saying quietly, "I'm going to go clear my head and think a bit. Will you bring Cason back when he's done with his lesson? We can talk more when you're home."

I didn't miss the way a glimmer of hope shot through his gaze. He cupped my face in his hands, pressing the softest kiss to my forehead. "Of course. I love you, Charlotte."

I murmured the words back before leaving him.

Tears hung in my eyes as I got in Sheldon's comet grey Tacoma—well, my Tacoma now since I'd started taking over the payments so it wouldn't get repo-ed. They slid down my cheeks as I headed out the drive and onto the main road. I needed to get out of there. Being so close to him, inhaling his familiar, wonderful scent, and hearing the timbre of his gravelly voice did dangerous things to my mind. I needed time to think clearly.

God, I wished Sheldon were here. To talk to. To tell me what to do. I didn't have anyone but Mama here, and Lord fucking knew I wouldn't be going to her with this particular problem. None of my friends back home would understand what I was going through. Besides, most of those friendships were superficial anyways.

My mind settled on a certain blonde cowgirl. Before I could think twice about it, I found her name in my phone—thank God she'd given it to me at the bar that night—and pressed on it.

The minute the dial tone sounded in my ear, I contemplated hanging up. She hardly knew me. Besides, she rode too. Was she just as crazy as Ryder? Cash would probably argue yes, because barrel racers, in general, were just a whole other level of crazy. But a little voice in my head told me to stay on the line.

She answered on the second ring, her smoky southern drawl a welcome sound.

"Hey, Cheyenne. It's Charlie. I know this is totally random, but are you uh…are you free to talk for a minute?"

"Of course, girl. What's up?"

I blew out a breath and launched into a retelling of what'd just gone down. Cheyenne whistled when I'd finally finished. "Well damn, girl… I'm sorry. But it ain't surprisin'. Ryder's one of the most stubborn, determined guys I've ever met."

I huffed a laugh as I drove down through town. "Stubborn and determined is an understatement."

Cheyenne's answering chuckle lightened some of the helplessness inside me. "So, what're you gonna do?"

"I don't know," I groaned. "I was hoping for some insight."

She laughed. "Well, shit. You've come to the *wrong* girl for datin' advice." A laugh of my own escaped me as she went on. "I see both sides. I *get* why Ryder did it. I don't agree with it, but I do get it. My daddy did that shit all the time. It's just somethin' that's done in our world…"

"That's what Mr. Mooney said."

"I ain't tryin' to justify his actions. He was an idiot, and lucky he didn't get more hurt. So, I get your side too. You have every right to be pissed. Especially with your past." She let out a deep sigh through the phone. "I guess at the end of the day, you gotta decide if you love him enough to give him another chance… I mean, Ryder ain't the type to do this shit. I've not known him in the past to do somethin' so stupid, and I think after this time, he won't try pullin' that again. But it's up to you."

"Yeah, you're right." I sighed, glancing out the window, half surprised I'd made it to the house. I hadn't even remembered driving through most of town… *Whoops.* I killed the engine when I pulled up in the driveway, and headed for the front door, placing the phone to my ear so I could hear her again.

"I mean, do you love him?"

"I do," I admitted plainly. "More than I fucking should, more than I'd like to admit, especially given how short of a time we've been together. I've never felt this way with someone before. It can't just be the honeymoon phase, can it? I've dated plenty of guys, not once have I felt like this with someone."

Cheyenne's laughter was warm and smoky on the other end of the line. "Girl, you got it bad…and you have your answer. The best things in life are hard to come by. You gonna give up on that kinda love, or work things out?"

I sighed, and unlocked the front door, hanging my keys on the rack as I strode into the house. "You're right. Thank you, Chey. Truly."

"Of course, girl. I'm glad you called."

"Me too." I smiled.

"Hey, once y'all kiss and make up, y'all should come up to San Antonio for the night. Celebrate Cash and Mav's overall win for ropin' in Austin."

My lips hooked up into a grin as I started tidying up the living room and kitchen. "Don't even pretend you really care if Cash, Ryder, or I show up as long as Maverick does."

Her laughter was infectious. If I could see her, a smile rivaling the sun in its intensity would be shining on her lips. "Guilty," she said, sobering.

"Tonight probably won't work because I have no one to watch Cason, but what about tomorrow? I'll talk to everyone and call you in the morning?"

"Sounds like a plan."

Hanging up, I scrolled through my music and put on a country station before getting to work on cleaning. I may not be able to control what Ryder did, but at least I could feel in control of *something.*

CHAPTER FORTY-SIX

The Devil Wears Lace

RYDER

WITH EACH MOMENT THAT passed after Charlie left, my anxiety rose. Higher. Higher. Higher. I wasn't the type to be nervous, but as the evening wore on, my worry only grew. I was wound so tight I was afraid I'd explode.

Cason seemed just as nervous as me on the drive home—his legs fidgeting restlessly, solemn gaze constantly landing on mine whenever I looked in the rearview. He'd been a step above crying for most of the afternoon.

Guilt festered in my gut. Well, damn. As if I didn't already feel like I'd disappointed Charlie, I'd caused problems for Cason as well.

I'd been stupid. So fucking stupid. How had I thought I could get it past her? How could I have thought it was a good idea?

"Uncle Ryder?" Cason's voice quaked.

I met his blue-eyed stare in the mirror. "Yeah, bud?"

"Are you and Auntie Charlotte okay now?"

I blew out a breath, my gaze flicking back to the road. I couldn't look him in the eye as I replied, "I don't know."

He didn't say anything else, but I heard him sniffling from the backseat, saw tears shining in his eyes when I glanced at the rearview mirror once more. The rest of the way that question kept racing through my mind, ratcheting up my nerves to a whole new level.

By the time I pulled up to the house, my heart danced against my ribcage. Charlie would kill me if she knew I thought this, but I was grateful the Banamine hadn't worn off yet. Between the nerves and pain, I wouldn't be able to function.

My boots felt like they were made of lead as I trudged across the driveway. Charlie's silhouetted figure leaned against the open door, warm, buttery light spilling onto the dark porch around her.

She greeted Cason with a big hug before he disappeared into the house. Trepidation coursed through me as I walked slowly up the steps.

"Hey," I murmured, coming up to her.

She surprised the hell out of me by pushing up and placing a soft kiss on my lips. But there was something guarded in her eyes, in her movements. I couldn't read her—usually an easy thing for me to do. But not tonight. She was a closed book as she pressed a hand to my chest.

"We okay?" I asked, wrapping her in my arms.

Another soft, brief kiss. "We'll talk after Cason goes to bed."

I nodded, even though my heart felt like it might beat out of my chest. Well, damn. I wanted this tension between us gone. Needed it. But I wouldn't push her. Not when she held all the cards. So, I trudged inside, quelling the burning need to fix whatever was going on between us.

I PACED CHARLIE'S BEDROOM, back and forth, back and forth, a part of me surprised I hadn't worn a path in the carpet. The door opened at eight thirty, Charlie slipping inside. Her gaze met mine, those stormy depths still just as unreadable as earlier.

"How're you feelin'?" I asked.

She shrugged, hugging her arms around her torso. "I'm tired."

I moved to her, reaching out a tentative hand. "Tired-tired or soul-tired?"

Tears hung in her eyes as she met my gaze and placed her hand in mine. "Both," she whispered as I pulled her to me, my arms caging around her. She melted against my touch. Had to be a good sign, right?

I tilted her chin up toward me. "Well, maybe this'll help."

Her brows furrowed as I released her chin and pulled her toward the bathroom. While she'd been putting Cason to bed, I'd grabbed all the candles I could find, drew up a bath, and turned on the jets in the jacuzzi tub. The scent of her favorite bath salts filled the room—lavender and vanilla.

She huffed. "So, you've decided to go with bribery to win me over?"

Fuck, my stomach clenched as I turned to meet her gaze. Damn, I'd only wanted to do something nice for her, I hadn't meant to offend her.

"I'm sorry," I replied, blowing out a breath. "I didn't do it for that. You've been doin' so much for me the past month, goin' above and beyond to take care of me…of Cason. You deserve so much more than this. I just wanted to show you that I see you. That I appreciate you."

Something glimmered in her eyes—warm and soft. She didn't speak though as she hovered before the tub.

"Go on, get in," I urged. "I'll be out in the room to talk when you're done."

She pursed her lips a moment, her fingers curling in the fabric of her shirt as she slipped it off her. Her leggings came next. All the while, her gaze never left mine. My breath hitched in my throat. My lips pulled up at the corners into the softest hint of a smile, my gaze taking her in. A goddess of tattoos and lace.

"What's there to talk about?" she finally said, slipping out of her bra and underwear before stepping into the tub.

I hated that I couldn't read her still. Challenge, mirth, a touch of sadness, and a hint of anger warred in her gaze, making it damn near impossible to figure out what was going through that mind of hers.

I blew out a breath and leaned against the granite countertop opposite the tub. "I'm sorry for what I did. I was stupid and selfish and I…I fucked up. You don't have to worry about me takin' it. I poured it out."

With her entire body from her throat down submerged beneath the bubbling water, she nodded, but said nothing as she pulled her damp hair up into a bun atop her head.

Desire and self-loathing battled within me.

"Last Sunday, when I came out of my mother's house crying after dropping Cason off…" I barely heard her weak whispers over the bubbles in the tub. "She said I'll never be good enough. That you'll always love the rodeo more than me. That I'll always be second best."

I pushed off the counter and knelt before the tub, a twinge traveling through my knee at the movement. Guess the medication was wearing off after all. "No, Charlotte. That…that ain't true." My heart clenched and twisted in my chest.

"I want to believe you, Ryder," she whispered, her gaze locking with mine. Pain and sadness shone plainly now.

I reached over the tub to cup her cheek. "What do I gotta do? Tell me. Please." Desperation clawed at me, shredding any lingering hope. Had I lost her? Had I let her slip through my fingers?

Her fingers gently curled around my wrist, her eyes fluttering closed for a moment as she leaned into the touch. "I won't pretend to understand why you felt the need to do it, especially when you're only a few weeks out from being okayed to ride again…" She blew out a sigh, meeting my gaze. "I'm still angry with you. I'm still hurt…but I love you. I love you so much it fucking hurts and the thought of not having you around…it terrifies me."

A broken sigh escaped me, relief soothing the worry knotted in my chest.

"But, Ryder…you do that shit again, and I'm done. I'm not kidding."

I pressed a kiss to her forehead. "Never again. I promise."

A flicker of doubt still burned in her gaze, but it was a challenge I'd gladly accept. I'd make her see. I'd make her trust me again.

"Get in," she murmured. A demand.

I fumbled with my boots, my belt, my jeans. Every movement sent a tremor of half-numbed pain through me, but I ignored it as I slipped into the tub facing her.

She shifted, straddling atop me so I could straighten my legs out. Her fingers traced over the lines of my brand. "Please don't make me regret loving you."

I slid a hand over her thigh, along the curve of her ass, before settling on the small of her back. Pulling her closer to me, I whispered, "I won't."

Charlie shook her head, her free hand slithering up my chest to cup the side of my neck. "Words mean nothing, Ryder. Actions…actions mean everything."

I nodded. "Anything—" I brushed my lips against hers. "Anything you want. I'll do whatever."

I don't know if it was the relief or desire talking at that point, but at least when it came to this, they were in total agreement. I'd do damn near anything to keep Charlie at this point.

Our mouths met, her body melding to mine as she moved against me, sending a groan up my throat that she stifled with her kiss. *Fuck*. Her touch was like fire. Searing, scorching, sizzling. And like a moth drawn to flame, I'd burn for her. Our mouths danced to a silent rhythm as I lost myself in her.

I'd thought I'd lost her.

From the way things went down, I hadn't expected this…but, damn, I wasn't complaining. Sliding a hand up her torso, I palmed her breast, earning a moan from her.

"Ryder," she breathed, her mouth leaving mine as her head fell back, exposing the curve of her neck. I pressed my lips to the corner of her mouth, along her jaw, down her throat, before grazing her collarbone.

Her hand found my cock, pumping up and down. A surge of pleasure coursing through me. I reacted on instinct—biting her neck. Not hard enough to hurt or draw blood, just a little nip. A whimper left her and she arched into me.

"Fuck." The word was nothing more than a breathy whisper on her lips, low and throaty. She ground her hips against mine; my cock pulsed with need. The need to be inside her, the need to make her say my name again.

"What do you want, Charlotte?" I murmured, leaning back against the tub to take her in.

Her hooded gaze raged like a summer storm. "I want to fuck you."

She sure didn't have to tell me twice. "Yes, ma'am." I obliged, settling my cock at her entrance. She slid all the way to the hilt, rocking in a slow, steady rhythm. My hands settled around her hips, my eyes fluttering closed as I let her ride me.

A curse fell from my lips. Damn, she felt good.

It didn't take long to get me close to the edge. Her mouth found mine, fingers knotting in my hair as she kissed the air from my lungs. She was the most gorgeous, sexy thing I'd ever seen or held. She was a treasure—one I'd do better with protecting in the future.

One thing was for sure, I needed Charlie Evans as much as the air I breathed. Without her…well, I didn't want to know a life without her.

Water sloshed around us, suds spilling over the edges, but she didn't seem to care, not as she worked me higher and higher, like a tidal wave surging before the shore. Just as I reached the precipice, just as my release was but a stroke away, she slipped off my cock and rose from the tub, a wicked smirk on her face.

"Charl—"

"This is nothing compared to the hell you caused me today, Ryder," she replied, her eyes sparking with amusement.

Oh, she was a savage, wicked thing. Shaking my head, I couldn't help but chuckle. I guess I deserved that. But fuck…I wanted—no, needed more.

With a smug grin, she wrapped a towel around herself and sauntered out of the bathroom, her hips swaying.

I fisted a hand at my side and slammed it against the bottom of the tub—the water drawing out the sound and intensity. I had two options: one, take care of it myself, though the last thing I wanted to do was jerk off in the bathroom alone. Or two, just give up. Settle on having blue balls and take the punishment.

Fuck. I dipped my head back against the tub, a groan of frustration escaping me. *No.* No, I wouldn't accept that. If I'd learned anything about Charlie in these last few weeks, she liked things being a bit of a struggle. Whether it be choking, biting, tying her up—damn, just the thought of that night made my cock throb—she liked that loss of control, I'd realized.

Surging up from the tub, I strode naked, save for the drops of water sliding down my skin, to the bedroom to find her lying stomach down on the bed, scrolling through Tiktok...as if we hadn't just been hooking up in the bathroom a moment ago. As if she hadn't ridden my cock and left me.

"I don't recall us bein' done," I bit out, my words low, guttural. God, she had me fired up and turned on at the same time.

She glanced over her shoulder, smirk still on her lips, challenge dancing in her eyes. "I am."

I balked at her dismissal. "Bullshit. It's time to finish what we started." My desire pumped hot in my veins.

Her smirk turned into a beautiful, wicked sneer. "Make me."

Her words, that look in her eyes...they absolutely broke me. Challenge and lust and excitement rushed through me, taking over all my self-control as I wrapped my hands around her waist and dragged her ass back toward me while I loomed over the edge of the bed. I wasn't gentle as I thrust my cock into her. The cry that fell from her lips made me still within her.

"Charlotte?" I asked, my voice trembling—with need, with worry, I wasn't sure which at this point. Shit, had Cason heard. My gaze flicked to the door for a moment, my heart racing.

A low, husky laugh fell from her lips as she thrust back against me. "More."

I slammed my cock inside her once more, launching in a hard, fast tempo. She took it, every thrust, with a smile on her face. Her back arched as quiet moans and filthy curses fell from her lips. God, she was gorgeous. And mine. That thought alone brought me right back to the precipice. This time, I wouldn't stop until I'd fallen over the edge.

Grabbing a fistful of her hair and tugging on it with one hand, I slipped the other down to her core, my fingers stroking and teasing her bundle of nerves there. She cried my name as she shattered apart, the sight and sound sending my own release crashing over me. Lightning tore through my veins as I came, my hips bucking wildly. My movements slowed after a moment, and her storm-cloud gaze flicked up to mine.

Dear Lord, I hope Cason hadn't heard.

"Was…was that too much?" I asked. I never knew if I went too far. If I was suddenly crossing over into dangerous territory.

She shook her head, the planes of her face soft, the curve of her lips just as gentle. She slid off me and collapsed onto her stomach before patting the bed beside her. A silent invitation to join her.

I did, scooping her up and drawing her into my chest. I inhaled her familiar, welcome scent, savoring the feel of her smooth skin against mine, and listened to the way her breathing pattern slowed.

"I love you," she murmured sleepily.

I brushed a soft kiss to her neck. "I love you too."

Dear Lord, I did.

chapter forty-seven

The Good Ones

CHARLIE

THE NEXT TWO AND a half weeks were hands down the best I'd had in my life. Ryder had been true to his word, there'd been no more Banamine incidents; there was more talk about the ranch he and the boys wanted to buy as opposed to just rodeoing in general. In fact, he hardly mentioned going back at all. I couldn't stop the traitorous, terrified little part of my heart that hoped he didn't. These injuries weren't even as bad as they could have been—seven weeks was nothing in the grand scheme of things—there'd be more injuries, *worse* injuries. The selfish side of me didn't want to deal with that.

The Banamine incident only made me worry more. He was so quick to do something so, *so* incredibly stupid, and for what? To ride a stupid practice bull? If he made it big, he'd have more pressure, higher stakes, would he do it again?

"...Charlotte?"

Ryder's gravelly voice drew me from my dark thoughts. "Hm?" I managed to get out, glancing at him in the driver's seat.

He frowned at me, his eyes covered by his Raybans. "You okay?" Worry rang in his words.

My lips drew into what I hoped was a reassuring smile, Not wanting to worry him with my fears and doubts and intrusive thoughts. This was all still new and, to be honest, I just wanted to ride out this wonderful bliss for as long as possible. "Yeah, just nervous."

Not a complete lie. Dinner with Ryder's parents was definitely a reason to be. Sure, I'd met them, but sitting at a table, in their house, with no escape from their questions… Just the thought made my stomach flutter nervously.

Ryder squeezed my thigh reassuringly, his thumb resuming its gentle, soothing strokes after. "Don't worry. They'll love you."

I blew out a breath. I hoped so. Somehow meeting Ryder's parents felt different than meeting any of my ex's family. It felt more real, more…important.

It scared the hell out of me.

Everyone always talks about instant-love and how love at first sight is a joke, but maybe they were the ones who were wrong. Maybe love found us when we least expected it, and you could either ignore it or embrace it. So, maybe our relationship was a bit rushed, but the way he treated me since meeting him was far better than how any other man treated me—than Cal treated me—in any of my past relationships combined.

So, let the haters talk. It wasn't their love story.

The Wright's house was picture-perfect as we came up the drive—a sprawling two-story plantation home with white wooden siding and black window panes and shutters. A wrap-around porch with twin rocking chairs and a swing in the front encircled the home, while a large barn loomed off to the left along with a huge pasture. Three horses grazed on the lush grass. To the right, was a greenhouse and lavender fields. As I slipped out of the truck and grabbed Ryder's waiting hand, the sweet, soothing scent filled my lungs and I breathed in a sigh.

"Wow," I said, looking around.

Ryder's lips quirked up, but he remained quiet as we walked up the brick-lined path leading to the house. We hadn't even made it to the top of the stairs when his mother opened the door, a welcoming grin on her face. She was just as pretty as when I'd met her at the memorial, even in a black t-shirt, jeans, and boots. Her turquoise and rhinestone studded ball cap matched the jewelry she wore.

"Dinner's almost ready." She held her arms out to Ryder.

"Hi, Mom," he murmured, drawing her into a hug.

I don't know why, but seeing him so openly show affection made my heart squeeze. It was so different than the cold, distant relationship my mother and I shared. Not going to lie, a part of me was a bit jealous.

"And, Miss Charlie…" She pulled out of his arms to offer me an embrace. I didn't have much choice as she wrapped me in a hug. Not that I minded. She smelled of lavender and citrus. "Welcome to our home."

"Thank you for having me," I replied. "Your house is beautiful."

She stepped back and opened the door wider, ushering us inside. "Well, thank you." She looked at Ryder. "Your dad's pulling the ribs off the grill."

Ryder's eyes lit up as he glanced over at me, pulling me to his side. "My dad can't cook to save his life…except for ribs."

Lori chuckled and led us through the foyer, formal living room, and finally into the gorgeous farmhouse-style kitchen. The place was gorgeous.

Stroker Wright—I still couldn't get over that name—came in through the French doors leading onto the back porch, a tray of meat in his hands. "Ribs are ready."

The resemblance between him and Ryder, again, shocked me; they were like carbon copies of each other, which wasn't a bad thing at all. Looking at Ryder's dad just proved that Ryder didn't have to worry about his looks diminishing as he got older. He'd age like fine wine.

Lori hurried over and grabbed the platter from him and fluttered about the kitchen getting plates and utensils ready. Stroker came over to us and smiled down at me. "How're you doin', Miss Charlie? Keepin' this knucklehead outta trouble?"

"Trying to, sir." I smiled back.

He looked at Ryder, gaze flicking up and down him as he held out his hand. "How're you feelin'? That was a nasty fall."

Ryder shook his hand and nodded. "My ribs still bother me now and then, but the eye socket's healed, and I finished all my physical therapy. Doctor was surprised with how quickly I bounced back.

I meet with him Monday, so hopefully I'll get cleared to compete again."

Stroker blew out a low whistle before settling his piercing gaze on me. "And how do you feel about him competin'? You're okay with it?"

"Dad." Ryder's tone held a warning note to it, the glint in his black eyes sharp. But if his father noticed he didn't react. Not much probably unnerved him.

I pressed a reassuring hand to Ryder's wrist at his side. "It's terrifying, sir. Especially since it's how my daddy passed away when I was younger. but someone once told me that the best opportunities in life should scare us a bit..." My gaze flicked to Ryder's. The answering emotion shining there stopped my heart a moment. How could just a look melt me like that? How could he have so much power over me? "And who am I to tell him what he can and can't do. If it's what he loves…if it's what he's good at…why wouldn't I support him?"

Stroker glanced between us and huffed, the barest hint of a smile lurking in the corners of his mouth. "Well, I applaud you for your bravery, Miss Charlie." He clapped Ryder on the shoulder before moving past us to open the fridge. "Wanna beer, Ryder? Charlie?"

ALL MY FEARS AND worries washed away the longer we stayed at the Wright's house. Lori was the epitome of Southern hospitality. She'd all but forced food down my throat—delicious, amazing, mouth-watering food—and told me story upon story of Ryder, most of them involving Cash and Maverick to some extent.

She'd pulled the photo albums out after dinner, taking the time to explain each and every single photo as she and I ate pie on the back porch. Ryder and his dad hung out at the other end, their conversation quieter and definitely not as carefree as ours. A silent tension lingered between the two of them. Neither looked angry or frustrated, just slightly uncomfortable. Like they didn't know exactly how to act around each other.

Lori paid them no heed.

"Oh, and this one was his first rodeo win," she said, pointing to a grainy photo. Ryder held a brand-new saddle almost the size of him. He couldn't have been older than Cason.

"How did he get into rodeoing?" I asked. "Did you or your husband compete?"

Lori laughed. "Stroker hates horses. The only reason we have them is because of me. I barrel-raced growing up, but never anything serious. Cash's dad, Clint, is the one to blame for Ryder's undying love of rodeos," she replied with a soft sigh.

I nibbled on the peach pie, waiting for her to continue. Each bite was like a little piece of heaven.

"Cash and Ryder have known each other their whole lives. Violet and I were part of the same bible study, and we'd bring the kids with us when they were little. It's always been the two of them—then Maverick got added into the fold, whether he wanted to or not, sweet boy.

"We always went and supported Clint anytime he competed close, but I remember this one time… Ryder was four and he looked over at me with this look of—" She shook her head, a small smile lighting up her features. "Pure determination on his face. He said, 'Mama, I want to be a cowboy'. He started taking lessons from Clint that next week and just never stopped. This photo was from that same rodeo a year later."

I huffed a laugh, a smile of my own pulling on my lips. "Sounds like Ryder. I've never met someone as determined as him."

She glanced his way. "His father still struggles with it. He doesn't understand how Ryder, for as determined and disciplined as he is, can be okay with a career that holds so much potential for disaster. I think at the end of the day, Stroker's just afraid—we all are—that if he falls, he may not get back up again."

My heart panged in my chest, the memory of my father and then Ryder's accident in Austin replaying through my mind. I nodded, a lump lodging in my throat. I completely understood. And with him being so close to fully recovered, everyday brought more and more anxiety, because come Monday, when he was cleared to compete, he'd be raring to go.

Was I ready for that?

Chapter Forty-Eight

In Came You

Ryder

"**S**HE SEEMS LIKE A good girl," my dad said from my side, nodding at Charlie across the way. Her and Mom sat on the outdoor couch rifling through old, embarrassing photos of me. It wasn't surprising they got along.

I nodded, taking a sip of my beer. "She is. Better than I deserve."

"You think you're gonna marry her?" he asked. "Or is it too soon to tell? I know you ain't been together long. But…you've never brought a girl home."

"If she says yes."

I'd been planning everything. Since the morning after the first rodeo. I found a ring by that next Wednesday. Crazy, I know. But I knew—I knew I wanted Charlie for the rest of my life. And if she wasn't ready, well, then I'd wait until she was.

She was it for me. Call it stupid, but it was true.

"So, what's the plan, then?" My dad's voice cut through my thoughts. "You gonna ask her to marry you, then leave her to go driftin' from town to town for a rodeo? Or you gonna force her to go cross-country with you? What about her nephew? He's got school here, don't he? You gonna pull him out and homeschool him? You plannin' on havin' kids?"

I'd known it was coming, had been waiting for it, but I still couldn't quell the annoyance that flickered to life in my chest.

He didn't even let me answer before he began speaking once more. "I know you don't wanna hear it—"

"So, don't say it."

"Ryder, that girl you got there may be strong, but she ain't invincible. Everyone in town knows how her father died. You gonna do that to her too?"

"Thanks for the confidence, Dad," I ground out, my jaw and fist clenching tightly.

"Ryder—" My dad pegged me with his heavy stare. "You're one of the most determined, smart, capable men I know. I'm just sayin' you could be so much more."

"You mean I could be you," I replied, careful to keep my tone low, respectful, but still letting that edge of anger poke through.

"Ryder…"

"I know I'm never goin' to be what you want. I've accepted that. But I believe in myself, even if you don't. You don't have to agree with what I do. You don't even need to support it…but this is my life. And I'm sorry if that ain't good enough."

I left him there, my boots clomping against the wooden floorboards as I came to sit on the edge of the couch beside Charlie. She leaned back against me, and I pretended to listen to her and Mom as they talked about my childhood, but I was checked out. Lost in thought.

I wasn't enough in my dad's eyes. What about Charlie's? Maybe for now I was. But would it always be that way?

Cash and Mav were waiting for me as I pulled up to the realtor's office Monday afternoon.

"Well?" Cash all but bounced with anticipation. "You get cleared?"

I had half a mind to tell them no, just to tone down some of Cash's ridiculous exuberance, but I couldn't. I was almost as excited as him. A wide grin tugged on my mouth. "Clean bill of health, boys," I all but crowed.

"Fuck yeah! Let's get ya some money! Where we goin' this weekend? We got a couple rodeos within a few hours of San Anton…couple out by Houston. Hell, I'm even down for a road trip outta state."

Mav placed a calming hand on his cousin's shoulder. "Dear Lord, Cash. Calm down."

I nodded to the realtor's office. "Well, did ya get 'em?"

Maverick followed my gaze and shrugged. "Get what?"

I leveled him with a hard stare.

A rare, full-fledged smile graced his face as he nodded. Excitement rushed through me.

This was it. This moment. This next step…it led to bigger and better days. To our hopes and dreams.

"You got the keys?" I asked.

Cash's grin sparkled like diamonds. "He's got the keys, bud."

"Well," I grinned. "What the hell are we waitin' for? Let's go."

SETTING FOOT ON THAT ranch, standing in that main house for the first time knowing it was ours…I don't think I'd had a prouder moment. Sure, the houses on the property were outdated and needed some remodeling, the fences needing mending, the barn needed a bit of fixing, but not even that could dull the sense of accomplishment thrumming through my veins.

"Well, boys. I say this sure as fuck deserves a toast," Cash said as he sauntered in through the front door and headed to the kitchen off to the left. He placed a black plastic bag on the counter and pulled out two single shots of whiskey and a can of Coke for Mav.

Cracking open the top of Mav's can, he held it out, saying, "Here ya are, mama."

Maverick rolled his eyes, but that smile hadn't left his face since we'd met up in the parking lot. He took it without a fuss though. I followed suit, grabbing my bottle of whiskey and twisting the top off.

"To dreams made reality," I said, holding up my shot. "Here's to the start of Mercenary Ranch."

They both murmured in agreement, placing their drinks to their lips. I knew it was just store-bought whiskey, but I'd never tasted anything better.

Cash drained his bottle dry and whooped before rifling through the bag once more. "I also had these made." He tossed a black piece of fabric at me.

"Oh god, not another one of your shirts." Catching it, I opened it up to inspect the writing.

"Ah, shut up. This one's serious."

As my eyes fluttered across the wording and image, I couldn't help but agree. It was our brand and logo. The gold imagery stood out against the black backdrop.

"Well, shit…Did Cheyenne do these too?" I asked.

Cash nodded.

"They look good," both Mav and I murmured as one.

"You told Charlie girl yet?" Cash asked.

I shook my head. "No, not yet, but I got a plan. I'm gonna show her tonight."

Maverick's jade eyes found mine, a seriousness in his gaze. "*The plan?*"

Blowing out a deep exhale, I nodded slowly. "First the good news about competin', now this…feels right to try for a third."

"Well, shit!" Cash clapped me on the back. "Our boy's gonna be a married man."

Maverick's congratulations wasn't quite as loud—a knowing dip of his head and a firm handshake. "You'll treat her good."

I intended to.

"Alright, now who's goin' to help me get this place presentable?"

Chapter Forty-Nine

All The Time

CHARLIE

I CHECKED MY REFLECTION in the mirror for what had to be the dozenth time in a twenty-minute span. Was this too fancy? Too casual? As always, Ryder had been tight-lipped in his instructions.

"Get dolled up, we're goin' out," was his only response.

I knew he was excited to have gotten cleared to compete. He probably wanted to go out and celebrate, even if it was a Monday night. Mama had agreed to take Cason, and I'd dropped him off without more than a word to her. We still weren't talking after our last conversation.

My stomach twisted and tightened with nerves, my heart dancing a fast staccato in my chest. I'd said I was okay with Ryder competing, and I was, but I was also scared. He didn't need to see that, though. He needed me to be there for him. To support him.

With a final glance at myself, I blew out a breath and shrugged. Hopefully a black chiffon sundress and sandals worked. It was too hot for anything else, really. It wasn't even summer yet, but the heat had rolled in with a vengeance…and the humidity. God, how could I have forgotten about it?

Ryder's truck purred up the drive as I walked out the front door. He'd barely placed it in park before hopping out and racing for me, no limp or flicker of pain on his face. Before I could even figure out what he was doing he picked me up, spinning me in his arms. A squeal escaped me as I clung to him.

"How're you, Miss Charlotte?" he asked, setting me on my feet while still caging me to his chest.

He saved calling me that for special occasions now. When he was feeling particularly seductive or happy. It still sent shivers down my spine. There was a lightness to him I hadn't seen since before he'd gotten hurt. He had that same glowing happiness shining from within him as the day that him and I first started dating.

It made me melt all over.

"I knew you'd be excited to compete again, but I wasn't expecting this." I chuckled, twisting my fingers through his midnight waves at the nape of his neck.

He dipped his mouth to mine, kissing me slowly, unhurriedly. The type of kiss that always led to desire swirling to life low in my belly. The type that always led to our clothes coming off.

"Come on." He grinned, releasing his hold on me, save for my hand.

Ryder led me to the passenger side of his truck and opened the door. I slid in, biting back a smile as he hurried over to the driver's side and hopped in. After pulling out of the drive, his hand found my thigh immediately—the touch so familiar by now.

"So, where are we going?" I asked, glancing over at him as we headed through town.

"You'll see." The sly smirk on his lips just about melted me completely.

Happy Ryder was almost as infectious as Cash, except nowhere near as obnoxious. I loved seeing him like this. A pang shot through me. That's how much hold the rodeo had on him. Would he—*nope, shut it down.* I wasn't letting Mama's fears and opinions worry me. I wasn't going to let them drag the night down.

I quickly checked off a couple locations on my list of potential places we were going—the Mooney ranch, a handful of restaurants, even San Antonio—as we headed west outside of town. Odd, we almost never came out this way. But Ryder wasn't giving anything away. With each moment, my curiosity grew and grew and grew, until I was a bundle of nerves practically vibrating with excitement.

Funny how things could turn to shit in an instant.

The setting sun caught the reflection off something in the center console. A clear, medium sized bottle with a silver lid that glinted in the light. Black letters all but mocked me as I gazed upon them.

Banamine.

Rage. Unbridled, unchecked, blinding rage filled me, ensnaring me in its vicious grasp. No, he wouldn't take it. He'd gotten a clean bill of health, why would he? *Maybe he didn't stop taking it.* Maybe he'd only told me he did. Maybe the Banamine was to help with the last bit of pain. He, Cash, and Mav were already getting ready for a rodeo this weekend. Would he take it?

Even though it was shitty, even though I had no proof, angry words spewed from my mouth anyway. "What the fuck is that?"

Ryder's hand stilled atop my leg as he glanced between me and the bottle. He frowned. "It's Banamine."

"Yeah. And why the hell is it in your truck?" I snapped.

His frown dipped deeper, brows knitting together as he switched between looking at me and the road. "Bad needed it."

I scoffed. "You sure about that?" My words dripped with sarcasm.

Was I being unreasonable? Was I being paranoid? Maybe, but Bad given Ryder the medicine once already. I wouldn't put it past him to try it again.

A muscle feathered in his jaw, his fingers tightening around the steering wheel, but when he replied, his voice was calm if not a bit condescending. "Yeah. One of his old mares cast herself. He needed me to pick it up from the vet on the way home from my appointment."

It seemed reasonable, and a part of me, the logical part of me, wanted to believe him.

But as he continued, whatever sense I had disappeared, my vision going red. "You do know it's used primarily to treat horses for pain, right?"

So, he wanted to be an asshole? Well, two could play that game.

"Really?" I asked, mock astonishment coating my tone. "I thought it was used by cowboys as pain killers."

Fury blossomed in his eyes, his irises blotting out all the light in them. His bottom lip jutted out as he locked his jaw. Ryder pulled his hand from my thigh and gripped the steering wheel tighter with both hands. For a long moment, he didn't speak, the tension building, building, building. "You're really gonna go that low, Charlie?"

I bristled at my name on his tongue. He knew I hated him calling me that. He knew it and he'd done it anyway. "Tell me the truth, Ryder," I growled.

"I am!" He smacked the steering wheel with a hand. "I ain't takin' Banamine. What more do you want me to say?"

Tears pricked in my eyes as I settled my sights on the road ahead. I should have believed him, but something—my stupid thoughts—planted seeds of worry and doubt in my mind.

"No," he ground out. "No, you don't get to ignore me now. You don't get to accuse me of that, then just drop it. Tell me what's goin' on. This ain't just about the Banamine, is it? It's me gettin' cleared to compete, right?"

I rolled my eyes, clenching my jaw tightly as traitorous tears slipped down my cheeks. *Say no. Say no.* But it's like my throat had collapsed. I couldn't get a single sound out, let alone a breath. Rage and hurt pumped through me, fueling my tears. Did it scare me watching him compete? Yes. But had I done it and would I continue to do it? Yes. Because I loved him, because I believed in him, because it made him happy, and he made me happy.

So, why couldn't I say that? My heart squeezed, screaming to *just say something.*

But my mind had finally won over my heart, it seemed.

I shook my head, unable to meet his stare. "I'm scared."

He scoffed, raising a hand to smack the steering wheel again, but instead clenched it into a fist and lowered it to his mouth. When he finally spoke, a cold, hollowness I'd never heard before rang in his words. "Why did you stay then, Charlie? You could have called it off over a dozen different times now. Why did you stay through the surgery? Through the physical therapy. Why have me move in or continue down this path at all if you don't want me doin' this…"

"It's not that!" I choked out. "I don't want to lose you! I don't want you to die."

A string of curses fell from his lips as he settled his gaze forward on the road for a long moment before pegging me in place. Icy black voids glared back at me. "Jesus Christ, Charlie, how many damn times—"

"You can't tell me that you won't die. You can't fucking promise me that." I sucked in a heaving breath, trying and failing to calm my breathing.

Some of the anger softened in his face, and for a moment hope bloomed in my chest—for what, I had no idea. Pulling off his cowboy to run a hand through his hair, he sighed. "This ain't gonna work…we just…we don't understand each other on this, and I'm afraid we never will."

"W-what?" The word was little more than a cracked whisper. "Are…are you breaking up with me?"

"I love you, Charlotte. More than anything…but I don't know what to do to ease your fears, and until you come to terms with them, we're just gonna continue havin' this fight."

Tears flowed down my cheeks, blurring my vision. It hurt to breathe as I struggled to get air down my lungs. My heart felt like it'd been crashed into and drug through gravel. He flipped a U-turn on the two-lane highway and headed back for home. Each passing second sent my anger rising. Was he so quick to give up on us? To leave me because I had baggage?

"You know, Mama was right about you…you'll always choose the rodeo."

He pulled off the road and slammed on the breaks before turning to look at me. "What do you want me to do, Charlotte? Give up my career, give up my dream to be your safe, cookie-cutter husband? Maybe become a sheriff like my dad and put rodeos behind me?"

"You say it like it's such a bad thing," I whispered.

"Because it is. It ain't *my* dream!" His voice broke. I'd never seen such wild emotion from him. It was so opposite of how he normally was. He sucked in a loud, deep breath and blew it out, his cold stare holding me paralyzed. "Maybe if you actually had a dream then you'd understand why I can't just give up mine."

Whatever sympathy I may have had for him in that moment dissolved into a cloud of dust. "Fuck you, Ryder," I snapped.

One of his brows rose. "Tell me I'm wrong. You're the one who admitted months ago you didn't have one. So, tell me I'm wrong."

It's you. He was my dream. Building a life with him. Being his wife. Raising Cason together. Having kids with him. Growing old with him. Maybe it was pathetic that he was my dream—I'm sure plenty of people would think that if they knew—but I didn't see it that way.

Not that I was going to tell him that now. The stubborn, hurt part of me retreated far into myself. I needed to get away. I needed to leave. I needed to do what I did best...

Run away.

"Take me home, please," I murmured, turning my gaze straight ahead.

He blew out another breath and settled himself forward. "That's what I thought."

We didn't speak as he drove me home. As he opened up my car door, like the annoyingly chivalrous gentleman that he was. Not even as I paused a moment to look up at him. My mouth popped open, my heart urging me to say something, anything...

Some of my anger dissipated on the twenty-minute drive, mostly sadness and devastation remaining now. But Ryder was right. Until I came to terms with what happened to Daddy, I'd never be able to look at rodeos without heaps of negativity. And even though I loved him, it wasn't fair for us to constantly have this fight. He deserved someone who'd be his cheerleader, his biggest supporter. Not someone who doubted him.

I thought it could be me, but I was wrong.

My head won out in the end. With a final look at Ryder, I shut my mouth and walked toward the front porch, the sound of gravel beneath my sandals overwhelmingly loud.

It took me far longer than necessary to open the door—damn my fucking tears. As soon as I got through and closed it, my legs gave out, sob after sob slamming into me, blurring my vision and tearing the air from my lungs.

I cried there until my throat turned hoarse, until I had no more tears to shed…and even then, I cried some more.

CHAPTER FIFTY

Quittin' Time

RYDER

I GRIMACED AS THE door to the bunkhouse creaked open, reveal-ing Cash and Mav sprawled on the couch watching TV. Fuck, I didn't want to talk to them. Didn't want to explain what had gone down. My mind still reeled, my heart heavy. How had things gone from so good to such shit in the course of a minute? How had I lost her? Like, really lost her?

I kept my steps silent as I made for my room off to the left of the kitchen. If I was lucky, they wouldn't notice until I'd closed the door. But Dutch, ever faithful Dutch, heard me and came barreling over.

Cash and Maverick's head snapped to mine in unison, looks of first surprise, then confusion washing over their faces. I could barely hold Maverick's questioning stare. What the hell did I say? Just a few hours ago they were helping me get the house ready for a proposal. I shouldn't be here.

Cash opened his mouth to say something, but one look from Mav stopped him. Shame roiled within me. Dipping my gaze, I made a beeline for my room. I hated that I couldn't talk to them. At least not yet. But I had no words. I'd…*I'd* broken up with her. I was still surprised that I'd been the one to call it off. But I'd been angry and defensive and just…tired. Tired of having that fight. Tired of trying and failing to ease her worries. And, a part of me had done it so she didn't have to.

I knew she was terrified of turning into her mother. She'd mentioned before that she didn't want to end up giving me an ultimatum…and even pissed as hell, I didn't want to put her in that position. So, I made the choice for her. A choice she probably hated me for, but it was better this way.

Is it?

I wasn't the type to cry. Tears just didn't come easily to me, they never had. But as I closed the door to my room and fell onto my bed, Dutch curling up at my side, my chest tightened. My eyes blurred.

Why was letting go so much harder than falling in love?

I TOSSED AND TURNED all night, sleep alluding me. Every time I closed my eyes I was consumed with thoughts of Charlie. The good times, the bad, everything in between. I missed her, fuck, I missed her.

Grabbing my phone off the nightstand, I checked the home screen. My heart sank as I let out a breath I hadn't even realized I'd been holding. *Nothing.* A part of me, the stupid, traitorous part of me, hoped to see a missed call or text with her name on it.

Wiping the sleep from my eyes, I changed into a fresh pair of clothes and strode out of the room. The savory aroma of bacon and eggs drifted through the main room of the bunkhouse as I went and let Dutch out and took a seat at the dining table. Maverick stood at the stove while Cash sat in one of the chairs backwards.

Silence swarmed me, suffocating me in its cloying intensity. The fact Cash managed to be quiet this long was a damn feat. One I might've applauded if I weren't in such a shitty mood. His hazel gaze met mine, for once that familiar grin of his completely absent.

"What happened?" he asked earnestly. So earnestly I'd expect it from Mav and not him.

Maybe that's why I answered. "It's over," I muttered, staring at the table as I fiddled with my hands.

Cash's questioning gaze seared me. "Why?"

Maverick suddenly appeared at the table opposite me, right beside Cash, two heaping platters in hand—one of eggs and one of bacon. He divvied up a couple paper plates from the center of the table, along with some forks in silence. But his gaze was just as intense as Cash's.

With a sigh, I recounted the night, reliving it yet another time. It hurt just as bad as the first.

Cash blew out a low whistle, grabbing a piece of bacon. "Shit…I can't believe you're the one to break up with her."

I huffed. That made two of us.

Maverick didn't speak for a long time. So long that I'd made myself a plate and almost ate everything off it by the time he finally spoke. "You should call her."

My brow furrowed, mouth drawing into a hard line. "Why? What's done is done."

Maverick rolled his eyes. "Oh bullshit, Ryder. Since when the hell are you the quittin' kind?"

"Weren't you listenin', Mav? She's too scared. It's just…" I blew out a breath, running my hand through my hair. "It's better this way."

Mav's mouth drew into a scowl, his dark brows knitting together as annoyance flashed across his face like a streak of lightning. "You're a damn fool," Maverick replied, pushing his chair out and standing up.

"What would you like me to do, huh?" I asked, anger of my own rippling to life in my chest.

He whirled around, disbelief and anger lining his features. "Fight for her. Do you understand what people would give for a love like that? For someone to look at them the way she looks at you? There ain't no doubt in nobody's mind…that girl was made for you. And after a few minor bumps in the road, you're willing to just let her go." He shook his head and shrugged. "Maybe you don't deserve her."

Whether it was the anger in his tone or the way his words hit me—I didn't know— but one way or another it sobered me. I scrubbed a hand down my face. He was right.

Blowing out a breath, I pulled my phone out of my pocket and clicked on her number. My heart beat wildly in my chest, a part of me hoping she answered, the other part hoping she didn't. What would I say?

"Ryder—" The weariness and raw edge to her voice made me wonder if she was just as miserable as I was. "What do you w—"

"Please, Charlotte. Just…just let me talk." I took the silence on the other end of the line as answer enough. "I was, well, I was an asshole last night. I said things I never should have said. I'm sorry."

She sighed, and when she spoke her words were tight, choked out. "I said things I regret too. I never should have accused you of taking Banamine."

Relief blossomed in my chest, and hope. A flicker of hope.

"But, Ryder…you were right." Her voice broke. "Th–this isn't going to work. I can't be what you need." She paused, sniffling. "I'm sorry."

And then she was gone.

She didn't even give me a minute to reply, to argue, to convince her, or ease her fears. She was just…gone.

I glared down at my phone, at her name mocking me in the call log. The rage lurking inside me bubbled up, boiling over and filling me so thoroughly I saw red. With a curse, I threw my phone across the room, the glass shattering as it crashed against the wall.

Maverick was right. I was a damn fool.

CHAPTER FIFTY-ONE

Pieces

CHARLIE

M Y FACE HURT FROM crying so much. I didn't even know that was possible. My heart ached, as if the entire thing had been shattered into a million, sharp pieces that I had no hope of ever fixing.

I hated that one call from Ryder had my dying heart fighting for life, the sound of his voice sending a swell of emotion through me. But in the end, I'd forced myself to think logically. I'd rushed headfirst into a relationship I had no business being in, and now I was suffering the consequences. As much as I loved Ryder, as much as I would treasure every moment I had with him, I wasn't what he needed. I wasn't sure I ever could be. And I loved him enough to let him go so he could find that someone.

Even if it killed me.

I pulled up to Mama's house and checked my face in the rearview mirror. Dear Lord, I looked a mess. There was no way to hide the red-rimmed eyes or the puffy cheeks. Hopefully she wouldn't ask too many questions. Like why I'd sent her a text last night saying I needed her to take Cason to school and pick him up.

She waited for me at the front door, her eyes cold and unfeeling as they settled on me. "You broke up with him." It was more a statement than anything else.

I bit my lip and dipped my head. Not entirely true, since he'd been the one to say it initially, but semantics, right?

She huffed, a hint of smugness heating her gaze. "Cowboys will always be cowboys… I told you, you'd always be second best."

"Jesus Christ, Mama! Shut the hell up!" The words erupted from me like a volcano spewing lava.

Mama's icy eyes widened, astonishment rendering her speechless as her mouth opened and closed like a fish on dry land. I was just as surprised as her by my outburst.

My eyes burned as I glared at her. She was such a huge part of the reason for why I was so insecure in the first place. Maybe without her hateful words, I wouldn't be so afraid of Ryder rodeoing. "What is wrong with you? Is being right really that important? You see that I'm hurting…you see that I'm in a horribly low place, and you'd rather kick me when I'm down than help me back up. You'd rather watch me fail than be a *fucking mother* and tell me everything's going to be okay." I wiped angrily at my cheeks. "You want to know why I left five years ago? Why even Sheldon getting pregnant couldn't make me stay? It was *you*. You're so much more worried about being right and making everyone else feel small. Even now, constantly reminding me that I'm never going to be good enough, instead of being there, guiding me, teaching me *to* be good enough."

"Charlo—"

"No. Save the fucking speech, Mama. I don't need your jaded life lessons or pathetic excuses. If you can't start acting like a mother instead of a goddamn judge, then I'll be out of your life for good." I didn't need to mention that she'd never see Cason again, as well. She understood from the pure devastation that shattered across her harsh features.

Tears…actual tears hung in her eyes. I don't think I'd ever seen her cry before. *Tears showed weakness*, she'd always reminded me. The anger swirling in my heart cracked. Oh God…I'd done to her exactly what she'd done to me my whole life. I'd gone for blood, fully intent on taking the wind from her sails.

And then Cason was there, his tiny voice cracking with emotion. "Auntie Charlotte…wh-why are you yelling?" Fear shone in his blue eyes as he came to stand between Mama and I.

God, I'd hoped he wouldn't hear any of this. I drew in a shuddering breath before exhaling and kneeling before him to be more at eye-level. "I was upset with your grandma and I said some mean things."

"Why?" he asked innocently.

I brushed a stray, dark lock of hair back off his face. "Because sometimes when people are angry or hurting, they want others to hurt just as bad as them."

"But that's mean."

I thought of Ryder for an instant. Of the tit-for-tat arguing we'd done last night. How we'd both gone in for blood. I wiped fresh tears from my eyes. "It is mean, and it's not okay. I owe your grandma an apology."

I rose and looked at my mother. Her expression was guarded, but something shone in her eyes—an emotion I couldn't quite place. It wasn't anger or hatred or fury…no, it was too light for that.

My words were soft, all the fire gone, as I spoke. "I'm sorry for shouting at you. That wasn't okay. I don't need someone in my life to constantly make me feel like a failure…life does that well enough without your help. I need a mother to love me, help me, guide me. I don't know the first thing about being a mom, about raising a child…but I'm setting a boundary. I will not be treated or talked to like you've talked to me recently. If you can respect that, I'd like to try and salvage this."

A single tear slipped down her cheek as she stepped forward and placed a hand to my face. I flinched, half expecting a slap, but her touch was as gentle as the soft lines of her face. "You're doing far better with that boy than I ever did with you." The admission cracked the icy armor around my heart, but the next words truly broke me. "I'm sorry."

Mama never apologized. Never. I'd never heard her utter the words in her life. Sorry's were almost as bad as tears in her book of weakness. To get both in one day…

"Come on in… There's some leftover chocolate cake. You can tell me what happened."

I wouldn't say things were fixed with Mama—we had an entire lifetime of trauma to sort through—but she was trying. She'd bit her tongue on multiple occasions as I gave her the abridged—very abridged—version of what happened the night before. She'd apologized that it didn't work out, which was still baffling to me, but I'd take it.

At least when Cason and I left, I didn't have to worry about another fight with her. I just had to worry about ruining Cason's whole world as he asked if we were going to see Ryder.

"No, bud. Mister Ryder isn't gonna be coming around anymore," I said, meeting his gaze in the rear-view mirror.

"What do you mean?"

A lump lodged in my throat. How did I explain a break up to a five-year-old? "Mister Ryder…um, well, he and I got into a fight. And we realized that even though we love each other, we don't agree on one very big thing."

"Him rodeoing?" Cason asked softly.

Okay, maybe it wouldn't be quite so difficult to explain. "Yeah," I replied, nodding.

"But that's giving up, isn't it? Why wouldn't you try to work together to come to an agreement? My teacher says if we disagree on things, we need to talk them out until we come to a solution."

A little swell of pride surged through me. *Kid's smart.* I blew out a breath, my gaze flicking to the rear-view once more. "Sometimes there is no solution, bud. Sometimes the best thing to do is agree to disagree and walk away."

His face scrunched up, his dark brows knitting together. "Does that mean I won't get to see Uncle Cash and Uncle Maverick or the Mooneys anymore either?"

The way his little voice shook pulled at every heartstring I possessed. But I couldn't let him see them all. That would just cause problems. If Ryder was there…if we were around each other and he apologized and tried to win me back, well, I doubted I had the self-control to say no. And then we'd just fall right back into the same cycle all over again.

"I'm sorry, bud. But yeah."

Tears spilled down his cheeks. "Why can't you and Mister Ryder just make up?"

"It doesn't work like that."

"Why not?" he shouted, the sound shrill as it bounced around the truck.

I blew out a breath, fighting back more tears of my own. "I'm sorry, bud."

"Who's going to give me lessons? Mister Mooney said he could have me ready for my first rodeo this winter."

"You're not going to rodeo, Cason. So, you don't need lessons."

"But… But…" His words dissolved into tears as he cupped his face and sobbed. Each wail was like a knife to the heart. But how could I let him rodeo when I'd broken up with Ryder for the very same thing? I just…I couldn't. I couldn't watch him go down the same path. Maybe if I stopped it now, he'd find a new passion. Kids were good at lots of things, right? Saying no to one hobby didn't mean he couldn't have others.

"You don't get to tell me what to do!" Cason finally shouted as we pulled up the drive to our house.

"Actually, I do," I tried to reason. "I'm sorry, but—"

"No! You aren't my mom! You don't get to boss me around!"

"Cason, please…" I couldn't take all of this fighting. First, Ryder, then Mama, now him? I hated confrontation, and yet it found me at every curve the past two days. "I might not be your mom, but she picked me to watch over you."

"Well, she chose wrong!" he yelled. "I hate you! I hate you! I hate you!"

His words drove into my heart and twisted so deep I couldn't breathe. I'd failed him. Failed him so thoroughly I deserved a medal for shittiest aunt of the year. He managed to wriggle his way out of his car-seat, and by the time I parked in front of the house, he was already opening the door and stomping for the porch. He glared at me as I walked up the steps and unlocked the door, all the while refusing to speak to me. The minute I got the door open, he shoved past me, darted for his room, and slammed it shut.

I didn't have the fight in me to try and reason with him.

I DIDN'T SLEEP AT all. Though I'd salvaged one relationship, I'd ruined two others. Cason had cried himself to sleep; I could hear his sobs through the entire house.

Was I really going to keep him from riding? Was I any better than Mama? Not letting Cason ride was as bad as her condemning me for dating Ryder. Tears of anger slid down my cheeks as I thought of Daddy. Why had he died? I wished he was here. So much would be different. I'd probably never have left Texas. I'd have grown up without this stupid, fucking hang up.

Why did you die?

I must have fallen asleep at some point, because nightmares of his death played on repeat in my mind. How could I get over it? How was his death so much harder to come to terms with than Sheldon's? It was terrible, but true. Maybe it was that Sheldon's death was inevitable because of the cancer. There was nothing that could be done. Daddy's death could have been prevented. Some would probably argue that when it was your time to go, it was your time to go. All death was inevitable, there was no telling when or how it would take you. Was that the way Daddy was always supposed to die?

Ryder's words in the church courtyard came to mind. *"I ain't gonna stop livin' my life out of fear. If I die, if it's my time to go, well, then… I'll be damned if it ain't doin' somethin' I love."*

I wondered if Daddy felt the same. Probably… He loved the rodeo.

My alarm on my phone went off finally, and I got out of bed, my limbs tight and sore, my head reeling. I showered quickly before waking Cason. He was still giving me the silent treatment as he got ready for school. Each second that passed between us made the tension grow.

I realized now how selfish I was being to tell him he couldn't ride. I didn't want to take him there because I didn't want to see Ryder or the Mooneys, or Mav and Cash…but the very same reason I wanted to stay away was the reason he wanted to go. Letting Ryder and his family—for all intents and purposes—into Cason's life, then taking them away was like giving him a glimpse into a toy shop then telling him nope, he couldn't go in. He'd just lost his mom. Now he was losing all of them too. Cason grabbed his backpack off the hook by the door and placed a hand on the door knob.

"Wait, Cason," I called, making my way over to him.

His cold stare landed on me. "What?" he muttered.

"Will you come here for a minute?" I asked, sitting on the couch, patting the spot beside me.

"We're gonna be late."

I waved him off. "It's okay."

With an audible sigh, he plopped down beside me, crossing his little arms over his chest. I bit back a smile at how precious he looked, even as sadness still clutched at my heart.

"I'm sorry for what I said last night. I was being selfish."

"It's fine," he grumbled, gaze set straight ahead.

"No, it's not." I turned to face him more. "It's my job to protect you, to keep you happy, and last night, I put my own wants and needs above yours. I failed at my job, and I'm very sorry."

He sniffled, wiping at his nose with the back of his arm. When he looked at me, tears shone in his eyes like diamonds. "It's okay. I'm sorry for saying I hate you. I don't hate you."

I pulled him into my arms, sobs wracking me as I clung to him. I murmured I'm sorry over and over and over into his hair, gently rocking him back and forth as we both sat there crying.

He pulled back after a time, a questioning look on his face. "Why do you hate rodeos so much, Auntie Charlotte?"

I bit my lip and wiped at my tears. "Did your mom ever talk about your grandpa?"

His brow furrowed, but after a moment he nodded. "I think so."

"He was a cowboy just like Mister Ryder, Cash, and Maverick. Like Mister Mooney too."

"What happened to him? Mama said he got in an accident."

I nodded. "He died in a rodeo. Do you know what that means? He went to heaven."

Surprise shone in his gaze. "Like Mama?"

Another nod. "Yes, but his wasn't peaceful like your mom's. He got trampled by a steer."

Understanding settled in his features. "Is that why you got so scared at the rodeos? Why you cried?"

Tears slid down my cheeks. "Yeah, bud. You see… I was there the day my daddy died. And every time I watch Mister Ryder compete, all I see is him dying too."

"But you love Mister Ryder, don't you? Why can't you just be with him?"

I let out a sad chuckle. "It doesn't always work that way. It's because I love Mister Ryder that I had to let him go. You know how angry you got with me when I told you last night that you couldn't ride…"

He nodded.

"Well, I don't want to make him angry too. He's going to ride, whether I want him to or not…and I can't bear to see him get hurt."

His face scrunched up again. "But Mister Ryder could still get hurt even if you don't watch him…and then he has no one to love him."

Well, if I wasn't a puddle of tears already, those final words completely broke me. How could a five-year-old be so wise? I had no response, his words rendering me speechless. I just squeezed him to me a little tighter.

"I love you, Auntie Charlotte," he murmured.

"I love you too, bud. So, so much."

Chapter Fifty-Two

Buckles and Broken Hearts

Ryder

"Everyone's loaded up?" I asked Mav as he hopped into the passenger seat beside me. Cash already sat in the back, though he remained almost as quiet as his cousin. Maverick simply nodded in response.

Things had been…strained, dour, since Charlie left. Everyone felt it at this point. Maverick was quieter than usual. Bad's mood was downright foul. Cash was the only one who still held a shred of his obnoxious self, but even that was tame in comparison to usual. Hell, even Dutch seemed down with no one to give her belly rubs or throw the ball to her.

We all felt Charlie's loss. And Cason's. They were a package deal, and everyone suffered without them around.

Emptiness hung around us like a shroud. Not even the rodeo this weekend could boost my mood. I should've been excited. I should've been pumped to be back, but knowing she and Cason weren't going to be there, well…

I shook the thought from my mind. *It's done. It's over.* She hadn't called. I hadn't talked to her since I shattered my phone four days ago. I needed to move on.

But just the thought of her sent my heart pounding, regret and shame pumping through my veins.

"You okay?" Maverick asked.

"Not even a bit." I put the truck in drive. Cash's hand cupped my shoulder before he sat back, settling himself into the seat.

You EVER HAVE ONE of those days where you just think, *I shoulda just stayed in bed?* Well, that was today. We got a flat on the way to the rodeo. Shouldn't have been a problem—I knew how to fix a damn tire—but the spare was flat. By the time we'd gotten it fixed, we were cutting it close. All the horses needed to be warmed up before their rides, not to mention we needed to stretch and get ready. Pulling into the rodeo grounds with half an hour 'til opening ceremony wasn't a good start to the night.

Cash's bronc run was shitty. I no scored—fucking no-scored—for my Steer Wrestling event. I'd missed the damn cow completely. At least Cash and Mav pulled out a second place for the team roping.

I sent up a silent prayer to at least get a score in bull riding. I couldn't afford another loss. I watched the other riders as they went down the lineup. Only a couple eight second rides. The bulls were rank as shit tonight. But as I stood there watching, waiting for my name to be called, all I could think about was *her*.

Stop. Stop doin' this to yourself. I needed to put her behind me. Ain't no use getting all wrapped up on what could have been. All that mattered was the here and now.

Mav and Cash were there as my name was announced over the loudspeaker. My nerves pulsed through me, flickers of images from my accident trying to push to the forefront of my mind. But I blocked them out. My dad didn't call me stubborn for no reason. Today might have been shit, everything sucked without Charlie, but I wasn't going to give up now. I could be miserable after my ride.

Focusing on my breathing, I drowned out the noise and settled myself on the bull's back while I got the bull rope ready. Eight seconds. That's all I needed.

"You got this, bud," Cash said, clapping me on the back as I glanced over at him. The high of the rodeo had finally gotten to him, bringing out more of his former self. It still wasn't the same Cash Mooney energy, but I appreciated the level of enthusiasm he showed.

But Mav's words hit me hard. About as hard as his intense stare did. "Make her see you were born to do this."

Determination crept over me, settling into my bones, my very essence. *Actions…actions mean everything.* Charlie's words lingered in my mind as I slammed the mask down on my helmet. I hated how it blocked out a lot more of my vision, but it was better than having a broken face, right?

With a nod, I lifted my hand…and the gate flew open. The bull launched out of the chute, my arm wrenching as I clung to the rope. A flicker of pain went through my ribs, but I ignored it, focusing on keeping my breathing calm and queuing the bull with my spurs and making sure I moved as one with the beast, instead of against it. The sights, the sounds of the arena, they all disappeared… Even my thoughts withered away to ash. In that moment, it was just me and the bull. Nothing else mattered.

The buzzer sounded, cutting through the haze of my focus, and I loosened my grip, wiggling my fingers out of the rope. I dismounted, landing on my feet in the soft arena sand. Adrenaline pumped through my veins.

For a day that started out as pure dogshit, it sure turned into one hell of a night. My gaze settled on the box Bad and Violet sat in, and for a moment, I thought *she'd* be there, Cason at her side, but no.

That just wasn't my reality anymore.

Chapter Fifty-Three

Better Together

Charlie

FIVE DAYS PASSED.

Five. Long. Days. The pain hadn't eased. Neither had the loneliness or regret. Funny… I'd been with Cal far longer than I'd been with Ryder, but I'd hardly even batted an eye when I broke up with him. In fact, the only tears I'd shed were for the time I'd wasted, and the fact I'd let myself be treated so poorly. After having all that time to build a life together, I only had a handful of actual happy memories with him.

But with Ryder…

We'd barely been dating, but that time had done something to my soul. I'd gladly take my time with Ryder over the years I'd been with Cal.

A part of me, a really large, desperate part of me, wanted to call him. Wanted to *try* and work things out. But I was still scared. What if we went right back down the same path we were going, falling into the same cycle?

Cason and I headed up the long driveway to our house after church that Sunday morning. I frowned, noticing a truck in the drive.

"Auntie Charlotte! Is that Uncle Ryder's truck?"

My heart leaped, hope blooming in my chest like a flower in spring. "Yea, it is, bud," I said slowly, as we pulled up to it. But my heart sank as I put the Tacoma in park and the cowboy who got out of the driver's seat was *not* Ryder. Maverick was dressed in all black as usual, his onyx long-sleeved shirt lined with gold. MRC was embroidered right over the heart.

Cason and I got out quickly, my disappointment turning to fear as it flooded my chest, drowning the air in my lungs. Why would Maverick be here and not Ryder? "What happened?" I breathed, tears forming in my eyes.

Maverick's jade stare softened, his hands flying up into a placating gesture as he made his way to me. "He's okay. Ryder's perfectly fine."

I blew out a sigh, but it didn't do anywhere near enough to calm my nerves. Cason came to lean against me. "That's good…w-why are you here, Mav?"

"How're you doin', Miss Charlie?"

My brow furrowed, but I managed to get out, "I'm fine."

His head cocked to the side. He'd always been the most observant. Not that it would take a therapist to see through my lies.

I sighed. "*Okay*, not fine."

"Ryder ain't doin' good either."

I shook my head. "If he wanted me, he'd have tried harder to work things out. He knows where I live."

Maverick dipped his head a moment. "You two sound exactly alike. Both of y'all are stubborn as hell."

A sad smile toyed on my lips, but died before it could fully form. "Why are you here, Mav?" I repeated.

He pursed his lips then knelt down to Cason's level before crooking a finger at him. Cason obeyed, hope dancing in his eyes. Maverick leaned in to whisper something I couldn't make out in his ear, but in the next moment, Cason tore the keys from my grasp and barreled off toward the house.

I frowned. Why was Maverick here? He had a rodeo this evening. It was obvious from his getup. Why the hell was he here and not Ryder?

He pulled the tailgate of Ryder's truck down and hopped up, patting the space beside him. I rolled my eyes, but followed suit.

"I'm here because I'm hopin' one of y'all has a lick of sense. And you and I both know it sure as hell ain't Ryder," he finally said after a long moment.

I blew out a soft laugh.

Maverick fiddled with his hands—no, not hands, I realized. He held a small piece of wood and a knife. I remembered he'd said he whittled.

His deep voice both soothed me and set me on edge as he spoke. "Did Ryder ever tell you how my family died?"

I glanced at him, but he wasn't looking at me. His gaze was fixed on the tools in his hands. "No," I said softly.

"I was eleven. My dad…well, he was a drunk. He was drivin' us to a rodeo, he needed to make some money. He uh…he hit a truck head on. Engine exploded, whole damn thing caught fire."

He paused, a muscle ticking in his shaven jaw as he clenched and unclenched it. "Somehow, by God's grace, or divine intervention, I lived. Mom and Dad died on impact. My sister didn't though. She burnt. I tried to get her out, but…" He blew out a breath. "She was stuck in the carseat and I was too late."

My heart clenched, constricting so tight I couldn't breathe. Dear God. I…I had no words. Nothing. My mouth popped open before closing. I pressed a hand to his arm. He looked at me finally, those light eyes of his shining with sadness.

"Mav," I whispered.

His lips twitched upward ever so slightly as he dropped his whittling tools in his lap. He reached over and wiped a tear from my cheeks. I hadn't even realized I was crying.

"I'm so sorry," I managed to get out. I'd thought Daddy's death was tragic, but what he'd gone through… I couldn't even fathom it. The pain. The suffering.

His hand dropped back to his lap. "I hate drivin' a trailer now. I'll do anythin' I can to avoid it. But there's times when I can't. When I have to buck up and do it. And it's scary as hell, and I get real damn close to psyching myself out, but I do it anyway. I don't let the fear win."

"Mav…"

"Tell me, Miss Charlie… Do you love him?"

Tears coursed down my cheeks. "I do…but it's not that simple."

"And why the hell's that?" The intensity of his deep voice sent a tremor through me. "Are you goin' to let your fears keep you from lovin' him? Are you okay with knowin' that you gave up the greatest thing in your life because you were afraid to be uncomfortable? Life has no guarantees, Charlie. No obligations to give you a long, safe life. Wouldn't you rather spend whatever time you have on this earth with the person you love?"

My heart cracked. "I'm scared," I admitted.

"I get that. Trust me, no one else gets it more than I do. But if I can do it, so can you. You're tough as nails. You've gone through shit that most people never been through. Can't even fathom. You can be scared and still love him. You can be scared and still support him."

I broke then, leaning my head against his shoulder, sobs wrenching out of my chest. He wrapped an arm around me, pulling me into his embrace. I'd never had any friends who'd lost a parent. No one who understood what I was going through or the toll it took on you. But Maverick did. Mister Mooney's words fluttered through my mind from the Austin Rodeo: *Everyone could learn somethin' from that boy, if they only took the time to watch and listen.*

I pulled out of his grasp and blew out a breath, wiping the tears from my eyes. "So, you came all the way down here to basically tell me to get my head outta my ass?"

He chuckled, lips pulling up into a genuine smile. "Yeah. And to drive you and Cason to the rodeo."

I laughed, bumping my shoulder with his. "That's mighty presumptive of you."

"Well…? You comin' or not?"

So many emotions writhed and tore through me—worry, fear, hope, happiness—they all clawed for purchase. I took a deep breath. Was I really doing this? Did I want this to work?

My lips drew into a smirk. "Let me get Cason."

But as I hopped off the back of the truck, Cason raced out of the house in his cowboy getup—hat, boots, and all.

I turned to Maverick. "Did you tell him to go change?"

Maverick just winked and nodded to the truck. "Come on, we gotta long drive between here and Houston."

M Y HEART DANCED AGAINST my ribcage as we pulled up to Ryder's trailer. Cash was there, a scowl on his face. "Where the hell have you been?" he all but shouted as Maverick got out of the truck.

I slipped out and undid Cason's carseat straps in the back. His little squeal of excitement stopped whatever Cash and Mav were arguing about.

"Little man?" Cash crowed, his gaze landing on Cason.

Cason hurled himself into his arms. "Uncle Cash!"

I smiled. How could I have ever thought to keep the relationships he'd made with these cowboys from him? He'd never known his father. These boys had filled that hole and then some. A twinge of shame threatened to rear its ugly head, but I pushed it down.

"Where's Ryder?" I asked.

Cash's lips pulled up into a smirk as he held his arms out to me. "What, you ain't gonna give Big Daddy some sugar?" I laughed, letting him fold me in his embrace. "We missed you, Charlie girl," he murmured in my ear.

I patted his chest. "Missed you too, Mooney."

"He's down in the competitor's area. Steer Wrestlin' just ended. They're about to start our event." He pegged Maverick with a hard stare. "You're lucky I got that bitch of a mare warmed up for you without dyin', or you'd be findin' yourself a new partner."

"Cash, words!" Maverick warned even as Cason giggled.

I laughed, a sense of contentment rushing over me. Fear lingered there too, but I wouldn't let it win. "You guys go. I don't want you to scratch. We'll go find Mister and Mrs. Mooney."

It didn't take long. They sat in a box along the front fence of the outdoor arena. I noticed Mrs. Mooney first, her loud outfit—amethysts and rhinestones this time, to match Cash's purple get up, I realized—sticking out among the crowd.

"Excuse me, Mister…Missus."

They turned as one to look at me, surprise warming Mrs. Mooney's features. But not Bad. No, he looked at me like he knew I'd be here all along.

"Well, what took ya so long?" he grumbled. "I was expectin' y'all back over an hour ago. Been havin' to cover Mav's ass all damn day." He held his arms out to me and enveloped me in a hug. The smell of aftershave and sweet tobacco drifted on the wind and my heart swelled.

"Sorry," I murmured.

"You're here now, that's all that matters. Ryder seen you yet?"

"No, sir."

"He's gonna piss his pants when he does. Better get my camera out."

I laughed as Cason settled himself next to Mrs. Mooney, little Bodacious hopping into his lap. "I gotcha some popcorn," she said, pulling out a massive bag of kettle corn from her purse.

I moved to the fence, Mister Mooney coming to my side. "What made you change your mind?" his gruff voice soothed my soul. God, I'd missed him. All of them. It hadn't even been a week, but they'd become such a huge part of my life in such a short time.

"You once told me that we all could learn something from Maverick, if only we took the time to listen."

CHAPTER FIFTY-FOUR

Forget about You

RYDER

I PACED IN THE labyrinth of pipe-stall. Where the hell was Cash? He'd run off right after my first event. No explanation. No warning, just up and left. Maverick had been gone since before I woke up—asshole just disappeared and left with my truck.

When I'd asked where he was throughout the day, Cash just waved me off, telling me he'd be here.

Well, their event had already started and they still weren't here.

Cash, I could understand missing an event. He's done it before—either because he was hugging a toilet, piss drunk, or because he was plowing some girl in the trailer. But Maverick… Maverick was never late. To anything.

Something wasn't right.

Worry roiled in my gut. Had something happened to him? Was he okay? I was about to head for the trailer to find Cash when they both charged up on horseback to the waiting area, letting one the rodeo assistants know they were there and ready.

I stalked over to them. "Where the hell have you been?" I snapped, my anger geared at Maverick.

He shrugged, a hint of smirk on his lips, some guarded, light emotion gleaming in his eyes as he slid from his saddle. "Nowhere," he replied, the word evasive. It was so unlike Maverick it made my worry coil tighter. What the hell was going on?

"Nowhere?" I growled. "You've been gone with my truck all damn day and you can't even tell me where?"

"Maverick Holstrom, Cash Mooney…you're up," the assistant called out.

Maverick swung back up onto Black Betty, who snorted and pranced, Cash already on a not as jacked up Playboy. The two of them leaned into one another, doing their little ritual. No point in trying to get an answer now. I wouldn't break their focus.

As the previous riders and steer were moved out of the arena, Cash and Maverick guided their two horses into the box. A steer wiggled in the chute, sending Black Betty into an absolute fit. She foamed at the mouth as Maverick held her back with one hand on the reins, the other preparing his rope.

And just like that, they were off. The chute slammed open, the steer darting across the arena, only to get stopped by Mav and Cash. I'd never seen two people work so well in tandem. It's like they read each other's minds. There was no explaining how well they worked.

I wasn't surprised they'd won with that time. Their overall points from both Saturday and Sunday earned them the number one spot. At least one of us would be going home with some money. I still had Bull Riding, but I'd performed like shit in Steer Wrestling.

I just couldn't focus.

I hadn't stopped thinking about Charlie. She was like a drug and I was a junkie. I couldn't get her off my mind… Had stopped trying to at this point. I'd always wanted this. Wanted to spend my life going rodeo to rodeo with my best friends, making money, and building a name for us. But as much as I still wanted that, I wanted something else too.

I wanted a family to come home to. A girl to love me. I wanted to build a life with someone.

No, not just someone…Charlie.

I wanted Charlie Evans.

Maybe Mav had been right over these past few days. I'd call her up after the rodeo. *Nah, you saw how callin' went.* Maybe I'd go to her house, and try to talk, beg, plead…whatever the hell I had to do to get her back.

Determination settled around me as I went into the final event. Not even the fact that I'd managed to draw Rockcrusher again could deter that. In fact, I reveled in the challenge.

My excitement grew and grew as each name was called. Not a single score tonight. Which left the odds in my favor. I just needed a score—not even a good one—to win tonight's event. Just an eight second ride.

"You ready, bud?" Cash asked, clapping me on the back.

I nodded, getting my bull rope ready. My gaze flicked to Maverick's. That mischievous glint in his eye still remained—reminding me more of Cash than his usual self. But I didn't press. Mav would reveal his hand when he saw fit. No prying or forcing him into it would work.

"I'm takin' your advice," I told Mav. "I'm goin' to get her back."

He nodded, but I didn't miss the way that his light stare shifted to Cash, or the secretive look they shared.

I didn't have time to press. Not as my name was called.

Chapter Fifty-Five

Long Haul

Charlie

I TAPPED MY FOOT on the wooden floorboards of the arena seating. It was all I could do to stop the nervous energy from swallowing me whole.

"And we have Ryder Wright ridin' Rockcrusher again. Folks, if y'all were at the Austin rodeo, you'd have seen that nasty fall he took off this bull. He's been out for a bit recovering from injuries, but he's back!"

My gaze flicked to Mister Mooney, a whisper of fear digging for purchase.

"He's got this," he replied, his hand covering mine on the fence.

I nodded, turning my gaze back to the arena just as Ryder descended into the bull chute.

He's got this. Don't let the fear win. Don't let the fear win. Don't—

He and Rockcrusher came tearing out of the chute. And even though I knew the bull wanted nothing more than to get him off his back, the way Ryder rode him…it was like they were one. Each dip and twist and buck flowed into the next, looking as effortless as breathing. An emotion snaked its way through me, gripping me tightly. But it wasn't fear, it was pride. Oh, the fear still lurked in the corners of my mind, but I wouldn't let it control me anymore.

The buzzer sounded and that pride swelled to new heights as he hopped off that bull's back, each movement as flawless as the last. I cheered from my spot, tears blurring my vision as he wrenched off his helmet and held it in the air. He made a slow circle, a look of pure joy on his handsome face.

And then his gaze found mine.

It's like the world stopped. The sound of the cheering crowd died away, time slowed, everything around us pausing, save for him and I. His feet ate up the distance between us, dirt flying in his wake. I clutched a hand to my chest as he climbed the pipe-stall fencing and pulled me to him from his spot on the other side of the railing.

His lips crushed against mine as one of his hands cupped the back of my head. I clung to him, savoring everything about the kiss. The touch, the happiness, the knowledge that I was his and he was mine.

How I thought I could move on from him was ridiculous. He was it for me. He was my happily ever after. My soulmate. My forever after all.

Time and sound morphed and sped up, the cheers and claps from the crowd deafening compared to the quietness of our moment, but I ignored it all as Ryder pressed his forehead to mine.

"You came," he whispered, breath sawing in and out of his lungs. Sweat covered him, dirt clung to his shirt and chaps, but I didn't care. I leaned back, cupping his face in my hands, taking in every inch of him. My fingers brushed over the scar slicing across his face, a soft smile coming to my lips.

"Yeah, well, there was this hot cowboy competing tonight and I wanted to see him ride."

"But, I thought—"

I pressed a finger to his lips. "You said I didn't have a dream the other day… But it's you, Ryder. Loving you, spending the rest of forever with you, making a family with you. I want it all. And I am willing to face whatever fears I need to, to make sure that dream happens…as long as I have you."

Unshed tears hung in his eyes like exploding stars. I kissed him softly, just a brush of our mouths. "I love you, Ryder Wright."

He held me to him tightly, his fingers knotted in my hair. "I love you too, darlin'."

EXCITEMENT AND EUPHORIA DROVE me through the rest of the evening. Ryder left me back in the box with The Mooneys and Cason as he went back to the competitor's area while the standings were announced and the rodeo finished up.

Not even the fact that hundreds of random people clapped, or patted me on the shoulder, or spoke in hushed whispers about mine and Ryder's heated moment of PDA could knock me off cloud nine. Mister and Mrs. Mooney led Cason and I through the throngs of people and back to where the contestant's all hung around. A few TV crews were interviewing cowboys—Ryder being among them.

Cash and Maverick spotted us and made a beeline over.

"Congratulations on your win, boys," I said with a smile.

Mister Mooney offered up about a dozen ways they could've improved, and all the things they needed to work on before the next rodeo, but in the end, he'd clapped both of them on the back, his hazel eyes shining with pride.

Anticipation ate at me as I waited for Ryder. I just wanted to hold him, feel him against my side. Inhale his familiar scent. The interviewer finally moved onto another contestant and Ryder strode for us, for me—his gaze holding a hunger in it that made desire swirl to life in my stomach.

But about a dozen or so paces away, a finely dressed cowboy stopped him. He wore a tailored gray sports coat over a crisp white shirt, and a ten-gallon gray felt cowboy hat. His bolo tie shone around his neck, the gemstones there accenting it speaking of his wealth. This wasn't just someone here at the rodeo. He was dressed too nice, and the air he carried didn't scream spectator, but businessman.

I frowned. "Who's that?"

"That's a sponsor." Mister Mooney's rough voice drew my gaze.

"Really? That's amazing." If anyone deserved it, it was Ryder. He'd win a World Champion title, I had no doubt about it. And with help from a sponsor, he'd get to go to more rodeos across the U.S.

"It's a great opportunity, but he's gonna turn it down," Cash added.

I whirled to him. "Why?" Why would he even think about turning that down? That's what he wanted. What he'd always wanted.

Cash and his father both offered me guilty looks. "Well, because of you, Charlie girl," Cash finally replied.

"Me?"

Mister Mooney's gaze was heavy as it held me in place. "He just got you back. He ain't gonna take a sponsorship if he thinks it'll keep y'all from being together."

No. No, he couldn't do that. Couldn't give up his dream. Not for me. Did the idea scare me a bit—okay, a lot? Yes. Did I want him gone? No. But this is what he'd worked his whole life for. I loved him, more than anything, and I wanted to see him happy, succeeding. So, I'd support him. Do whatever I needed to do.

Setting my gaze on Ryder once more, I closed the distance between us. He wouldn't be giving up any dreams on my part.

Not if I could help it.

CHAPTER FIFTY-SIX

Thank God

RYDER

"**R**YDER WRIGHT, IS IT?"

I turned to the cowboy who'd said my name. He reminded me of Goodie, Bad's brother. A blend of cowboy and businessman. My heart skipped a beat. I knew his kind. Excitement bubbled to life in me.

"Yes, sir. That's me," I replied, turning to face him as I held out my hand.

His handshake was firm. "Leroy Jenkins. I gotta team of bull riders and we gotta spot to fill. I've had my eye on you for a while. Your skill, your determination, it's impressive."

I nodded, biting back the excitement rippling through me. "Thank you, sir."

"I'd like to talk more about you joinin' us."

My heart swelled, but the lightness turned to dread in an instant. The boys and I had just gotten the ranch. Not that they weren't capable of managing it without me. Not to mention, the extra income would help speed up some of the repairs. But what about Charlie? I'd just gotten her back. I wouldn't just be rodeoing in Texas and a couple other states anymore. I'd be all over.

I couldn't leave her. I *didn't want* to leave her.

Taking off my hat, I ran a hand through my hair and blew out a breath before placing it back atop my head. "Mr. Jenkins, sir. I'm... I'm real honored. Truly. But..."

A warm hand touched my shoulder, and Charlie's lavender and vanilla scent enveloped me. I glanced down at her by my side. Her gaze wasn't set on me though, but Mr. Jenkins. "Excuse me, sir. I'm sorry to interrupt, but can I speak to Ryder for a moment."

Mr. Jenkins smiled. "So, you're the lucky lady. Y'all put on quite the show tonight. Some might say an even better one than the rodeo itself."

Her cheeks flushed red but she offered him a polite smile back as she held out a hand. "Charlie Evans, sir."

He chuckled, shaking her hand. "Go ahead, I'll be right here."

I dragged her out of earshot, confusion whirling within me. "Charlotte, what're you doin'?"

"I know that guy is a sponsor. Are you going to take it?" Her stormy gaze was intense, her expression unreadable.

"I...I don't know. No, I don't—"

"Take it," she said, cutting me off.

I frowned, rocking back at her words. "What? But, I—"

She grabbed my hands in both of hers, her smooth skin scraping against my callouses. "Take it. I'm not going anywhere. Do not give up this opportunity because of me."

"But..."

"No buts, Ryder. If you won't say yes, I'll accept the offer for you. This is everything you've ever wanted."

I let go of her hands to cup her face. "You're sure 'bout this?"

She leaned up on tiptoe, pressing her lips to mine. Warmth and love wrapped around my heart, settled in the pit of my stomach. "I'm positive. Go and ride for me. Win for me."

I kissed her once more, quick but no less intense. Grabbing her hand, I returned to Mr. Jenkins. "I'd love to talk more with you, sir."

Mr. Jenkins smiled and nodded. "Great."

THE NEXT DAY, CHARLIE and I sat in my truck once more. The sense of Déjà vu was overwhelming as we drove down the highway towards the ranch. But things were different this time. Funny how only a week separated the two but so much had happened.

"Where are we going?" she asked from the passenger seat.

I offered her a secretive smile as I squeezed her leg. "We're almost there."

She still didn't know about the ranch, but that all would change tonight. Cash, Mav, and I had spent every second of today getting things ready once we'd gotten home. Trying to keep Charlie from finding out had been damn near impossible, but we'd managed somehow.

Charlie groaned. "Can't you just tell me."

"Patience is a virtue, darlin'," I chuckled.

She scoffed. "Not for me."

I glanced over at her. She looked gorgeous. In black, as usual. Her tattoos and a sinful amount of skin on display. Her sundress had cutouts on the waist, exposing flashes of her wildflower tattoo. The heart-shaped neckline dipped low, revealing the one on her sternum as well. As much as I loved that dress, I couldn't wait to get it off.

There'll be time for that later, I reminded myself, pushing down the desire sparking within my chest.

The weight of her ring in my pocket brought me back down to reality. I'd never been more sure of anything in my life. With us getting back together, with this new sponsorship with Mr. Jenkins, everything felt right.

We turned off the highway and down the county road until the main gate came into view. A surge of pride gripped me as my gaze landed on the sign Cash, Mav, and I had worked so hard on erecting over the entrance. Mercenary Ranch with our brand between the two words.

"Is this—Did you guys buy the ranch?" Her words held a sense of disbelief and awe in them.

I ran a tongue over my lips and grinned, gripping her thigh tightly for a moment. "We sure did."

"Oh my God, when?"

"Last Monday."

Her gaze snapped to mine, her storm cloud eyes full of emotion. She covered her mouth with a hand, a little gasp escaping her. "You were bringing me here," she breathed.

I slipped my free hand into hers and squeezed reassuringly, before pulling it over to press a kiss to the back of her palm. A silent way of telling her it was okay.

She turned back to look out at the property once more. "Oh my god, Ryder. This place is beautiful. And that house…"

The houses had always been the biggest selling point. Three identical sprawling ranch-style homes made of solid red brick with black and white shutters and trim. The other two were scattered across the sixty-five acre property. One for each of us.

I put the car in park as we came up the circular driveway, and helped her out right before the brick steps up to the porch. We'd hung twinkle lights along the porch trim, their warm glow catching on Charlie's copper hair and making it shine like a burning sunset.

"Wait right here," I told her at the front door as I pulled out a key and unlocked it.

"Ryder—"

I pressed a kiss to her lips, trying and failing to push down the desire raging inside of me. "Count to sixty, okay?"

Her bottom lip jutted out, a pout forming on her mouth, but she sighed with an eyeroll. "Fine." Amusement and curiosity danced in her gaze.

Kissing her one last time, I slipped inside the house, careful not to let her see anything. We'd covered the large windows with black curtains so she couldn't peek. My gaze scanned the room. The rose petals hadn't moved, the words will you marry me still perfectly clear. I pulled a lighter out of my back pocket and set to work lighting the dozens upon dozens of candles.

"Sixty!" she called, her voice muffled from the wall separating us.

"Give me another minute!" I shouted.

Another groan escaped her. I laughed as I finished lighting the last couple candles. Readjusting my cowboy hat on my head, smoothing out my shirt, I took a deep, calming breath and kneeled down on the hardwood floor.

I pulled the ring from my pocket, gripping it tightly in my hand.

You got this. You got this—

"Come on in, Charlotte."

Chapter Fifty-Seven

Forever After All

Charlie

My heart beat like a war drum in my chest, my nerves coiled tight like a cottonmouth in my stomach. He'd bought the ranch. He, Cash, and Mav had done it. A flicker of guilt gnawed at me. He'd been trying to bring me here last week when we'd gotten in that fight.

My mind whirled as I dutifully counted to sixty.

Was he going to propose? It explained his nervousness. The evasiveness. The request to get dolled up.

"Sixty!" I called out.

"Give me another minute."

Yep, he was definitely proposing. Butterflies fluttered in my stomach, a soft smile pulling on my mouth. *You've got this. You know you're going to say yes.*

But nothing could prepare me for the overwhelming sense of awe as Ryder told me to come in and I opened the door.

I gasped, my hands coming up to cover my mouth as tears pricked in my eyes. The house was barely furnished, but I didn't focus on that. Not as my gaze scanned the four words shaped out of fresh roses.

Ryder knelt beside them, dozens and dozens of candles surrounding him.

My feet felt like lead as I strode for him, tears already streaming down my cheeks.

He reached a hand out, to which I happily took as my legs gave out beneath me. I had to kneel to stay upright, my chest feeling heavy with emotion.

"From the minute I saw you in Jacks, I knew the course of my life would forever be altered. You make me want to be better. Want to work harder. You made me see that there's more to life than just rodeos and buckles. I want you in my life. For the long haul. For forever and again. Please…please make me the luckiest man in the world and say yes."

"Oh, Ryder," I choked out, cupping his face in my hands. "Yes. Fuck yes."

He grinned, a husky chuckle escaping him as he gripped my chin between his thumb and forefinger. "You and your mouth," he murmured against my lips.

I laughed, clinging to him. "You know you love it."

Another kiss to my lips, this one all but a whisper as he pulled back and held something out in his hand. My gaze dipped to the ring, a gorgeous black diamond surrounded by smaller ones, gleaming on a rose gold band. Everything about it called to me.

"I bought this a week after I met you," he said, grasping it between his fingers and holding it before my left hand. "May I?"

I nodded, trying and failing to hold back tears. "You knew all this time?"

"All this time," he murmured, slipping the ring onto my finger.

The last bit of restraint in me broke as I launched into his arms, knocking him to the ground.

He laughed, his arms banding around me as he flipped us so that he hovered over me. I leaned up and kissed him. Hard, deep. Telling him everything I felt without words.

"You ready to be Mrs. Wright?" he asked, his calloused hand cupping my cheek.

I laughed. "I do very much like the sound of that."

He kissed me. "Good, me too."

And as his mouth met mine, as he took me right there on the floor of our home, I was never more certain about anything in my life…somethings were meant to be forever after all.

Feel Like This: Epilogue

RYDER

A MONTH.

It'd only been a month, but it felt like a lifetime as I raced for home.

Right after Charlie and I got engaged, I'd gotten sent off to a string of rodeos with Jenkin's team. It had taken some getting used to. New people, new places…I was used to rodeoing with Cash and Mav, and while they'd come to a few of them, their usual constant presence was missed.

The Mercenary Ranch sign came into view down the old dirt road and a thrum of excitement swelled up inside me. A month without Charlie was too long. Too. Damn. Long.

I'd barely put the truck in park when the front door opened. Cason came barreling out, a wide grin splitting his face as he took the brick steps two at a time.

"Uncle Ryder!" he shouted, slamming into me as I held out my arms to him.

The air knocked from my lungs, and I grunted before pulling away to ruffle up his hair. "Hey, bud. How're you doin'?"

I glanced up at the front door, a smiling Charlie waiting at the threshold. God, she looked gorgeous. I urged Cason into a walk beside me as I made my way up the stairs. He told me all the things he was doing. How Cash and Mav were teaching him how to mend fences and repaint the barn now that school was out. But I couldn't focus. Couldn't think of anything other than Charlie waiting for me at the top of the stairs.

She held her arms out to me as I made it up the last step. I moved to her, hooking a hand around her waist, kissing her deeply. Her arms snaked around my neck and she arched into me.

"Ew!" Cason gasped. "That's firkin disgustin'! I'm goin' to find Uncle Mav and Funcle Cash."

Charlie threw her head back and laughed, the song a sweet, sweet melody I'd sorely missed.

"He's startin' to talk to like a cowboy," I murmured in her ear.

She chuckled, her stormy eyes meeting mine. "He sure is. Speakin' of cowboys, how're you?"

"Good, now that I'm home." I nipped her earlobe. "How've you been, darlin'?"

She huffed. "Sick."

I pulled back, a frown forming on my lips. "You okay?"

"Don't worry," she laughed, her hold on me not loosening. "Not that kind of sick."

"What do you mean?" My brows furrowed.

A soft smile curved on her mouth and she released her hold on me. She reached into the back pocket of her shorts and pulled out a long, thin piece of blue and white plastic. My heart stopped. Full on stopped as understanding dawned on me.

"You're gonna be a daddy," she whispered, tears hanging in her eyes.

My lungs seized as I grabbed the pregnancy test with trembling fingers. Sure as shit, the word pregnant stared right back at me.

I was…I was going to be a father. Excitement and terror and pure joy fought for hold over my heart. Was I ready? Would I be any good at it? We'd just gotten engaged and I was on the road and—

"Say something, Ryder…" Charlie's voice quaked, the excitement in her eyes dulling to worry. "Please."

"H-how?" It was the only word I could think. The only one I could bring to my lips.

And it sure as hell wasn't the right word, I realized, as sadness settled in Charlie's stormy gaze. "I don't know exactly…birth control sometimes fails…and we never use a condom. I'm—I'm sorry." She hung her head, tears streaking down her cheeks.

"No, no, Charlotte, darlin', no I ain't mad." I cupped her face in my hands, forcing her to meet my gaze. "I'm just surprised, is all."

"Do you not want it?" Fear shone in her gaze, lingered in her words.

One of my hands drifted down to her still flat stomach. Just the thought of her pregnant with my child…desire flared to life within me. I kissed her, long and slow and soft. "Of course, I do, Charlotte."

"I know we aren't ready—"

I kissed her again, hoping, praying I could ease her worries. "We ain't ever gonna be ready. But I want this baby. I need you to know that."

Her answering smile was brighter than the sun. She kissed me, stealing the air from my lungs. I pulled away, only far enough to hold that soft, stormy gaze of hers, and I knew…I just knew I saw forever in her eyes.

Don't miss Maverick's story...

Don't worry, this is only just the beginning for the boys of Mercenary Ranch. Next up, is Maverick and Cheyenne in a tale of heartbreak, healing, and growth.

(Title to be revealed at a later date)

You can read their story chapter by chapter through Kindle Vella starting November 1st. Paperback and Ebooks will be available in late Spring 2024!

Acknowledgements

This book wouldn't have been possible without the help of some seriously amazing people.

To Cody: My sweet courage. My biggest cheerleader. My best friend. Your constant love, support, enthusiasm, and general amazingness is the main reason this book even exists. Ryder and Charlie's story will always hold a special place in my heart, as so much of their love story was inspired by you and I. The way you saw me, time and time again, at my weakest, most broken, and vulnerable moments and loved me anyways, is exactly what I strove to imbue in Ryder. I hope I did you justice my love. Thank you for the constant late night plotting discussions. Thank you for helping me rewrite scenes and tweak characters and alter story lines to make this book what it is. Thank you for believing in me on the hard days, and showing so much excitement and dedication and love for these characters and this story.

To Clare: Not everyone gets to have an amazing critique partner, let alone one who becomes their best friend. Thank you for your constant kind, encouraging words. Thank you for the late night chats, the countless writing sprints, the gushing about my characters, and pushing me to produce some of—if not the best— work of my life (not trying to toot my own horn). You are such a gorgeous gem of a human being and a top notch author that I am so incredibly lucky to call my best friend! Without you, this book wouldn't be what it is today!

To Savanah: Girl, you are proof that the best friends come from the most unexpected situations. Despite the short time we've known each other, your friendship has meant absolutely everything, and I am so incredibly grateful to call you one of my best friends and one of the most passionate, inquisitive, and honest critique partners I've ever had. Your love of my writing and characters gives me life, just like every single one of our daily conversations. Thank you for your constant support and for being such a ray of sunshine in my life. I don't know what I'd do without you.

To Amy and Hammy: Thank you both so very much for reading this book and giving me some of the most amazing, honest, and helpful feedback! Getting to send you chapters and hear your thoughts was such an amazing, fun part of this process, and your words of encouragement and critique was absolutely amazing!

To my family: Amanda, Dad, and Nana, thank you all for being such amazing supporters of my work. Even if you don't always understand or vibe with what I write, you still support it, and for that I am so incredibly grateful!

To my editor, B.C. Fajohn: Thank you for your top notch editing skills and helping hone this thicc boy into the story it is today! Your thoughts and suggestions were so helpful and appreciated!

About the Author

Just a thirty-one-year-old who loves tattoos, dogs, crystals, and writing steamy romance. For as long as she can remember, story telling has consumed her soul. She's a California transplant living in small town Uvalde, TX with her super talented author husband, a sweet-as-pie son, and a sassy little girl. When she isn't writing, she's working as a teacher, a freelance editor, and a gymnastics coach. She loves rodeos, country music, and Texas sunrises, all of which inspired her series.

You can follow her on her website and social media at:
http://www.hailiercamarillo.com

tiktok.com/h.r.camarillo

instagram.com/h.r.camarillo